Miranda is the author of thirteen books, including six *Sunday Times* bestsellers. Her books have been translated into ten languages, selling over a million copies worldwide. She has been shortlisted for the RNA Novel of the Year and Contemporary Novel of the Year awards and is the winner of the 26 Project Writer award. She is the founder of *WriteFoxy* and the host of the online show, *Fab Night In Chatty Thing*. Miranda lives in The Black Country with her husband and daughter.

Also by Miranda Dickinson

Miranda
DICKINSON

ALL MY LOVE

ONE PLACE. MANY STORIES

HQ
An imprint of HarperCollins*Publishers* Ltd
1 London Bridge Street
London SE1 9GF

www.harpercollins.co.uk

HarperCollins*Publishers*
Macken House, 39/40 Mayor Street Upper,
Dublin 1, D01 C9W8, Ireland

This edition 2023

2
First published in Great Britain by
HQ, an imprint of HarperCollins*Publishers* Ltd 2023

Copyright © Miranda Dickinson 2023

Miranda Dickinson asserts the moral right to be
identified as the author of this work.
A catalogue record for this book is
available from the British Library.

ISBN: 978-0-00-844078-7

MIX
Paper | Supporting
responsible forestry
FSC™ C007454

This book is produced from independently certified FSC™ paper
to ensure responsible forest management.

For more information visit: www.harpercollins.co.uk/green

This book is set in Caslon by Type-it AS, Norway

Printed and Bound in the UK using 100% Renewable Electricity at
CPI Group (UK) Ltd, Croydon, CR0 4YY

For the hopers, the dreamers and the
making-the-most-of-it-ers.
May this story bring you joy xx

One word frees us all
of the weight and pain of life.
That word is love.
—SOPHOCLES

Say yes and you'll figure it out afterward.
—TINA FEY

One

ESTHER

'This feels right. Being here. You know how sometimes you just *know*? That's how it feels. It's exactly what I needed. I've had a horrible year until now. Losing my last job, I mean. I thought my mother was going to have a coronary when I told her – well, you can imagine . . .'

'Mm-hm.'

My new manager, Marjorie, strides ahead of me. *Blimey*, she's fast.

My breath quickens as I pick up my pace. 'My mum thinks this job is a comedown – no offence, by the way, that's her problem, not mine – but it really isn't. I'm excited. Really keen to get started. It's a challenge I'm going to relish. Expanding my horizons, learning new skills . . .'

'Skills, right.' Marjorie wheels a cart between us, unsmiling. 'Mop. Bucket. Cloths and dusters in the basket, polish and sprays up top. Vac's power switch is tricky so just kick the bastard if it stops.' She gives a brief nod and starts to leave.

'Great, thanks, but . . .'

I see her shoulders hunch and she slowly rotates back to face me. 'But?'

'Aren't you staying?'

Marjorie's eyebrows rise into her bottle-red fringe and I think I catch the ghost of a smile. 'Staying? I have six floors in this building, one cleaner to each, and we have to be done by eleven. So no, sweetheart, I'm not staying.'

'But there was supposed to be an induction? Mr Grove said—'

'Mr Grove?' That eyeroll of hers is worthy of its own show. 'Right.' Marjorie clears her throat and sweeps her hand across the darkened expanse of the open-plan office. 'Clean *this*—' she points at the bright yellow cleaning cart beside me '—with *that*.'

And then she powers past me towards the lifts.

Heart hammering, I call after her. 'But what do I do when I finish?'

I'm answered by a large bunch of keys flying at me that I barely manage to catch.

Stunned, I turn back to the office floor, clutching my keys like a first-day nursery kid grasping their teddy, one side of the enormous blue tabard apron I'm wearing drooping off my shoulder.

'That's it?' I ask the dark expanse.

Sleeping computer screens stare blankly at me. Empty chairs face away. From somewhere in the shadows a low buzz drones.

'Seriously?'

Marjorie Ollerenshaw wasn't the warmest of managers I've met, but even her company would be preferable to this. Tears threaten, but I blink them away. I am *not* going to cry on my first day . . .

First night.

'*Night cleaner*,' Mum repeated yesterday when I told her I'd got the job. She said it like it was the sourest-tasting word to ever grace her tongue.

'I get a tabard,' I'd offered with a grin, thinking it would help. It didn't.

I look at the bright yellow cleaning trolley, with its scuffed edges, peeling labels and bleach-stained wheels. It's jolly, in a beaten-up way. And, apparently, it's my new work colleague.

I think I'll call it Fred.

'Hey, Fred,' I say, patting its rubber handles, not caring now that I say it aloud because there's nobody to hear me. 'Pleasure to be working with you. Fancy showing me around?'

The gut-kick of realisation doesn't last, thankfully. The spark returns as I pull out a roll of bin bags from Fred's tray and survey our new kingdom.

This *is* a good thing. Yesterday morning I was unemployed and camping out in my sister Naomi's cramped attic bedroom because I lost my flat; an unofficial childminder-housekeeper-dogsbody because I can't afford to pay her to stay there. Tonight, I have a job. The other stuff remains, of course, but this is one change for the better. One item off the list.

My list is folded up in the back pocket of my jeans (wearing jeans to work! Another plus!) but I know the items by heart. I wrote it on the day I moved out of the canalside apartment I'd called home for four years. My *Get My Life Back* list:

1. Find a job.
2. Save money like a BOSS.
3. Find a new flat.
4. ~~Escape~~ Leave Naomi's place.

5. Stop thinking about M.
6. Move on.

I have a job. I can start to save money. And it might take months but I *will* save enough to rent somewhere and finally rescue my things from storage. When that happens, I will kiss my three nieces goodbye and wait until I'm out of view before I run like hell from my sister's home.

5 and 6 might take longer.

My mood dips.

5 might take forever . . .

I push the thought away and fix my smile.

'Right, Fred,' I say, grabbing his handles and pushing him towards the rows of desks. 'Let's do this!'

Two

ARCHIE

Jessie Edmonds is a goddess.

I watch her across the office while I wait by the photocopier for the meeting notes to print. She's holding court by the coffee station, the usual suspects buzzing around her like . . . like . . . flies around a bin . . .

No! Jessie is not a bin!

I kick myself for my poor word choice. No wonder they won't let me near a column here. I'd send the scant remaining readership of *The Herald* running for the hills.

Rubbish, Archie Quinn. *That's* why she never notices you.

I shove the familiar voice in my head away and focus on the most beautiful woman in the world. Her blonde hair is loose today, defiant despite the storm raging beyond *The Herald*'s office windows. It's draped over one shoulder, in that way that makes you think she arranged every hair to obediently lie in place. Her green suit jacket makes her eyes flash like sapphires, her matching skirt revealing just the right amount of endless leg.

My face flushes and I look down. She is so much more than just her perfect body. She's smart; she writes like a dream; she can spin a line that leaves every other hack in this place in the dust. And Jessie Edmonds is my soulmate. She just doesn't know it yet.

'*Quinn!* Coffee!'

'Coming,' I call back, hating my mousey tone. I only ever hear it when I'm at work.

One day I will walk out of here to find a job I adore and finally prove what I can do.

That day is nearer than anyone thinks.

Especially my boss.

'What were you doing, waiting on a hillside for the coffee beans to ripen?' John 'Jock' Callaghan doesn't look up from the layouts on his desk as I carefully balance the mug of coffee on his beloved Wigan Athletic coaster, which is far too small to accommodate it.

'Here are the meeting notes you wanted,' I say, holding out the stack of papers. When he doesn't acknowledge them, I place them on the sole uncluttered corner of his desk.

'Not *there*,' he barks. 'In the conference room. One per seat. Do I have to explain this every time?'

'No, Jock.'

'Good.' He deigns to look up at me. 'Something else?'

I wasn't going to say, but it's an open door I wasn't expecting. 'Actually, yes. I heard Elvis is leaving?' I check myself. 'Sorry, *Brian* Presley. Retiring. So there'll be a vacancy in Editorial?'

Callaghan's eyes narrow. 'And why would that concern you?'

I straighten my shoulders, imagining my grandfather slapping my back like an Irish version of Rocky Balboa's trainer in the ring. *Go on, lad! Sock it to 'im!* 'I'd like to be considered for the role.'

'Reporter?'

'Junior reporter.'

'You?'

'I have a portfolio. I've been doing citizen journalism for the past two years, got some articles up on BuzzFeed and—'

'No.'

I hold my ground. 'At least take a look?'

His face relaxes into a grin that's not altogether friendly. 'What's it worth?'

'Sorry?'

'I give you a shot at an interview, what do I get?'

'A fresh voice for *The Herald*. New ideas. Hard work.'

'My car. Cleaned. In your lunchtime. Every Friday for a year.'

'Done.'

I say it before I think better, instantly cringing. Washing Callaghan's car in its premium parking space, right outside the canteen where everybody will see. And still no guarantee of a job – just an interview. He could still turn me down. I am a prize idiot he saw coming from a mile off.

Callaghan's nicotine-grated chuckle follows me as I slope out of his office.

At my desk I sit and seethe. *Bastard!* I do not deserve this. Three years I've been at his beck and call, the carrot of a non-existent writing job dangled in front of me whenever he thought I might be tempted to leave. But working for him isn't the prize . . .

'Hey, Archie.'

My head snaps upright in time to catch the waft of perfume as Jessie Edmonds passes my desk. The vision of her and the way she speaks my name in that honeyed voice of hers are the push I need.

Enough.

Callaghan pushed his luck too far today. It's time to go.

I grab a sheet of paper and start to write. This is *it*: time to write the letter I've written and rewritten in my mind for two years. I don't let myself stop for a moment in case my nerve should go, taking my words with it.

Jessie,

You are incredible. A light on the darkest day. A brave, sparkling flame in the coldest place. The world is at your feet and nothing is outside your grasp.

I think you could ask the stars to fall for you and they would.

I would.

We talk about truth in this place like an inconvenience, but here's one truth you can trust: you have my heart, if you want it . . .

I stare at the words. They swim on the page – and my mind goes blank.

What am I thinking? None of these words are right.

Heart crashing to the floor, I snatch up the note and screw it into a tight ball. It lands in the bin by my chair with a soft thud of defeat. I kick the metal basket into the shadows far beneath my desk.

I couldn't do it. I couldn't tell Jessie the truth.

Why did I ever think I could?

Three

ESTHER

Stevie Wonder makes *everything* better.

It's my seventh night on the job and I'm really getting into the groove. Cleaning an entire empty floor of *The Herald*'s newspaper offices is so much easier when you're bopping to 'Sir Duke' and 'I Wish'. Headphones are my saviours in my new role, I've discovered. Also, those small packs of custard creams you get in B&Bs, which I found a box of in one of the cupboards beneath the coffee station. Stevie, biscuits and Fred are the perfect companions to a night's work.

It did occur to me that helping myself to biscuits might be theft, but, considering the state *The Herald* staff leave their coffee station in every day, I reckon I'm owed a little sweetener. Yesterday it was such a tip it took me nearly half an hour to get coffee stains out of the carpet and off the cupboard fronts. Cleaning up other people's mess certainly gives you an insight into them.

Like the bloke – I'm assuming it's a bloke because it's so random – who shoves empty sugar sachets down the tiny gap between the backrest and seat cushions on his office chair. Why would anyone do that? Who looks at the perfectly good metal bin right by their desk and decides wedging their sugar packets into their chair is preferable?

One desk always smells of expensive perfume, often so strong that I half-expect the owner to appear beside me as I'm cleaning. They fold every bit of rubbish, too: crisp packets folded into tiny balls like a bar manager once showed me when I worked pub shifts at university; envelopes concertina-folded like the paper fans Naomi and I made as kids. That's *weird*.

I love it, though. Guessing who owns which desk, imagining their ghost seated there as the circus of daily life in a newspaper office continues around them. I can almost see the movement: the people who circulate and the ones who stay still, the watchers and the scene-stealers.

And the sugar-packet-stuffers and wastepaper folders, doing their thing in secret . . .

I bend down to peel off a rogue sticky note that Fred's picked up on his wheel and my lower back groans in reply. I'd expected some aches and pains from my cleaning shifts, but I hurt more than I ever did after a gym session. I noticed Marjorie wears one of those fitness tracker bracelets this evening when she did her start-of-shift powwow in the entrance lobby. I bet she walks some miles around this building every week. Maybe I should get one. See how many steps I clock up . . .

The ache isn't just from my shifts, though. It's the legacy of almost a whole day of washing, ironing and picking up three girls from school. I love my sister for letting me stay, and I love my nieces, but I never intended to be quite so involved in their lives as I am.

'We all chip in,' Naomi had said, when I first moved in.

Except what I think she meant to say was, 'we all contribute to the work you're going to do for us'. I'd agreed to washing and ironing, thinking it was a once-a-week affair, but it's more like twice a day. I never see Naomi and the girls changing into four outfits every day, but the mountainous pile in the washing basket suggests whole fashion shows being conducted out of my sight. And while I expected to pick Issy (nine), Molly (seven) and Ava-May (five) up from school occasionally, I don't remember agreeing to cover every school run.

One of the mums at the school gate this morning asked if I was my nieces' 'other mum' because she hadn't seen Naomi in the three months I've lived with her, implying that I'd shacked up with my brother-in-law, Gavin, and nicked my sister's kids, which is *horrific*. Not least that my sister found the most boring bloke in the whole of Greater Manchester and then married his even more tedious brother. I mean, Gav's a decent enough bloke – his heart is in the right place and he loves Naomi and the girls to death – but his choice of conversation is so dull it could bore drying paint straight off the walls. And as for his potential as a love interest – no thank you! I might be single, but I haven't had a full-frontal lobotomy . . .

I shudder at the thought now and turn my attention back to the next desk to clean. Ah. No prizes for guessing where Fred's lime-green wheel accessory came from tonight. I've christened this desk The Post-it King because it's more brightly coloured sticky note than desk. I don't think I've ever seen so many messages on one small six-foot desk before. Lists, mostly – someone after my own heart – good lists, too; lists with tick boxes next to them, each one given a comic-style drop shadow. My cousin

13

Joe, who's a TV screenwriter, would be in awe. We once spent almost an entire family Christmas debating the elements of a perfect list. 3-D tick boxes are *ninja-level* stuff.

Whoever Post-it King is, he's in demand. Most of the lists are things he has to do for other people. There's only one that seems to be for him: a DayGlo orange note with a shopping list:

Pasta	☐
Mince	☐
Garlic	☐
Wine x 2	☐
Toothpaste	☐

The last item makes me giggle. If he's planning a date with all of that, he's thought of everything. Nothing worse than a garlic-meat-and-wine snog at the end of a meal . . .

It's definitely a bloke because there is a much-loved pair of red Converse sneakers under his desk. I mean, it could be a woman, but I don't imagine there are many female office workers in this city with size 11 shoes.

So, he has great taste in shoes, is a grandmaster of lists and has really lovely handwriting.

I think Post-it King is my favourite of all *The Herald*'s invisible employees.

He's messy today, though. There are even more screwed-up sticky notes on his desk than usual. They form a teetering pyramid precariously close to the edge. I'm guessing Fred's green sticky note toppled from the summit. I scoop them into my hand and look down for the bin.

That's odd.

It's *always* here, to the left of his chair, just in front of the lowest desk drawer. The metal wastepaper baskets at every other desk move each time and I'm used to hunting for them to empty. But not Post-it King. He's so reliably predictable with his bin placement that I could locate it with my eyes closed.

Not tonight.

I stare at the round indentation on the office carpet where the bin usually sits. Where has he put it?

I check under the next desk – the one where Perfume Ghost sits – just in case their bins are hanging out together. But hers sits in splendid isolation, weirdo-folded waste bits in place.

Groaning, I wheel Post-it King's chair to the side and plonk down on my knees to peer under his desk.

What's it doing back there?

The bin is right underneath the desk, half-leaning against the backboard. The red Converse sneakers have been shoved to the side, one shoe upside down. Sticky notes and screwed up paper are strewn around it, where they must have fallen when the bin tipped up. It must have taken some effort to push it that far back. It's almost as if it's been kicked there.

Fixing a wayward earbud in place, I take Stevie with me on my dark and shadowy under-the-desk rescue mission. It's so gloomy under there, the half-light of the deserted office barely reaching halfway. Stevie's voice soothes as I grapple around to scoop up all the detritus and pull the bin back to its usual home.

I'm triumphant, if a little ruffled, when I re-emerge, the skin on my knees feeling scuffed where they met the carpet through the rips in my jeans, and that blasted tabard drooping off me like it was designed for someone four times my size. Thank goodness I'm alone – save for Fred, of course, and he doesn't seem alarmed by my appearance. Grabbing Post-it King's chair, I push myself upright and fetch the bin bag from Fred's side.

I've almost emptied the rubbish when a ball of paper bounces clear of the bag and lands at my feet. I bend down to pick it up and I'm about to chuck it in the bin bag when something catches my eye.

His lovely handwriting, laid out like a poem. Is Post-it King a secret poet?

I'm about to take a closer look when I stop myself. This isn't one of his ninja lists. There are no tick boxes in sight, just lines of carefully penned thoughts. It was screwed up at the bottom of the bin: clearly he didn't want anyone else to see it.

But he doesn't know about me. Nobody sees me.

By the time he comes back in the morning, I won't be here. The office will be clean and tidy, the carpets vacuumed and the coffee station no longer a health hazard – and pretty much everyone won't give it a second thought. I'm supposed to be invisible; part of the machine that keeps everything ticking over at *The Herald*.

If I see it, he'll never know.

Besides, I just did a deep dive under his desk to rescue his bin. Surely I deserve a little reward?

My curiosity wins. With a quick glance about to make sure I'm not being watched, I smooth out the violent creases in the paper and sit slowly on Post-it King's chair as I read.

Jessie,
You are incredible. A light on the darkest day.
A brave, sparkling flame in the coldest place.

The world is at your feet and nothing is outside your grasp.

I think you could ask the stars to fall for you and they would.

I would.

We talk about truth in this place like an inconvenience, but here's one truth you can trust: you have my heart, if you want it . . .

Oh. My. *Goodness.*

My breath catches.

I turn the page over, hoping more of the message is on the other side. But it's blank. Turning it back, I read the words again, my heart thumping so loud in my ears now that even Stevie can't compete.

I can't believe he stopped writing.

I sit back, stunned. Because this is the most perfect love letter I have ever read. And because, instantly, my heart recognises the battle. He's trying to tell Jessie he loves her. This was his moment to finally express everything he'd carried in secret. Why did he stop?

Tell me, Es. Tell me why I shouldn't marry her . . .

I dismiss familiar tears with the heel of my hand.

I know what it's like to miss that opportunity. I wouldn't wish it on my worst enemy.

I stare back at the perfect words. And I know what I have to do.

Taking an envelope from the pile in Post-it King's in-tray, I carefully fold the letter and place it inside, sealing it so that nobody in the office can see the words. Then I select a lime-green sticky note from the top of the stack by his pen pot and stick it to the front. Borrowing a black biro from the pot, I scribble a note:

> <u>Don't</u> stop writing this.
> You're almost there.
> Kind regards, . . .

My pen pauses. Should I sign it? Write an initial? I glance at Fred, then the office clock on the wall behind him. I need to get going – there's only twenty-five minutes left of my shift. And I'm supposed to be invisible, so the less I say, the better. Decision made, I write the final words:

> A friend x

Four

ARCHIE

I didn't sleep last night.

I just kept thinking about that letter – about the words that should have been there. And bloody Callaghan's smug face when he stitched me up. I have come to an earth-shattering conclusion: I am completely rubbish. I've suspected it for a while but yesterday I magnificently proved it.

It's my own fault: I made The Vow.

Two years ago, I vowed that I wouldn't leave *The Herald* until I'd told Jessie Edmonds how I feel about her. Back then, I reckoned I'd summon the courage within weeks – that making The Vow would be the final push I needed. But then it all became too risky, too outfacing. And I started thinking about everything else that keeps me here: my rent, my bills, my not wanting to accept defeat. Before I knew it, two years passed and here I am.

Yesterday I was furious enough to make it happen. But I failed.

I've been walking around the city for an hour, trying to decide what to do. I should go in and tell Callaghan to stick his job. If I can't tell Jessie how I feel, I should just get as far away from her as possible.

But how would I live without seeing her every day?

I check my watch. Thirty minutes before I'm due at *The Herald*. Ordinarily I'd go in early, continue my woeful attempt at impressing my way into a writing job. But not today. Callaghan can take a long jump off a short plank if he thinks I'm going to suck up to him anymore.

I stride past the entrance to *The Herald*'s faded building, limbs fired with defiance despite the fact that nobody else will be in the office yet so my rebellion is pointless. I carry on, kicking into the wet pavement like a recently landed Viking off to claim his kingdom, making a wide circuit around my workplace, for the next ten minutes. But my resolve saps with each lap until, fifteen minutes later, I give up and slink into the building like a defeated lettuce . . .

Lettuce? Even my metaphors are limp this morning.

Norman, the security bloke on reception, looks up as I swipe my pass against the barrier.

'What's up, lad? Someone piss on your chips?'

Now there's a man who can wield a phrase.

'Several people. A positive party of pee,' I reply as I pass. Even Norm's boombox chuckle in my wake can't lift my mood.

Slumped against the side of the lift, I catch sight of my many-mirrored reflection. I look pathetic. Why did I ever think Jessie would take me seriously?

'You're a total joke, Archie Quinn,' I mutter. The myriad mirror versions of me snarl back.

The screens on the news-floor are blank when I emerge from the lift, desks empty and every chair neatly returned to its place. There's an unmistakeable tang of antibacterial cleaner and spray polish in the air and the coffee station is the cleanest I've seen it in months. We must have a new cleaning company, I muse, as I take the coffee filter jug to the water cooler to fill it. That must be a thankless task, cleaning this place. It might start passably tidy most mornings, but it's a pit by the end of the day.

Coffee made, I head to my desk. At least it's quiet. Callaghan won't be in for another two hours, while Jessie will arrive bang on eight o'clock. Which means an entire sixty minutes of perfectly perfumed loveliness beside me unsullied by our boss. Silver lining for the day, or as my grandfather would say: *one blessed crack in the shite shower.*

I can't help but grin thinking of that. Granda Brady is a one-off, a true original whose straight-talking wisdom and dubious Irish sayings brighten my days. I'll see him later today, along with the other old guys. Another good thing to hold on to. I sit with a sigh, the last of my fury carried out on the exhale. That's what I've got to do today: focus on the positives, not the rest. I can't spend my entire life being angry. It's not me. I need positives to keep me going. I need . . .

Hang on.

What's this?

The old sticky notes have been cleared from my desk and in their place is a single white envelope. There's a green sticky note stuck to the front, a handwritten message on it.

> <u>Don't</u> stop writing this.
> You're almost there.
> Kind regards,
>
> A friend x

Don't stop writing what?

My heart crashes against my ribcage as I open the envelope, my fingers faltering as I recognise the letter inside. My letter to Jessie. But how? I threw it away and my rubbish bin is empty like all the others nearby.

A thought grips me and I glance right at Jessie's desk where her notepad lies open. But my heart sinks when the handwriting doesn't match the note. Of course it's not from Jessie.

I look at the envelope again. So who sent it? And how did they get hold of the note?

Don't stop writing this. You're almost there.

Almost where? It's a failed letter. The words didn't come. *Almost there* is worse than nowhere at all. Why would a complete stranger fish a screwed-up letter out of a bin and send it back to me?

My head swims as I take it in.

'You're always so quick to believe the worst,' Granda Brady's voice singsongs into my mind. He's forever pulling me up for fast judgements. 'The world isn't conspiring against you, Archie Quinn, whatever you think. You're not that important.'

I smile despite myself. Granda's compliments always come with added bite. I love him for it, despite the wince that follows each helpful comment. Okay, so what would he tell me to do? I check my watch but it's too early to call him. Besides, my colleagues are due to arrive at any moment. I can't risk being caught on the phone.

I picture him in my mind instead, grinning beneath his Donegal tweed trilby that's seen far better days, that twinkle in his green eyes as he speaks.

Flip it, son. Turn that thought on its head.

Right. Here goes.

A complete stranger found my letter – I still don't know how – but they saw something in it that I missed. They rescued it, put it in an envelope and wrote me a note. Whoever my 'friend' is, they believed in me.

A lump appears in my throat. Surprised, I swallow it down.

They believed in me. In my words. That's more than anybody else has in this place.

You're almost there . . .

Am I?

And if they know where *there* is, do they know how I could reach it?

I take the Post-it note off the envelope and stash it safely in my desk drawer. Then I peel an orange Post-it note from the stack by my pencil pot and stick it to the letter inside.

If I'm going to do this, I need help.

Brandishing my pen, I write:

> *Dear friend*
> *How do I get there?*
> *Help me!*
>
> *Archie x*

I don't even hesitate about signing my name. Because the more I think about it, the stronger the idea becomes. It's completely unexpected, but I find I can't do this alone. Maybe what's been missing for the past two years – besides my own lack of courage – is someone to advise me. I don't know who my friend is, but it just might be that they arrived in my life at exactly the right time.

I tuck in the envelope flap and write *To my friend* on the front.

They might not reply. But I've been kicking at locked doors for too long and this is the opening I need. I stare at the note and something burns inside that I haven't felt in forever . . . hope.

Behind me a bell chimes and the lift doors open to usher in my colleagues. I watch them storming into the office, loud voices filling the place with sound. And it's only when the tide of bodies is almost at my desk that I remember the note still in my hand. At that moment, Jessie Edmonds emerges from the crowd and starts to stride towards me. Panicking, I grab one of my red Converse sneakers from beneath the desk and push the envelope inside, kicking it back underneath as Jessie and my colleague Liam Whittaker reach their desks, which flank mine on each side.

'Quinny!' Liam booms, shoving a grease-stained Greggs bag at me. 'Steak bake for brekkie!'

'Um, really? Thanks . . .'

'Call it research.' He grins, flakes of pastry dancing across his bottom lip and tumbling onto his beard as he speaks.

'Research?'

'*Ten Surprising Breakfast Alternatives* – I saw your article on MyManc, man. Impressive.'

I'm genuinely surprised. Normally if it doesn't have a connection to Formula One or his beloved Manchester United, Liam doesn't see anything. I didn't think he knew the local citizen journalism site existed, let alone read it. 'You did? Wow, thanks.'

'Total lack of pastry-based goods, mind,' he continues, chomping a sausage roll. 'And you coming from a family bakery? They'd excommunicate you if word got out.'

I grin back at him.

'Did you write something, Archie?'

My heart rate quickens as I turn to Jessie. Her jacket is already on the back of her chair, her pen in her hand and her work loaded up on her monitor.

'It's just a community site,' I say, my world spinning slightly as our eyes meet.

'What's the addy? I'll look it up.'

That smile will be the end of me.

I don't trust my ability to reply coherently, so I fetch another sticky note and scribble the MyManc web address in frankly awful handwriting. My smile mirrors hers as I hand it over, the tip of her thumb brushing mine when she takes the note.

'Thanks,' she says, turning back to her monitor.

I go to reply, but somewhere between my brain and my tongue the words get tangled, so all I can manage is, *'Nnhgyurrwlcmnthanx . . .'*

Liam sniggers into his Greggs bag. I stuff my steak bake into my mouth before I embarrass myself any further. But, as we all start to work, the knowledge of the envelope in my shoe takes away some of the sting.

I'll wait until everyone else has gone tonight and then I'll leave it on my desk, exactly as I found it.

I just hope my friend visits again . . .

Five

ESTHER

'What's that?'

Issy, my eldest niece, is all questions today. I'm folding washing in my sister's utility room and she's hovering at my elbow. It's an inset day at school, so I have the pleasure of her company all day, along with her sisters. I love her, but it's like constantly entertaining a coiled spring today.

'It's washing.' I grin, enjoying the mock groan she gives in reply.

'I know *that*. I mean the blue thing on the top.'

'It's a tabard,' I reply.

'A what?'

'An apron that covers your back and your front. I wear it for work.'

'Cool! Can I try it on?'

Knowing my niece, she won't give up until I say yes, so I don't even bother to argue. 'Sure. Just don't get it dirty, okay? I need it clean for my shift tonight.'

Of course, my work uniform swamps her, but Issy is delighted, dancing off out of the kitchen, pulling up the slipping shoulders as she goes.

I pile the rest of the folded washing into my sister's artisan-woven wicker washing basket, shaking my head at the ridiculous multi-looped 'rustic gingham embellishments' tied to both handles – Naomi's latest entrepreneurial venture. *Making Cleaning Cute*, according to her Insta posts. She's aiming to become the queen of decorated household goods, each item bedecked in ribbons and silk flowers. Good luck to her, I say.

I can hear Issy's giggles out in the garden through the bifold doors from the kitchen as I bring the beribboned basket into the large open-plan space. As temporary accommodation goes, I can't really fault this house. It's light and spacious and much better when the girls are home from school, their noise and energy bouncing off the artfully grey walls.

'Issy Martins, what *are* you wearing?'

My heart sinks a little. I can hear my sister hurrying across the lawn from her 'garden office' (aka the large pastel-painted shed at the bottom of the garden). She won't be happy about the kids being out there, but it's a lovely day and for once they are all getting on.

'I'm being Auntie Esther,' Issy protests.

'Oh right. Because being a cleaning lady is such an aspirational career choice. Take it off.'

'But it's a *tabard*, Mum!'

'It's ridiculous. Take it off.'

I take a long breath and walk out into the garden.

Naomi is shielding her eyes from the late afternoon sun with one perfectly manicured hand, the other outstretched to receive my uniform as Issy struggles out of it.

'I take it this was your idea,' she says as I pass her to help my niece.

'Issy asked if she could try it on.' I gently ease my niece's long blonde hair from the knot of fabric it's wrapped around. 'No harm done.'

My niece beams quickly at me before she runs over to her sisters.

'Don't,' Naomi snaps.

'Don't what?'

'I think it's great you've found work, Es, but don't bring your lowered standards to my girls. I want them to achieve more.'

My hackles rise, as they always do. 'It's just a tabard. It's not an attack on your ambition. And anyway, I *have* achieved more. I achieved for seven years—'

'And I haven't?'

'I never said that.'

'You didn't need to.'

Here we are again, where we've been too many times before. Why is everything always about my sister? Why does she see my success as some kind of commentary on her life?

I don't want to fight today. I can already feel weariness tugging at my limbs and I still have my shift ahead of me. 'That wasn't my intention. You know it wasn't. I'm hugely grateful to you for taking me in, Naomi. I was just having fun with Issy, that's all.'

For a moment, I think she's ramping up for another round, but then she rolls her eyes and takes a step back. 'Right. Can you put dinner on for me? I just need another thirty minutes to finish this thing I'm working on.'

'Sure.'

*

It's a relief to drive into the city, two hours later. Dinner was tense, to say the least, Naomi shooting me evils at every opportunity, my brother-in-law Gavin droning on about roadworks he'd encountered on his way home and rolling his eyes at everything else, while the girls chatted on, oblivious to it all. I miss the days of lazy dinners in nobody's company except my own and whoever was playing on my music system. I miss a lot about my old life, not least the choice to be alone if I wanted to be, but I shake off the weight that the memory of it always hangs on my heart. I can't look back. I daren't.

My shift seems to take an age tonight. Time stretches between the desks and the bins, my slow progress around the otherworldly night-time office feeling like an uphill climb. I can't find the right song to listen to. I trip over invisible obstacles. My feet drag. My body protests with aches and grumbles.

But there's one difference that makes it all vanish.

It happens when I reach Post-it King's desk.

I've left it almost till last this evening, a reward for completing the rest of my tasks. And the moment I arrive there, my heart leaps.

There's a white envelope in the centre of his desk, the area around it spotlessly clean. Bless him. Has he worked out what my job is? Whether he has or not, this singular kind act means the world.

Written in his lovely handwriting are three words that make me smile:

To my friend

I glance behind me, relaxing when I see only Fred there, then I sit on Post-it King's chair to open the envelope. Inside is his original letter and, on a bright-orange Post-it note stuck to it, a message for me:

Dear friend
How do I get there?
Help me!

Archie x

Archie. I like it.

Archie the Post-it King of *The Herald*. He sounds friendly. Mind you, I don't think it would have made a difference what his name was; I've already decided he's my favourite *Herald* employee. He had me at the tick box lists. And that impossibly wonderful love letter . . .

And now he wants me to help him finish it.

I *love* that. Even if I'm not sure what to tell him.

I need to think about this.

I look over to the coffee station, which, as usual, is a *pit*. Cleaning that will help me mull over my reply, I decide, putting Archie's letter safely in the front pocket of my tabard – the garment my sister branded 'ridiculous' earlier. *It's not ridiculous now*, I tell her in my head. It's proof I'm getting back on my feet. And it's now a keeper of treasure.

I can't hide my smile as I head over.

What do I tell Archie? I know how his letter made me feel but how do I help him find the words to match? Scrubbing at stubborn coffee stains, I watch the tide of water and soap bubbles changing from clear to brown, the shine of metal so dulled by the mess slowly returning beneath my cloth. My thoughts swirl with the water, memories rising to the surface.

Memories of Matt.

I wince as the old familiar pain re-emerges.

The chances I missed. The words I swallowed. The time I wasted.

By the time the coffee station is clean, I know what to tell Archie.

Half an hour later, I'm walking away from *The Herald*'s building, a warm glow inside despite my body being ready to drop. It took longer tonight to do my cleaning than it has before, but I don't mind leaving late. I'll be quicker tomorrow night. Besides, I haven't felt this excited about anything for months – I'm determined to enjoy it.

My stomach growls and I remember I haven't eaten. Dinner this evening became so excruciating I made my excuses and left the table having only nibbled a few bites of bread. There's a Turkish chippy not far from here that stays open until half past eleven. Do I have time to get there before it closes?

I lift my denim jacket sleeve to check my watch – and my heart crashes to the floor.

My bracelet is missing. The one Molly made for me when I first arrived at Naomi's. I've worn it constantly ever since, the sight of it on my wrist above my watch enough to brighten my toughest days. A length of felt with a fastening made of a plaited embroidery cotton loop and a primrose-yellow button, it's lovingly stitched in the wonkiest way, with Molly's own design of daisies surrounding my name. Where's it gone?

Panic rising, I force my mind to replay the events of this evening, trying to picture where I had it last. I'm hoping I didn't drop it on the journey from the car park to work – if it fell in the street it's lost forever. But then I remember the button scratching across the edge of Archie's envelope as I wrote the note to him.

It has to be in the office.

I don't stop to think. I turn back and race to the building, praying the night watchman hasn't locked the main door for the night. I have to find it – with any luck I can slip back inside, hunt for it and get out again before anybody notices.

Thankfully the door swings open when I yank the handle, the front desk empty as I run past. Using the fob on my building pass, I summon the lift and dash inside, tapping my impatience out on the hammered steel floor as it creeps too slowly to the fourth floor. I don't remember seeing the bracelet when I put my coat on, which means it must have dropped between Archie's desk and the cupboard where Fred lives along with all the cleaning supplies, where I stash my coat and bag while I work. The loop that fits over the button fastening has been getting more saggy over the weeks I've worn it and I've been meaning to put a couple of extra stitches over the end to secure it. All I can think is that the button slipped out, causing the bracelet to fall off.

The lift doors finally part and I hurry into *The Herald*'s office, blinking away the glare of the lift lights until my eyes focus on the dimly lit space beyond. There's no sign of Molly's bracelet in Fred's cupboard, so I quickly retrace my steps across the darkened office floor towards Archie's desk. In the half-light, I can't see anything out of place. I'm almost at the desk when a bell sounds behind me.

I lose my breath.

Someone is coming up in the lift.

Damn it!

I can't let anyone find me here, not after I've signed out. I can't afford to lose my job over this.

I hurry to Fred's cupboard, only just managing to slip inside and shut the door as the clunk and heavy slide of lift doors sounds beyond it. Holding my breath, my heart slamming in my ears, I lean against the door and listen.

A high giggle.

A low snigger.

Then two elongated *shussshes*, the kind fuelled by too much alcohol and shockingly few inhibitions.

'What if *sss*omeone comes in?' a woman's voice slurs.

'*Isss* cool, babe,' a bloke's voice replies. '*Shh*cool. We're *to-o-odlly* alone.'

I hear more sniggering and the pop of a champagne cork, followed by a clatter of crockery in the coffee station.

Great. So much for cleaning it earlier.

But if I think a dirty coffee station is my biggest concern, I'm quickly proved wrong.

Because it gets worse. The giggles and sniggers merge into murmurs and mumbles . . .

Oh no . . .

Then *much* worse. The mumbles become moans . . .

Hell, no . . .

A low one followed by a high one, over and over like a demented game of tennis without the ball-thwacks.

My stomach churns. *Ball-thwacks* was definitely not the word to spring to mind right now.

Bloody hell, no!

I'm trapped, aren't I? I can't leave without Molly's bracelet and, judging by the sounds floating through the door that I *really* wish I wasn't hearing, my path would be blocked by the couple who sound like they're just the other side.

A sudden bump and the crash of objects tumbling to the floor from the workstation nearest Fred's cupboard confirm my very worst suspicions.

I'm going to have to *completely* disinfect that desk before I leave. Wearing two pairs of gloves . . .

At any other time I might find this hilarious – and maybe one day this will become a funny story I tell my friends – but right now I'm tired and stressed and I just want to go home. Even the thought of Archie's letter waiting on his desk for him to find doesn't take the edge off the horror.

I back away from the door – and the unmistakeable noises the other side of it – and retreat into the dark depths of Fred's cupboard. Edging round his comforting bulk I hunker down on an unopened palette of paper towels and jam my earbuds in, blasting my music as loud as I can bear to drown out everything else.

This is horrific, but it can't last forever. I'll hide here until they've gone, straighten everything up, find Molly's bracelet and get the heck out of the building.

The noises beyond the door start to rise again towards a gut-wrenching, inescapable crescendo. Wincing, I pull my jacket over my head and put my hands over my eyes . . .

Six

ARCHIE

Hi Archie,
I don't claim to be an expert
but I think if you start with your heart,
the words will follow.
So what does your heart want Jessie to know?
Your friend,

Esther x

Esther. Great name.

And that's a cool reply.

My new friend is officially cool.

I, on the other hand, didn't even attempt to be cool about dashing here this morning. I'm an hour early and it has nothing to do with trying to impress my boss. I wanted to see if my friend had replied.

Esther. I wanted a reply from Esther.

I'm not surprised she's a woman. Her handwriting was too flowery to belong to a bloke and it just felt like a female sort of answer. I groan. No wonder I can't find the right words if that's the kind of lame response I make in my own head.

I'm thrilled she replied, though. Even if her advice leaves me no closer to completing Jessie's letter. My heart is a woeful tumble of mess most of the time, especially concerning Jessie Edmonds. I don't know how to start unravelling it all to find out exactly what it's trying to say.

I'll give it a go, though. Not least because I finally have somebody who thinks I can do it.

I was thinking about this last night, as I sat with the lads in the community hall, trying my best to keep up with the latest tune we're all learning. My banjo's seen better days, but that's not surprising considering I climbed into a skip to rescue it. As I was plucking along – getting about one note right in every seven – it struck me that my secret friend is unlike anyone I've ever met before. Because she is, isn't she? She saw my letter and read beyond the words. If that isn't remarkable, I don't know what is.

My grandfather had clocked it immediately, of course. He'd winked across the circle of ageing musicians at me, that old Donegal tweed hat of his at an even more rakish angle than usual.

'What's her name?'

'Whose name?'

He'd chuckled. 'Whoever she is who found your grin.'

'I'm not grinning,' I'd protested, but Granda Brady was having none of it.

'Are you not? Strange.'

'What's strange?' By then, everyone in the circle was watching us.

'Put it this way, lad, you look awful happy for a man murdering a banjo.'

I'd dismissed his jibe, naturally, but he was right, wasn't he? Turns out my letter-advising friend *is* a woman. She knows nothing about me and yet she believes I can write this letter. That's incredible – and I'm not about to pass up the opportunity to seek her advice. Maybe this is the moment things change. With her help I could finally tell Jessie Edmonds how I feel and plan to get out of this place.

I'm about to write a reply when I spot something in my wastepaper basket. It's spotlessly clean as usual – thankfully not reeking of disinfectant, as some bits of the office are this morning. But there's a brightly coloured scrap of fabric draped over one side. I pick it up and turn it over, my pulse kicking up a gear when I see what's stitched across it.

Six daisies, three on each side, and a name in the middle . . .

✳ ESTHER ✳

There's a bright yellow button on one side of the green fabric and on the other a loop of braided yellow, orange and white threads that supposedly fits over the button. The loop is frayed and a bit grubby and the stitching looks like it was done by someone either inexperienced or drunk. Did Esther make it herself? It feels odd to be holding something of hers. I must be right about her being a night cleaner – the fact this has been dropped in a clean bin overnight and the new message on my desk are dead giveaways.

I'll send it back to her in my reply. But, first, I need to work out what to say next . . .

I glance at the clock. I still have half an hour before anyone arrives. I'd better get a move on.

I smooth out the letter to Jessie on my desk and reach for

a pen. But my elbow catches the edge of my mug, sending it tumbling off my desk, the contents splashing a dark puddle of coffee over the blue office carpet.

Shit!

Stuffing the letter and the envelope into my pocket, I jump up from my chair and look around for something to soak up the spill. A half-empty packet of tissues on my desk does nothing to help and ripped sheets from my notepad are useless, too. I have to clean this up before anyone else sees – if Esther is a cleaner and Callaghan spots this mess she'll be out on her ear. He's sacked people before for less. The night cleaners are provided by a contractor – Callaghan's favourite people to harass. We've been through two water cooler bottle companies and three cleaning contractors in the last year alone. If they're not employees, they're fair game for his vitriol.

I can't let that happen to the friend I've only just found.

I sprint from my desk to the cleaning cupboard, hoping it isn't locked. The previous company guarded their cleaning supplies like the crown jewels – a zealousness that was ultimately their downfall when Callaghan couldn't get into the cupboard to get bin bags and went ballistic.

As I reach the cupboard I notice papers and a spilled pen pot on the floor by the desk nearest it. That's odd, especially with the rest of the office being so tidy. I scoop the bits up quickly, placing them neatly back. Then I return to the cleaning cupboard.

The handle sticks a little, causing me a heart-stopping moment of panic, but finally it relents with a squeak of protest. I don't bother switching on the light, spotting the large roll of blue paper towels as soon as I open the door. I snatch it up with relief and am just reaching for the spray bottle of antibacterial cleaner hanging on the handle of the yellow cleaning truck when a sound stops me in my tracks.

I freeze.

Nothing happens.

Man, I am far too jumpy for my own good. Laughing at my own daftness, I pick up the spray bottle and turn to leave.

Behind me, the noise comes again.

Is that – a snore?

I follow the sound, edging around the cleaning trolley that dominates the space, look down – and pause.

Lying on what looks like a huge, cellophane-wrapped stack of rolls of blue paper towels is a person. Curled up on their side, their face obscured by the collar of a faded denim jacket; they are wearing ripped jeans and, just visible underneath the jacket, what looks like a blue tabard apron like the one my mum wears when she works in our family bakery's shop. A tumble of dark curls is splayed out across one edge of their paper towel palette bed, while Jaffa-orange Converse sneakers dangle off the other. They look both cosy on their makeshift bed and painfully uncomfortable at once. I'm tempted to leave them sleeping, but people will be coming in soon and I can't risk them being found.

Tentatively, I reach down and give their arm a gentle shake. There's a loud snort of a snore and they sleep on. When I put down the paper towel roll and spray bottle and lean closer, I spot an earbud in their ear, bright white against the chocolate curls. Crouching beside the sleeper, I gently lift the earbud out.

'Hey,' I whisper. 'Wake up.'

And then everything happens at once.

The body jumps, right arm flailing out, their forearm connecting with my nose with a crack. Shocked, I rock back, clutching my aching face, just as they try to sit upright and slide off the plastic-wrapped roll stack, landing in a heap on my feet.

'Ow!'

'Argh!'

'What are you . . . ?'

'Get off me!'

We jump apart and suddenly I'm face to face with a startled girl, her amber eyes staring wide at me through a veil of scattered curls. She looks horrified. I scramble aside, holding her earbud towards her like a pathetic olive branch.

'Sorry – *sorry* – you were asleep and . . . this is a cleaning cupboard and . . . this is yours.'

The wild stranger snatches the earbud and I notice rainbow-painted varnish on her nails as her fingers brush mine. For a moment I'm worried she'll attack me, but then her eyebrows rise and her hand flies to her mouth.

'I'm still here, aren't I?'

I stifle a smile. 'As far as I can tell . . .'

'No, I mean I'm still *here* – at work.' Her eyes lift to the ceiling. 'In Fred's cupboard . . .'

'Fred?'

She blinks and I watch a slow blush claim her cheeks. 'I am so, so sorry! I shouldn't be here. I only came back for my bracelet . . .'

The bracelet? So is this . . . ?

'You mean this?' I scrabble in my pocket, my fingers forgetting how to work for a moment. My mind is racing, my heart thudding along beside it. Finally I feel the warm fabric between my fingertips and pull the bracelet out.

'That's mine,' she breathes. 'Where did you find it?'

'In the bin by my desk,' I say, taking in this person who has appeared physically in my life as suddenly as her words appeared before. 'Hi, Esther. I'm Archie.'

She gives a slow blink and then it's as if a light snaps on inside her, a smile blossoming across her lips. Realising I'm staring, I grin back, my own cheeks burning now.

The air warms between us. For a moment I forget everything – the surprise of finding her here, the strong smell of disinfectant from the trolley behind us, the fact we're crouched *in a cleaning cupboard* . . . It all vanishes. It's just her and me, flush-faced, wide-eyed and grinning like loons.

In that moment, I know my life has changed.

I can't explain it. I just know.

. . . And then I hear the bell chime above the lift doors.

'You can't stay here,' I rush, my hand touching hers without thinking.

She doesn't flinch, but her smile vanishes. 'I can't be seen. I'll get in trouble if I am. Can you help me?'

I can hear voices now, the familiar bark of Liam's laugh as it passes the cleaning cupboard door. How am I going to smuggle Esther out without being spotted?

Think, Archie!

And then it comes to me: a bright, blessed flash of inspiration that's so blinkin' genius it brings a bubble of laughter to my voice.

'How do you feel about being an OAP?' I ask.

'A what . . . ?'

'Here we go, Mrs Stanhope, you just grab my arm and we'll see you out, okay?' I call loudly as we shuffle out of the cleaning cupboard together. Esther's head is bowed beneath the hast-ily tied blue paper towel headscarf, her body swamped in an enormous beige mackintosh that's lived in the lost property pile at the back of that cupboard for as long as I've worked here. She's bent her back over, rocking a little as she totters beside me. From behind, she could easily pass as an elderly lady battling painful hips to walk. At least, that's what I hope. Our steps quicken as we reach the lift, though, just in case any of my colleagues are more alert than usual this morning.

By the time we're inside the lift, the doors safely closing us in, we can no longer contain our laughter. Esther grasps her stomach, doubling over, eyes brimming with tears as she pulls the paper scarf off her head.

'I can't believe that worked!'

'Me either.'

'That was brilliant, Archie.'

'I only thought of the costume. You made it work. Don't take this the wrong way but you make a cracking old lady.'

She snorts and gives a bow. 'Cheers. I'm just hoping your friends didn't spot these.' Her multi-reflection in the mirrored lift wiggles a myriad of orange sneakers.

'So, you're a cool old biddy.'

'Apparently I am.' Her eyes twinkle and then, with no warning whatsoever, she hugs me. A full-on, no-holds-barred embrace. Arms tight around my body, her cheek against my chest. 'Thank you,' she murmurs.

It's such a surprise I almost lose my footing.

The lift continues its slow descent, our bodies pressed together.

Instinctively, my arms wrap around her, the folds of the too-large mackintosh gathering beneath my hands. I smile against her curls. 'You're welcome.'

Seven

ESTHER

We only pull apart when we feel the lift start to slow. I'm breathless with laughter and the sheer audacity of what we just did to get out of *The Herald*'s offices, but also that I hugged him. I *hugged* Archie – the Post-it King who, without ever knowing it, has been making me smile since I started working here.

'Better pop your headscarf back on, Gran.' He grins, nodding at the little screen above the lift door that has flicked to G for the ground floor.

I do my best to replace the crumpled paper head covering, giggling as I take Archie's arm and we hobble out into the foyer. He talks loudly to me the whole way, even though nobody we pass appears bothered, until we clear the entrance doors and emerge into the pale Manchester sunlight. I keep my arm tucked through his until we round the corner of the building, out of sight.

Laughing, I shrug off the mackintosh and offer it back to him.

'Keep it,' he says, pushing it back to me.

'But it needs returning.'

Archie folds his arms. 'And how's it going to look if I go back up there with this, eh? They'll think I mugged you for your mac.'

'It's a nice mac.'

'It is. But not worth robbing an old lady for.'

We trade grins again, my heart so full it could finally fit the raincoat. 'I really appreciate you getting me out . . .' I begin, but Archie holds up a hand.

'Don't mention it. I'm glad we met at last.' His gaze drops to his feet – to the cherry-red sneakers I recognise from their usual resting place beneath his desk. He isn't at all like I thought he'd be, yet somehow he absolutely fits the feeling I've had about him. He's taller than me, with a mop of sandy-brown hair and eyes the colour of my jeans. He blushes when he smiles, managing to look like a cheeky five-year-old boy and a grown man simultaneously.

'Me too.'

He reaches into his pocket, producing the envelope I know so well already. 'I – um – replied.'

Now this is weird. I accept it and unfold the extra sheet of paper wrapped around the half-finished letter to the love of his life.

'"*I wish I could reach inside my heart and pull out the perfect words to explain how I feel*",' I read. Archie is *really* blushing now. I force my eyes back to his words. '"*I just don't know how I'll ever express it. My words work for everything else, but not this.*"'

'"*Can you help me, Esther?*",' he choruses with me as I read.

I look at Archie at the moment he dares to meet my gaze. I see it then: the pain my heart knows too well. It's etched into his skin, it weighs down his brow, and I want to reach out and smooth it all away. Because I've carried that for a year and nobody should ever have to experience it. Especially not Archie.

'Yes, I'll help you. I don't know how we'll do it, but we'll find the words.'

'Could be fun.' He smiles, his eyes still haunted.

'Could be.'

'*Will* be. But not if it's done with envelopes and sticky notes.'

What's he suggesting? 'How, then?'

'Meet me. To chat. One day soon, before your shift. If you like,' he adds, as if there were ever any chance I'd refuse.

'I start at eight.'

'So meet me at half six.'

'What's open at half six around here?'

'Rossi's – it's a little café that does meals till nine. It's a block away from here, right by the river. Do you know it?'

'I can find it. But I can't afford a meal, Archie.'

'You don't have to. My mate Ciro owns it with his brother. He won't mind us just having coffee and cake. My shout,' he adds quickly before I can protest. 'We could meet once a week, maybe, and in the meantime I'll work on the letter. What do you think?'

It's completely unexpected. It will mean missing dinner with my sister once a week and finding a plausible excuse why. But I like Archie – and I want to help. Maybe if I can help him win Jessie's heart, the universe will forget the mistake I made in my own life and I can finally stop punishing myself for it.

'I think you have a deal,' I reply.

His hand is warm as it shakes mine.

My phone is totally dead, the battery drained by the all-night music party in my ears while I slept in Fred's cupboard. I don't want to think about the messages lurking on there from my sister or the huge row already brewing at her house to greet me on my return. So she will have had to take her own children to school for once? Big deal. I never agreed to do it every day and maybe she needs to appreciate that. All the same, I'm not relishing seeing her.

All I want to do is drink a pot of tea, curl up in bed and sleep until I have to go back to work tonight. I don't fancy my chances of that happening, not with my sister on the warpath, but it's a nice thought to drive home with.

As are thoughts of Archie.

I can't believe he got me out of *The Herald*'s building – or that he did it in such a brilliant way. He didn't have to do that. He could have minded his own business. I hope he doesn't get in trouble for it. My manager Marjorie reckons Jock Callaghan is terrifying. He ousted at least two cleaning companies before ours got the contract. How does Archie work for someone like that?

What I can't quite get my head around is how Archie felt like a friend I'd known forever. There was no standing on ceremony, or hesitation to crack jokes. It's like we knew each other and had an ease between us that normally comes from years of friendship. I never had *escaping from a building dressed as an old lady* on my list of expectations for my new life after losing my job, that's for sure. It was fun, though. I haven't giggled like that with anyone since . . .

I brake sharply as the traffic lights change to amber ahead.

. . . since *Matt*.

What would Matt have made of my doddery old dear disguise?

I can't help the thought arriving: it's a natural impulse I'm still not cured of. I fool myself that what Matt thinks doesn't concern me anymore – because no matter what, despite everything, a defiant part of me still wants to know. I want to call him up and relay the story, embellishing every detail until I'm rewarded by his booming laugh. For years he was my go-to person for every crazy, random thing that happened in my life. Overheard conversations in coffee shops, bonkers things Mum said, the latest gossip from work – it didn't matter what it was, Matt was the first person I told. A year without that constant communication has stung more than anything.

I should be over him. But I'm not.

I'm scared I'll never be.

Matt Hope was my partner in crime since the day we met at primary school. He arrived in my third year, a fascinating newcomer in our class of firmly established friendships. Everybody wanted to be his friend, but Matt chose me. From then on, we were always together.

We danced around dating in our teens, sharing the odd drunken snog at the end of parties but never anything else. He dated, I dated, and we met in the middle when we'd both been dumped. At college it was the same. And even though we went to different universities, they were still in the same city, so we carried on.

And I loved him.

I loved Matt from the beginning and I secretly hoped we'd be each other's natural conclusion. Just over a year ago, I thought it was going to happen. I'd promised myself that I would finally tell him how I felt. But when the perfect moment appeared, I didn't speak.

And then, six weeks later, he married someone else.

It was a whirlwind, he told me, one of those moments when the stars align. And it didn't matter that they'd only dated a week before he proposed because when you meet the love of your life, what's the point in waiting?

I'm almost at the turning for Naomi's street now. I snap on my hazard lights and pull over to the kerb, tears blurring my vision too much to drive on yet. As the hum of disgruntled morning traffic snakes past, I pull my jacket sleeves over my hands and press them to my eyes.

I blame *When Harry Met Sally*. I lost count of the number of times we watched it together over the years, first on a dodgy VHS Matt's mum had taped off the telly, then a DVD we replaced three times as each one wore out from overuse and Matt's inability to ever put discs back in their boxes. He loved Harry's big line at the end and did a pitch-perfect impression of Billy Crystal saying it at every opportunity.

And then he pretty much used that line to justify marrying Nina. *I just want the rest of my life to start as soon as possible, Es . . .*

When he put it like that, what could I say?

That's why I want to help Archie. I don't want him throwing away his chance to speak, like I did. When I saw that pain wash over his face today, it was like looking at myself. Except Archie still has time to tell Jessie he loves her. I couldn't save my heart: maybe I can save his.

'Where *the hell* have you been?'

I don't even get to step inside before she starts. Naomi is incandescent, her fury clearly honed over the three hours she's had to process my absence. She is going to have her say and nothing between heaven and hell is going to stop her.

'I'm sorry, I got caught at work and—'

'You finish at eleven, Es. *Eleven*. Are you telling me you slept there?'

If only you knew.

'I was delayed and a friend let me stay over.'

A friend called Fred. He let me kip in his cupboard . . .

My sister's hands slam onto her hips; her ever-perfect nails digging into her Instagram-perfect cashmere sweater. 'Oh really? A *friend*? Who's this? Some random you met in a bar?'

'What?'

'I don't believe you. I think you sat outside Matt's house again. All night.'

I bristle. She has no right throwing that at me. It happened once. *Once.* And he wasn't even there. Will I ever be allowed to forget it? 'Sod off,' I growl, pushing past her and heading for the kitchen.

'I had to take the girls,' Naomi barks behind me. 'When I have so much work today. Do you have any idea how much of an inconvenience that was?'

I snap the switch on the kettle, hoping it will drown out her voice. 'They're your kids.'

'What was that?'

'Nothing.'

'There are three loads of washing that need doing and Gavin needs shirts ironed for his conference tomorrow. And the school run, unless you want your nieces stranded again like they nearly were this morning. I get that life is tough for you, Es, but in this house we show up and we get the work done.'

I close my eyes as the steam builds. Weariness has slammed back into my body and I can't push it away. If I don't sleep now I won't be able to work later. 'It will have to wait,' I reply, my voice merging with the boiling kettle.

'It can't!'

I spin around to face her and see her falter for a nanosecond when she sees my expression. It's enough to push my advantage. 'I'm exhausted. I need to sleep. I'll iron Gavin's shirts before I go to work tonight but if you want the washing done, you'll have to do it. You'll have to collect the kids too, just for today . . .'

'Are you seriously telling me . . . ?'

'. . . Because here's the thing, Naomi: if I don't sleep now I'll get ill, my body will call a time out and I'll be in bed for a week. Now you can either give me one day to rest or lose me for seven. Your choice.'

She has no answer for that. I knew she wouldn't. Calmly I make a pot of tea, fill a jug with milk and put the pot, the jug, a mug and a pack of biscuits on a tray. Naomi stares back, her mouth open and useless as I ease past her and head to my room.

I don't like fighting with my sister. I'm genuinely grateful for her opening her home to me. But I haven't fought back since I arrived and today something changed. I've missed being in control of my own life, of having a purpose beyond just getting through each day.

Now, I have something.

Someone.

First, I'm going to drink tea and get some sleep.

And then, I'm going to work out how to help Archie.

Eight

ARCHIE

Callaghan is out for blood today. He's like a bear with a sore head, and, if I didn't know better, I'd swear he was hungover. He's not the only one, either. If there was a pub blowout last night I must have missed the memo. Jessie is quiet, too. And Sarah from Accounts, who popped in an hour ago and avoided eye contact with everybody. Even Liam is keeping his head down.

'Callaghan's got woman trouble, I reckon,' our senior reporter, Brian Presley aka Elvis, mutters to me when we're standing by the coffee station.

'Ugh, thanks. Way to make my coffee unpalatable.' I grin back. 'I can't believe any woman would find *that* attractive.'

'They don't. They see desperation, a disposable income and a moderately pathetic amount of power as attractive. Old Jocky has all three in spades.' He laughs as he pats my back. 'And on that note, I'm off.'

'What's the job today?'

Elvis grimaces. 'Puff piece for a local MP. Going to take all my professional detachment to resist punching the bloke.'

'Good luck with that.' I mirror his expression as if I share his pain, but, in truth, his job sounds like a dream to me.

'It's the constant questionable glamour of my job, Archie. A cross I have to bear.'

I like Elvis. He's always been happy to chat to me about the job he's done since the age of seventeen and I like the way he sees it. If I ever get to be a reporter, I want to be just like him.

I definitely don't want to be like my editor. As the morning drags on, Callaghan's ire grows – and nobody is exempt from his wrath:

'Quinn! Where's my coffee?'

'Am I the only poor sod in this place able to understand basic grammar?'

'I'm not asking for a Pulitzer Prize-winning article, Jessica. I just want a business roundup of the council meeting this afternoon. You think you can do that?'

'Why are these files not in order? Quinn!'

None of it touches me. Not like it normally would. I take Callaghan his coffee, find the file he needs, duck out of the room as he launches his vitriol at Jessie and Liam, and get on with the crazy long list of tasks I've been given, oblivious to everything else.

Because I have a friend. And a way forward.

It's only when Callaghan storms out for what will no doubt be a long, liquid lunch with Steve Parnell, *The Herald*'s MD, that the mood lightens and Liam wheels his chair over to my desk.

'So, what was all that this morning?'

'All what?'

'Smuggling an old lady out of the office.' He grins through a great mouthful of sausage sandwich, tomato sauce dancing at the corner of his mouth and crumbs between his teeth. 'Didn't have you down as a granny-botherer.'

'Nice.' I brush the crumbs he's sprayed off my desk. 'She came in wanting to place a classified ad.'

My colleague frowns. 'Classifieds are downstairs.'

I lean back in my chair, nonchalant as you like, praying Liam can't hear my heartbeat crashing in my ears. 'I know that, you know that, but Mrs Stanhope didn't.'

His eyes narrow. 'Stanhope?'

'Yep.'

'I see. First name *Vera* by any chance?'

Ohhh crap . . .

I thought the name felt familiar . . . Straight from my favourite books by Ann Cleeves and the only TV show I refuse to miss – facts I've discussed at length with Liam over the last two years.

'Enid, actually,' I rush, chucking the first old lady name I can think of at him. 'What are the chances, eh?'

'Indeed.' Liam observes me for a minute more than is comfortable, then shrugs and takes a swig of coffee to wash down his sandwich. 'What's up with Jessie today?'

'No idea. She said anything to you?'

'Nope. Thought you might have been able to charm a smile out of her.'

'What's that supposed to mean?'

'You're the entertainment, aren't you?' When I frown, he laughs and slaps a heavy hand on my shoulder. 'Chill, mate. I'm just joshing.' He leans closer, even though Jessie is out at the council chambers and can't hear us. 'I reckon she likes you best, that's all.'

Does she?

The question dances around my head all afternoon. I'm so used to believing Jessie Edmonds hardly notices my existence, but what if that's my own doubt speaking? Liam is hardly the most observant of people, but, if he's noticed, might it be more obvious than I thought?

Jessie returns an hour before the end of my shift, harassed and flush-faced. I make her tea in her favourite mug without being asked, placing it on her desk as she regales Liam with the details of her afternoon. When she finally flops down on her chair and sees it, her smile is the best reward.

'Did you make this, Arch?'

'Thought you'd need it.'

'It's perfect. My hero.' Her eyes sparkle and her hand is cool when it rests on mine. My face, by contrast, is a furnace. If they ever invent a pill to stop you blushing, I'll be first in the queue. Mum reckons it's endearing; I think it's a curse.

She keeps her hand there while she takes a long sip, her hair falling back over her shoulder as she drinks. I have to look away to save what little dignity I still possess. On the other side of me, I swear I hear Liam chuckle.

When I see Esther next, we're going to nail that letter . . .

On my way back home I pop into Mum and Dad's shop. We talk on the phone every day, more or less, but it's been almost a week since I saw them last. I've had my tiny flat for four years now but it's still weird not living with them. I know it's not supposed to be cool to admit you like your folks, but mine rock.

It helps that their lives are like a constant soap opera. Weatherfield has nothing on Quinn & Co, the Quinn family bakery. My sister Dacey often jokes that the theme tune from

Coronation Street should play whenever the door opens because, no matter what day or time of the year you visit, there's always drama. Never life or death stuff, you understand, but my folks can make the most mundane happening into a drama that has you on the edge of your seat. It helps that they live at the heart of a community and the shop is a conduit for the best gossip in Greater Manchester, so if they have no dramas of their own to contend with, they can easily nick someone else's.

Today is no exception. Mum meets me at the door with a mug of tea, a Belgian bun and the latest controversy.

'Doreen Metcalfe's next-door neighbour was mugged!'

Not even over the threshold yet, I don't hide my smile. 'Who?'

'Doreen,' Mum repeats, still not letting me in. 'You know her.'

'Do I?'

She gives a sigh Dame Judi Dench would covet and thrusts the mug at me. 'Comes in every Tuesday. Three split tins and a custard tart.'

'Can I come in?'

'Broad daylight it was! Can you believe it?'

'Love you, Mum.' I lean in and kiss her cheek, the magic gesture to break the spell. She gives a rueful grin as she steps back to let me pass.

'Well, I love you too, kid.' She locks the door and flips the OPEN sign to CLOSED, turning back to cast a critical eye over me. 'Are you eating? You look thin.'

I gesture with the bun. 'I'll be fine once I have this. How's things?'

'Oh, you know, bobbling along. Your dad's out back. Flour order was late. *Again*. I reckon the delivery chap's moonlighting.'

'As what?'

'Who knows? He could be Uber Eating on the side.'

I love her. Comedy gold, every time. 'Don't ever change, Mum.'

She rolls her eyes but her smile is as wide as the welcome.

I love coming home. Walking through the bakery conjures a million memories, the space retaining the scent of the day's work as if it's infused into the walls. My earliest memories are scented with butter and flour, my darkest days brightened with sugar and hope.

This place was Great Aunt Margaret's before it came to Dad. He and Mum moved in before us kids arrived, living on two floors above the bakery and shop. I don't think they expected to have to squeeze three small Quinns in with them, but Connell came first, then Dacey and, three years later, me. Even now, as I munch my bun and follow Mum through the bead curtains to the bakery's kitchen, I sense the shining shadows of us as kids weaving around me, stealing cherries from the pot behind the counter, being chased out by Dad's cousin Brigid or any one of the parade of family members who worked alongside my parents over the years. I hear our shrieks of delight, the thunder of our feet on the wooden steps leading to upstairs and safety; still feel the breathless thrill of a successful raid.

Dad is wiping down the large aluminium prep table when we arrive in the kitchen. He drops his cloth and wipes his hands on his apron, beckoning me over for a hug.

'Archie Quinn, as I live and breathe! Come and give us a squeeze.'

I love his booming Mancunian accent, crazily at odds with the rest of our collected family, whose Irish accents refuse to yield to any other influence, despite half of them being born here. He gives proper hugs, too. Not the self-conscious frantic backslaps I used to see the other dads give their sons at Sunday junior league football matches. Dad's a Northern giant, all muscles and moxie: if he hugs you, you *know* you've been hugged.

I laugh as he squeezes the air from me, the flour from his apron tickling my nose. 'Leave some air for the lungs, Dad.'

'Ah, they'll be reet.' He releases me. 'Didn't squash your bun, did I?'

'No fear of that.' I produce my half-eaten treat from behind his back like a magician and we trade satisfied Quinn-grins. The banter is what binds us. Never more than five minutes away from a joke. I love that.

I help Dad sort the last of the baking utensils from the dishwasher, lining them up ready for tomorrow morning's work, and then the three of us head upstairs.

'What's this? Bakery Open Day?'

There in the middle of the living room is my big brother Connell – Conn to everyone who knows him.

Surprised, I hug him; his usual hearty backslaps are almost as powerful as Dad's hugs. 'What are you doing here?'

He grins. 'Delivering that.'

I follow the point of his finger to a new coffee table – a chest-like box with rope handles at the sides. It's made of cross-laid planks of what looks like vintage advertising hoardings.

'Oh man, that's something else.'

'Isn't it grand?' Mum chirrups, slipping between us to deliver kisses. 'Your brother's a genius. Chippendale has nothing on him.'

'Isn't that the chap with the Velcro trousers?' Dad quips from the kitchen.

'Come off it, Dad, the only person who'd see me with removable slacks is Elodie and she'd never pay for it.'

'She'd probably want a refund,' I joke, ducking my brother's swipe. 'How is your lovely El?'

'Driving me insane decorating the new flat. I didn't realise I was moving in with Kelly Hoppen.'

'Cheeky git.' Mum cuffs his ear, which is no mean feat considering Conn is a good foot taller than her. 'You should be over there helping the girl, not hiding out with your family.'

'Sorry, Mum.'

'But you'll stay for a cuppa and a slice of something now you're here.'

'Try and stop me.' Conn grins and kisses the top of her head, then sits down on the old armchair nearest the window.

Dad makes tea, Mum slices malt loaf, Conn hunches over his phone and I get the third degree from all of them.

'How's the love of your life, Archie?'

'*Mum . . .*'

'I'm just asking. We hear so much about this Jessie girl but never of her taking the initiative. I just don't understand it. Any woman deserving of my Archie's heart should be breaking down doors to get to him.'

'She's a beautiful young lady, not Jason Statham.' Dad chuckles as Mum glares back.

'Have you told her yet?' Conn doesn't even try to hide his grin. They're all enjoying this, clearly.

'No,' I begin, bristling at their identical eyerolls. 'But . . .'

Dad's eyebrows make a bid for the ceiling. 'There's a *but* now?'

I wasn't going to tell them about Esther today. It's all so new and she could still change her mind about helping me. But for the first time I have a way forward and I want to shout it to the city. '*But* I met someone today who is going to make all the difference.'

That wipes their smirks away.

Mum flaps a hand in front of her face. 'You met someone?'

'Not like that. I—'

'Oh, *Archie*, a young lady, is it? That's perfect! Someone who sees my baby for the treasure he is! Not like that lazy Jessie. Someone who will be proud to be on your arm . . .'

I'm losing her already, her eyes wide and sparkling in the way they do when her mind is running fifty miles ahead of where it should be. 'She is a young lady, but she's not interested in me. Not like that.'

'Whyever not? What's her problem?'

'Mum – *Mum* – Esther is a friend. A lovely, sweet friend who is going to help me write the perfect letter to Jessie.'

My family exchange looks I'm not altogether happy with. After an uncomfortable silence, Mum shifts a little and turns her smile back to me.

'A lovely, sweet girl who's helping my Archie? Well, she sounds like a dream.'

'She is.'

'Good for you, Arch,' Dad says. 'Keep us posted, okay? You know we like to know these things. Talking of which, how's work?'

'Same as usual,' I say, grateful for the reprieve. 'My boss was vile today, but we survived.'

'Has he given you anything to write yet?' My brother doesn't even bother to look up from his mobile when he asks.

'Nope.' I flop down onto the sofa, pushing four brand-new

scatter cushions to one side so there's room for me. I don't know where Mum stashes all her hundreds of cushions, but every time I visit there seem to be new ones.

'What is he thinking?' Mum tuts, serving tea from a tray she's put on the brand new coffee table Conn made. 'Has he even read your stuff? Eejit.'

'Loved that latest one.' Dad beams, sitting beside me. 'Up on MyManc last week? Cracking bit of writing, that.'

'Thanks, Dad. I didn't know you'd seen it.'

Dad's laugh erupts like a depth charge. 'Seen it? Your mum's had it pinned to the noticeboard in the shop since it went up.'

'It's lovely, Arch,' Mum says. 'I could hear your voice in every word.'

I love how much faith my folks have in me. I don't know anyone else whose chief online fans are their parents. Which makes it a million times harder when I have to admit how much I'm *failing* to be a writer.

But that's going to change now I have Esther.

A sudden recollection of her dark curls bouncing around her face beneath that paper towel headscarf as she pretended to be Mrs Stanhope arrests my thoughts. I catch Mum's quizzical look and stuff the remainder of my bun in my mouth to hide my smile. Esther really did make a cute old lady . . .

Nine

ESTHER

Naomi still hasn't forgiven me.

Not that I'm surprised. I stuck to my guns about the washing and the school run, even if I did relent on Gavin's shirts. I felt like a traitor ironing them, but by then I'd had five hours' sleep and was feeling far more charitable.

I haven't heard from Archie yet about meeting up. We exchanged numbers before I left the other day and he promised he'd call to arrange it. Half of me wants to see him soon, to get started. But the other half is glad of the delay. I still don't know what to tell him. How do you write the perfect letter to win someone's heart? I hardly know anything about Archie, but the sadness that stole his smile tells me everything. He's such a lovely soul, from what I've seen. A real sweetheart. Nobody should feel lost like that – especially not a treasure like him.

Besides, I have to work out how to broach the subject of missing dinner with my sister. I don't think I can outright lie to her, but I don't want to tell her about Archie, either.

It's going to be tricky.

'Auntie Es, have you seen Ava-May?' Molly asks, appearing in the kitchen in that ninja way she does. I thought seven-year-olds were supposed to make their presence felt at all times – not my middle niece. She is a master of sneaking into a room, which, considering the entire ground floor of my sister's home is covered in wood, slate and tile, is no mean feat.

'I haven't, Molls. Is she out in the garden with your mum?'

'I doubt it,' she replies, instantly seven-going-on-thirty. 'Mum's got a right one on her.'

'Ah.'

Molly gives a world-weary sigh. 'I'm just keeping my head down with my colouring.'

'I don't blame you,' I sympathise. 'Want me to help you look?'

My niece beams and grabs my hand. Together we make a slow circuit of the lounge, the kitchen, the utility room and up the wood-and-glass staircase to the first floor. With the girls' bedrooms and the master bedroom all checked and found empty, we head up to the attic and the only room left to explore.

The moment I walk into my bedroom, I spot my youngest niece's dark eyes peeking out from the gap in my wardrobe doors.

'Hey, you,' I say, kneeling down beside her. 'Everything okay?'

Ava-May nods slowly, her face crumpling when her nod becomes a shake.

'Oh, poppet . . .' My heart swells and I gently slide the door back. 'Want a hug?'

Of my three nieces, Ava-May is the tender heart. She makes her way through her world heart first and I love that, but I'm scared for her, too. She's just like I was as a kid. Maybe that's why she's the one I feel most protective of. I recognise the blessing and the danger wrapped around that lovely heart of hers.

She curls into my lap, her floppy-limbed rabbit toy clutched

62

to her chin. Molly sits beside us, her hand resting on her sister's knee.

'What's up, chucky duck?' I ask. It usually makes her giggle and I see the faintest bobble of her shoulders now before she snuggles tighter against me, shaking her head.

'Was it Mum yelling?' Molly asks, mirroring my tone. She glances up at me. 'Mum yelled at us for taking the lid off the sandpit.'

'It's a bit chilly to play in there,' I begin, not wanting to contradict Naomi's authority, even if I'd have been tempted to play in the sandpit, too. 'And you're both still in your uniform.'

Molly isn't swayed. 'It's not *that*. She was trying to take a *brand photo*.'

'A what?'

'For her Instagram.'

'Ah . . .'

'I just wanted my bucket,' Ava-May murmurs. 'I didn't mean to make Mum mad.'

'I don't think your mummy's mad at you,' I begin, but then the words I need to follow it desert me. Navigating the perilous seas of female politics as an adult is bad enough. How are you supposed to explain it to a five- and seven-year-old? I stroke Ava-May's soft curls, so like my own, only blonde where mine are dark, and give her a squeeze. 'Listen, A-M, your mum loves you very much. All of you. And she's doing what she thinks is going to help everyone . . .' It's a stretch, but they're still with me. The last thing I want to do is drive a wedge between them and Naomi because of our row. In the end, I opt for the truth. 'I think your mum's cross with me. It's okay and we'll be fine in the end. Just right now we don't agree. You know how it is.'

'Sister fights,' agrees Molly, in that knowing way of hers. 'They *suck*.'

I snort with laughter, which sets both Molly and Ava-May off, too. I should probably pick Molly up on her vocabulary, but she just hit the nail on the head.

'Yes, they do,' I agree. Then I have to bite my lip as tears threaten my eyes – because my first thought is how much Matt would laugh at Molly's word choice. And how much I want to tell him . . .

His number is still in my phone. It really shouldn't be, but there it is. I catch myself flicking to it absent-mindedly later, as I wait in the kitchen for the kids' tea to cook. So many impulses I can't break, learned over years. I open the entry in my contacts list, my thumb hovering over the *Delete* option. I think of my *Get My Life Back* list and Point 5. I can't stop thinking of Matt Hope if his number remains here. I can't move on until he's gone.

I haven't spoken to him for months. He broke contact shortly after their honeymoon. I still don't know why. I drove to his house one time – the house he shares with Nina now. It was in darkness when I arrived, so I parked across the street and stared at its darkened shape for hours, sobbing my heart out and eventually crying myself to sleep. If it hadn't been for a clattering milk truck waking me just before dawn, Matt and Nina would have returned to find me there.

I wish I hadn't told Naomi that. I should have known she'd store it up as ammunition for a future row.

As it has done every other time, my resolve falters, my thumb swiping away from Matt's entry. Why can't I just delete it?

I can fool myself that I'm okay, that I'm picking up the pieces and rebuilding my life, but, until Matt leaves my shattered heart, it will never heal . . .

My phone judders, its screen illuminating so suddenly it makes me jump. A name appears as the ringtone sounds – a name that makes me forget everything else:

ARCHIE calling

'Hi, can I speak to Mrs Stanhope, please?'

It's so good to smile again. 'I'm afraid she isn't here at the moment. She's off at her skateboarding lesson.'

Archie's guffaw on the end of the line buzzes against my ear. 'Is that so?'

'She's hoping to nail a one-eighty.'

'Legend! Oh well, I guess you'll do.' I can almost hear his smile. 'Hi, Esther.'

'Hey, Archie. Written that letter yet?'

'Nope. So how about that meet-up?'

I glance past the kitchen island to the garden beyond, pleased to see it empty of any interested ears. 'Let's do it. When?'

'Tonight? Half six at Rossi's. I'll text you the address.'

'Great, thanks.'

'Thank *you*,' Archie rushes, so quickly his words overlap mine.

There it is, then. My first step to getting Matt out of my head once and for all . . .

Ten

ARCHIE

I arrive early – mainly because I've been counting the minutes to this meeting, but also because my mum would throttle me for being late.

'You don't keep a lady waiting,' I hear her say as I fiddle with the folded napkin and check my watch for the hundredth time.

'She's fit, then?' Ciro Rossi is grinning when I look up.

'She's just a friend.'

'Yeah, yeah, and I'm Lionel Messi.'

'Don't you have posh cooking to do?'

My mate chuckles. 'No, considering you're only ordering cake today. Cake your mum makes for us, might I remind you.'

'Mum says hi.' I grin back.

'Tell her she breaks my heart with each new delivery. And if she's ever in the market for an Italian toy boy . . .'

'Argh! Enough!'

He holds up his hands in surrender. 'So, what time's she coming?'

'My mum?'

'Your *amica*.'

I consult my watch, even though I know exactly what the time is. 'Any minute now.'

'Cool. You want a coffee while you're waiting?'

I shouldn't. My body is four-fifths caffeine already after the amount I've drunk today. I might not sleep for a week if I have more. I'm just meeting Esther for a chat over cake – it's no big thing. Except, of course, it is. If my gut feeling about my new friend is correct, she is going to make the difference I've needed in my life. I accept Ciro's offer, as much from a need to get him away from the table as to imbibe yet more caffeine. He already knows too much about this: if there's one thing my mate loves it's ribbing me about my love life – or lack of it.

Esther *isn't* my love life, I correct my train of thought. But she is as far as Ciro Rossi is concerned. All my mates will know about this by the time our meeting ends. Let them talk. My dignity disappeared years ago: no use worrying about protecting it now . . .

I have to calm down.

I'm just meeting a friend for coffee and cake.

That's all it is. No big deal . . .

The door opens and there she is. Same denim jacket I remember from our first encounter, black T-shirt underneath this time, with those very ripped jeans and bright-orange Converse again. Her hair is tied back today, a couple of corkscrew strands bouncing around her face as she raises a hand and heads over. Without the veil of curls I can see the shape of her face, the curve of her cheekbones and chin . . .

I drag my gaze away as I struggle to my feet.

'Am I late?' she asks, reaching the table.

'Right on time,' I reply.

Neither of us knows if we should hug: we end up doing a strange shoulder-dipping dance until Esther thrusts her hand towards me and I gratefully accept. We sit and Ciro is there like a shot, his far-too-attractive Italian brown eyes drinking in the sight of Esther. I watch her smile and politely accept his offer of espresso and Cake of the Day. When he finally leaves us alone, Esther turns her smile on me.

It's quite something.

'How did Mrs Stanhope get on with her skateboarding?' I ask.

'Slammed it. She showed the young 'uns a thing or two.'

'I'll bet she did. See, those Converse should have tipped me off about how cool she was.'

Esther giggles and sticks one foot out from under the table. 'They're ace, aren't they? Absolutely ancient but I love them.'

'They're cool,' I say. I want to add, *they're very you*, but I don't because how would I ever know that? 'So, how have you been since . . . ?'

'My sleepover?' She seems to shimmer when she smiles. And it's weird because I knew she would just from the way she wrote that first note to me. 'All good, thanks. I slept for five hours straight when I got home.'

'Sounds like bliss.'

'Mm.' Her expression flickers a little. 'So, ready to do this letter?'

My stomach somersaults. 'Ready as I'll ever be.'

'Excellent!' She grins and rubs her hands together, then reaches into her bag and pulls out a notebook and pen. I don't know whether to laugh or be *really* scared.

'Oh, okay, we're doing this with notes, are we?' Nerves skip through my question.

'Yes, we are. We need to do this properly. So, Archie from *The Herald*, tell me about Jessie.'

Wow, straight in, then . . . Where do I start? I stare at Esther, take a breath. 'Her name is Jessie Edmonds. She works at the next desk to mine and I've been in love with her for almost three years.' Spoken aloud it sounds so much worse than I expected it to. 'She's thirty-one. Blonde hair. Blue eyes. Incredible body – sorry, that's probably too much information . . .'

Esther's hand stops writing and rests on her notebook, her eyes very still as she watches me. 'It all counts.'

'True. She's amazing. At everything. Work, friends, office chat, *life*. Next to her I feel an abject failure.'

Her brow knots. 'Why?'

It hits me then: the hopelessness of it all. In my head I can pretend I have a hope in hell of being with Jessie. Saying it out loud makes me realise how impossible it is. My sigh flutters the pages of the menu propped against a wine bottle candle between us. 'Because she's everything to me. Because I know exactly how I feel about her and yet I turn into a babbling weirdo the moment I have the chance to speak.'

'Everyone gets nervous when they fancy someone . . .'

I shake my head. 'Not like this. It's debilitating – I'm totally trapped. Because I can't talk to her, let alone tell her how I feel. And until I do, I can't move on.'

Esther shifts a little. It's a tiny dimming of her light but I feel it like a kick. Is she regretting offering to help me?

'I'm sorry. This is probably a bad idea . . .'

'No,' she says, louder than I'm expecting. Over by the bar Ciro looks up from the stack of napkins he's folding. I watch the steady progress of pink pass across Esther's cheekbones.

'Sorry. I don't think it's a bad idea. I think you're closer than you think . . .'

You're almost there . . . her note had said.

'How am I? Half the time I can't even manage a complete coherent sentence when I'm with her.'

'Your heart knows, Archie. Those words you wrote . . . I *felt* them. Like your heart was beating through every one. That's close. Really close. We just have to find a way to let your heart take over your pen.'

When she says it like that, it sounds easy.

'Your coffee. And your cake.' Ciro is back, grinning between us as he puts down espresso cups and two of the most enormous slices of cake I've ever seen. 'Just call me if you need anything, okay?' He flashes the full charm of his smile at Esther, only slightly ruining the effect of a smooth Italian when he gives me an enthusiastic ten-fingered *ten out of ten* sign over Esther's shoulder as he's leaving. I glare at him, quickly reverting to a smile when Esther clocks me.

'Friend of yours, is he?'

'Known him since school.'

'Ah, right. He's – charming.'

'He can be.' I'm still thinking about that dip in Esther's smile a while back. I want her to help me and I think she's my best chance of ever sharing my heart with Jessie, but there's something she's not telling me. I sense it, just out of reach. 'Can I ask you something?'

'Sure. As long as it isn't *can I have a bit of your cake*, because this baby is all mine.'

Nice attempt at deflection, I note. 'Why do you want to help me?'

She observes me, the cake fork halfway to her mouth. 'Because I know how you feel.'

'About being in love?'

She nods. That shadow passes across her face again, just like before.

'Are you in love, too?'

'I was.' This time the fork returns to her plate, its cargo undelivered. 'I still am.'

I wait for more: I don't feel I can ask unless she offers it. Sure enough . . .

'His name is Matt. I've known him forever and loved him for as long. He is – was – my best friend, the one person I turned to first. I had the chance to tell him how I felt, but . . .' She swallows hard.

My throat burns and I realise I'm holding my breath. 'But . . . ?'

'I didn't. I couldn't . . . And then, Matt married someone else and I watched him do it.'

'No . . .' My hand is on hers before I can think better of it.

Our eyes lock – and in the unspoken moment so much is said.

Her hand slips away. 'Being on the other side of that decision, Archie, it's the worst. Nobody should ever have to feel that way – *you* shouldn't have to feel it. I believe you still have time.'

'And you don't?'

She shakes her head. 'I can't move on from Matt, no. Not unless . . . okay, this is going to sound dreadful, so please don't hate me, but maybe if I can help you *not* make the mistake I made, it will cancel it out in the universe. Karma restored, or something like that. Because I have to do something, Archie, or I'll never get my life back.'

This is *huge*.

Not only that Esther wants to help me win Jessie, but also that she's doing it to heal her own heart. I'll admit, I've battled asking her to help me because it felt so selfish. But now I understand. Esther's heartbreak is palpable when she talks about Matt: in this moment I promise myself I will do whatever it takes to take her pain away. She's wonderful – in only the short space of time we've been friends, I know this beyond doubt. I don't want Esther to ever feel alone. She deserves the best. And if I can help make it happen for her, I'll do it.

This is no longer just about me.

It's the two of us – Esther and me – figuring out our own hearts by helping each other find theirs.

On our own we've already failed.

But maybe together we can change that . . .

Eleven

ESTHER

I can't believe I told Archie about Matt. I mean, I hardly know him.

But the more we talk, the better I like him.

Archie is a sweetheart in every sense – funny, self-deprecating, respectful and kind. Don't ask me how I've figured all this out from the thirty minutes we've been chatting: I just *know*. The very fact we started off with the heavy, make-or-break truth bit and now are happily chatting about all the other stuff most people begin with before they dare to get personal, marks him out as special in my book.

'So you live at home?'

I shake my head, polishing off the last of my cake. There's enough sugar, butter and cream in it to have me jigging into next week, but I'll take the hit. 'With my sister and her family. Temporarily. Until I can afford my own place again.'

'Again?'

'I had to give the last one up when I lost my job.'

'That's – that's awful,' he says – and, bless him, he looks genuinely upset about it. I haven't had that response before.

Mum directed her fury about it at me because she didn't know how else to process the news; Dad just went quiet and mumbled stuff about everything happening for a reason. Even Naomi approached it with practical impassion, too caught up in the business of finding me an alternative to acknowledge what I was feeling. But it *hurt* – almost as much as losing Matt did first. Nobody ever seemed to acknowledge that. Not until now.

'It could be worse. I'm choosing to see it as an opportunity,' I say quickly, still taken aback by Archie's reaction. This meeting is already so much more than I thought it would be. I told Naomi I was meeting Marjorie, my manager, before my shift, but I don't know if she believed me. I'm going to have to be creative with my excuses from now on because this meeting with Archie is definitely not a one-off thing. Meeting here was a genius idea. We can formulate a plan and create the perfect letter in lovely surroundings. And if regular meet-ups come with cake as good as this, why would I ever want to miss them? 'How about you?'

'I have my own place. It's microscopic, but I don't mind. My folks live twenty minutes away so I see them whenever I can. They own a bakery.'

'Really? Wow.'

Archie points to my empty plate with his last forkful of cake. 'You've just eaten one of Mum's creations.'

My mouth drops open. 'Your mum made this? Tell her I love her!'

He laughs and I notice his good-looking waiter mate smiling over at him from the bar. 'I will. She'll be chuffed. So, what did you do before you lost your job?'

I click my pen closed and stretch back. 'I was an account manager for a PR company.'

Archie's expression is exactly what I expected. Months after I lost my job, that part of my life feels like it belonged to someone else.

'Yeah, I know. You'd never picture me there, right?'

He looks sheepish. 'Sorry. It's just I can't imagine you doing that.'

'The funny thing is, neither could I once I lost my job. I mean, I was great at it, I'd worked so hard to get there and I was proud of all the work I did but – I don't know – I just got sucked into the whole promotion ladder thing without ever really asking myself if it was what I wanted. I liked the salary, I loved the apartment I was able to rent because of it, and those were the things I missed when it ended. I hated leaving my home. That was the worst. Especially after Matt . . .'

I stop because I don't want to say the rest. That I'd thrown myself into work because I needed to be too busy to consider the rest of my life without him. Losing my job – and then having to give up the apartment – were the biggest blows after I'd lost him.

Archie nods, as if I've told him all of this already. I like that. I like a lot about him.

'How about you, though? Working for *The Herald*. That must be exciting. Did you always want to be a journalist?'

To my surprise, his smile vanishes. 'Still do. Haven't exactly got there yet.' Seeing my confusion, he continues, 'Officially, I'm Assistant to the Editor, which sounds impressive. Unofficially, I'm the dingbat hanging onto a dead-end job in the hope I'll get a writing position at the paper one day.'

'But you have a great way with words. And *gorgeous* handwriting . . .' Realising what I've just said, I shut my mouth quickly.

His eyes go super-sparkly when he's amused . . . 'That's kind of you to say.'

I'm blushing like a trouper now but his reaction is so lovely I press on. 'It was your handwriting and your letter that made this happen,' I say, vaguely waving a hand between us. 'And your tick box lists are second to none.'

'My lists . . . ? Have you been nosing around my desk?'

'It's kind of my job.' Okay, if I'm going to embarrass myself I may as well go the whole hog. 'I liked your desk. It stood out from my first night shift. I have to clean the whole floor by myself, you see. And I'm a fan of lists. So your Post-its made me smile.'

Archie is staring at me, eyes like the saucers our espresso cups rest on. 'You noticed my lists?'

'I'm a sucker for a tick box – and yours have drop-shadows.'

'Oh my *life*, you're a list-geek!'

Laughing, I hold my hand up. 'Guilty.'

'I can't believe you noticed.'

'I notice everything. I have to do something to make the hours pass.' I glance down at the notes I've taken so far and one thing Archie said about Jessie catches my eye. 'Hang on, you said Jessie works at the next desk to yours?'

'Yes. Why?'

'Which side?'

Archie frowns, closes his eyes for a moment as if trying to picture himself at his desk, pointing his hands out either side. 'My right. If I'm sitting at the desk.'

'Perfume Ghost? You're in love with Perfume Ghost?' It's out before I can stop it and now Archie is staring at me like I've lost the plot.

'What?'

Brilliant, Esther. Now you have to explain yourself . . .

'The desk to your right is Perfume Ghost because the scent of perfume is so strong it's like its owner is still there.'

He folds his arms. 'Amazing. What about the desk to my left?'

Here we go . . . 'Sugar-Packet-Stuffer . . .'

Archie's sudden burst of laughter makes me jump. 'Man, this is brilliant! That's Liam! He does that weird thing with shoving his sugar packets into his seat . . .'

'I know! Who does that?!'

'What about the desk directly opposite mine in the next row?'

That's the desk that's meticulously tidy apart from one old, chipped *Welcome to Nashville* mug absolutely stuffed with old pens, chewed pencils, bent paperclips and bunches of elastic bands bound around the handle. 'Opry Man.'

'That's Elvis!'

'Elvis works at *The Herald*?'

'Brian Presley, senior reporter. Everyone calls him Elvis. He loves it. This is so cool! How about the desk in the big office off the main one?'

'That's Boss Man – not very imaginative, I'm afraid.'

'Don't worry, neither is he. That's Jock Callaghan, my boss.'

'His desk is pretty gross. I daren't move anything so I just dust the gaps between the piles of stuff and spritz polish in the air above it.' Judging by Archie's expression I don't think there's any love lost between him and his boss. I think of what else I found in Boss Man's rubbish bin last night and can't resist telling him. 'Also, I think he trims his toenails in his office because last night when I was emptying the bins . . .'

'*No!*'

I love this. I love making Archie laugh, love seeing his horror and delight right now. He hasn't once been rude about my job, which is unlike everyone else in my life. Him asking for details makes me proud to share them. Watching him now as he mimes throwing up at the thought of boss toenail clippings in the bin, I realise this is the first time I've been able to share the fun I've discovered in my unexpected career change. Naomi wouldn't want to know any of this. Mum would be horrified. If I was still talking to Matt, I reckon he'd take a dim view of it, too. He was always the one pushing me to go for the next promotion, insisting I never settle. At the time I thought it was because he wanted the best for me, but was it, really?

'So, what about me?'

'Sorry?'

Archie grins. 'Every other desk has a name. What's mine?'

I should have seen that coming, shouldn't I? 'Don't laugh.'

'Can't promise that.'

'Post-it King.'

He holds my gaze for a moment, his head shaking a little. 'I love it. I am the Post-it King of *The Herald*. And there was me thinking I wasn't important.'

The air leaves me. Because I think Archie just let the truth slip.

'You are important,' I reply, and I mean it. 'Don't ever think you aren't.'

He stares at me. 'I don't know what to say to that.'

'I know. But I think you'll have to believe it or you'll never find the words to say what you want to Jessie.'

He says nothing, just reaches for his espresso cup. As I watch him slowly drink, I let the silence settle between us – he needs to think and I have to let him. I resist the urge to click my pen on and off, which is what I always do when I'm nervous and silences are stretching uncomfortably. It's an effort to let the moment be.

The door to the kitchen swings shut and, when I look to the bar, Archie's friend has gone. It's just my new friend and me, heavy words hanging in the air around his head. Beyond the bistro windows, the city rumbles on, colour and life and movement and noise continuing, oblivious to the two of us sitting here and the vastness of what Archie is considering right now.

Finally, his eyes lift to mine.

'Esther?' he says.

'Yes, Archie?'

'How the heck are we going to do this?'

I wish I knew. But I have to find a way – for Archie and for me. 'We just have to work out how to write the perfect love letter.'

'Could be impossible.'

'Maybe. But it could be fun.'

'So where do we go from here?'

I've been thinking about this since Archie called. 'Research. We need to talk to everyone we know, find out what they think.'

'What if they think love letters are lame?'

'Then we find more people to ask. People have been declaring their love by letter for hundreds of years. You're just the latest lovelorn soul stepping into a noble tradition.'

Archie's smile returns at the exact moment his friend reappears from the kitchen. Both are a welcome sight. 'You'd better write that down. We might need it later.'

Twelve

ARCHIE

Beethoven wrote letters to his 'Immortal Beloved'. He signed one, 'Ever thine. Ever mine. Ever ours.' How lovely is that? E x

> You've been re-watching the Sex and the City movie again, haven't you? A ☺

It's called RESEARCH, Archie I-Don't-Know-What-Your-Last-Name-Is.
Do you want to write the perfect love letter or not? E x

> I stand corrected, Esther I-Don't-Know-Yours-Either.
> A thousand apologies ever thine, love Archie QUINN x

You're forgiven, Archie Quinn. Love, Esther HUGHES x

> Hughes and Quinn. We sound like private detectives ☺

Private detectives of LOVE! ☺ ☺

I smile at my phone. This is fun, even if neither of us is any closer to finding the magic formula for the perfect love letter. Since our first café meeting at Rossi's four days ago we've been trading messages, sharing snippets of what we've found. I don't know how useful any of it will be, but it's lovely to have a constant flow of inspiration. It's a game that's brightened every day since we started.

'You're wearing that smile again.'

I look up from my phone and realise the whole room is watching me. Granda Brady chuckles, his eyes bright over his battered accordion. Mirth passes around the circle, each musician adding to it, a gentle ripple of gravel-edged amusement.

'What smile?'

'The one that says you got the cream off the milk before the cat got the chance.' Eric laughs, drumming his many ringed fingers on the body of his scuffed guitar.

'Leave the lad alone. He's in love,' says Robert, aka Old Bob. The smile he shares with his new husband William, aka Li'l Bill, is a lovely sight.

'I'm not in love,' I shoot back, but none of The Old Guys are listening. This is the moment they all pretend their hearing aids are playing up so they can get away with whatever they want to say.

Through the serving hatch of the community hall, the centre manager Marta sends me a sympathetic smile. I roll my eyes and feign offence, but it's impossible to really bear a grudge against them.

'Are we learning this song or not?' Jim, our reluctant musical director, gives me a comradely wink and shoulders his fiddle. His sharp Glaswegian bark has a miraculous effect. One by one, the ragtag band drop their mocking of me and quieten down. I love how Jim does that – forty-five years of teaching in some of the biggest secondary schools in Greater Manchester evident in his ability to restore order. He has his work cut out with this lot, that's for sure.

I flash Jim a smile then return to the task I was attempting before Esther's message arrived – trying to wrestle my rescued banjo back into some kind of tune.

I've loved hanging out with these guys since I was a teenager. Granda Brady first told me about his mates and their dodgy music club when I was fourteen and I begged and begged him to take me to a meeting. He relented eventually, but only after I'd undergone an initiation, as every member of The Old Guys must. It involved me, a skip and a leg-up from Granda Brady and his cousin Pádraig, followed swiftly by a victorious rescue of a dented, stringless banjo and a breathless dash from the scene when the foreman of the building site gave angry chase. That's not what we told Mum, of course. She thinks we found Béla Fleck the Banjo at a humble church jumble sale . . .

Every instrument being played in the circle in which I now sit has been rescued from somewhere else. Skips, charity shops, family lofts, car boot sales, house clearances. The more daring the rescue, the more respect it has. Consequently, the sound we produce is eclectic, to say the least, and tuneful if we're lucky. But it's exactly what Granda Brady wants.

'This way no one gets left behind. If we're all shite, we're equal.'

We're certainly fulfilling his wish today. I wince as I stumble-pick my way through 'Jim Ward's Jig', which sounds more like 'Jim Ward's Trudge' at the moment. I try not to notice the grimaces of my fellow players, but the worse we play the funnier it gets.

'Okay, okay, let's give poor Jim a rest from his ordeal,' Granda Brady calls eventually, much to everyone's relief.

'Is he talking about the Jim on the sheet music or me?' our Jim asks, grinning widely when the room erupts with laughter. 'Because we're both in pain.'

'Break time!' Marta calls from the kitchen. Instruments are gratefully laid down; chairs scrape back on the old vinyl floor and the exodus begins. I sit back in my chair and flex my aching fingers.

'So, tell me who the smile's for.'

Granda Brady is beside me. He can move surprisingly quickly for an eighty-year-old when he wants to. He is also like a Jack Russell with a slipper when he's after information. There's no point deflecting his questions anymore.

'I've met someone – not like *that*,' I add quickly, before my granda's brain spins into overdrive. 'She's a friend. She's going to help me write a letter to Jessie.'

'Jessie your woman at work?'

'Jessie – my colleague – yes.'

Granda's green eyes narrow. 'What do you need a letter for? Just tell her.'

'I've been trying. For two years. I've failed every time.'

'But this new girl can help?'

'I think so.'

'Ah, right.' I watch my granda take this in. 'Of course I'm going to need more details from you.'

Of course he does . . .

'My friend's name is Esther. She's brilliant and she believes in me.' *She thinks I have gorgeous handwriting*, I add in my head. I still can't get over that one. It's a massive compliment. My writing is *me* – the point where I meet the page. She couldn't have moved me more if she'd called *me* gorgeous.

'That so?'

'Yup.'

'Well, I like her immensely already. Where did you meet?'

'At work. Sort of. Esther's a night cleaner. She found one of my abandoned letter attempts and told me to keep going.'

'A cleaner, you say? Well, isn't that perfect!'

'Why?'

'Your Esther sounds like just what you need, Arch. She's going to clean up your act. Brush you into shape. Polish your words . . .'

He's so chuffed with his own jokes I can't pretend to be offended. 'Go on.'

Granda wrinkles his nose. 'Can't. I got stuck at a Hoover metaphor.' He chuckles as he stands. When I join him he ruffles my hair, just like he's done every day I've seen him. I duck out of it as I always do, but there is nothing better for making me feel I'm home. 'Good on you, Archie boy. So when will you bring her here?'

I stare at him as we walk over to Marta's kitchen. 'Here?'

'Sure, why not? Might be inspirational. We play love songs all the time.'

'The last two months we've been learning murder ballads.'

My granda bats this away with a wave of his hand as we join the refreshment queue. 'Ach, murder, love, they're all the same.'

'Such a poet, your grandad.' Kavi laughs, turning round in

the queue to beam at us. He's the best guitar player we have by a long way and I strongly suspect he pretends to play badly when he's with us just to spare our blushes. 'You bugging your poor grandson again, Brady?'

'He has a new lady friend helping him declare his love to the woman of his dreams,' Granda Brady replies. 'Convoluted as that sounds. And I'm just saying, if she wants to see our lad in his natural state, he should bring her here.'

Kavi grins. 'Oh aye, that'd be a treat.'

'Who's he bringing?' Isaac, Old Bob and Li'l Bill are all joining in now.

'Delightful new lady,' Kavi informs them.

'Bring her!'

'She'd love it! Marta would love it, too,' Jim says, now at the front of the queue by default, taking advantage of the distraction by piling three slices of coffee cake on his plate. 'What d'ya say, hen? Another lassie at the club?'

'Fine by me,' Marta calls through the hatch.

I'm about to dismiss the idea outright when I think back to something Esther said when we met at Rossi's: 'We just have to find a way to let your heart take over your pen'. So much of my heart is here, in this old, shabby building abandoned by the council years ago and adopted by Marta and the community. I found my heart sitting with these guys, who couldn't be more different in life experience, background and upbringing. This is where I learned so much about me just by hearing them talk and laugh and play together. If Esther is going to help me find my heart for Jessie's letter, this is a perfect place to start the search.

'I'll ask her,' I say, rubbing the back of my neck self-consciously as The Old Guys cheer. 'She might say no.'

'Tell her there's cake and a bundle of eligible gents,' Li'l Bill calls.

'More like *illegible*,' Granda Brady shoots back.

As their banter rises over my head, I sneak away and find my phone.

Hey, E. Got an idea of where to look. Call you later? Ax

Thirteen

ESTHER

'How about meeting somewhere different?'

I frown against my phone. 'Sure. Was there a problem with your mate's place?'

'No, no problem at all. We're still on for meeting there this Thursday. I just thought we could book in an extraordinary meeting as well.'

This could be tricky. I want to see Archie but getting away early one day of the week is difficult enough to swing. Now he wants two? 'I can't do another early evening in the week,' I begin, imagining Naomi's fury if I tried it. We're only just back on an even keel from the night I slept in the cleaning cupboard; I don't want to risk another row so soon.

'I'm not talking a weekday,' he interrupts. 'How about next Saturday morning? Around eleven?'

'That could work. Where were you thinking?'

I hear him give a nervous cough before he answers. Why is he nervous?

'You said we have to find a way to get my heart on the page for Jessie's letter, right?'

'Right.'

'So I want to take you to a place that *is* my heart. Maybe if you see it, you'll help me find the words for what you find there.'

A day later, as I'm doing my rounds in *The Herald*'s offices, I'm still wondering what on earth he meant by that. But also intrigued by how he said it. This really means something to him. And he was able to say it to me, just like that: *I want to take you to a place that* is *my heart*. I don't think I've ever met a bloke who can speak straight from the heart like that, which is crazy because this is the same lad who believes he can't write a love letter. Archie doesn't realise how much further down that road he is.

How much further along he is than Matt ever was.

I hate that my head goes straight there whenever I've considered this.

I don't want to compare Archie with Matt Hope because my relationship with him is totally different. But my head keeps linking the two of them. Maybe it's because of the connection I instantly made with Archie. It was just *there*; from the moment he rescued me from the cleaning cupboard. The only other time it's been that immediate with anyone was when I met Matt. It was the connection that made me believe he could love me like I loved him. Except I never got the chance to find out, did I?

Maybe I see in Archie what I might have seen in Matt if I'd told him I loved him?

No, hang on. That's ridiculous. I have to remember why I'm doing this. It's to move on from Matt, not find another excuse to think about him. I'm helping Archie believe his words have the power to change his life – hopefully without sounding like an Instagram motivational guru.

I catch sight of my reflection in the newly polished chrome of the coffee machine in *The Herald*'s coffee station, which I left till last to clean tonight.

'Stop it,' I say to the wobbly mirror-version of me. 'Archie isn't Matt.'

My sigh fogs my face from view.

The drive home seems to take an eternity, my car finding every red light between Central Manchester and Naomi's place. I have to double-blink to keep my focus on the rain-soaked road ahead and my whole body is complaining. Manchester rain is unlike any other for sheer epic determination, and tonight it's chucking its most impressive deluge directly at my windscreen. My wipers are working at double speed and still not shifting it, the streetlights and oncoming headlights of cars merging and blurring within the flood. It's a relief when an impatient driver overtakes from behind in a cloud of spray because their angry red rear lights streaking ahead of me become guide-lights for my eyes to follow.

My shoulder muscles are tied up in macramé-tight knots when I arrive home. I'm so exhausted I can't even find the energy to run to the front door, cold rainwater seeping into the denim of my jacket as I plod slowly across the gravel drive.

I'm about to put my key in the door when it flies open. Startled, I look up to see my sister bathed in the soft glow of the hallway. What's she doing up so late? It's almost midnight – an hour I didn't think Naomi knew existed, being a fully paid-up member of the In Bed By Ten club.

'You're soaked! Get yourself inside, quick!'

She ushers me into the house, taking my bag from my shoulder and relieving me of my sodden jacket. I'm so surprised I just stand there and let her do it, like a kid. Like I used to do for her when we were little. My little sister being a mum is strange enough to process – having her mother me is a whole other level of weird.

'Kick your shoes off and wait there,' she commands, heading upstairs while I dumbly obey.

She returns with a pair of her cream lounge pants, a large white T-shirt adorned with a gold foil star and a white fluffy towel for my hair, standing there while I change in the hall. The clothes look strange on me, jeans and tees and sneakers being my comfort zone when it comes to clothes, but it's a sweet gesture I'm not going to challenge. Especially given how frosty things have been between us lately. We might be chalk and cheese in every respect, but I love my sister. I'm not sure where this benevolence has come from, but I'm prepared to go with it.

Pleased with the result of her kindness, Naomi scoops up my discarded clothes, sneakers and tabard and smiles at me. 'Let's put that kettle on, shall we?'

When we're sitting on the cream sofas in the open-plan lounge, curled up around huge steaming mugs of tea and a stack of hot buttered toast each, my curiosity finally gets the better of me.

'How come you're up?'

'I wanted to see you.'

'And that's lovely of you, Nai – really lovely. But why?'

The steam dances in billows from the top of her mug as she sighs. 'Because I've been an arse to you lately.'

'No, you haven't . . .'

'Bollocks I haven't. All that fuss when you didn't come home. I overreacted.'

'You didn't know where I was. My phone was going straight to voicemail. You had a right to be worried.'

My sister picks at her toast. 'I shouldn't have said that thing about Matt. It's just – with you losing him and then your job and your home and all – it changed you. I was scared you'd do something daft.'

I'm shocked to see her eyes mist.

'I'm okay now.'

'Are you? Because I'm worried, Es. Everyone is.'

'You mean Mum.'

'Everyone. You were always the one who had it together. The career, the five-year plan. I watched you sail through college and university and into one successful job after another and I thought you were invincible.' She shakes her head. 'And then that business with you camping outside Matt's house . . . '

Irritation bristles my spine beneath the unfamiliar clothes. 'I told you: it was one time . . . '

'But what about sneaking off early last Friday? The sudden *pre-work meeting*? If you think I believed that then you've got wool between your ears. And the texts you keep getting? I see the way you look when they arrive. The way you hurry out of the room. Is Matt calling you again?'

'No.'

'Is your night cleaning job a ruse to meet up with him?'

'What? How can you even think that?'

'Because it all looks a bit *convenient* to me.'

'Convenient? I'm working every hour I can, on top of everything I'm doing here. When do you think I have time for clandestine meetings?'

She rolls her eyes and instantly battle lines form on the white ash floor between our sofas. 'Oh, come on, Es, you have to see how odd this is. You get a night cleaner job, of all things, and now you're getting secret messages and sloping off hours before your supposed job starts? What am I meant to think?'

'I don't care what you think.' I slam my mug down on the wide oak coffee table and struggle to my feet. 'I'm going to bed.'

'You haven't answered me.'

'Because you're insane!'

She's on her feet now, too. So much for our truce. 'If you stay under my roof I have a right to know. I don't think that's unreasonable.'

I should just walk out now. Leave her to stew with her bloody horrible accusations. But if I don't meet it head on, this is going to hang over us for days. I am done fighting. 'I work hard, Naomi, harder than I ever did in my last job. I am entitled to an evening off. Weekends, too. And no, not because I'm secretly seeing Matt. I haven't seen him since I watched him marry someone else.'

My words sting the air around us. Naomi shrinks into her oversized spa robe. 'I shouldn't have said . . . '

'Well, you did.'

'Es . . . '

'I need to sleep,' I begin, shocked into silence when my sister grabs my hand.

'Stay, for a bit longer? Please? I didn't mean to yell.'

My resolve ebbs with my anger. 'I don't want to fight with you.'

'Neither do I. I'm not a monster, Es.'

'I never said you were.' I sit slowly beside her. 'You know how grateful I am for you taking me in. As soon as I have enough to look for a new flat, I'll be out of your hair. But you have to let me have some life of my own while I wait for that to happen.'

She nods. 'Okay, I'm sorry. I was just worried.'

'I know. Don't be.' I look at my sister, still looking immaculate despite the flush of her face from our row. I shouldn't have to tell her anything about my private life, but I don't want her thinking I'm sneaking around with Matt. 'The texts are from my friend, Archie. I met him at work. I'm helping him with something.'

'Is he a cleaner, too?'

'No, a journalist.' I *think* I can call him a journalist – it's what he wants to be, anyway.

'What are you helping him with?'

I lean into the too-soft cosiness of the sofa cushions. 'He's in love with someone and I'm helping him write a letter to her.'

Naomi's mouth drops open. 'Another guy in love with some-one else?'

Said like that, the comparisons to Matt are unavoidable. 'I know how it sounds . . . '

'It sounds like you need to revise your type.'

I laugh, despite the lingering hurt from our earlier exchange. 'Except the difference this time is that I'm not in love with Archie.'

'Are you sure?'

'Yes, I'm sure.'

I catch the smallest glimpse of mischief in my sister's expres-sion. 'You seem very happy when he contacts you.'

'Because he's a friend. A good friend. I haven't had one of those for a long time, not one that didn't come with a whole world of extra baggage. And I'm helping him, which makes me feel good.'

'Okay, sorry.' Naomi holds up her hands in surrender. 'So you're writing a love letter for him?'

'With him. I'm helping Archie put the words down.' A thought occurs to me, something I've never asked Naomi before. 'Did Gavin ever write to you? When you started dating?'

'Gavin? Write love letters? It's not really his style.'

'I suppose it's a stretch to think he might.'

'He's a man of few words at the best of times.' She snuggles into the sofa. 'Although there was one thing he did when we first met that you probably won't believe.'

'Do I want to know this?'

'Oi, you!' She picks up a cushion and chucks it at me. 'It was something sweet. At the beginning we were just mutual friends in this big group. We chatted, hung out, the usual stuff. But once we swapped numbers he started texting me. Twice a day, regular as clockwork. First thing in the morning, last thing at night. I mean, it was nothing profound, just *Have a lovely day* and *Sleep well*, but it might as well have been a sonnet each time. Because nobody had ever bothered to check before if my day was lovely or my dreams were sweet. It meant the world.'

I can't imagine my dour brother-in-law being romantic. But it's a huge gesture for him. I'm struck by the power such a small act had on my sister. His words – and his heart behind them – made the difference. That's what Archie has to do. He'll have to be more lyrical than two texts a day, but if Gavin Martins can woo the woman of his dreams through the power of his texted words, *anything* is possible for Archie Quinn . . .

Fourteen

ARCHIE

I'd forgotten about the car-cleaning thing.

I'd hoped Callaghan had forgotten it too, his days since our 'little chat' in his office taken up mostly by him ranting about the quality of our recent headline stories. But no, Jock Callaghan instead proved that he can multitask like a despotic ninja – yelling at Liam, Jessie and Elvis while also delighting in belittling me.

What he can't do, however, is make me feel unimportant.

Not today.

Not even in Manchester's finest rain, which has been happily pelting the city for the last week and is now chucking its best at me.

I see Callaghan gurning triumphantly at me from the windows of the staff canteen, so I beam back and give him a double thumbs-up. The sudden disappearance of his mirth is a trophy to me.

You see, Jocky-boy? Nothing can stop me today.

I am invincible, if a little soggy. In a few short hours, I'm meeting Esther at Rossi's to work on our plan. I *will* write the letter I've dreamed of and I *will* win Jessie's heart.

And I'll get to do it with the help of the loveliest friend I've known.

She texted me this morning, telling me about the words her brother-in-law used to woo her sister. It was like sunshine illuminating my phone screen as I read it.

> Gavin is the world's most boring man. If he could find words to win the love of his life, you definitely can. You're a million times more interesting, for a start. Also, you don't think that alphabetising the tools in your shed constitutes a hobby. So, you win x

Esther's been talking to people – her sister, the next-door neighbour, some of the mums at the school gate when she's been waiting to pick up her nieces – and gathering their stories to share with me.

> I have so much to tell you. Make sure you ask people, too. Research is our deadly weapon. Hughes and Quinn investigate! x

Hughes and Quinn. I smile as I crank up the power on the pressure washer Callaghan handed me this morning and aim it at the soapsuds already chasing each other down the bodywork of his Jaguar as the cold rain hammers me and everything else. Each blast of water is a victory and I imagine Esther and me annihilating every doubt, every barrier to uncover the words to win Jessie's heart.

When I glance back up at the canteen window, Callaghan has gone.

An hour later, back in the office, Elvis beckons me over to his desk.

'Nice bit of car cleaning you did there. You should charge him for it.'

'It's supposed to be getting me an interview for a writer's job.'

'That right?' Elvis pats the vacant seat next to him. 'Pull up a pew, lad. Tell me more.' As I sit, he produces a tin of biscuits from the bottom drawer of his desk. 'Bit of snap?'

'Very kind.'

'Help yourself. I've only Rich Teas and knock-off Nices, but it's all sugar in the end, eh?'

The biscuits may have been in that tin for a while, judging by their floppiness, but I am never one to turn down free food, however it comes. I select two sad-looking Rich Teas and a broken shard of sugary Nice biscuit.

'So this job you're washing cars for, that'll be mine, I suppose?'

Nice one, Archie. I hadn't even thought about whose job I was aiming to take. Nobody wants Elvis to leave. He's a legend at *The Herald*. I don't want him thinking I'm hovering on the sidelines waiting to jump into his boots. He doesn't look offended, but I hope that's not just him putting on a brave face.

'Junior reporter,' I say quickly, my mouth too full of biscuit to form the words properly. 'For – later.'

'When I'm gone? Don't look so horrified, lad, I'm not daft. Makes good financial sense for His Nibs to do that. Me retiring will save this place a decent penny. Hiring a junior instead – well, that's both cost-effective and risk-proof.'

'Risk-proof?'

'Aye. Right now they can't fire me unless they're ready to acknowledge my forty years' service. They can get rid of you for a couple of grand at most.' He pops a whole Nice biscuit in his mouth as he chuckles.

'Well, that's a comfort.'

'You're welcome.'

'There's not a hope in hell of me getting it anyway,' I say. 'I mean, I've hardly written anything . . .'

'You've written plenty, by the looks of this . . .' Elvis twists his laptop to face me and the familiar banner of MyManc appears. I watch him scroll down the page of search results for my name – months of my life dancing up the screen.

'I didn't realise you knew about that.'

He keeps his gaze trained on the articles. 'I happen to be senior reporter of *The Herald*. It's my job to know these things. It's good work, Archie. Much better than Old Grumpy Dick in there expects.'

'Wow, thank you. I mean, it's all voluntary and most of the articles are throwaway content. They're just . . .'

Elvis turns to face me, his pointed finger suddenly millimetres from my nose. 'And you can stop that for a start. "*They're just . . .*"? There's no *just* about them. They're good. They fulfil the brief; they're entertaining, well written. Never apologise for your own work. First and most important lesson about this job: don't be so cap-doffing humble about it. You *mined* those words from the depths of your soul. Don't cheapen them by suggesting they don't matter.'

'I'm proud of them,' I reply, touched by the enormous compliment he's just paid me. 'But they won't mean anything to Callaghan.'

'Maybe not if you tell him. But if *I* say they're good, he might just listen.'

The suggestion dances between us.

'You'd do that for me?'

'I reckon you have what it takes. Rough *as* right now, but we can fix that. I'm going to request your help on a couple of jobs, okay? Can't promise they'll be earth-shattering exclusives, given today's headline—' he points at a mock-up of *The Herald*'s front page beside him, which reads **BOLLARDS TO THAT!** above a photo of a local councillor frowning at a row of them across a street '—but you'll learn a lot whatever the story. You up for it?'

I can't believe it. But I'm not going to turn him down.

'Yes – yes, I am.'

'Right y'are.' Elvis gives me a slow nod, which is his equivalent of a victory lap around Anfield. 'If you're making coffee, lad, mine's black with two.'

At the coffee station, my head whirs in time with the bubbling of the filter machine. This is *such* a break! It's all coming together: meeting Esther, forming a plan to win Jessie, standing up to Callaghan this morning and now a real, proper, cast-iron opportunity to learn from the best in the biz.

'You look happy.'

I look up from the brewing coffee and there she is: the reason for everything.

'I am.'

Jessie smiles and I feel heat spreading across my chest. I could bask in that smile for several lifetimes . . .

'At least someone in this place is,' she says, her gaze drifting over towards Callaghan's office. 'He's going to have a coronary if he carries on raging at everyone. That editorial meeting this morning was brutal.'

'I heard. Liam's been in a sulk ever since.'

'Yeah, well, when your lead article's been deemed "trash not even fit for chips" it has that effect.'

I wince with her. 'That's got to hurt.'

'It comes with the territory. Trust me, Arch, you do right staying away from Editorial. At least what you do matters, even if the boss moans at you.'

I know I'm staring at her, but I can't quite believe what she said. 'I didn't come to *The Herald* to make coffee and run errands: I'm here because I want to write.'

'Oh, I didn't mean . . .' Her fingers are soft and warm where they rest on my bicep. The room seems to undulate a little. 'If you want to write, write for someone who appreciates what you do. Jock Callaghan stopped caring years ago.'

I watch her walk away, unease tightening my stomach. Does she think I can write? Or was she suggesting I deserve better? I was about to tell her about what Elvis just offered me, but it suddenly doesn't feel right. Instead, I deliver coffee to Elvis, grab my phone and jacket from my desk and hurry out of the office.

'Hello?'

'Es, you'll never believe what just happened.'

'What? Tell me?' Esther's excitement warms my ear as I shelter under the entrance canopy from the persistent rain.

'Only our senior reporter offering to take me under his wing!'

'Oh, *Archie*! That's incredible! I'm so chuffed for you!'

It *is* incredible, isn't it? Forget what Jessie said, Esther's right: this is huge. I'm not going to let anything stop me enjoying it. 'Thank you. I knew you'd understand. We still on for half six?'

'You bet! And this time, cake's on me.'

Fifteen

ESTHER

I've been excited all day since Archie's call, counting down the hours till we meet.

I park my car and race from the car park to Rossi's. I don't even care that I'll be flushed as anything when I arrive. My friend has just had great news and I can't wait to celebrate with him.

He's already at the table when I get there, his wide smile beaming a welcome. We've texted every day and spoken every other but seeing him is just the best.

We don't even worry about how we greet today. It's just a huge bear hug that's warm and safe and so welcome. 'Congratulations.' I smile against his T-shirt, the soft pad of his heart against my ear.

'Thank you.' His voice buzzes against the top of my head.

We giggle when we part and I pull out the notebook from my bag as we take our seats, placing it on the table before him. 'My research so far, Detective Quinn.'

'Excellent work, Chief Inspector Hughes.'

'I get to be Chief Inspector, do I?'

'You're the one that's done all the legwork so far. Your

professional partner is slacking. If I were you I'd have a word with me.'

See, this what I love: the chat, the jokes we trade that happen so fast it makes your head dizzy. Nobody else in my life does that. I watch him flicking through the notebook, the shifting of his expressions as he reads each entry. How have we only just met? I feel like Archie Quinn has always been here, like this.

'Oh, this one is marvellous,' he says, turning my notebook to face me. I recognise the story immediately but it makes my spine tingle when he reads it out loud:

'"*Cloris, the crossing lady at my nieces' school, went on a date with her now husband because he left a note tucked inside her ballroom shoes at the waltz class they both attended. The note read:* If you'll be my partner, I'll make everywhere you step a dance floor."'

'It was an evening class,' I tell him, enjoying the gentle smile that eases across his lips. 'Cloris had been widowed for a year and her daughter persuaded her to go to the dance class to meet people. Stav was a confirmed bachelor after caring for his mum for years – he joined the class when she passed away. He fell for Cloris the first time they danced together and, when they kept being paired up, he took his chance. Cloris said she'd taken off her shoes at the end of class and left them with her things while she was chatting to a friend. When she got home and unpacked her dance bag, there was Stav's note.'

'I love that. How did you get her to tell you her story?'

I chuckle. 'I had to cross the road with her about seven times.'

I loved it, too. I'd barely chatted to Cloris before, just saying hi when we passed on the school run. But as soon as I asked her how she'd met her husband, I was *in*: pals for life.

The mental image of me going backwards and forwards across

a zebra crossing with a lollipop lady while scribbling notes in my notebook has an immediate effect on my friend.

Archie is one of life's serious laughers. Head back, huge guffaws rattling his chest, tears that follow easily. Making him laugh is quickly becoming my mission. On our phone calls, the sudden burst of his laughter is a reward I look forward to.

'What did you say to him?' Archie's friend Ciro asks, arriving with cake and coffee.

'I just told him a story,' I reply.

'Some story,' Ciro says, clamping a tanned hand on Archie's shoulder. '*Breathe*, mate. It's kind of important for staying alive.'

'I'm good,' Archie gasps back, wiping his eyes with the heels of his hands.

'If you say so. Try not to kill him with comedy, eh, Esther?'

'I'll do my best.'

As Ciro slopes off back to the kitchen, Archie's laughter gently ebbs away. Then we sip espresso with surprising synchronicity and a subtle silence settles between us. I watch his gaze return to the notebook, knowing exactly what's written there.

The bloke at the post office who wrote a poem in a Christmas card for his next-door neighbour to declare his love. The check-out assistant in our local supermarket who found a love letter written on the back of a till receipt with a returned item. The mum at the school gates whose girlfriend proposed with a paper trail of notes leading from the front door, through their terraced house, to the middle of their tiny garden where her partner was waiting on one knee, surrounded by tealights. In my tiny patch of the city, so many words being exchanged to win hearts.

And, with each one I collected, more evidence for my conviction that Archie can do this: his words can win Jessie's heart.

'Have you asked anyone yet?' I ask him.

'Not yet, but I will now. My folks, for a start. They're bound to have heard stories in their bakery from customers. And The Old Guys.'

'What old guys?'

He closes the notebook and leans in, as if the information he's sharing might be stolen by enemy elements. 'The old guys I want you to meet. On Saturday.'

'Where on earth are you taking me, Archie Quinn?'

He laughs. 'Okay, first you need to know two things about me: one, I love being surrounded by people – my family are Irish and I have relatives pretty much all over the city; and two, in my spare time I love nothing better than playing the banjo badly.'

I wasn't expecting either of those things. 'How badly?'

He shrugs. 'You'll see. I rescued it from a skip.'

I laugh in surprise. 'A *skip*?'

'Yep. I'm in a band – kind of – with my grandfather. Granda Brady. You'll love him. All of us play instruments we rescued from somewhere. We're rubbish at playing them but pretty awesome at everything else and that's where you'll find my heart.'

Oh my goodness. Spoken over the phone it was powerful enough: seeing Archie say it in person is incredible. I love that passion, the shy smile that accompanies it, the tiny gestures – the circles his thumb traces on the back of his hand, the gentle tap of his cherry-red sneakers on the floor beneath our table – that reveal what this really means to him.

It's like he opened a door just for me.

Like he'd trust me with his heart.

Tears sting my eyes. I look away.

*

Later that evening, alone in *The Herald*'s office, I'm still thinking about that moment. Fred's familiar wheel-squeak is a comfort, his cheery bulk trundling along in front of me a companion I need. I don't know why I was moved like that when Archie told me about his grandad's music club. It shocked me, to be honest. I wasn't ready to show him how emotional it made me feel. I think I covered it up well enough, but I can already sense danger around this. I can't get carried away with emotion: I'd be no good to Archie if I became distracted by it. But the way he's spoken about his family, about how close they all are, has already made me compare it to mine without wanting to. And one thing has become clear: I need to talk to Mum.

I've avoided it for long enough.

But, this time, I'm not going to try to persuade her to be proud of my new job: I'm just going to show her what it means to me. I'm getting my life back, one lonely shift at a time, and I should be proud of that. I love what I do – and I love who I've met because of it.

As I reach Archie's desk, I spot something in the centre, surrounded by a starburst of pens all pointing my attention to it.

A sticky note. Bright yellow this time.

> ESTHER,
> You're amazing.
> Don't let anyone tell you otherwise.
> You rock, partner! X

Sixteen

ARCHIE

Something's going on.

I spotted it the moment I arrived – fifteen minutes late, thanks to a big crash on the road in, but thankfully here before the boss.

Liam and Jessie, deep in conversation.

Nothing new there – they write together so a lot of their work is shared. But what set alarm bells ringing was the way they sprang apart as soon as they saw me. Almost *guiltily* . . .

Now it's like they're opposing magnets moving around the offices. If Liam sits, Jessie moves. If Jessie heads for coffee, Liam ducks away. They've been like this for hours, like some strange, demented game. And yet when I've asked them if everything's okay, they've both assured me it is.

Could they be *together*?

I kick myself under my desk. Of course they aren't, idiot! Liam is happily settled with Lou, a primary school teacher he met a year ago. He can be a git sometimes but he'd never cheat on her. Besides, I know Liam knows how I feel about Jessie because I made the mistake of getting drunk at the Christmas party and blurting it out to him, huddled in a heap by the photocopier in full-on, alcohol-induced maudlin state.

No. Liam isn't with Jessie.

So what else could it be?

Since I asked them how they were, they've both resolutely avoided making eye contact with me. We're now sitting at our desks like the oddest version of the Three Wise Monkeys: *see nothing, ask nothing, acknowledge nothing*.

'So, what'll we get old Elvis when he retires?' Liam pipes up, far too chirpily for him.

'Blue suede shoes and a hot dog?' Jessie suggests.

'Hot dog?'

'Safer than giving him a hound dog.'

'Ha ha! That's right!'

Neither looks up from their screen. I sit between them wondering what planet I've dropped onto.

'He's not retiring yet,' I say, crossing everything that Elvis hangs on long enough to teach me everything he knows.

'Aye, I know, but it doesn't hurt to plan . . . ?' Even Liam's voice is unconvinced by the topic of too-bright conversation, judging by the way it rises apologetically at the end.

'I guess so . . . '

A weird silence shifts its way between us and stays there for an hour until Liam mumbles something about needing nicotine and hurries out of the office. I risk a look at Jessie: she's staring at her screen that I swear hasn't changed in all the time we've been sitting here.

'I thought he'd quit?'

'I guess he hasn't,' she replies, eyes still on her screen. 'Mind you, the way Callaghan's been this week is enough to drive anyone back to cigs.' Her nails tap on the desk and I notice her bite the edge of her lip a little, as if she's considering saying more.

I look away again. I'm doing pretty well in this conversation for a change and watching her do *that* is not going to help me stay calm. Jessie flicks her hair back over her shoulder and I'm treated to a gentle breeze of her perfume. *Perfume Ghost* . . . Esther's nickname for Jessie's invisible desk owner comes back to me: *The perfume is so strong it's like its owner is still there . . .*

'What is it?'

I'm startled to find Jessie watching me when I look back. 'Sorry?'

She twists a little so her chair faces mine. 'You just laughed.'

Did I?

'Er, I was just – thinking – about Callaghan– being an arse . . . ' I splutter, my face, coincidentally, being an utter arse too by blushing against my wishes. I was doing so well . . .

'What's got into you lately? You've been the only person smiling in this place.'

'Someone's got to . . . ' I begin, but my brain is fast descending into a blur. She noticed? She's never noticed anything about me before – not that she's ever said.

I'm still reeling from this bombshell when she drops another.

'You have a lovely smile, Arch. You should wear it more often.'

Dead.

I am *dead.*

A Quinn ghost melting beside the Perfume Ghost.

I try to reply but clearly my words left my body when the rest of me did. 'I – um – well, I . . . '

She smiles and for a split second I think I see a patter of pink across her cheeks. Is Jessie Edmonds *blushing*?

Before I can see for certain, her phone buzzes. Checking the screen she swears and stands, flashing an apologetic smile at me. 'I've got to run. Press conference at the Town Hall. Would you be okay to shut my Mac down for me?'

'Sure . . . ' I manage, gazing up at her loveliness.

'Hero,' she breathes, her hand warming my shoulder for the briefest time before she shoulders her handbag and hurries out.

I'm left in her sweet-scented wake, wondering what the hell just happened . . .

'*Quinn!* Backside in here, *now!*'

Ah well, it was fun while it lasted.

Jock Callaghan is glowering between the paper skyscrapers crowding his desk when I get there, his balding head a Belisha beacon of simmering rage.

'Yes, boss?'

'I've just talked with our senior reporter,' he says, through gritted teeth, as if Elvis's job title hurts him to mention it. 'Apparently he wants you with him on his next assignments.'

'Does he?' Do I look surprised? I hope so.

He eyes me like a boxer sizing up his opponent. 'I'm guessing this wasn't your idea?'

'Nothing to do with me. I'll do it, though,' I add quickly, sealing off any routes of escape for him.

'Too right you will. And you'd better be bloody good at it, too, or you'll have me to contend with. Also, this does not change our previous agreement.' A smarmy smirk spreads across his face.

'I did a good job on your car, then?' I risk with a grin. His teeth vanish beneath pursed lips.

'You'll do better next time. And less of your lip, okay? This stuff with Elv— *Brian* – is a privilege, not a right. Remember that.'

He hates this, I think to myself, careful to hide my smile until I'm gruffly dismissed. *He bloody hates it but there's nothing he can do about it.*

Pulling my phone from my back pocket, I text Esther. She is going to adore this news!

> Boss just said yes to me working with Elvis ☺ A x

I don't even make it back to my desk before her reply arrives:

> I bet he hated that! ☺ x

I chuckle and swing into my seat as I text back:

> He did! Went so red he looked like a furious beetroot! x

> Love it! It's a sign, Archie. Everything's going to go your way now ☺

> If it is, it's because of you. I reckon you're my lucky charm ☺

> Do lucky charms wear orange Converse?

> They do now x

Man, I love this. The faith she has in me when she still hardly knows me.

'Now that's the grin of a man in demand.' Liam flops onto

his seat beside me, stretching out. Considering he's been outside for a fag break, there's no scent of smoke on him, although his aftershave intensity seems to have gone up a gear. 'You've got something good going on there.'

'I have,' I reply, scrolling back through Esther's messages. 'I think she gets me, you know?'

''Bout time, I reckon. Can't have you mooning over her forever.'

He's so relaxed he's almost floating above his chair. I give him a look, which he doesn't see, his eyes closed as his hands fold behind his head, but he smiles like he knows it happened.

'I'm not *mooning* over anyone. It's just nice to be liked.'

'Oh, I know it is. Make the most of it, I say, before she changes her mind.' As I'm pondering this, he changes tack. 'Did I hear right? Is old Elvis taking you out?'

Liam always does this – talks just enough for you to say something interesting, then moves on to the next juicy topic. It's a good job he mainly writes sub-columns and advertisement features – he doesn't have the concentration span to write entire stories. I once heard Elvis refer to Liam as *Captain Pull-Quote* and I don't think I could sum him up any better.

'He is now the boss has agreed.'

Liam's nut-brown eyes flick open. 'How did you swing that?'

'I didn't. Elvis did.'

'Blimey, you *are* in his good books. First the Biscuit Tin of Dreams, now this? You want to watch out, Arch, he'll own you like the Godfather before you know it. Don Presleyone – a hunka, hunka bossin' journo!'

. . . And cheesy headlines. Liam is king of those.'

'Nice.'

My phone chimes as another text arrives. Liam raises an eyebrow. 'That'll impress her, though.'

'She doesn't need impressing,' I reply, only then considering whether I should have. 'She likes me already.'

'Does she now?' Liam gives a gravel-edged chuckle and slaps me on the back. 'Good for you, AQ. Carry on.'

Seventeen

ESTHER

Come on. Just get out of the car . . .

I huddle in my seat, peering up at the house for the umpteenth time. I should go in. But I'd banked on so many things delaying me and now I'm here – early, completely unhindered by anything during my journey over – I'm wishing I wasn't.

The universe is conspiring against me in every conceivable way today. The traffic let me down: every temporary traffic light that's plagued my journeys for a month disappeared overnight. The post-school-run dash to work hasn't happened either, the roads frustratingly clear. Even the weather hasn't had the decency to be consistent today. I'd fully expected Manchester's finest rain to accompany me here, the torrent enough to let me hide in my car for a long time before I dared to go in. Instead the sun is bright and warm, ushering me out into it.

Now the only thing delaying me is *me*. And I'm a poor substitute for a viable 'sorry-I'm-late-but' excuse.

I'd like to start the engine and drive away, but the problem is that Mum's expecting me. She's probably clocked me already from the edge of her curtains, watching her eldest daughter pretend she isn't parked on the road the other side of the clipped privet hedge.

You're pathetic, Esther Hughes. Just walk in there, like you promised yourself you would.

It was all very well planning this meeting, calling Mum to arrange it, adopting my most grown-up, confident voice to show her I meant business. But my resolve crumbled to dust as soon as I actually had to make it happen.

I'm overthinking, aren't I? Or maybe this is a great big mistake. Maybe I'm not ready to . . .

. . . Oh, stuff it. I'm just going to go in.

I lock my car and walk quickly up my parents' block-paved drive. When I reach their new pale oak front door, I press the doorbell and wait. Exactly ten seconds later, Mum answers, her arms folded tight across her body.

'What were you doing skulking out in the car for so long?'

Great. I knew she was watching.

'And on the road, too, when we have a perfectly decent drive to park on. What will the neighbours think?'

If they know you, they'll understand, the thought sneers in my head. Annoyed, I squash it and force a smile. That's the kind of thing Mum would say and I am *not* my mother. 'Bertha's exhaust is a bit dodgy. I didn't want it dropping gunk on your drive.'

Mum tuts and steps back against the door – her version of an invitation inside. '*Bertha.* Who calls their car Bertha?'

'Dad thinks it's cool,' I say, as I pass her.

'Your dad would,' she mutters behind me.

This wasn't the easiest house to grow up in but returning always brings a pang of longing for the past. It's been redecorated countless times since Naomi and I moved out, but new paint, flooring and wallpaper can't erase the memories infused into every room. The stairs are where we raced up and hurtled down – sometimes with a banister slide, others a bum-bumping descent – the hallway a place that echoed sibling rows, much-practised tap dance routines and teenage tears of the newly dumped. Even the smell of this house has remained, unchallenged by redecoration or Mum's never-ending quest for the perfect air freshener. It's a heady mix of dust – though you'd never find a speck – recently made toast, despite it being hours since anyone ate breakfast, and the burr of sun-warmed carpet.

Mum hasn't said yet, but I know where Dad will be. I hear the faint drumming from the small box room directly above the front door. Dad, typing his memoir. I've lost count of the number of online courses he's taken, the webinars on autobiography and ancestry he's watched. Mum thinks it's a mid-life crisis come twenty years late. I know Dad needs a reason to get up in the morning now he's retired, and he's not quite ready to volunteer to drive the local Red Cross bus or sign up for shifts at B&Q yet.

'*Phil!*' Mum barks up the stairs, leaning on the newel post at the bottom.

The muffled typing stops. '*Mmwhaaa?*'

'Your daughter's here.'

'*Mmnaommi?*'

'No, not Naomi. Your other one! I told you she was coming.'

'*Mmnokay. Mmnown in a mo . . .*'

There's a pause, and the typing resumes, much slower, as if Dad thinks he can sneak another fifty words into his work-in-progress before my mother notices. Mum groans, lifting her eyes heavenwards.

'He'd better sell that blasted book at the end of all this or I might just leave him.'

I hide my smile as I follow her through to the lounge.

Now I'm inside, I feel calmer. It helps that sunlight is bathing the room in soft-focus glow, the happy ghosts of my sister and I weaving in and out of the furniture that, while different to when we grew up here, occupies the same spaces. It amuses us that when Mum redecorates she just changes colours and textures, but the layout remains sacrosanct. Naomi reckons she's measured the footprint of every piece and heads to the furniture store armed with the measurements.

Mum brings in an already brewed Emma Bridgewater teapot, cups and saucers – not a hint of a mug in this house – together with a Victoria sponge cake she definitely hasn't made herself. She sets it all down on a coffee table I've never seen before.

'Sit,' she says. 'Any chair'll do.'

I perch dutifully on a leather armchair near the window and accept a cup of tea.

'Cake?'

'No, thanks.'

'You have to eat.'

My smile slips free of its restraints. 'I do eat. I'm just not hungry.'

She frowns. 'Who said you have to be hungry to eat cake? You'll take some home with you, and no arguments.'

'Fine. Thanks.'

She settles back and observes me as she sips her tea. 'So to what do I owe this pleasure?'

'I wanted to see you.' I ignore the cynical rise of her eyebrows. 'I didn't like the way things were left last time.'

Mum blinks but stays quiet.

It's been almost three weeks since *that* conversation, when I told her I'd found a job – and what it was. I suppose I shouldn't have been surprised by her reaction – Mum has always pushed me to be the best at everything – but the fury with which she dismissed my night cleaning job shocked me. It hurt. And I wasn't prepared for that.

Since then we've exchanged brief messages and one fleeting phone call – during all of which she never once mentioned my new job or the row we'd had because of it. But I haven't been back to her house since.

Until today.

I steady my breathing and face her. Now is the moment to say what I planned. I think of Archie and what I'll tell him when this is done. Of all the people in my life, I know he'll celebrate with me. I picture that smile of his, the way he leans towards me when I'm telling him something, as if he doesn't want to miss a second of it. I hold him in my mind's eye as I begin, my nerves becoming excitement as I do.

'I don't want to fight with you, Mum. That was never my intention. I know you worry about me, that you want what's best – and that's lovely, honestly it is. But the only way I'll move on from everything is if I figure out my own way forward.'

'Cleaning offices at night?'

'If that's what it takes.'

'You could work anywhere . . . '

'I like working at *The Herald*.'

'Cleaning other people's mess. Like a – a . . . '

'Skivvy?' I catch the flare of indignation in my tone and wrench it back. If I draw the battle line here, I'll never win. 'The thing is, Mum, when I left the agency I lost so much more than my job. I lost my confidence, my identity, my whole way of life. And that hit me harder than I ever thought it would.'

Her eyes don't leave me but some of the fire in them does.

'I took the cleaning job because I needed to do something. And actually, it's been such a blessing – no, don't roll your eyes, Mum, it has. It's given me money to save, new things to learn and time to think about what I want the next part of my life to look like. And I've found a friend – a great friend – which has been the biggest serendipity of them all.'

'A friend?'

'His name is Archie. And no, he's not *that* kind of friend. But he's asked me to help him with a project so we're working together.'

It sounds far more formal than it is, but it's piqued my mum's interest.

'An important project?'

I nod. 'It is to us – to him. What I'm trying to say is that I'm really enjoying my job. And while I know it isn't what you wanted for me, I would love it if you would trust my instinct on this.'

'Instinct on what?' Dad is leaning against the open doorway when I look up.

'The mystical properties of a night cleaning job,' Mum says drily.

'Ah. How's the tabard working out, kid?'

In my peripheral vision, Mum bristles. I smile at Dad to deflect my irritation. 'Bit floppy on the shoulders but we're getting on. And I have a cleaning trolley called Fred.'

His grin is wide and warm and wonderfully *Dad*-ish. 'Excellent! Definitely my daughter if you're naming things.'

'Well, I have to uphold the family tradition.' I grin back.

'Your *father's* tradition,' Mum corrects. 'I will never understand the appeal of naming inanimate objects.'

'That's because you've never been properly introduced to any of them,' Dad replies, far too fast for his own good.

His audacity makes me laugh despite my better judgement.

My mother watches us, her eyes snapping between Dad and me. 'Oh yes, go on, mock your poor daft mother!'

I stuff my amusement away. 'Mum, it isn't like that . . .'

'It is, Esther. It always is. Now, I'm glad you think you're happy. And it's nice you've found a friend. But when I think of all that hard work you put in over the years that you just threw away. All because of *that lad* . . .'

My teacup clatters back onto the saucer. I don't mean it to, but I'm shaken. I can't believe she's brought Matt into this. She hasn't spoken about him for months: why start again now?

'Lynne. That's not fair.'

'No, Philip, it wasn't fair! It wasn't fair *that lad* messed with our Esther and then disappeared. It's no wonder she went to pot . . .'

'I'm still here?' I say, but the argument is no longer mine.

'*He* chose to stop talking to her, remember? And our Essie picked herself up and went to work instead of letting it ruin her life. And what did that company do? Kicked her with redundancy. If anybody should feel aggrieved, Lynne, it's your daughter. Now, drop it please. We haven't been together for weeks: let's not ruin it, eh?'

I love my dad. I love my mum, too, but she needs reminding that berating someone you're worried about doesn't actually help them. It comes from a place of love, I know, and there will always be a part of me that's restless for better things, like she is. Maybe that was the problem: I pushed myself on and never settled for what I'd achieved because that's what I'd learned from Mum. And I went along with Matt's wedding plans after my own heart was shattered because I wanted to make everyone happy – exactly what I learned from Dad. And all that did was make me doubly unhappy: stuck on a career trajectory I was never sure I really wanted; and making myself watch the man I adored exchanging vows with someone else, a part of me dying inside.

I stand by everything I've said to Mum today, but I didn't come here to fight. If I leave with us still on opposing sides my visit will have achieved nothing.

'Mum,' I say, softening my voice and fixing her with my stare. 'I know you worry and that you care about me. I love that you do, but I'm doing my best to put all of that behind me. So, trust me to do it, please?'

She gives the slightest nod of her head, a huge concession in her world.

'Thank you.' I sigh. 'The reason I'm helping my friend Archie is so I can finally move on from Matt. I'm helping him write a love letter to a woman he's loved for ages. I know this won't make sense to you, but doing it is changing how I feel about Matt. It's putting things into perspective. And that's helping everything else.'

Dad beams at me, then he moves to sit on the arm of Mum's chair, wrapping his arm around her shoulder. 'There you go, love, you see? Our Essie has it all worked out. Takes after her mother for that, of course.'

He means this as a soothing compliment but *ouch* . . .

And then I witness the age-old miracle. Mum leans into

Dad, gives an overblown sigh and just like that the danger is past. I've seen this happen countless times but it still amazes me. She can be incandescent with rage and Dad can calm her in an instant. I asked him once how he did it: how she could have ranted undeterred for hours before it happened. He'd smiled and said, 'You just have to be a storm-watcher and pick the right moment to jump in.'

'So, love letters, eh?' Dad says, the swift topic-change the work of a master. 'If you need any advice, I've been known to pen a few.'

'Is that how you wooed Mum?' I risk.

He shifts a little. 'Summat like that. Swept you off your feet, didn't I, love?'

Mum's expression lifts. 'Not sure I would describe it quite like . . . '

'Casanova Hughes, they called me in school. Silver-tongued charmer from Crumpsall. Your mother was lucky to get me. In demand, I was. Fighting them off.'

'Don't listen to your father,' Mum tuts. 'He reckons he's a complete romantic and he may well be, but the fact is if I hadn't started the ball rolling I'd still be waiting for him to do something about it.'

The atmosphere finally lifts in the room, the sun's warmth returning. 'Is that right, Dad?'

Dad shrugs. 'It is.'

How have I never heard this before? 'What did you do?'

Mum is about to answer when Dad cuts in. 'She sent me flowers. A great big bunch of them, with a note she wrote herself.'

'You smooth operator, Mum!'

She bats this away, but she's properly smiling at last. 'Your gran nearly disowned me. "Sending a chap flowers? Who does that? Next thing you know you'll be wearing th'suit at th'wedding!'"

'Ever the equalitarian, your gran.' Dad chuckles. 'We almost had matching suits for the wedding just to give her a shock.'

'Well, I had to do something. All the other girls were letting their lads walk over them. Sitting doe-eyed while they faffed around. I wasn't about to join that club. I knew he liked me – he told me once by the bike sheds – but months went by and nowt happened. So, I thought I'd do it.'

'I had to go out with her after that. I was terrified not to,' Dad says, chuckling when Mum elbow-digs him in the ribs. 'You know I don't mean it. Honestly, our Essie, it blew me away. Nobody'd ever written to me before, not like that. Her note said: "*I'd rather spend forever with you than waiting for you. So why don't we give it a go?*" How could I refuse that?'

It's typically Mum in tone, yet so unlike her in action. I love it – even though I can't help being reminded of Matt's excuse for marrying Nina.

An hour later – duly armed with a Tupperware box packed with slices of cake from Mum – I hug them goodbye and hurry back to my car. I feel taller than when I arrived, glowing that I made headway today – a bumpy ride for sure, but I said what I wanted to and got a startling new anecdote about love letters into the bargain. Not bad for an afternoon's work . . .

Archie is going to love this . . .

I send a text to him before setting off home.

Another one for the top secret Love Letter file, Detective Quinn! From my PARENTS (can't believe it!). Also, I had a breakthrough. Will explain next time we speak, but it's

huge and I just want to thank you. I wouldn't have done
it if we hadn't met. Chat soon! E x

I've barely driven a mile down the road when my mobile buzzes
on the passenger seat. Indicating quickly, I pull off the main road
onto a side road that runs alongside a park. Finding a space,
I pull in and kill the engine, answering the call just before it
stops ringing.

'Explain now,' Archie says, and the thrill of his voice makes
me wriggle back into my seat.

So I recount the story, loving his excited reactions to everything I say.

'That's great, Es! How do you feel?'

'Lighter. Stronger. I've played out that conversation in my
head for weeks but I never thought I'd get the chance to say it
for real.'

'I think it's amazing. *You're* amazing.'

The heat in the car seems to increase and I can't blame the
sun for it. 'Give over.'

'No, come on, take the credit! You don't let stuff pass by: you
just go for things – it's inspirational. Okay, that sounds lame but
I mean it. I love how you do that.'

'It helped to know you believed in me.' It feels huge to say
it, but it's true.

His voice is lower when he speaks next, like he's moved closer
to my ear. 'I feel the same. About you. I've failed for so long
but not this time. That's down to you, that is. I think you're
wonderful, Es.'

'Good job we're both brilliant then, eh?' I say, too quickly, too brightly for it to be anything other than a deflection. Because what Archie just said means more than I have honest words for.

'Totally.' Is that relief I hear in his voice too?

When the call ends, I sit back in my seat and breathe in the feeling. My heart is thudding ten to the dozen and I can't stop the smile that's taken residence. I want to frame this moment, right now, knowing that I've made a major step forward and it's been in the company of a truly remarkable soul. *This is how it can be*, I tell myself, courage and hope and delight coursing through me. *This is the future.*

I've hidden away for too long, keeping all the injustice and hurt inside without sharing it. I don't want to live like that anymore. I'm *better* than that. And now I have a friend who sees me for who I can be, not assuming I can never change.

I catch sight of Bertha's dashboard clock and realise I need to get going. I need to be at the girls' school for 3 p.m. and it's twenty-past two now. Friday traffic is unpredictable at the best of times – I can't afford to get caught out.

Firing up the engine, I'm just pulling my seatbelt back across myself when a glint of sunlight on the windscreen catches my attention. I turn my head . . .

. . . and everything freezes.

I know this park.

These houses.

This road.

It isn't a random turn-off I chose to park in and answer Archie's call: this is *Matt's* neighbourhood. I'm a street away from his house.

Shit!

Why did my stupid subconscious mind bring me here?

I haven't driven anywhere near since *that* night. Why return today?

Where my palms grip the steering wheel, cold sweat beads. I have to get out of here . . .

And then, just up ahead, a figure steps out, his arm pulled forwards by a shaggy grey dog straining at its lead. Halfway across the road, he looks over towards my car and stops dead. The dog protests but he doesn't move, raising a hand to his brow to shield his eyes from the sunlight that's streaming across the road between him and me.

I lose my breath.

I can't move.

Matt Hope stares straight at me, as if he's trying to read Bertha's number plate.

But he doesn't have a dog, my mind argues. He didn't before but it's been a year since I last saw him. Anything could have changed in his life since then. There's no mistaking him: his height, his frame, the coat he's worn for years that we used to joke made him look like a police detective going to court . . .

He's still staring at me.

Then he yanks the dog's lead and starts walking down the middle of the road towards me . . .

Wrenching back control of my body, I slam the car into reverse to escape his advance, then push it into first gear, swinging Bertha around. Her wheels clatter over the kerb and skid across the grass verge, the ancient springs complaining. Over the screech of tyres I hear a shout, but I don't stop, flooring the accelerator until I'm away, Matt's figure shrinking in my rear-view mirror.

My whole body is a knot, my mind a mess. When I reach

the school, with fifteen minutes before I have to meet the girls, I lock all the doors and drop my head into my hands.

All the triumph from today gone.

All the warmth from Archie's call stolen.

In their place, a gnawing, empty ache I thought I'd left behind.

What does any of it mean when I return to this, over and over again? And what chance do I have of moving on when my heart still aches for Matt?

Eighteen

ARCHIE

I'm ridiculously early.

But I need to be.

Something happened after I spoke to Esther. I'm sure of it. I sent a couple of jokey texts to her, following on from our amazing call, but she didn't reply. I know she was working, so I wished her a good shift and then sent another message at half past eleven, when I knew she'd be heading back to her car. Still nothing.

I figured she was busy, or maybe her phone had run out of charge like it did the day we met. So I went to bed, a little confused but thinking she'd probably reply this morning when she woke.

And she did reply, but straight away I knew I should've trusted my gut.

Sorry I missed your messages.
See you later.

That's it: no *hey Archie*, no smiley-faced emoticons, no cheeky kisses. And every text she's ever sent me has had those things. So there has to be a reason why my sunny-sounding, irresistibly chuffed friend from yesterday afternoon changed into a two-short-sentences sender.

I've got to admit, I'm worried.

I've been waiting in the car park outside the community hall for an hour, watching all my friends slowly arrive and head inside. And the longer I've waited, the more nervous I've become. Esther said she'd see me later, so I have to assume she's on her way. But what if she's upset? What if she's only coming over to say she won't come in?

I have got to get a grip. I'm sounding like an obsessive boyfriend instead of a concerned friend. I just can't escape the feeling that Esther isn't happy.

Ten minutes later, a flash of sunlight heralds the arrival of her car. I don't think I've ever been so relieved to see anyone. I resist the urge to jump out before she's parked, waiting instead until I see her driver's door open. Then I grab my banjo case and walk over as slowly as I can bear.

'Hey,' I call.

She turns – and my worst fears are confirmed. Esther's face is pale, her hair a curtain of curls across it. Her smile slips a moment after it appears and when she speaks her voice is tight.

'So, I made it.'

I reach her side. 'Are you okay?'

'Yeah,' she replies, but even she doesn't look convinced. Then she sighs, her body sagging as if all the air is leaving with it. 'No. I'm sorry, Arch, I don't think this is a good idea – going in *there*, today. I'm just not . . . I don't think I can . . . '

Her eyes are glistening now. I am not good with tears. But this is my friend who is hurting and I *knew* she was hurting before she even told me. I can't let that happen on my watch.

'Come here,' I say, pulling her into a hug.

She doesn't protest, just curls herself into my arms. As I hold her, I feel the first judder of her shoulders.

'Want to talk about it?'

She presses in as if my arms are the only things anchoring her to the ground. 'I failed.'

'Failed at what?'

'Everything links to him. I'm meant to be moving on, proving I can do it to everyone. I was so certain I was on the right track, but . . . ' Esther pulls back, her eyes lifting slowly to meet mine. 'I saw Matt.'

'When?'

'Yesterday. Just after we spoke. I pulled over to take your call and it wasn't till it ended that I realised I'd driven into Matt's neighbourhood. And then there he was. With a *dog*.'

'A dog?' It's such an incongruous thing to end with that I laugh, instantly wishing I hadn't.

'A dog. That he doesn't even have.'

'A *ghost dog*?'

She laughs and clamps a hand to her mouth. 'I mean, he didn't have a dog before. But he does now. I shouldn't even laugh about it, it's so awful.'

'Why?'

'Because the moment I saw him, I knew it wasn't over. All

that hurt and boxed-up anger just flooded back.' She moves away, my hands falling to my side as she leaves.

I watch her pace along the line of parked cars, not really sure what to say. I'm glad I made her laugh, but beyond that I don't know what I can do. For the first time since we met, I'm aware of my own shortcomings, suddenly clumsy beside her. 'I'm so sorry that happened to you.'

'It wasn't your fault.'

'I know, but . . . I hate that it happened right after you were so excited. Standing up to your mum was amazing. It still is.'

'But Matt . . . I can't believe I drove there without realising. One street away from his house – what was I thinking?'

Her hand runs through her hair, which bounces back defiantly. I know she told me about this guy before and I guessed it was bad, but seeing it in person, in real time, is a total kick to the guts. Esther is the loveliest person I know. I don't want her to hurt. But the longer this goes on, the less likely she is to come with me to meet The Old Guys. I need to help her out of this – but how?

'Everybody drives places they used to go. I spent weeks driving past my flat and finding myself at Mum and Dad's bakery. It's automatic – a force of habit. It doesn't mean anything.'

She presses her fingers to her closed eyes as if trying to keep the tears inside the lids. 'But it was *Matt* . . . '

I jump in before she can continue, hoping the right words arrive. 'It's just one sighting. I know it hurts – I get it, more than anyone – but it was a one-off. You haven't failed, Es. You said what you wanted to your mum. And look what happened here, with us. That's why you need to go in that hall and meet everyone.'

'I don't think I can.'

'I know you can. And I know you're going to love it.'

She pulls back a handful of curls from her face and observes me. 'How do you know?'

'Because they always make me feel better. You and me, we're the same, I reckon. We think the best of life even when it's kicking us. Also, if you don't come in you'll never get to experience quite how disastrous my banjo playing is.' I hold my hands wide. 'And I reckon that's a treat nobody should deny themselves.'

I don't know if I've said the right thing, but at least I said something. Esther doesn't reply and for a moment I think she might still leg it. We're late already – not that Granda Brady and the lads will mind – but something has to move because we can't stay out in the car park forever.

Esther's eyes narrow. 'Just how bad are we talking?'

'I've moved listeners to tears and hardly ever in a good way.'

Her hesitant smile is the loveliest, brightest gift. 'Sold. I have to hear this.'

Delighted, I shoulder my banjo case and dare to offer her my hand. 'Shall we?'

Inside the community hall is a loud, echoing mass of happy noise and activity. Jim's booming laughter punctuates the chat, dodgy tuning and overloud moving of chairs, while Granda Brady is already bargaining with Marta for refreshments to happen before they begin. Eric and Isaac are the first to spot us as we hover by the door, Eric striding over to greet us.

'Well hello.' He beams. 'You must be the lovely Esther.'

Esther looks at me, surprised. 'Yes, I am. Hi . . .'

'This is Eric,' I tell her, only considering now that I should have given her the lowdown on The Old Guys before we arrived. 'Guitarist.'

'Getting there slowly. But we all try, don't we, Archie?'

'We do.'

'Come and meet everybody,' Eric says, beckoning for us to follow as he heads back to the circle of chairs. 'This is Isaac, demon of the ukulele. Kavi, fellow strummer. Old Bob and Li'l Bill, mandolin and bouzouki, almost as harmonious in music as they are in love . . .'

'We're a sight better at the love bit, thankfully.' Li'l Bill chuckles, shaking Esther's hand. 'Lovely to meet you, Esther.'

'And this Caledonian giant is Jim.'

'MacLennan,' Jim booms, tucking his fiddle under one arm to offer his hand to Esther. It dwarfs hers when she accepts. 'Musical director of this midden, for my sins.'

I watch my friend taking all this in, aware of my two worlds colliding. Esther looks completely at home as The Old Guys surround her, her smile thankfully back in place. A flush of pride swells in my chest. I knew this would work.

Would Jessie Edmonds be as at home here?

Surprised, I kick the thought away. Where did that come from?

'Okay, put the poor girl down,' says a familiar voice. As The Old Guys part, Granda Brady strolls between them. 'Esther, I'm Archie's grandfather. Diarmuid Brady, but mostly everyone calls me Brady. Player of the squeezebox, or, more accurately in my case, the *wheeze-box*. I'm delighted to make your acquaintance.' He tips his trilby and gives a slightly jerky bow. I know his hips will be complaining but you can't fault his attempt at chivalry.

'Lovely to meet you. Archie's told me a lot about you.'

Granda Brady casts a glance in my direction. 'That I don't doubt. I'm happy you came despite the tales.'

'I wouldn't miss it,' Esther replies and I see approval ripple through the group.

'Now, hard as I've tried, Marta will not part with her cakes and tea until after we play, so apologies, gents – and lady – I'm afraid we must endure pain before pleasure.' Granda raises his hand in reply to the groans. 'Let's start with "The Wishing Tree" and hope the title inspires.'

Everyone takes their places and Isaac brings over an extra chair for Esther, putting it between his and mine.

'Don't say I didn't warn you,' I whisper, sliding on my thumb and finger picks.

'Can't wait,' she whispers back.

It's predictably awful, but the atmosphere makes up for it. To Esther's credit, she keeps her smile steady and never winces once, despite the high proportion of ear-jangling bum notes. We subject her to three more tunes before Jim signals for us to stop. Relief is palpable around the room.

'We've murdered every note as planned. Only Marta's cakes and tea can save us now.'

On cue, the creaky steel roller shutter over the serving hatch to the kitchen rolls up and instruments are abandoned in a gleeful dash for refreshments.

'Well, Esther, what do you think?' Granda Brady winks. 'Is there any hope for us?'

'Absolutely. I don't think it's as bad as you all say.'

'You're kind but have you had your ears tested lately?'

Esther grins. 'I think I just did.'

My granda's laugh echoes in the hall. 'Ach, perfect! You've a good one here, Archie. Let's reward her with the best cake in Greater Manchester.'

As we walk over, I bump my arm against Esther's. 'Thanks for being here.'

'Thanks for asking me.'

'I love them, these guys. I've been coming here with Granda Brady since I was fourteen and they've always accepted me. I've played in high times and low points, and whenever I've questioned who I am and where I find my strength, this is the place I've found answers.'

'You're different here,' Esther says. 'Calmer. More sure of yourself.'

Am I? I feel it, but I'm surprised Esther sees it so clearly. 'Despite the dreadful banjo abuse?'

'That's part of you, too. Does Jessie know you play banjo? Or the story of how you rescued it from a skip?'

'No.'

She shrugs. 'Maybe she should.'

'It doesn't make me sound weird?' I ask it before I've thought the question through. Now I wonder if the asking confirms my concern.

'Not at all. Put it this way, you've got to really be committed to your dream if you're prepared to climb into a skip to get it.'

I burst out laughing, causing the assembled Old Guys to look over with amused smiles. 'Stick that on a motivational fridge magnet!'

She laughs, too. 'No, listen. Your heart leads you. That much I know already and being here has just confirmed it. Now if I wanted someone to fall in love with, I'd want someone daft enough to jump into a skip for what he wants. Or rescue an instrument most people would bin. I would want someone to see value in me that others haven't – and to be proud that they're with me. Because, ultimately, we all want to be cherished.' She flushes a little, her curls falling over her face as she dips her head. 'That's just what I think.'

If I had clever words prepared for this moment, they're gone. I smile back dumbly because I'm stunned by what she just said. How has Esther worked all that out from just one funny story about a banjo rescue and a single visit here?

Ahead of us, Granda Brady beams. I reckon he heard it all.

Nineteen

ESTHER

Dear Jessie,
    I climb into skips to rescue banjos.
    And I think I'm falling for you . . .

'No.'

'It's the truth,' Archie protests. 'And you said I should tell her about the skip.'

Archie Quinn is impossible when he's feeling vulnerable and using humour to mask it. 'You should tell her that, just maybe not in the letter you want to win her heart with,' I say, unable to stop myself smiling. 'And that sentence followed by the *falling for you* line makes it look like you're falling into a skip for Jessie.'

'Ah. Now you mention it, it does.' He reaches over and steals a handful of crisps from the packet beside my glass of lemonade.

'Oi, get your own!'

'Brain food,' he replies, his mouth already full.

'Cheek!'

I'm still shaken about seeing Matt, but this is helping. Every time I can laugh or joke or muck around with Archie it distracts my attention from the uncomfortable eddies of emotion just under the surface. I get the feeling Archie knows it, too: I'd had a tough morning battling memories of Matt before coming to meet Archie and my new friend has been a Quinn-on-a-Mission ever since. I see the shimmer of delight in his eyes every time he wins a smile from me. I was a little worried he'd grill me over the whole Matt thing today but his determination to take my mind off it is such a welcome surprise.

He studies the notepad on the pub table between us and jabs a finger at the lines he's just written. 'So the skip bit is a no-no?'

'Definitely a no.' I feel mischief waggle-dance from his side of the table to mine. 'Besides, you don't want to hit her with that pearl too early.'

'*Pearl*!' Archie chokes a little as he laughs. 'Go on then, O Wise One: why not?'

'Well, you'd always be wondering if she loves you for yourself or your skip-jumping ability.'

Man, I love making him laugh.

I love all of this.

We've been meeting regularly for the last week, Naomi grudgingly accepting that this project will call me away from her dinner table until the letter is written. In return, I'm doing every school run both morning and afternoon, and hanging out with the girls until Gavin gets home from work at 5.30 p.m. My sister has made no secret of what she thinks, but she can see how happy I am. I don't mind that it makes my days busier and my body achier as the week goes on: I'm flying. The more time we spend together, the more I understand what a huge responsibility Archie's entrusted me with; how important it is to make this happen for him so he wins Jessie and I can finally move on from Matt.

Today we're in a pub next door to the community hall – a real 'spit and sawdust' place, as Dad would call it – after my second meeting with The Old Guys. For a Saturday lunchtime it isn't very busy, but Archie assures me it never is. There's something lovely about wandering into a half-empty pub with someone who knows it well. Being with Archie makes me feel safe like that. This is his world and I'm welcomed further into it with each new meeting.

For that reason walking into The Old Guys meeting was completely different today. After feeling so conspicuous and new last Saturday, this week I strolled in, chatted with Granda Brady, Old Bob, Eric and Marta like we'd been friends for years and had taken my seat beside Archie in the circle of musicians before I'd realised how easy everything had been.

'It's like you've always been with us.' Granda Brady had smiled, shouldering his accordion. 'We should get you an instrument next time.'

'Spoons!' Jim had suggested, the room erupting with good-natured laughter.

I'd have a go, too, now I feel at home there . . .

Since Archie and I met, more things in my life have had that ease. It's like everything in his immediate vicinity relaxes to fall in step with his rhythm.

It's happening at home, too. I feel closer to the girls, who now chat happily to me during the school runs. I'm learning that Issy likes the extra ten minutes we have together at the school gate before her class goes in, to talk about the latest soap-opera shenanigans playing out among her girlfriends. Molly is impressed by how much I know about Snoopy and Charles M. Schulz, finding ever more obscure facts to quiz me on, while Ava-May saves up questions during the school day to quick-fire at me on the fifteen-minute car drive home.

Even Naomi seems more relaxed around me, albeit still ready to grumble when it suits her, but I haven't heard her bicker with Gavin as much as they usually do, or snap at the girls when she's got things on her mind. It might be my imagination, of course. Seeing everything through Archie-hued specs because of the change he's wrought in my life. I'm not going to overanalyse it, I've decided. Better to put away the microscope and just enjoy the ride.

It hasn't solved the Matt Problem. But every minute I'm *not* obsessing over that man is a step closer to leaving him behind.

Archie wipes his eyes as his laughter finally subsides and spins the pen around his fingers like a baton. 'Okay, how about this . . .'

He flips the page and starts to write.

'Be serious this time,' I say.

'I'm always serious.'

'Are you heck!'

'Ssh, Detective Hughes, this is delicate work.'

'Sorry, guv.' I sit back and watch him, the bubble of fun waiting to be set free. 'Your handwriting is lovely.'

He doesn't look up, but I can see his smile from here. 'You said.'

'Maybe just write: *If you think this handwriting is sexy, you should see the writer . . .*'

Archie snorts. 'Remind me why I asked for your help?'

'Because if it weren't for me, you'd be wooing Jessie with skip-jumping anecdotes.'

'True.' He clicks the ballpoint pen closed and pivots the notebook on the table to face me. 'How about this?'

> Jessie
> I think you're amazing.
> Would you go out with me?
> Esther says you should and she's
> pretty scary so best not upset her, eh?
> Regards, Archie x

'Ha ha. You're supposed to be taking this seriously.'

'I am taking it seriously.' He slumps in his seat and reaches for his beer. 'It just stops between my heart and my head. And when it reaches the page it's dreadful.'

'Stop overthinking. Let's look back at the research, see if anything inspires you.'

We turn a few pages back in the notebook to find the stories we've collected. People we know well, people we've chatted to in the street, friends, family, co-workers, strangers we've encountered.

'I love this one,' I say, pointing to an online magazine feature I'd printed out and stuck in the book. '"*Geoffrey Salter Ellis, a young Yorkshire RAF navigator flying sorties in Wellington and Lancaster Bombers during World War Two, proposed to his sweetheart Doris Parker by sending her a small length of blue wool with his letter from the airfield he'd been posted to. 'Tie this around the third finger of your left hand, knot it and send it back to me,' he wrote. On his next leave he produced an engagement ring he'd had made to the size of the wool loop*" . . . How smooth is that?'

'Geoff sounds like a dude. I hope Doris said yes.'

'She did. He died hours before their sixtieth wedding anniversary.'

'Wow. I need to channel Geoff then.' He leafs through the pages. 'And also my brother Conn.'

I peer at the page. 'I don't remember you telling me that one.'

'That's 'cos he only told me yesterday.' Archie grins. 'My big brother is a dark horse when it comes to romance. I just assumed he'd got together with his partner Elodie in a bar somewhere – that's usually his style. Turns out she used to work in a café round the corner from his furniture workshop and every lunchtime he ate in there he'd write a little thank you note on a paper napkin with a tip for her to find.'

'Aw, that's sweet.'

'Forget sweet: for a great big hulk like him, it's miraculous. I asked him when he'd finally had the courage to ask Elodie out and he said he never got the chance – she brought his sandwich over one day and she'd written on the napkin, *Here's a tip for you: ask for my number today*. That was four years ago and they're still blissful.'

'So, it's in your genes,' I say.

'Or maybe it weakened with each of us and there's none left for me.'

'Stop it.' I glare at him. 'You know you have it in you. I wouldn't be here if you didn't.'

'What's this, kids? Homework?' The gravel-voiced landlady clearing glasses from the next table nods at our notebook.

'Research,' Archie says – and I'm struck by how quick he is to answer. Nobody stands on ceremony here: if someone has a question, they ask it. One of the many things I love about this part of the world. You can get someone's life story in the supermarket till queue, purely by virtue of the fact that you've stood next to each other for a few minutes.

'Not one of them secret shoppers, are you?' she asks, eyeing us both.

'No, you can rest easy. I'm a journalist investigating how love letters bring people together.'

'Love letters, is it now? You want to ask my old man how he wooed me, then. Derek!'

A bald-headed man-mountain restocking beer bottles behind the bar looks over. 'What is it, my precious?'

'Tell this lad how you asked me out.'

Derek leans on the lager pull and chuckles. 'Now there's a tale. All it took were one beer mat and a biro I borrowed from Old Trev who used to do the crossword on the end of the bar.'

'What did you do with them?' Archie asks.

'I wrote, *NEXT ROUND'S ON ME* on the beer mat and slid it across the bar to her. I'd been trying to catch our Lil's eye for months. Turned out I only had to offer her a pint.'

'Forget three little words. My Derek found the magic four. Knew he were a smooth-talking beggar from that moment on. Put *that* in your article, son.' Lil winks at us as she heads back to the bar.

We giggle and Archie writes a new attempt:

> *Hey, Jessie*
> *Next round's on me.*
> *(Lil said that worked for her.)*

'Classy.'

'It's simple.'

'True. Does Jessie like pints?'

Archie is doodling around his mock love letter now, undulating ink seas dipping beneath the words and pairs of lovebirds flying overhead. 'No idea.'

'Maybe you should find out?'

'Hm.' He stabs the page as if he's just remembered a vital clue. 'You said I was sexy.'

'Eh?'

'Just now. You said, *if you think my handwriting's sexy . . .* '

My cheeks burn. I did say that, didn't I? I was joking, of course, but quoted back it sounds far more forthright than I would ever be. I raise my chin. 'I said your handwriting was sexy. Completely different.'

'My hand's connected to the rest of me—' he raises a suggestive eyebrow '—last time I looked, anyhow.'

'Shut up.'

'Maybe I could quote you. The ultimate pull-quote: *He's so sexy – Esther Hughes.*'

'Oh yeah, that would work.'

'Worked on you, apparently.' He's enjoying this, isn't he? I want to squirm but the sheer audacity of his game is irresistible. 'I mean, if there's anything you want to tell me, Esther . . . '

'*I'm* not writing the letter. You are.'

He leans on the table. 'So what would you say? If you were writing to me?'

'I would say . . . ' I mirror his gesture, squaring up to him, adopting the softest, breathiest voice I can, while resisting the urge to giggle and ruin the effect. He leans closer too, the smallest hint of uncertainty creeping into his stare. 'Archie, there's only one thing I want you to do for me . . . '

He makes to rest his chin on his hand, his elbow almost missing the edge of the table. 'What?'

I pick up the pen and slowly, deliberately offer it to him. 'Write the letter to Jessie.'

'Very funny.' He scowls and rocks back. 'Like it's that easy.'

'It is easy.'

'How? The words are too hard to find.'

The fun seems to have vanished all of a sudden and in its wake I'm a little shaken. 'Oh really? *Jessie, I think you're amazing. Would you go for a drink with me? Love Archie* . . . How about that?'

That shuts him up. He glares back.

'Write the letter, Arch.'

He fiddles with the pen as if remembering the words I cooed when I was winding him up. 'And miss out on all this?'

'What's that supposed to mean?'

'I like this – the research. The word-wrangling. With you.'

'I like it too.' I say it quietly because it's the truth. And so is what has to follow. 'But you can't do all the things you've promised yourself until you tell Jessie how you feel. That's what you said. Is that still the case?'

His sigh sends tiny specks of salt skidding across the silver lake of the opened-up crisp packet.

'Of course it is. You're right.' He lifts his head. 'You're always right.' There's something in the way he looks at me that sets question marks spinning like the tiny bits of crisp-salt . . .

Twenty

ARCHIE

We're getting closer, I think.

To the letter, obviously, I correct myself, the hint of a different meaning sending a hot shot of adrenaline through me. Closer to *writing the letter*. Not closer together . . .

'Who stomped on your pie?' Liam is frowning at me.

'Sorry?'

'You look like someone nicked your season ticket.'

I manage a wry smile in reply. 'Lost on me, that analogy.'

'Right.' He frowns. 'I forgot you were one of the weirdos born without a football gene.'

I give a head-bowed salute.

'You okay, though?' He's wearing the kind of uncertain concern that begs me not to say I have a problem. Bless him for asking, though.

'Yeah. Always okay, me.'

He glances at my desk. 'Tell it to your notepad.'

When I follow his line of sight I see that the blank sheet of my notebook is now covered in angry stabs of black ink. Some of them have passed through the top sheet and marked the one below. I didn't even realise I'd made any of them.

'Just . . . testing my pen.'

'Alrighty . . . ' Liam swings his chair back to his desk. 'Remind me never to be reincarnated as a Bic Cristal biro.'

I *am* okay. But we're getting closer to writing the letter and it's just dawning on me: once it's done, what happens with us?

I think – I *hope* – we'll be friends for a long time. Already Esther is streets ahead of any other friend I've known. We found one another at the right time – you can't walk away from that. But if we succeed with the letter, how will that change what we have now?

We'll still see each other. We'll send each other daft texts and meet for occasional cake and chat. But our mission will be over, the purpose that brought us together gone. Can I be happy with a casual acquaintance where this friendship has been?

It's still playing on my mind later, when I head over to Wythenshawe to have tea with my granda at his house. I don't manage it every week, but since my nanna died nine years ago, I've tried my best to join him for a home-cooked meal as often as I can. I assumed my grandparents would always be there, fighting fit in body, mind and wit. Nanna was such a formidable force of nature, gathering her kin to her with a strong love bordering on scary. Losing her suddenly as we did – two weeks after an unexpected fall – shook me to my foundations. I didn't see her as often as I should, taking her constant, larger-than-life presence for granted. I vowed not to have the same regrets with Granda Brady that have haunted me with Nanna.

Every time we sit down to eat in Granda's house, I feel closer to Nanna. It doesn't sting like it used to but every now and again a memory will floor me. Maybe it's the carpet that's the same one they had laid in the 1980s, or the three-piece suite Granda refuses to be parted from, despite it being a fire hazard due to its age. Sometimes it's the plates we eat our meal from – a sudden recollection of the six plates in the set balanced on every available flat surface in their tiny kitchen while Nanna served dinner, with an extra mismatched Willow-pattern plate for Granda on top of the fridge. Nanna's always here, no matter what. And that's a comfort as much as a barb.

It helps that Granda discovered a hidden flair for cooking when Nanna finally relinquished sole charge of the catering. It's never a chore eating one of his meals.

Tonight, it's brisket with onions and gravy, mashed spuds from the tiny veg plot behind his council house and a cheeky bottle of beer he's not supposed to have. So far, we've hidden this detail from Mum, who polices her father's health with terrifying tenacity.

'To your dear Ma.' Granda winks, clinking the neck of his beer bottle with mine and taking a swig. 'Ah, *rebellion*. There's no better flavour.'

'You're a bad man, Granda.'

'That I might be, but I'm a happy one.' He takes a mouthful of meat and potatoes, watching me as he chews. 'And what about you, Archie Quinn? Are you happy?'

'Always.' It's too quick, too defensive and he's on to me.

'Well, of course you are, lad. Happy little soul from the day you were born and you made everyone who met you happy, too. But that's not what I meant.' Bushy eyebrows shadow his eyes. 'How's the auld heart?'

'It's good,' I say, shovelling a forkful of food into my mouth to prevent me saying more.

'I see.'

I give him a closed-mouth smile hoping this draws a line underneath his questioning.

Some hope . . .

'Now let's try the version I'm actually going to buy.'

'Honestly, Granda, things are good. We're getting really close to finishing the letter and then I'm going to give it to Jessie.'

'Define "we".'

'Esther and me.'

'Mm-hmm. Now tell me again the name of the lass you're writing the letter for.'

'Jessie. Jessie Edmonds.'

I'm about to make a joke about Granda Brady getting forgetful in his old age, when his bony index finger wags at me. A sure-fire sign that a lecture is imminent.

'*There.*'

'Where?'

His finger waggles again, inches from my nose. 'You flinch when you say Esther's name. That doesn't happen when you mention the other one.'

'Jessie,' I say, realising too late that I've tumbled into his trap.

'Nothing, again.'

'Maybe I'm calm saying Jessie's name because I love her.'

He pulls a face, the accusing finger still aimed at me. 'If it helps you to believe that, go right ahead. In my experience, the flinch comes with the heart-skip.'

What is he going on about? I make a mental note to start bringing alcohol-free beer for our weekly tea dates. 'My heart doesn't skip when I say *Esther*.'

'Flinch!'

'I don't flinch! Esther and I are just friends.'

'Flinch again!'

I will stillness into my body. 'If you think I'm secretly lusting after my friend you're bonkers. I love Esther as a friend. Esther is . . .'

'Flinch! Flinch!'

'Would you stop that?'

Chuckling to himself, he holds up his hand. 'Done.'

'Good, thank you. Now eat your tea.'

'Yes, boss.' He obediently resumes work on his plate and the living room falls quiet, the symphony of his housing estate sweeping into the room – screeches of kids playing in neighbouring gardens, a dog barking, the distant *woomph-woomph-woomph* of a car stereo bass line.

I return to my own meal, pushing away the niggle Granda's words have nudged into my mind.

'Here's what I know . . .'

I groan and drop my head into my hands. He's going to go right ahead and say whatever he wants regardless, so better just let him get on with it. And the most annoying thing is that this is exactly the conclusion Granda Brady wanted me to reach. 'What do you know?'

'Women, Archie. Wily customers, I've found. But nowhere near as sneaky as your own heart where they're concerned. See, that pesky beggar called love tends to go hand in glove with the utter bastard that is abject fear. You love the women. But you fear them more. That's the sign of true love, Arch. Lord knows I adored your nanna, but she could scare the living shite out of me on a whim.'

'I'm not scared of Esther – I *didn't* flinch,' I say quickly as the finger appears again. 'But when I'm with Jessie I forget how to speak.'

He dismisses this with a mash-laden fork. 'Not the same thing at all. You lose the power of speech when you're lusting because the blood is required *elsewhere* . . . ' Completely unnecessarily, he gestures downwards.

'Ugh, Granda!'

'We are men of the world, Archie. That wee fella is responsible for a lot of trouble and I know you know this already.'

There is no polite response to that. So I eat instead, chewing my irritation along with potatoes and gravy. He's quiet for a while, too. A strange silence settles between us.

I know he thinks he's helping with his dodgy advice, but I don't need it today. Except – he's hit a nerve. I don't want to admit it, but I'm struck by a need to talk whatever it is out of my system. Better my granda than anyone else . . .

I glance at him. 'I am scared. About Esther. But not because I'm in love with her.'

'I've met the girl. She's not scary, son.'

'She can be when she's trying to get me to write.' Our shared smiles blow the tension away that had hung over the dining table. 'But it isn't that. I'm scared I'll lose her.'

Granda Brady says nothing, but he's waiting for more.

'When the letter's done. When Jessie has it. What will we do then?'

'Stay friends.'

'But what if we don't?' I let out a sigh as I push my plate away. 'We agreed to finish the letter together. And we're really close now – so close that I'm busy hurling roadblocks in our path that we don't need, just to keep . . . *this*.'

'That's the fear, Arch.'

And suddenly, I feel it – terror in the depths of my guts, a wrenching, writhing sensation that sends cold waves of dread washing out from my core. I can dress it up any way I like, but the thing that's made life so much brighter lately hasn't been the letter. It's been the person I've been writing it with.

'I don't want to lose her, Granda.'

He gives a slow nod, pulling the napkin from the collar of his shirt and wiping his hands before setting it down on the table. I watch his sun-weathered, time-bent fingers moving across the white linen, marking fold lines and twisting the fabric into a neat rectangle. I've seen him do this so many times, a meditation while he gathers his thoughts.

My heart aches as Nanna's voice drifts into my head. 'Uh-oh, now he means business. Stay quiet and watch, Archie, there's magic being made in that auld head of his . . . '

When it's done, he nods to the napkin as if thanking it for its assistance, and looks up at me.

'Then don't lose her.'

I wait for the next part of his wisdom, but his smile is all I receive. Is that it? All of that *Granda-magic* show for four words?

'Not helpful,' I snap. Granda's surprise makes me regret my tone.

'Make it imperative that she stays. Give her a reason, Arch.'

'Like what? Help me out here, please.'

'Okay.' He rescues a stray pea from the table and sends it spinning back onto his empty plate. 'Well, you could tell her what she means to you—' seeing my reaction, he chuckles '—but given your track record of telling women how you feel, maybe a different approach would be advisable.'

'Such as?'

'You know, I was saying to The Old Guys only last week what a lovely thing it would be to get some new blood into the band. Besides yourself, of course. And also to – as you young people say these days – address the woeful gender imbalance we currently have.'

'You've lost me.'

'Talk about slow on the uptake – a glacier would speed past you sometimes.' He leans towards me. 'If she had an instrument, she could join us. She would have to come to practice every Saturday morning at eleven. We'll let her off Tuesday evenings because she's working. Regular attendance would be necessary – from you, too. So there would be a legitimate, *ongoing* reason for you two to be in the same room at least once a week . . . And so you wouldn't have to stop seeing her.'

I take it all back. Granda Brady is a magician of the highest order.

Big Jim had joked about Esther playing spoons last Saturday and she'd found it funny but seemed to be up for the challenge.

Is she looking for a reason to keep seeing me, too?

I've caught her without her smile sometimes, as we've been thrashing out words for this letter. And there are long pauses that appear from nowhere, which neither of us seems able to fill. I thought I was imagining it, but what if I wasn't?

If I can find Esther the perfect instrument and offer it to her, I'll know by her response if she's feeling the same as me.

It can't be spoons, though. Esther Hughes deserves more than spoons.

*

Knowing the instrument must adhere to The Old Guys' initiation rule of being rescued makes procuring the perfect one for Esther that bit trickier. Overnight, all the many skips near my flat vanish and searches through the free-to-a-good-home classifieds on the MyManc website prove fruitless. I scan the piles of unwanted household items left for collection on the side of the road as I drive into work each day, praying something vaguely musical might be tucked up with the battered bookcases, boxes of odds and ends and single dining room chairs.

Finally, I sneak out of *The Herald* at Friday lunchtime, safe in the knowledge that Callaghan is off on a long golfing weekend, with Liam assuring me they'll manage without me for an extra twenty minutes if I need it. I think he was amused to discover I was hunting a battered old instrument for my friend. What I might have lost in dignity in admitting this to him, I gain in vital extra search time. It's a trade I can live with.

Charity shops are my last, best hope now. Tomorrow I'll see Esther at The Old Guys and I need to have something to give her. The letter might be complete next week and then it will be too late. I need this to look like it's just a serendipitous suggestion, not a desperate last-ditch attempt to keep Esther in my life.

Because that's exactly what this is now.

As I've searched ever more unsuccessfully, that sense of dread has grown. What if I'm too late to ask her to stay? What if she only wanted to hang around for as long as it took to complete the letter? And what if I've imagined those pauses, those rare smile-slips on her part?

The only musical thing I find in the first four charity shops I visit is a strange mini keyboard you blow into and play at the same time. I'm a confirmed fan of charity shops, but some items in them you should never put your lips around.

And then I strike lucky.

In the farthest, junkiest corner of a tatty cat rescue shop, half-buried in a red plastic bucket beneath a tumble of naked Barbie dolls, I spot the stringless neck and tuning pegs of a tiny guitar. When I carefully extract it from its wild-haired companions, I discover it's not a guitar, but a ukulele. At one time it must have been painted, a few flecks of sunset yellow and old gold clinging stubbornly to the scuffed bare wood. There's a makeshift shoulder strap tied between its head and the small button on the lower end of its body fashioned from red and white twisted butchers' string.

It has a 20p sticker stuck across its naked fretboard. Ghost-lines of grime are the only evidence strings were ever there. It's scratched, dented and grubby.

And it's *perfect*.

On the way home that evening, I drop in at Marlon's, the tiny music shop half an hour from my home and one of my favourite places in the world. Since I rescued Béla Fleck the Banjo, and fell in love with playing, the delights of this musical treasure trove have called me back time and again.

'What the *chuff* have you got there now?' Marlon booms, as I walk in with Esther's ukulele.

'Another daring rescue,' I say. 'I want to do it up for a friend and I haven't much time.' I hand him the instrument, which looks even smaller in his large hands.

'Impulse buy, was it?'

'You could say that.'

'Bloody Nora, Arch, you've your work cut out with this one. Give us a min and I'll see what I've got in the back.'

While I wait, I scan the crowded walls for new stock. My gaze drifts up to the rows of stage passes hanging from lanyard cords on hooks all around the perimeter of the ceiling, collected by Marlon during his years of being a touring guitar tech for just about every major band you've heard of. Then I spot a gorgeous guitar below them. It's a beauty – frets marked by half-moons and tiny stars of inset abalone, a varnish so smooth and clear it's a mirror to the other instruments around it.

'Is the mahogany six-string a new one?' I ask.

'Came in last week,' Marlon's voice replies from the stockroom behind the counter. I can hear boxes being moved around and rummaged through back there. 'Lakestone. Father and son team down in the Midlands. Bespoke stuff, but boy, she plays like a dream. You'll not find one of them beauties in a skip.'

'I'll bet.'

'Right, here y'are.' He strolls back into the shop with a shoe-box and a small roll of tools. 'I have a set of decent strings, some varnish and there's a load of odds and sods in this box you can have for free. Were you thinking of painting it?'

It hadn't entered my mind but now the sad excuse for an instrument is lying on the counter, I can see its possibilities. 'I might. Looks like it was painted before.'

'This kind of thing always is. I've some tester pots of colour you can have – just paint the body then top with a couple of layers of varnish to seal it. The strings are easy enough to fix, but I know you've done that before. I can't promise it'll sound good, but knowing you and your lot I imagine that isn't important. We'll make her look the part at least, eh?'

*

I start work as soon as I get home. Over takeaway pizza I search through the box of dubious wonders Marlon gave me and find a tester pot of bright-orange paint the colour of Esther's beloved Converse sneakers, and a sheet of glittery flower decals Marlon reckons one of his exes left when she hightailed it with a roadie. Piece by piece, layer by layer, it comes together. I grab a couple of hours' sleep while the topcoat of varnish dries, then wake at 6.30 a.m. to fix the strings in place.

By the time I arrive at the community hall, only caffeine and sugar are keeping me upright, but adrenaline is giving me the biggest buzz. I can't believe I pulled it off but it's done and it's sitting in my car next to me, waiting to meet Esther.

She waves as her car passes mine and I make myself stay in my seat until she's parked and has climbed out.

'You look happy.' She smiles, walking over to meet me.

'You too.' I'm almost knocked over by an urge to take her in my arms and dance her around the car park. She can't refuse the gift, can she? I'm crossing everything that the ukulele is the invitation Esther's been seeking as much as I have.

'I like it here,' she replies, turning to walk towards the hall.

'No – wait, Es. I have something for you first.'

She turns back. 'Oh?'

'Close your eyes.'

'Why?'

'Just trust me, okay?'

She looks at me like I might have a flamethrower hidden behind my back. But then, with a mock groan, she obliges.

'Hold out your hands.'

'I'm not a kid at a birthday party, Arch . . .'

'Do you want your present or not?'

'Present?'

'Close your eyes!' I laugh.

'They're closed.'

I pull the ukulele from behind me and gently lay it across her outstretched palms. The bow I tied around it looks ridiculously huge and the bright sunlight reveals how questionable my painting skills really are. But it's too late to stop now. 'Open them.'

I watch her fingers tentatively fold around the body of the ukulele, two lines appearing between her eyebrows as she tries to decipher her gift by touch alone. 'What is it?'

'Have a look.'

She does – and it's the loveliest thing. I see waves of surprise, joy, emotion and fun pass across her face like the cloud shadows being blown across the sun-drenched car park.

'Oh *Archie*,' she breathes. 'I love it! Did you make this for me?'

'Yes.'

'Why?'

'Because you deserve it.'

'Don't be daft.'

'I'm not being daft and you *do* deserve it. You keep saying I don't know my own worth, but neither do you. I think we're the same, Es. Both of us don't realise what we have. Maybe if we did, the people we love wouldn't hesitate to be with us.'

She stares at me for a moment, the lightest suggestion of pink brightening her cheeks. 'I don't know what to say. Thank you. Where did you get it?'

'I rescued it yesterday.'

'Rescued? Then is it . . . ?'

'It's an invitation,' I rush, excited and thrilled and terrified to be saying it out loud. 'To join the band.'

Her eyes meet mine. I catch my breath.

'Me?'

'The guys love you. I love you – being here . . .'

She strokes the instrument's body, which looks completely at home in her hands. 'Orange, like my shoes. And glitter stickers? Where on earth did you get those?'

'From a friend. I wanted it to fit you. Bright and colourful and unapologetic about sparkling, no matter where you are.' She blinks and I'm tempted to shut up, but unless I say everything I've planned now, I might never get the chance to express it. 'I don't want to stop seeing you once the letter's done. I would love you to be a part of this – not as a visitor, like you have been, but as a proper member of the band. What do you think?'

Her smile is warm and immediate, delight transforming her whole body like the decorations across the old-new instrument in her hands. 'I think I'd better learn to start playing badly.'

Twenty-One

ESTHER

My fingers sting from where I practised my ukulele for two hours yesterday.

The girls love it; my sister thinks I've lost the plot.

Ava-May and Molly kept creeping up to my room as I was playing, their little noses peeking through the gap in the door. In the end I invited them in, laughing as they danced and twirled to my less-than-melodic melodies. Issy's already asked Naomi if she can have a ukulele for her birthday next month, which went down like a lead balloon with my sister.

'And have to listen to you murdering it every day like your Auntie Esther does? I don't think so.'

'But I'd get much better than Auntie Esther much faster,' Issy had protested in true Issy fashion. It wasn't meant as mean and I didn't take it that way. Issy learns everything at warp speed – she was simply stating fact. I don't know if I'll ever be able to make my instrument sing. Playing it makes me smile though, even though my progress is so slow. When I see Archie and The Old Guys next Saturday I want to be able to adequately stumble through the two pieces Archie gave me to learn.

I love that he got it for me, even if its origin story will never beat Béla Fleck the Banjo's daring skip rescue. I love it most because he made it mine. Those sparkly flower decorations, using orange paint to match my shoes – thought has been poured into every detail. Nobody has ever done anything like that for me before.

The supermarket is quiet today. I check the list Naomi gave me this morning and realise I've already passed the organic aisle. Spelt flour is her latest obsession – evidenced by the recent series she's posted on YouTube and Instagram. I never knew there were so many recipes for the stuff – however tenuous their link with the past.

'I read that Ancient Mesopotamians baked with this nine thousand years ago,' she replied stuffily when I'd made this remark.

'Were they making lemon Bakewell bars and quiche though?'

'If they'd had the recipes, they might have.'

I grin to myself remembering her consternation.

Doing the supermarket run today is my self-nominated penance. We may never be joined at the hip, but we're closer than we have been for a while. Naomi is trying her best and I appreciate that more than I'll ever tell her. It's a peaceful equilibrium I want to protect.

The organic aisle is actually half organic products and half strange seasonal goods, the conscientious groceries at odds with inflatable flamingo pool toys, plastic skittle sets and half-price bottles of Baby Bio. What kind of customer heads into this aisle, I wonder? Do the organic lovers steer clear of the novelty goods set or do they meet halfway in a strange, eclectic truce?

Finding the spelt flour after some searching, I turn to head towards the tills as another customer enters the aisle. I see their shoes first – definitely organic side, I reckon. Confident I'm correct, I lift my gaze past the black jeans, half-empty green supermarket basket and striped shirt over a white T-shirt, towards their face and . . .

'Es?'

My world screams to a halt.

No . . .

'I thought it was you.'

Don't look at me. Not like that . . .

'The things you find in seasonal goods, eh?'

This can't be happening.

Matt Hope is too close to walk past, a shopper behind me blocking any chance of retreat too. I can't avoid him this time.

'It's good to see you,' he ventures, raising the tone of the last word to a gentle question, urging my reply. He looks tired, weary smudges beneath his eyes and the furrows in his brow deeper than I remember. He doesn't look like he's shaved in days and close up I notice his clothes are creased. He's so unlike the Matt I watched leave his wedding reception, immaculately attired to match his elegant wife.

But that's the kick: the man he was no longer exists outside of my memory. I have no place in his life, no right to know anything about him. He made that abundantly clear by disappearing from my life the moment he married *her* . . .

I don't answer. I can't. I manage to blink and breathe but beyond that there is nothing.

'Can we talk? Please?'

'I've got to get this back to—'

'*Please*? There's a café past the tills. Have a coffee with me. Ten minutes, that's all I'm asking.'

I'm about to decline, the warm safety of my car calling to me, but then I remember what Archie said when he gave me the ukulele:

'I wanted it to fit you. Bright and colourful and unapologetic about sparkling, no matter where you are.'

That's how Archie sees me. Right now, not months or years down the line when I finally get over Matt. It's happening already and I feel it. So, I have a choice: I could run like I did the other day or stay and show Matt who I am now. Archie sees it, my sister sees it; even my mum can't ignore it.

If I'm ever going to prove I've moved on, Matt has to see it.

'Okay,' I say, forcing my head high. 'Ten minutes.'

We take neighbouring lanes at the tills. I keep my back to him as I pack and pay for my shopping, but I'm conscious of his gaze burning into me the whole time. When I thank the cashier and turn, Matt's still paying, fumbling in his pockets for screwed up fivers and change, so I'm stuck like a stranded boat in a sea of fast-moving trolleys while I wait. It's a relief when he joins me, but only because I can finally move.

At the entrance to the supermarket café, he picks up a tray and nods at the mostly empty tables.

'I'll get these. Find us somewhere to sit?' He asks the question like it might offend me.

My hands are shaking as I sit down. I stow my shopping bags at my feet – a barrier to where his feet will be. It isn't much of a defence but any fortification is better than none.

You're doing the right thing, I tell myself, even though right now it feels like the biggest mistake.

Matt hurt me by breaking contact like he did: a coward's way to step back from a friendship. That hurt is real, but it's behind me. I've lived a whole year without him and I'm still breathing. More than that, I'm discovering a life beyond him far more exciting than it ever was before.

'You keep saying I don't know my own worth, but neither do you. I think we're the same, Es. Both of us don't realise what we have. Maybe if we did, the people we love wouldn't hesitate to be with us.' The memory of Archie saying that on the day he gave me my ukulele is a warm embrace around my heart.

Matt arrives and I imagine Archie's words as guards lining up between us.

'Do you still drink cappuccino?' he asks, too late considering he's placing a mug in front of me.

'I do, thanks.'

'I asked for cinnamon because you hate chocolate,' he says proudly. He's wrong, of course. It's the other way round, has been for all the time he's known me. Cinnamon is for apple pie and Christmas biscuits, not floating clumpily on top of steamed milk. I don't say anything, but I store it away. It's ammunition against any stray thoughts about him – proof he's not the friend I thought he was.

The sharp scrape of his chair jars my ears. Two older ladies at the next table tut loudly and aim their judgemental stares at him. *'Annoy a Northern woman at your peril,'* my gran used to say, *'but do it while she's drinking her tea and she'll have your guts for garters . . .'*

'Here we are, then.' He's finished fidgeting with his chair, the teaspoon and his mug now, folding his hands on the table and finally daring to look at me. 'Crap, Es, I've missed you.'

'How's Nina?' It's blunter than I anticipated but the words strengthen my spine.

He pales. 'She's – she's good, yeah. You still over in Salford Quays?'

He doesn't know what he's said, but it's a direct hit.

'No, I'm at Naomi's now.'

'Bit of trek to your job though, isn't it?'

I jam my heels into the tiled floor, pushing the hurt and anger downwards instead of across the table where its intended target is sitting. *If you hadn't broken contact with me the moment you married, you would know this.*

'I lost my job,' I say, the effort to keep my tone cool hurting my sides.

'No! Es, I had no idea! When?'

'Couple of months after your wedding.'

He sits back in his chair as if winded by the news, rubbing a hand across his brow. '*Shit*. I should have known.'

Yes, you should. A friend would have. 'You couldn't have.' There's a world suspended from those three words.

'What happened?'

'The company folded. Went into receivership so I had no redundancy payment and that meant the apartment had to go. I didn't have any savings and couldn't afford anywhere else. I'm lucky Naomi took me in.'

'You couldn't go to your mum and dad's?'

My shoulders prickle. I shouldn't have to explain any of this to him. He lost the right to demand information about my life the day he walked out of it.

'I'm at Naomi's,' I state. The air stills between us.

Matt grabs his coffee mug and drinks. I do the same. This is so much more painful than I thought it would be. Have I done enough to leave now?

'What did you want to talk to me about?'

His mug lowers to the table and I see him swallow hard. 'I just – it's so good to see you. After the other week . . . That was you, wasn't it? By the park?'

'I wasn't coming to see you . . . ' I begin, far too defensively.

'I didn't say you were.' I know that look he's giving me: I saw it a thousand times over the years when we'd had a row and he didn't want to concede defeat. 'I've missed you, Es. We were best friends once – all those years. You were best woman at my wedding . . . '

Enough. Matt can spin this in his favour any way he likes, but I won't sit here and agree. 'And then you left on honeymoon and stopped talking to me.'

His gaze falls.

'I called, I texted. Expecting you to just bounce around like you've always done. All the time we were preparing for your wedding you kept telling me it changed nothing; that we were Es and Matt, buddies for life. And then you ghosted me.'

'It . . . was complicated . . . '

'Was it? And you couldn't have just told me that? Sent me a text, answered a call?'

'I never meant to hurt you, Es. I made a mistake and I'm sorry.'

I have waited a year to hear those words and now they're said I'm not sure how to feel. I look at Matt Hope – at this spectre from years of my life that loomed so large in his absence, holding me back from everything – and I'm shocked by how little a presence he is now.

I've hidden away for months because of this man. I've taken his disappearance as proof of my own mistake. I made myself believe my life was worthless without him. Why did I do that?

I can leave here feeling defeated or I can show Matt who I am. I'm not putting my life on hold for him any longer.

'You really hurt me. But it wasn't my fault you walked away. I don't know why you broke contact, Matt, but it's done and we have own lives.'

'I've missed you,' he rushes. 'So much.'

I don't reply. I can't.

'I know I've been a git. Please don't hate me, Es. I don't think I could bear it if you hated me.'

I meet his stare. 'I don't hate you. But friends don't abandon each other.'

'No.' He shakes his head. 'I'm sorry.'

'Thank you for saying it. I'll always be glad I had you in my life. But I have my own life now. I'm getting back on my feet and, actually, things are pretty good.' My heart swells as I say it. I picture Archie standing behind Matt, grinning and cheering me on.

'You look – incredible. Happier than I've seen you in a long time.'

'I am. And you?'

He says nothing for a long time. 'Oh, you know.'

I don't – but then I realise, I don't want to. I don't need to be party to every twist and turn of Matt Hope's life anymore. He's not my responsibility. He stopped being that the moment he walked away. The revelation fires my heart and slides steel into my spine. *I don't need you*, I tell him in my head.

I drain the last of my coffee and gather my bags. 'I need to get going.'

He scrambles to his feet. 'I'll walk you to your car.'

I'm taller when I walk across the car park. The air seems

fresher around me, the overcast day brighter than before. When we reach my car and Matt hesitates, I hug him. It's spontaneous and he takes some time to reciprocate, but I'm not hugging him: I'm hugging the rest of my life.

'Take care of you,' I say against his jacket.

He squeezes back. 'You too. I'm so glad we met today.'

When we part, I smile and get into my car. In the rear-view mirror Matt Hope gradually diminishes as I drive away, shrinking from view like he's retreated in my mind.

The tears that follow aren't pain flooding out from my body. They are a celebration, a laying to rest of ghosts from my past.

I did it.

I'm finally free of Matt's shadow.

And I can't wait to tell Archie.

Twenty-Two

ARCHIE

'I did it, Archie!'

I smile at my phone, the sunny burst of my friend's voice as welcome as a break in the clouds. 'Did what?'

'Guess! You'll never guess. But guess!'

Whatever Esther is on, I want some. 'You bungee-jumped from the top of Beetham Tower.'

'Ha ha, nope.'

'You wrote my letter for me?'

'Not likely!'

'You could though, you know, if you wanted to.'

'I couldn't.'

'Why not?'

'Because I'd make Jessie fall in love with me and how does that help you?'

You have to hand it to her: Esther wields comebacks like verbal nunchucks. And while I know she's joking about Jessie, I'm pretty sure Esther Hughes could make anyone fall in love with her.

'I give up. What did you do?'

'I spoke to Matt.'

I stop dead in the street, holding my hand up in apology when a bloke walking behind almost topples over to avoid me, unleashing a torrent of abuse. 'When did this happen?'

'About an hour ago.'

'Bloody hell, Es.'

'I know!'

A million questions swarm in my head. 'How? Where? What did you say?'

'I'll tell you later. I've a night off tonight – you've got Maintenance in fixing the lights so they've said no cleaning. Fancy a drive somewhere? I can tell you it all then.'

'Love to. Where do you want to meet?'

'I can pick you up?'

'Great. I'm on a shout with Elvis till five. How about I meet you about half past five where you usually park?'

'Okay. I'll text you what floor I'm parked on. Thanks, Arch.'

'What for?'

'This thing I did. I couldn't have done it without you.'

What did she mean by that?

Half an hour later I've bought the coffees I almost forgot to get when Esther called me, and I'm standing outside Old Trafford football ground next to a very disgruntled senior reporter. We're all waiting for news of a potential signing to the club, but so far all we've got in reply is deafening silence. Around us groups of similarly miffed journalists are doing the same.

'Well, this is a chuffin' waste of time,' Elvis says, taking a swig of coffee and grimacing. 'How many sugars did you put in here?'

'Three? That's what you asked for.'

'Tablespoons, was it?' He shudders. 'Oh well, just don't tell the wife. We're meant to be sugar-free this month. If she finds out I've had half a hundredweight of the stuff in my coffee, she'll have me doing laps up and down the stairs till midnight.'

'You're secret's safe with me, boss.'

We share grins.

'Scout's honour?'

'Always. Why are we here again?'

Elvis sighs. 'We are here to wait for a statement about something the club has absolutely definitely no comment on.'

'Why don't they just say, "no comment", then?'

'Because it's all part of the game, see? If they dismiss the rumours too quickly, nobody bothers with them. We all shuffle off to bigger stories at other clubs. But, if they strenuously keep their traps shut, while saying a comment is imminent, us poor sods all hang about like idle lemmings waiting for a big story. Can't rush the mystique of the summer transfer window, remember that.' He sniffs. 'Did you bring any biscuits with you?'

'Yep, sorry.' I hand him a tiny multipack bag of Party Rings, slightly warm and crumpled from my jacket pocket. Elvis holds it between his thumb and forefinger as if it's radioactive.

'Party Rings? Do I look five to you?'

'They were all they had in the coffee shop,' I protest.

'*Mini* Party Rings? What kind of insanity is this? As if the full-size ones weren't depressing enough.' He rips open the packet and takes out a little biscuit that looks comically miniscule between his thick fingers. 'Look at that, would you: despondency in biscuit form. Pretty apt for the occasion. I've more chance of getting a calorie from this than Man United have of signing Gerard Villanova.'

'You think?'

'Trust me, kid. It's all bollocks.'

I try not to laugh as Elvis blesses each miniature biscuit with a scowl before eating it. 'You know so much stuff. Did you ever consider being a sports pundit?'

He splutters into his coffee. 'No fear! I wanted to break news, not lig about in TV studios regurgitating daft opinion. You just pick up stuff as you go along, that's all. Hang on to what you do know, blag what you don't.' He wipes his chin and looks at me. 'Is this what you want to do? Reporting?'

I nod. 'It's all I've ever wanted to do.'

'And Callaghan knows it. That's why he's got you on the never-ending apprenticeship. Reckon he knows you're good, too.'

'Then why stop me doing it?' I ask, the old frustrations pushing the question out into the afternoon air.

'Jealousy. Arsiness. Barefaced spite. What you need to know about Jock Callaghan is he never made the big leagues and he reckons he should've. Plenty like him in this business, 'specially in the hyper-locals like *The Herald*. A free paper that's more adverts than news. It's the way things are now and it's a dangerous eddy to find your career in. He'll never get out now: he's too old to go for the bigger papers. Like I said, experience costs and the newspaper owners don't want to pay.'

I think about my boss, holed up in his messy little kingdom, forever shouting the odds and trying to keep us all on our toes. Knowing he wanted more but found himself eddied there makes it all a bit tragic. I don't bear him any ill will but discovering his attitude towards me is from his own issues (and not my lack of talent, as I've always assumed) is a revelation.

'Here's what I know, Archie, for what it's worth: in this gig you have two choices – be professionally grateful and get precisely nowhere or push the envelope to get what you want.'

'Professionally grateful?'

He clamps a hand to his heart and adopts a weak, trilling voice. '"Yes, Mr Callaghan, thank you, Mr Callaghan, let me wash your car every Friday lunchtime, Mr Callaghan" . . . Sound familiar?'

'Ouch.'

'Exactly. Make him work to keep you, not t'other way round. Your words have power, lad, and you have a choice: advance or retreat. Don't waste it on the likes of him. What're you working on right now?'

I think of Esther's excited phone call and our conversations that have dominated my thinking lately. It's a writing project unlike any I've attempted before. What does Elvis think of love?

'Love letters,' I dare. 'What makes the perfect one.'

Elvis sips his coffee, eyebrows making a bid to meet his receding hairline. 'Bit of a departure from *Surprising Breakfast Alternatives*, that.'

'Just a bit. You ever sent a love letter to your missus?'

I'm expecting him to laugh off the question or tell me to get lost, but to my surprise his expression stills. 'I did, aye.'

'What did you write?' I ask, checking myself and adding, '*Sort* of things. Not specifics. I didn't mean . . . '

'She told me she dreamed of finding a message in a bottle,' he says. 'So I wrote one, put it in an empty beer bottle with the cap wedged back on and set it floating in her dad's fishpond.' He turns and grins. 'Luckily her mum found it, saw who it was for and got Geraldine out to fetch it before my father-in-law saw it. We didn't tell him till years later and you should have seen his rage. *Not in my water lilies!* The shock almost did him in.'

I laugh with him, not least because Elvis is the last person I would have expected to do something so cute. 'That's very cool.'

'I reckon it is. Everyone should be a romantic idiot at least once in their lives. Want to know the words that stole my Geri's heart?'

Of course I do. 'Go on then – if you want to . . .'

A wistful smile passes across his lips. 'I wrote, "*If I were oceans away, I would send my love sailing on the seven seas to reach you. As I only live over the road, this'll have to do. But six steps or six thousand miles makes no difference: I am yours. Be mine, Geraldine.*" Not bad for a young upstart who'd just been given a thesaurus, eh?'

'Brian Presley, you Romeo!'

'Words, Archie. Like I said. Powerful beggars when you use them right.'

My heart is thumping as we turn to face the stadium. 'So, what would your advice be to a young upstart wanting to write the perfect letter?'

'Do it.'

'How? I mean, for the article.'

'Of course. *For the article*. I would say, let your heart speak. Don't overthink it. Stop putting it off and just write the bastard . . .'

When I dare to glance back, he's smiling right at me.

'Because waiting only makes you walk away. If you love her, tell her. You can quote me on that.'

'Oi! Statement's in,' one of the journos yells and suddenly everyone is checking their phones, loud curses ringing out as fifty journalists see the death of the rumour confirmed on Sky News.

'Told you,' Elvis tuts, depositing his empty coffee cup in the deep pocket of his mackintosh. 'Right, lad, we might as well bunk off early. The glamour of this job, eh?'

I reach the car park an hour before I'm due to meet Esther, perching on a low wall to wait for her. Elvis' advice is still ringing in my ears. *Stop putting it off and just write the bastard* . . .

How many times have I delayed writing a piece only to find a flow when I finally sit down to write it? And why haven't I figured out before that I'm doing exactly the same thing with Jessie's letter?

It's time to change that.

I fetch the little A6 spiral-bound notebook I keep in my back pocket for ideas and find a clean page.

Don't overthink it. Just write . . .

There's an ancient Bic biro in the bottom of my rucksack. I fish it out, praying it still has ink for me. A tentative scribble in the top right-hand corner of the notebook page makes me sigh with relief.

I am going to bloody well do this. And then I'm going to show Esther when she arrives.

My pen hovers over the paper.

No more delays, Archie Quinn. *Just write the bastard.*

Here goes nothing . . .

> Jessie
> I think you're amazing.
> I've loved you for a long time.
> Could you love me too?
> Archie x

I stare at the words I've written.

It's . . . promising.

It's . . . short. Too short, maybe?

Should I add caveats? Umm . . . okay, try this:

Could you love me too?
If no, that's okay.
If yes, I'm yours.

No. Too apologetic. If it's no she'll tell me to my face. Jessie would do that.

I score out the extra lines.

The page flutters where my fingers hold it.

It's exactly what I want to say and completely true. It doesn't hide behind flowery prose or try too hard to be romantic. It's my heart, on the page.

So why do I feel there's something missing?

Twenty-Three

ESTHER

When Archie suggests we get chips and go up on Crompton Moor to eat them, I'm happy. I've been so excited to tell him about meeting Matt I've hardly eaten all day and now I'm starving.

He's very quiet on the drive up.

I've been careful to hang on to my news so far, not wanting to blast him with all of it in the first thirty seconds after he got into my car. He's smiling and joking, but I think his head's somewhere else.

Maybe he's hungry, too.

The moor is gorgeous tonight, bathed in the honey glow of the slowly setting early evening sun. This time of year it's light till almost eleven some nights, and on a clear evening like this the last of the daylight won't be darkened too early by cloud.

'Dad used to bring us up here when we were tiny,' I say, as we park the car and walk up the path. 'He'd come home from work with fish and chips and Mum would grab the folding chairs and a picnic blanket from the garage, swaddle us up in three layers of woollies and we'd all pile into the car to drive up and eat tea on the moor.'

'Bet you loved that.'

'I did.'

Near the top is the bench my family always headed for. Heaven only knows how long it's been here. One of those green-painted steel benches the council used to put everywhere. What it's lost in paint it's gained in words: new and fading graffiti scrawled across the slats and backrest, and older messages scratched deep into the metal itself.

'Hi, Auntie Sue,' I say, patting the bench.

'Auntie who?'

'Auntie Sue.' I point at the small brass plaque screwed to the backrest. 'Subject of the coolest epitaph in the history of bench dedications.'

Archie crouches in front of Auntie Sue's bench to read it, bursting out laughing when he sees what's written there.

'Oh wow, that's *epic*!'

> Dedicated to the memory of our Auntie Sue.
> Born 1926, Died 1992
> As she said in life, we write here too:
> "Sit on me and enjoy the view!"

I smile as I sit, handing Archie his packet of chips. 'My mum had a hard time explaining that to us as kids, mind you, but Dad found it hilarious. I reckon Sue was a bundle of fun. That's what makes the dedication so joyful.'

He tears the paper packet open and juggles a steaming hot chip. 'New life goal: live a life that inspires an epitaph like that.'

'Amen.'

We blow on our chips and gaze out at the evening-shadowed valley.

'It's lovely up here.'

'Even better when all the lights come on in the valley. I used to call it Fairyland when I was a kid. If it's warm enough, the heat haze makes the lights twinkle. And even though I understand the science behind that now, I still find it enchanting.'

Archie nudges me. 'You're such a romantic.'

I nudge him back. 'If you haven't worked that out about me already I'm shocked.'

'So,' he says, munching chips and licking grease from his fingertips, 'what happened with Matt?'

Delight sparkles from the top of my head to the tips of my toes and it's all I can do to remember to breathe. 'I met him. By chance.'

'Where?'

'In a supermarket. Miles away from his home.'

'Which aisle?'

I catch the mischief in his tone and feel the thrill of the story shared. 'Organic and Seasonal.'

'I see.' He nods wisely.

'What do you see?'

'You can tell a lot about a chap from the aisles he frequents.'

'Well, he stopped dead between the bagged almonds and a shelf of inflatable flamingos, so draw your own conclusions.'

Archie's laugh is instant and wonderful. It's the loveliest sound: a full-throttled belly laugh that shakes his body and throws back his head. 'My point magnificently proved. Did he buy one?'

'Nut bag or flamingo?'

'Either.'

'I don't recall if he did. But feel free to embroider this part of the tale with your own theory.'

'Noted.' He looks at me. 'How was it, though?'

'Weird. I didn't know what to say at first, just stood there, unsure what to do. And then, Matt asked me to have a drink with him in the café. I wanted to say no, I did. But then I kept thinking about what you said about me, when you gave me my ukulele. And that if he saw that in me, he'd think differently. I wanted to show him who I am now. So, I went.'

'And?'

'I felt so different, Arch. I couldn't believe it. For months I've dreaded seeing him, like it was the absolute worst thing that could happen. I built up that fear into this monumental, insurmountable obstruction that dictated everything, influenced every thought I had about Matt, about my own heart . . . But there he was: this tired-looking chap across the table from me. I just kept thinking how *small* he was. How unlike the monstrous version of him I'd let live, rent-free, in my head.'

'Wow, Es.'

'I know.' I take another mouthful of chips, their heat, salt and steam giving me a moment to regroup, my hammering heart a chance to calm.

'Did he apologise?'

'He tried to. I told him I didn't hate him – because I honestly don't. But I said I have my own life now and I'm happy. And then I said goodbye.'

'You're incredible, Esther.'

'You helped me. With what you said.'

He shakes his head. 'You did it all yourself. Drew a line. Shone bright. I knew you could do it.'

'I knew you believed in me. Thank you.'

'You don't have to thank me.'

'Too late: I just did.'

We share grins.

Far away, the sun begins to dip beneath the soft curves of the distant moor. We watch the deepening colours bleed across the ice-blue sky, shadows lengthening away from where we sit. The gentle breeze that greeted us when we arrived has now dropped, the stillness startling. The far echoes of traffic from the valley below fade with it. It's just the two of us, on Auntie Sue's bench, drinking in the view.

I don't know how long we stay there in companionable silence, but as the first lights shimmer into life in the city below, I feel the air between us shift. Archie's smile is gone, his eyes fixed on a point beyond the sunset.

'The lights are coming on,' I say, folding the remains of my chips into the paper and scrambling up onto the top of the bench backrest. 'Come up here – you get the best view.'

It's where Naomi and I always perched as kids, stretching up as high as we could in a bid to see the most lights. It felt daring and decadent to be sitting on the back of a bench rather than the seat. And Mum, usually such a stickler for these things, always let this one rebellious act slide. It still feels daring now: with Archie clambering up beside me it takes on a new sense of adventure.

But he doesn't say anything, even though his expression suggests many words he's considering.

'You okay?' I ask, finally, as gently as I can.

'Mmm.'

I press on. 'Arch? What are you thinking?'

He blows out a long sigh. 'I'm thinking I don't want to this end.'

What does he mean by that? The change in him is unnerving.

'Might get a bit nippy on Auntie Sue if we sit here all night,' I say, nerves dancing in my reply.

A smile tugs a little at the edge of his lips. 'That's not what I meant.'

'So, what then?'

'I meant, once we've written Jessie's letter . . . '

'Once *you've* written it,' I correct him. Where is this going?

'Yep, once *I* write it . . . I don't want it to change things.'

'With Jessie?'

'No. With us.'

I stare at him. I can't help it. All my nerves are on edge now, the change in my friend startling. 'I don't know what you mean.'

He turns to me, his eyes searching my expression for – what, exactly? Something he hopes to see or something he fears he'll find?

'I'm scared, Es.'

'Scared? Of what?'

'I'm scared that once I send that letter, I won't have *this*. With you.'

My heart contracts. How can he think that? Tears appear – I couldn't halt them if I tried.

'I will always be here for you, Archie. You don't lose me because you get Jessie.'

'But I thought . . . '

'Listen to me. You arriving in my world changed *everything*. How I saw life. How I saw myself. How I felt about Matt. But more than all of those things: you gave me a friend like nobody else I've ever known. And a rescued ukulele, which is possibly the nicest gift I've ever had.'

He smiles at that. Then he reaches for my hand, his fingers taking mine. Gently, he lifts our hands together up to his lips. Instinctively, I close my eyes and just feel: sudden warmth, the whisper of breath and the soft brush of his kiss across my skin. Startlingly tender, breath stealing, *right*.

And in that moment, I know two things: one, Archie means more to me than I thought before; and two, he isn't mine to want that way. I promised I'd help him win Jessie. I have to see it through.

It's heartbreaking and resolve-strengthening all at once.

We will always have this, I tell myself. But the story isn't done yet.

Archie has to follow his heart – and I have to help him do it.

Our hands return to the cool steel of the bench, fingers laced tight together, a hundred thousand words rendered useless as the sky above us flames with colour and light.

Twenty-Four

ARCHIE

I couldn't tell her I'd written it.

I was going to. But Jessie's letter stayed hidden in my pocket, its words complete. I had the perfect moment to share my breakthrough, just after Esther had shared hers. It could have been the perfect celebration for both of us up there on Auntie Sue's bench, gazing out at that sky.

But the moment I tried to speak, I lost my nerve.

I didn't want to send the letter.

I wanted to bury it in the litter bin by the car park with our screwed-up chip papers and just forget I'd ever completed it. I wanted to leave it there on the top of the moor, cast it free as we drove away.

What the hell is wrong with me?

Everything Esther and I have done has been about writing that letter. Finishing it. I've stared at it for so long when I blink I can see the outline of the words imprinted on my retina. It doesn't need any more words. It's done. But it doesn't feel like I thought it would.

'Archie, talk to me.'

I'm startled to find Jessie Edmonds standing by my chair, arms folded across her pristine white shirt. What has she seen? What does she know?

'What about?' I stumble, sounding guilty even though I've no idea what of.

She leans against my desk with an irritated sigh. 'Anything, so long as it isn't bloody football. Tell me I'm not the only sane soul in a summer transfer window frenzied sea.' She nods at Liam, glued to Sky Sports while taking notes as talkSPORT jabbers away in the background, and Elvis, grudgingly writing updates for the website despite only just having had his first coffee of the morning.

My smile is one per cent amusement and ninety-nine per cent relief.

Though I've kept my head down since I came in, I've been aware of Jessie wandering aimlessly around the office. But I never expected her to seek me out.

'What shall we discuss then?'

'Did you watch telly last night?'

'A little.' Truth is, the TV was on in my lounge, but playing away to itself while I tried to process what happened on the moor with Esther. 'You?'

She brightens a bit and fiddles with the highlighters on my desk. 'I watched the first episode of that *Evie & Seth* – on BBC 2? It's by one of the writers of *Eye, Spy*, but it's not a thriller. It's a kind of will-they-won't-they love story. I think it's going to be good. Gabriel Marley's in it.'

I smile. 'Then it's bound to be good. Or if it isn't, you just get to look at Gabriel Marley doing his sexy dark and brooding act for half an hour.'

Her laugh is delightful. Heck, everything about Jessie is delightful. I think of the words now safely returned to my back pocket, my best shot at winning her heart. When should I give it to her? In person or left on her desk? These are the questions I should have asked Esther last night, right after I'd let her read it – neither of which I did.

I *have* to stop thinking about Esther.

What she did when she saw Matt was nothing short of brilliant. But she said it wouldn't have happened if it weren't for me. I know she did it all herself, but it's a result of the project we hatched together: for her to move on from Matt by helping me write to Jessie. Her side of it is done: all that's needed is me to sort mine.

Jessie Edmonds *is* lovely. She's so close to me I can smell the shampoo she's used, mingling with the scent of fabric conditioner on her clothes beneath the cloud of her usual perfume. She's playing with a narrow gold necklace at her throat as she looks at me. My eyes follow the forwards-backwards motion of her perfectly manicured index finger as it dances along the chain.

'What do you think, Arch? Are love stories your thing?'

Bloody Nora . . .

'I'm—' I give a slight cough as I wrestle my thoughts back into the newspaper office '—I'm not averse to a bit of that.'

I sound like I'm talking about pie. It's the kind of thing Dad says when Mum offers us a sample of her latest recipe for the bakery.

'The will-they-won't-they bit is the best,' Jessie continues. If she's aware of the effect she's having on me, she isn't letting on. 'When you're yelling at them to just tell each other how they feel.'

I stare up at her, my heart thundering loud. 'Don't you find that frustrating? The waiting, I mean?'

'Are you joking? That's the best part.' She gives a self-conscious laugh and shakes her head, soft waves of her butter-gold hair dancing around her shoulders. 'I sound like a right div now.'

'No, you don't. I think it's lovely.'

Her features soften into a smile. 'Well. Thank you. You can get back to the football chat if you want.'

'I'm not a football fan,' I say. It's the truth: a source of great consternation in my family, who are football through and through, despite supporting rival teams. Mum and Dacey are Man City devotees, Dad's Man United all the way and Conn offends them all by loving Liverpool. I reckon I saw their endless fights and chose to support rugby instead because it was safer.

'I thought everyone here was.'

'I like rugby. And golf on TV. And I like talking to you.'

'Do you?'

I nod.

Jessie glances back at the other end of the office, where Liam and Elvis are now both glued to the TV screen watching the rolling news. 'Listen, Liam said something, the other day . . . You don't have to answer if you don't want to, but . . . Is there anyone special right now?'

Crapping hell . . .

'Special how?' I manage, fast losing my grip.

'For you.'

'Well, I . . . '

'Because there was for me. For a long time. But there isn't now. So, you know. In case you were wondering . . . '

'Archie!'

Liam's bark jolts me out of wherever my head was heading.

'What?' I call back, my eyes locked with Jessie's deep sapphire gaze.

'Come and see this!'

'In a minute.'

She's closer, all of a sudden. I can see the rise and fall of her breathing, the soft undulation of the pulse at her neck . . .

'Jessie! Put the lad down and both of you come here,' Elvis commands – and that's it: game over.

Exchanging flushed smiles, we walk across to the others. I don't know how my legs work, but I get there in the end. Liam and Elvis don't even look up from the screen.

She knows, doesn't she? Liam's told her. And that was an open door, waiting for me to accept. I need advice – I can't blow this chance. I need to call Esther, tell her everything that's happened, but there's no way I can sneak out yet.

'I'm telling you, that rumour's got legs,' Liam insists, jabbing a thumb at the screen.

'Nah, it's bollocks, lad. Sergio Totti signing for Man City?'

'They've the money for him.'

'He's not even in the country.'

'So *he* says.'

'And his management. And his club. Star striker for AC Milan, still with eighteen months left on his contract, transferring to City? Dream on, sunshine. It's never happening.' Elvis turns to me. 'See, this is what I was saying yesterday: we're heading into full-on loony days now.'

'Who's reporting it?' I ask, very aware that Jessie is beside me, so close our arms are millimetres apart.

'Nobody so far. Just rumours.' Elvis stares back at Liam.

'*Rumours*, Liam. From pundits too enamoured of their own voice.'

'TalkSPORT has had three callers already reporting sightings of Totti.'

'Oh aye? Where?'

'Two at Manchester Airport, one at Heathrow.'

'Baggage handlers going for their ten minutes of glory. I've heard it all before and it's never true.'

Liam slumps a little. Elvis clamps a comforting hand on his shoulder. I will my rapidly reddening cheeks to calm down and the rising hairs on my forearm tantalisingly close to the warmth of Jessie to stop reacting. The letter in my back pocket calls to me – the link that could finally bridge what little gap remains between us . . .

'Don't sweat it, kid. It's all part of the magic.' Elvis winks at me. 'Mind you, that's not to say I don't wish this one were happening.'

'Are you a City fan, Brian?' Jessie asks, stepping away from me to look at the scrolling news on the screen. My whole body wishes her back.

'No fear! Stockport County forever, me. But imagine breaking that story. Not many of those left for me now.'

As their conversation shifts to Elvis's retirement plans, I sneak my phone from my pocket and fire a text to Esther. We haven't planned to meet today, but I need to talk to her about the letter – and what just happened with Jessie.

Hey Es, long shot but are you up for a chat before work?
I REALLY need to talk to you. A x

Twenty-Five

ESTHER

'Tonight?'

I nod, braced against the rumble of the oncoming storm.

'Why can't you just see him on Saturday at the music thing?'

'Because he needs me now.'

Naomi groans and continues her pacing along the length of the kitchen island. 'And this is what you do for him, all to write a letter to another woman?'

'He's my friend. He wouldn't ask if it weren't important.'

'*We're* important. The girls and me. And Gavin, who is coming home early tonight specifically for family dinner. You've been so preoccupied lately with that tiny guitar and your own head it's like we never see you.'

'It's just for tonight.' I keep my voice as soft and calm as possible, despite the urge to answer back. 'You can have me Saturday night. Gavin will be home then, too. We could do a movie night.'

My nieces gasp as one.

'Can we, Mum?' Issy begs. 'And have popcorn and snacks?'

'And watch it in our pjs?' Molly chimes in. 'And make Dad wear his, too?'

'And the movie will be *Frozen*,' Ava-May states, eliciting a chorus of *No* from everyone else.

'But Mu-um!'

'You have watched that a lot,' Naomi says, but her youngest daughter has flung her arms across her chest and is eyeballing us all.

'You're s'posed to watch it *lots*,' she shoots back.

'Not with the sound off and you doing all the script and voices,' Issy argues.

'I'm good at them, that's why. You're just jealous 'cos you don't know all the *speaky bits* . . . '

Just as the kitchen fills with loud protest, I cut in. 'We'll decide on Saturday, all right? But only if you're good for your mum and dad tonight. Stop the arguments and help with the washing up after tea, or the deal's off.'

My sister shakes her head at me but she's smiling. 'You heard your Auntie Esther. Now go and change out of your school clothes, please.'

We watch three delighted girls dash off upstairs.

'They're good kids.'

'You're great with them.'

'So are you.'

Naomi flicks the switch on the kettle and leans against the white marble work-surface. 'Just be careful, Es. With Archie.'

'Careful?'

'I know you care about him and when you make a promise you see it through to the bitter end, but are you really just dashing to his aid now because he's a pal?'

Something in her tone sets my nerves on alert. It doesn't help that I'm still reeling from my revelation about Archie up on Crompton Moor. 'Of course. It's what friends do.'

'It's what *you* do. With Archie. With *Matt* . . .'

'That's not fair.'

'I just want you to think about being this available for Archie. It's more than most people do for their friends.'

'Well, I'm not most people.'

She sighs. 'No, you aren't. Just ask yourself if the reason you're racing over there is because he's just a friend or because you want him to be something more.'

I'm rattled as I drive into the city. This isn't Matt all over again. Why can't Naomi see that? I promised I would help Archie and he needs me. Whatever the reason, he needs me.

The traffic around me slows, a broken-down vehicle in a bus lane ahead causing late afternoon chaos as cars, taxis and buses try to navigate around it.

He needs me.

Is that what I want?

Last night, that moment when he'd kissed my hand and we sat there watching the sunset, that wasn't just friends, was it? Friends would have goofed their way out of the moment. Friends wouldn't have kissed hands in the first place.

I felt it then and I feel it now: the danger.

I'm not in love with Archie Quinn. But last night was the first time I wondered if I could ever be.

I hate to admit it, but my sister is right.

Last night I sensed something new between us. But that's what I felt with Matt. Am I exchanging one unrequited love-crush for another?

I don't want this to end . . . I'm scared that once I send that letter, I won't have this. With you . . .

Finally it's my turn to navigate the bottleneck around the stranded car. And as I pass the frustrated driver pacing the tarmac as he yells into his phone, it occurs to me: did Archie feel the danger last night and that's why he wants to see me now? Knowing what he does about my history with Matt, does he want to nip things in the bud before they have a chance to bloom?

By the time I reach the car park and leave my car, I'm a bag of nerves.

Nearing Rossi's, I'm surprised to see Archie waiting outside for me. Isn't the place open yet?

'Hi,' I say, surprised when he hugs me without hesitation. 'How come you're not in there?'

He grins. 'Ciro said we're to meet him round the back.'

'Sounds dodgy. His family aren't Sicilian, by any chance?'

'Don't be daft! Follow me.'

We leave the front entrance and head back down the street until we reach a tiny alley I've never noticed before.

'Down there?'

'It's quicker than following the road round. You look scared to death, Es; trust me, okay?'

Reluctantly, I follow him down the narrow passage between an estate agent's and a bank. The red bricks look darker here, older than the building facades on the street. We emerge on a small road marked with double-yellow lines on both sides, with groups of industrial wheelie bins pulled in front of small parking bays and delivery entrances to the shops and businesses surrounding Rossi's.

Ciro raises a hand as we reach Rossi's plot, the stub of a hand-rolled cigarette clamped between his teeth.

'Tradesmen's entrance, eh?' Archie quips, greeting his friend with a backslapping hug.

'Well, you guys have been coming regularly enough. I reckoned you've earned VIP status.' He grins at me. 'Just don't mention it in our Tripadvisor review, all right?'

Archie nods at the open back door of the restaurant. 'So, what's up?'

'My old man's had a booking for the whole place. Couple of businessmen wanted a sole dining experience. So the restaurant's closed for public dining.'

'It's okay, we'll go somewhere else,' I offer, not wanting to put him in an awkward situation.

'No need.' Ciro stubs out his cigarette on an old tin ashtray balanced on top of a large blue wheelie bin. 'If you don't mind staying in the kitchen, you guys can have coffee and cake there. On the house, to apologise for the disruption.'

Archie and I exchange looks.

This should feel like an unexpected adventure, but after my building nerves on the way here and the sudden change of restaurant entrance, I'm completely on edge.

'I'm game if you are?' Archie asks. 'I'm not likely to turn down free cake and coffee.'

'Me neither,' I say. I have to stop worrying. There's no trace of whatever was going on last night in Archie's expression now.

We follow Ciro through the door into a storage area for boxes and then a pantry that looks like a foodie's ultimate dream, emerging into the bright light of the kitchen. Ciro pulls two stools up to the large steel preparation table in the middle of the room and motions for us to sit.

It feels wonderfully decadent to be granted a seat in the

beating heart of the restaurant, but I'm surprised to see the stoves empty and no activity in the kitchen.

'Are your guests eating here?' I ask.

Ciro is about to answer, but then he puts a finger to his lips, sidles up to the door leading to the restaurant and nudges it open a tiny way. When he's satisfied by whatever he's seen in there, he returns, hunching down between Archie and me, his hands resting on his knees.

'They're not. My dad's not best chuffed: he'd cleared tonight's bookings because he thought they wanted to take over the restaurant all night. Turns out they just wanted sweet antipasti and endless coffee.'

'That's awful!' I say. 'Did they pay you for having the restaurant to themselves?'

Ciro snorts. 'They did, but we should've charged them more. Dad was under the impression the payment was to ensure exclusivity and they'd be ordering meals on top of that. No way is it going to match what we could've made from a whole night of covers.'

'I bet your dad was railing at them,' Archie says, turning to me. 'Ciro's dad is the loveliest man but I swear the few times I've seen him angry is scary stuff. He launches into full Italian but you can guess every word.'

'I told him you were coming. That made him smile. He'll probably come and say hello in a bit.' Ciro grins. 'I'll go and get your drinks and cake. Make yourselves at home.'

I wait until the swing door closes behind him and I'm alone with Archie before I bite the bullet. 'Why did you want to see me?'

His smile pales just a little.

Please don't let this be bad news.

'I wrote it.'

'Wrote what?'

'The letter for Jess.'

'Oh.'

Of all the many answers I've anticipated on the way over here, this wasn't one of them. Which is crazy, because that's supposed to be why we're here.

'I wanted to tell you yesterday but . . . It wasn't the right time.'

I'm thinking I don't want to this end . . . I'm scared . . .

That's what he was talking about last night, wasn't it? He'd written the letter, so he thought our work was done. It wasn't ever about me being anything other than a friend.

Part of me is devastated, another part hugely relieved. I've worked myself into such a muddle over this when it turns out I didn't need to. And I realise then, as we take in the magnitude of Jessie Edmonds's finished letter, that I should have trusted Archie. He's been the loveliest, most loyal friend since the first time we met. He was never going to walk away from me; neither was he going to throw a curveball at me by wanting us to be something more.

He's *not* Matt.

And I am not teetering on the precipice of another heart mistake.

It's just Archie. And me. And a letter for the woman he loves.

'So, when are you going to give it to her?' I ask, surprised by a crack in my voice.

'That's why I wanted to see you.' His gaze is wide and searching as it meets me. 'I don't think I can do this. Not alone.'

'Yes, you can. Writing the letter was the tough bit.'

'Doing something with it is worse. There's no going back after it's delivered.'

I hope my smile soothes him more than it's soothing me. 'But that's a good thing – you're not going back, you're moving forward. It's what you wanted, Arch. What we both wanted. That's why we're here.' I focus on my friend, this tender soul who crashed headlong into my life and made everything better. And I make a decision. 'And if you think I'm letting you do this alone, you're mistaken.'

'What do you mean?'

'Let's deliver it together.'

'When?'

'Today. Before my shift. You can let us in. My manager Marjorie doesn't arrive until six, so we can be in and out before she sees us.'

Archie's mouth gapes like I've just suggested we rob a bank. 'We can't . . . '

'We'll go up there, now, and leave it on her desk. *Together.*' My heart thuds in my ears as I say the word.

'You'd do that for me?'

'Hughes and Quinn always see a case through till the end.' I smile.

He laughs and runs his hand across the back of his neck, which is already flushing red. 'Wow, that's . . . I don't know what to say.' He leans a little closer, as if his next words are only for us to hear. 'I need to say something though before we do it.' I see the quickening rise and fall of his chest beneath his T-shirt, see his hand reaching for mine . . . 'The thing is, Es, I—'

'Archie Quinn!'

We jump apart as the swing door crashes open so hard it's

almost wrenched off its hinges and a tall, tanned man with an impressive sweep of silver-streaked jet-black hair strides into the kitchen. He's an older version of Ciro – the family resemblance unmistakable.

'Jacopo!' Archie scrambles to his feet, the hand he holds out completely ignored as he's kissed emphatically on both cheeks and drawn into a powerful man-hug that practically lifts his feet from the ground.

Ciro edges round his father and Archie, rolling his eyes at them. 'I swear my papa thinks he got the wrong son when Archie's around.'

'*Zitto, figlio*! I love this boy like he was my own.'

I grin at Ciro, while he sets out our coffee and two slices of cake even bigger than before, feigning insult. 'Archie gets away with more than I ever did.'

Jacopo Rossi releases my friend and ruffles Ciro's hair. 'Honorary sons always do. I don't make the rules.' He looks over at me. 'Forgive me. I love these boys.'

'This is Esther, Jaco.'

'*Bellissima*,' he replies. 'You are a sight for sore eyes on a day like this.'

'Are they all in now?' Ciro asks.

'*Si.*' His father grimaces. 'Four of them. They ordered espresso and cannoli. Literally the smallest things on the menu. Cheapskates. And that *cretino* calling the shots for his "client" is clicking his fingers at me! Me! In my own *ristorante*!'

'That's dreadful,' Archie says. 'Who are they?'

Ciro beckons us over by the door. 'Come and look. Total bastards taking up the whole space.'

We line up beside him as he opens the serving door a crack.

In the sliver of restaurant view I can see four men, three in suits and one in a hoodie, white beanie, joggers and bright-white trainers. He is slouched in his seat looking completely bored while the three suits talk loudly over him.

Beside me, Archie swears.

One of the suits looks up and Ciro quickly closes the door.

'What's up?' I ask him. 'Do you know them?'

Archie appears to be struggling for breath. 'Yes, I . . . *know* them. That's only Sergio bloody Totti!'

I blink at him. 'Who?'

He flaps a hand in front of his face. 'He's not supposed to be here. He's meant to be out of the country . . . This is *huge*!'

'Totti from AC Milan?' Jacopo exclaims, instantly hushed by Archie and Ciro. 'You're kidding me!'

'That's Sergio Totti, his sports agent and the football director from Man City. I don't know who the other guy is, but . . . I need to tell Elvis!'

'Elvis?'

Archie shakes his head as if to dislodge rogue words that have caught there. 'Brian Presley, our senior reporter. We call him Elvis, obviously. He's retiring soon and this would be the best present . . . ' He turns to Jacopo, grasping the restaurant owner's hand. 'Did they ask you to sign anything about them being here? A nondisclosure agreement?'

'No. I would have definitely charged extra for that,' Jacopo replies, sneering at the door.

'Okay. How would you like to tell the world about Rossi's?'

Ciro and Jacopo wear identical, bright-white grins.

*

Brian 'Elvis' Presley is not exactly how I'd imagined the owner of the Nashville mug-strewn desk at *The Herald* to look. But maybe that has more to do with the deep red of his face from the dash across from the newspaper offices to get here. Archie ushers him to sit down and Ciro brings a glass of water.

'Are they still in there?' he pants.

'They just ordered more coffee,' Ciro says.

The anticipation in the kitchen is palpable as we watch Elvis drink slowly. When his glass is drained, he places it on the steel table. 'Right. Mr Rossi, I don't want there to be any comeback on you for when this story breaks. So here's what we're going to do: me, Archie and – I'm sorry, love, I don't know your name . . . '

'Esther,' I reply.

'She's the one helping me with my project,' Archie says.

The reporter's bushy eyebrows rise. 'Oh. I see. Well, miss, if you don't mind helping out a couple of greasy hacks like us?'

'I'd love to.' I have no real idea what's happening apart from the people in the restaurant being a story that will make Brian Presley retire happy. But it doesn't matter – the thrill is infectious as we huddle together around the table, trading excited whispers.

'How are you with a camera?'

'Okay, I think.'

'Right. Let's get going, we don't have long.'

After a quick briefing, Elvis shakes hands with Jacopo and Ciro, and Archie leads us back out the way we came in. We hurry along the narrow alley and emerge into the street. It's that strange time when the two versions of Manchester meet – the end of the working day and the start of the city's night life – so most the people we pass are in a hurry to get home. Nobody is standing near the large window of Rossi's or the shops that flank it.

'Right, are we all ready?' Elvis points to a spot in front of the window and Archie and I line up as we agreed – me standing by Elvis, facing Archie who is nearest the window, holding up his phone with the screen facing us. As we pose for him, we can see the image over his shoulder into the restaurant beyond.

'Bit to the left,' Elvis mutters between clenched teeth as he grins and poses next to me. From our vantage point we can see the shot lining up as Archie moves it. 'That's it, lad! Press that button! Zoom in a bit. Take another! Again!'

To anyone inside the restaurant we are just three people taking daft photos in the street, Totti and the others too distracted by Jacopo suddenly arriving to serve them surprise complimentary cake to realise that Archie is aiming the shot to a particular table inside Rossi's.

'Check them,' Archie says, showing us the screen. Four photos, three of them crystal clear.

'Perfect! Bloody brilliant!'

'Do a video, Brian,' Archie says, handing me the phone as we'd agreed. 'We can do it while they're looking at Ciro's dad.'

'Right. Esther line up the shot.'

I do as he says, and Elvis moves over to Archie, throwing a comradely arm around him as they fake-pose for me. I see the senior reporter glance at Archie with a look of real pride. Then, slowly, he steps away.

Archie stares at him in horror. 'What are you doing? We have to do this now!'

'Your gig, son.'

'No! This is your parting shot, Brian! The thing you wanted . . . '

Elvis chuckles. 'I was here for the scoop. That's what counts. And I'm going to call it in for you. I still have some contacts in the national press, you know. But you're just beginning. Now take the damn video or we'll miss the shot.' He nods at me. 'Start filming, love.'

Archie stares at his mentor, his mouth moving but making no sound.

'Go on, Arch!' I urge him, hitting the red button to start filming.

He takes a shaky breath and straightens his jacket. 'Right. Here goes nothing . . . I am here outside Rossi's Italian restaurant in the heart of Manchester, where right now a meeting is taking place between star AC Milan striker Sergio Totti and representatives of Manchester City Football Club. Talks that both the club and the striker's management have strenuously denied are taking place. We were told Totti wasn't even in the UK, but it appears negotiations have been ongoing. This surely has to be the major signing of this year's summer transfer window. Archie Quinn, *The Herald*, Manchester.'

I can't take my eyes off him. He's so self-assured, despite being a bag of nerves seconds before he started to speak.

'Zoom in,' Elvis hisses in my ear. 'Time for the money shot.'

Just as I film the party at the table, Totti's football agent looks up and yells. The four men jump to their feet, joined by Jacopo and Ciro who dash with them to the front door and make a huge show of unlocking it, grinning at us through the glass.

'Last lesson, Archie,' Elvis pants as we start to run. 'Get what you need, then run like crap!'

We duck and dive around bollards and speed down side streets, our laughter echoing off walls and buildings as we dash past. I daren't look over my shoulder in case they're chasing us, but ahead of me Archie makes frequent glances back. When we round the next corner and hurtle into a side alley, Elvis holds up his hand.

'It's okay,' he manages between huge gulps of air. 'We're clear.'

Buzzing with adrenaline we lean against the dark brick wall to get our breath back. My calf muscles hate me and sweat is tricking down my spine, but I've never felt more alive.

'Show us the footage, lad,' Elvis says, holding out one hand for the phone while the other rests on his knee.

We fall silent as we huddle over the screen, our rapid breathing the only sound in the alley. The photos are perfect, the faces of the footballer and the football director crystal clear and indisputable. Grinning like a puffed-out Cheshire cat, Elvis pulls his own phone from his jacket pocket and dials a number.

'Greg, Brian Presley. Aye, it has been a while. No, I have something for you, provided the terms are acceptable.' He winks at us. 'What if I told you I have conclusive photographic and video proof that Sergio Totti is in advanced talks with Manchester City?' He holds the phone away from his ear as a loudly enthusiastic string of expletives barks from the phone. Nodding at us, he puts the phone back to his ear and strolls out of the alley. 'That's what I thought you'd say. Now the lad with the scoop is a protégé of mine and I wouldn't be happy for him to surrender it to anyone else . . . Right. One moment . . . '

'What does he say?' Archie asks.

'He says he wants to talk to you.'

Elvis passes the phone to Archie and we watch him walk a few steps away.

'Watch this,' Elvis whispers.

'Hi, yes. I took three photos and a video, plus a piece to camera . . . Yes, it's HD . . . I'm Archie Quinn. Q-U-I-double-N, that's correct. Yes, I'd be happy to. Thank you, sir – *Greg*, right. Thanks, Greg. Will do . . . ' He hands the phone back to Elvis, who saunters out of the alley like an expert negotiator, naming his terms.

I stare at Archie. 'Well?'

He blinks. 'They'll show it on Sky News, tonight. And I get the byline anywhere it's printed.'

We stare at each other. And then we're yelling and laughing and screaming, our arms wrapping around one another as we jump about like fools. I am so thrilled for Archie, so utterly proud of him. But it's more than that. I'm also delighted for me: that I got to be part of his dream coming true. I helped make it happen. So I hold on and giggle and whoop and allow this moment to take over.

I've been too long without magic. Archie too. But right here in the heart of the city we love so much, it's found us.

We stumble a little as we land, the alley wall buffering us as our bodies bump together. We're hanging on to each other, our laughter subsiding a little now.

Archie lifts his head from my shoulder, pulling back to look at me.

I look at him, too.

And I think how wonderfully blue his eyes are.

How safe it is here. This close to him.

How soft his fingers are when they brush my cheek.
And how warm his smile is as I lean into him . . .
Then our lips meet.
And I forget to think about anything else . . .

Twenty-Six

ARCHIE

I'm kissing her.

At last.

Maybe I should be shocked, but I'm not. I just want to stay here, our mouths pressed together, the intensity and heat startling. We told ourselves we were just friends, but who were we kidding? This has been inevitable all along. All that matters – all that ever mattered – is *this* . . .

Her fingers are in my hair, mine are moving over the warm dip of the small of her back. We *fit* like this. It's right.

It's . . . Esther . . .

Wait.

Stop!

I'm kissing *Esther* . . .

A light snaps on in my head at the same time she pushes me away. And now, we're a step apart, breathless, our shock and horror mirrored in each other's expressions.

'Shit, Archie, I . . . '

'No, I never meant to . . . '

'I don't know where that came from.' Her lips tremble as she speaks. Why am I staring at her lips? I force my gaze back to her eyes. 'I am so, so sorry . . . '

'It wasn't just you.' My mind is racing at a thousand miles a second. 'You've nothing to be sorry for, Es. It was both of us.' I reach for her hand, our fingers brushing before they part again.

How did I let this happen? My heart took over, that's the only explanation, because of what I wanted to say to her before the Totti story kicked off. It's all I've been thinking since last night on the bench. The words I'd prepared, the confession I should have made:

Do you want me to go for Jessie? Because I'm not sure it's what I want any more. I think I'm falling for someone else . . .

I never got the chance to voice the doubts I've had for weeks. But my heart had other ideas. That kiss was right – for me.

But Esther looks devastated.

How did I get it so wrong?

'We just got caught up in the moment,' she says, but her expression doesn't match her words. 'Didn't we?'

'I think we might have. But it was lovely.'

'It was.' Her smile flickers back into action. It's a beautiful smile . . .

My nervous laugh reverberates around the alley walls. 'Imagine what Jessie would say!'

Esther's smile vanishes.

What the hell did I say that for?

Archie Quinn, you absolute bastard.

'We don't have much time,' she says, and I sense doors slamming around us. 'You need to be ready for when the story breaks.'

'We have time. I think we need to—'

'Read me the letter,' she says, the last syllable a snap that cuts the air.

'It doesn't matter now.'

'We see this through to the end. Read the letter.'

She means it. After what just happened, I can't refuse. So I take out the letter, my heart aching like it did when I wrote it, but not for the same person. I clear my throat and read: *'I think you're amazing. I've loved you for a long time. Could you love me too? Archie x . . .'*

As I read each word, it all makes sense. I found the words not because Jessie inspired them, but because Esther did. That's why I've been able to talk to Jessie lately. And why I've faltered when trying to talk to Esther. My heart wasn't talking to Jessie, despite her name being at the top of the letter. How have I only worked this out now?

Her hand flies to her collar. 'Oh, Arch . . .'

'It's short,' I say, needing to say something but sounding pathetic.

She nods. 'It is. But it's perfect. It's – your heart.'

It is, I want to say. *And it's all because of you.* But the words don't come now they're on the letter. 'Thanks. We should probably find Elvis.'

'We should probably deliver this letter, like we agreed.' A glimpse of her old spark is enough to silence me. 'If we go now, we can do it before the world and its wife descend on Manchester looking for you.'

'Archie! Can you be ready in half an hour?'

I turn to see Elvis dad-jogging towards us.

'For what?'

'Live bulletin, Sky News. Then BBC. Then ITV and, if Greg is as good as his word, pretty much every other news agency after that.'

'Thirty minutes is enough,' Esther hisses beside me.

'I can,' I call back. 'I just need to grab something from the office.'

'Well, bloody hurry up! Breaks like this don't come often.'

Esther grabs my hand. 'Let's go.'

She doesn't let go all the way back to *The Herald*. We walk in through the foyer together, wait for the lift together, step in together when it arrives. But we aren't together – not in the way I thought possible minutes ago – and as the lift rises to the newspaper office I realise this is where we began. Us, in this lift. Only where we dashed and laughed and felt victorious for sneaking Esther out of the building before, now we move slowly, determinedly, silently. Where the lift journey dragged before, today it's far too fast. All of this is. It's spiralling out of my control, impossible to halt.

I know Esther's right. I know we got caught up in the moment. It feels like more than that, but is that just nerves talking? I wish I knew.

She doesn't speak beside me but her face is set firm and her hand is tight around mine. She's not letting go yet.

The toll of the bell when we reach our floor sounds like a death knell. As the doors slide open, Esther's hand slips away.

'Right,' she says, a smile in her voice, at least. 'Are you ready?'

No.

'As I'll ever be.'

'Come on then. And try to smile, eh? This is weird enough as it is.'

So let's not do this now. Let's wait and talk and . . .

'How's that?' My smile feels like someone mixed theirs up with mine. It doesn't fit right; it slips too easily.

Esther stops walking and looks at me, her face finally brightening. 'You look scared to death.'

'I am.'

I'm scared of losing you . . .

'Only a few more steps, Archie. You've come such a long way.'

I have, haven't I? We both have. The kiss aside, we did it: we did what we set out to do. I've spent two years failing to do that. But with Esther, it's happened.

I promised her I'd write Jessie's letter if she helped me. I owe it to her to see this through.

Beneath the confusion and the screaming questions jostling for space in my head, my original regard for Jessie Edmonds is still there. It has to be. Just a few hours ago, I thought my heart would give out when I stood next to her. She is beautiful. She's finally noticed I exist. This is the moment I make everything happen, right?

Right?

We've crossed the office now. One more step and we'll be at Jessie's desk. I take the letter and slip it into an envelope from my desk drawer. Keeping my eyes on Esther, I seal it and write Jessie's name on the front. Esther is glowing beside me, her smile wide and warm. Her eyes are strangely still. But this is huge for us, so I understand that.

I take a breath in, willing my following exhale to sweep my nerves out of me. 'Is this really what I should do?'

'You know it is. Everything we've done has led us here.'

I take in the sight of her: my selfless, huge-hearted friend. And fear curls around my heart. 'Do I still have you, Esther?' It's the question I asked her last night, sitting together watching the moorland sunset, a lifetime away.

She blinks and her lips part. For a moment I think she's going to say something. My breath halts.

Then slowly, gently, she places her hand on the back of mine. The lightest pressure from her causes our hands to descend as one towards Jessie's desk, the letter held by my thumb. We deliver the letter together. *We see it through to the end.*

When it's there, we stare at it, ethereally white against the dark grey desk. In the strange half-light of the empty office, it almost looks like it's floating.

I should feel relieved. I should feel lighter.

I should feel *something*.

But I'm just numb.

'You need to get going,' Esther whispers.

'Yeah, I do. Are you staying here?'

Esther lifts her head and looks around. 'This is the time your world becomes mine. Less light, better music.' She reaches into the pocket of her denim jacket and produces a pair of earbuds. 'I'll be just fine with Stevie and Fred.'

Stevie Wonder. Fred the cleaning trolley she named.

Oh, Esther . . .

'If you want, I could hang on a bit? Make you a coffee?'

She laughs. 'You have a news story to break.'

I look at my watch and panic courses through me. 'I have to go.'

'Go. Be brilliant.'

I should say something now but I have five minutes to get out of the building to meet Elvis. 'I'll call you, Es. Later tonight?'

She gives a tight-lipped nod. I squeeze her arm – possibly the lamest parting gesture in the history of awkward moments – and run for the lift.

I don't look back.

I can't.

Twenty-Seven

ESTHER

The lift doors close.

I sink into Archie's chair and stare at the space where he last stood.

What happened with us tonight?

Maybe the kiss was what he wanted. Maybe it was what I wanted, too. But all I know is that, at the moment he could have chosen anyone, he chose Jessie.

I can't be angry, much as I want to be. All Archie did was follow his heart. That's what we've worked on all this time – we found the words, he wrote them down and we delivered it together. It's lovely, if you only consider that.

So why do I feel like I just lost him?

The news story muddled everything. If a world-famous striker hadn't taken over our regular meeting place, Archie would have read me the letter, I would have agreed to deliver it with him and everything would be done.

I laugh at myself, despite the hurt.

If a world-famous striker hadn't got in the way . . .

One phrase I never imagined saying. My dad would love that.

I don't have long before Marjorie arrives. It's not enough time to start my round because I'd miss the nightly briefing she always gives us in the building's foyer. I need to get back down there and preferably be waiting outside for her arrival.

Besides, I need some air.

During the lift's creaky descent I cross everything that the foyer is empty – of both my best friend and my manager. I'm relieved to discover my prayer has been answered. I hurry outside, walking halfway around the edge of the building before leaning against the wall to catch my breath.

Is Archie doing his national news report now?

The dipping sun washes the windows of *The Herald* a rich, prospector's gold, making the once grand place shine like new.

I watch the evening glow; so different from the view I shared with Archie last night. It's still the same sun, but I don't feel its warmth now.

No. I am not going to think like that . . .

I stuff the thought away as I shrug off my jacket and pull off the long-sleeved top I've worn over my work tabard. I push all thoughts of Archie Quinn into its folds and punch it down into the dark, biscuit-crumbed depths of my bag, sucking air into my lungs as I replace my jacket. Whatever happened this evening is over. I need to move on.

I wait ten minutes there, letting the sounds and rhythms of the city gently blow everything else from my mind. People think Manchester is all fuss and bluster, all *Madchester* attitude and Northern grit – but to me it's also humour, grabbing life by the scruff of the neck, being unafraid to speak your mind. Everywhere I go in this city, people surround me who just get on with stuff, who don't lie down and let life trample them. I'm cut from the cloth of innovators and industrialists, of optimists, dreamers and bloody hard grafters. I've lost sight of that for too long.

I will the moxie of Manchester into my lungs, my muscles, my bones.

Brush off the dust, kid. Straighten your smile. Get moving.

'You're early.' My manager doesn't look up from the stack of printed sheets she's reading as she passes me.

'Traffic was light driving in. I figured I'd come straight here.' I smile as I follow her into the building.

'Don't know which road you came in on. I hit every ruddy red light and pothole going. Hold this for us, would you, kid?'

I take the bag she gives me and wait as she signs in with Sanj on the main desk and collects the strong box of keys for the cleaning team. Sanj grins at me over Marjorie's shoulder.

'Lovely evening for it, Marj. Almost like the Bahamas out there.'

'Oh, aye, we're strapping margarita glasses to the cleaning trolleys tonight so we all get in the party spirit.'

Marjorie's humour is so dry it could out-parch Death Valley. Sanj raises his eyes to heaven over her shoulder.

I catch myself smiling.

It's better already. What I said to Archie is true: this is my domain now, where only his desk-ghost inhabits. He isn't here and for once it's a blessing.

Marjorie has arranged the bunches of keys into floor order on the front desk and is back to scowling at her reading matter.

'Absolute pile of *guff*,' she mutters to no one in particular. 'Beggars belief, this.'

'What is it?' I ask, not sure if Marjorie will hear me.

To my surprise, she looks up and thrusts the sheets at me. 'Just look at this, will you? Give me your honest-to-God opinion. Because I've been staring at the damn thing for hours and I still can't make hide nor hair of it.'

I hand her the bag she gave me and turn my attention to the source of her consternation. It appears to be a layout for a brochure of some kind, the text roughly blocked between scrawled images. There are pages of it. The first thing I notice is the opening paragraph made up of three versions of the same sentence; the next are the typos.

CLEANIGN, for one.

PROFFESIONAL for another . . .

'Well?' My manager is watching me with a mixture of amusement and disdain.

'It's a mess.'

'No shit, Sherlock.'

'What's it supposed to be?'

Marjorie groans. 'Brochure for new clients. Our esteemed lord and master found someone ridiculously expensive and remarkably dim to knock this up for him. Says the images will sell it, apparently.'

'Don't you mean *a*-parent-*ly* with one *p*,' I say, pointing at another glaring error in the text.

'Exactly. Call me picky, but if we're meant to be professionals you'd expect us to be able to spell the damn word.'

'How many pages is it supposed to be?'

'Twenty-five. I told him, we don't need that many. I love my job but I'd be hard-pressed to write twenty-five bloody pages about it.'

'You could do something really smart with eight,' I say, my

mind whirring now, instincts from my old life clicking straight back into action.

Her eyes narrow. 'How?'

'It would look like – hang on,' I say, rummaging in my bag for an ancient biro. Flipping the pages over I draw four double-page layouts, quickly sketching out the picture in my head. 'Front page, back page, introduction, testimonials, list of services, letter from Mr Grove and the rest you could fill with really arty stock photos of offices and work environments. Stuff like that.'

When I look up, Marjorie and Sanj are staring at me.

'What? What did I do?'

'How come you know this stuff?'

I fold the papers and hold them out to Marjorie. 'The last place I worked. I had to brief promotional material as part of my job, work with designers, copywriters, that kind of stuff.'

Marjorie doesn't take the papers, her arms folding as she observes me. 'How long did you work there?'

This is a conversation I never expected to have with Marjorie *Clean-This-With-That* Ollerenshaw. But today has been a mine-field of surprises. 'Seven years. I started as a junior office assistant and worked my way up to account manager. It was a PR company.'

'Then how the bloody hell did you wind up cleaning offices?'

'The company went bump. And I love this job.'

'Well, you've got guts, kid; I'll give you that. Reckon you could mock summat up for us, like you just did? Words an' all?' When she sees me start to refuse she adds, 'Paid. I'd see to it your time was covered – properly, no mates rates. I've been telling Peter – *Mr Grove* – that he needs to get a professional on this for months. Reckon we just found one.'

'Bet she can spell it, too,' Sanj adds, with a wink.

By the time I reach *The Herald*'s office, I'm exhausted. Can this day chuck any more twists at me? The sight of Fred almost brings me to tears. Reliable, always sunny, never-changing Fred. The biggest curveball he ever throws at me is an occasional new squeak. I can live with surprises like that.

'Why can't everyone in my life be like you, Fred?' I ask as I wheel him out of his cupboard. And then I have to smile because, on this crazy day, me chatting to a cleaning trolley is the sanest thing I've done.

The job Marjorie just offered me is an opportunity I won't ignore. Something to shift my focus from other things I definitely don't want to think about. It's been a year since I worked on any promotional material but I could probably do it with my eyes closed. The extra money will come in useful, too. All part of the *Get My Life Back* list. I need to start carrying it with me again. It's on my bedside table hidden in the latest book I'm reading, safe but out of sight. I exchanged it for a folded chord sheet Granda Brady gave me for the piece I'm learning. I've taken to reading through it several times a day when I get chance, like I used to do with the List.

Archie wanted to know if he still had me. For the music, he does. I'm not sure about the rest yet. I need to complete this day, get whatever sleep I can and tomorrow work out how the hell to move on from this. I want to keep playing with The Old Guys – I don't want all the practice I've done to be wasted and, besides, time spent playing music with Archie is time we can't spend talking about *other* stuff.

I work methodically around the floor, my route so instinctive now I don't have to think about it. But tonight I put off cleaning Jessie Edmonds's desk until last. It means an obvious break in routine that jars slightly, but it's necessary.

I'm going to call her Perfume Ghost again when I'm working here. It makes her less real. Through Archie I've thought of her too much as we've worked on the letter together. First she was my touch point with Archie, then my shot at redemption with Matt, then the ultimate goal for making my best friend happy.

And now?

I've reached her desk. I can put it off no longer: everywhere else is clean.

Now she's a slammed door.

I don't want to think like that. I want her to be an ethereal sweet-scented shadow again, there for my own whimsy with no other concern attached. I need to deal with this, soon. And I will. But tonight, it's okay for me to hate her a little.

My fingers rest on the envelope, already missing the warmth of the hand I guided to place it there.

'Don't let him down,' I urge Jessie through the paper. 'Treasure his heart. It's a good one.'

Enough now.

Heart aching, I wheel Fred around and push him slowly back to his cupboard.

It's time to go home.

Twenty-Eight

ARCHIE

'*Archie Quinn in Central Manchester, thank you.*'

'And – we're out,' says a voice on Elvis's phone. It's the director of the last TV segment of the night, on speakerphone. 'Great work, Archie, thank you. If we need a follow-up, are you good to go?'

'Sure, no problem.'

'Okay. I'll let you go. Cheers – and thanks, Brian.'

Elvis yawns. 'Pleasure, Tom. Keep me posted, yeah?'

'Sure.'

He ends the call and shakes his head at me. 'Well, *bloody Nora*, Archie Quinn. You're a national sensation.'

I laugh. 'I don't know about that.' My entire body aches from holding myself upright for what is now seven live TV news reports, my face muscles so tired from smiling they've lost the will to move. 'Is it always that mad?'

'Worse now than when I was working on the nationals. Now you have twenty-four-hour rolling news, endless online stuff, everything changing a million times a minute. It's a young man's game now, for sure. Although you look fit to drop, kid. Fancy a bite of something to eat? Omar's is still open if we rush.' Elvis grins. 'Mountain of cheesy chips and a kebab – triumphant meal of gods, eh?'

I should go home, the drive back already looming like a Herculean task, but the last thing I ate was cake at Rossi's, hours ago. It's just past eleven now and I'm famished.

'Yeah, go on then. But I'm paying.'

'You'll not hear me complaining about that.' Elvis chuckles as he slaps a hand against my back and we start to walk.

The city is still damp from a downpour an hour ago that we powered on through, the pavements and roads dark mirror-glass studded with flares of light from shops and streetlights. I'm glad we weren't asked to do any of the reports from the Etihad. It's gridlock all round the stadium now, according to Elvis, who has been tracking events on Twitter in between live pieces. Fans gathering, journalists crowding the entrance, satellite trucks blocking the car parks. Chaos, by all accounts. The rain-drenched city centre is genteel by comparison.

'Hey – I just seen you on the telly!' Omar beams as we both drip steadily by his counter.

'Lad did good for his first scoop, eh?' Elvis grins, accepting the steaming takeout cup from the owner.

'That your first one? How you going to top that, then?'

'Not sure I will.'

'It were definitely him, then? Totti? In Jacopo's place?'

I nod, swaying a little in the warmth of the kebab shop, the soothing spice of cooking food irresistible.

'I knew it!' Omar turns to his son sullenly shovelling chips beside him. '*No way Totti's going to Man City*, you said. That's a tenner you owe me.'

'Take it out me wages,' his son mutters, glaring at the fryer.

'You lads want to eat in? You can sit on that table if you like.'

We turn to look at the single plastic table and bench seats between the counter's end and the buzzing soft drinks fridge with its chipped-paint cola bottle handles. Three heavy-looking textbooks, their pages opened and marked by many coloured sticky-note dividers, cover it.

'You're using it, don't worry,' I begin, but Omar is having none of it.

'Khalid's doing his uni stuff, that's all.'

'I can take it out back, it's no problem,' Omar's son says, still not smiling. He looks like a knackered zombie. I know how he feels.

They insist and neither Elvis nor I have the energy to protest, so we watch the young man and his father clear everything from the table and wipe down the surface. When we sit, Omar brings over our news-scoop-delayed dinner and slides onto the bench next to my startled colleague.

'Great, now we're cosy, you have food, so . . . tell me *everything*!'

I'm not sure how I get home, only that it's heading for 1 a.m. when I slip my key into the Yale lock of my front door.

That's odd . . .

I don't remember leaving the hall light on.

Dumping my rucksack and jacket by the front door, I kick off my rain-splattered shoes and peer into the flat. More light edges the closed kitchen door and in the living room something blue is flickering . . .

Is there somebody here?

I look around for something to protect myself, finding a very old, very broken golfing umbrella that's leant against the wall by the coat rack for as long as I've rented the place. Spurs of broken spokes swing out as I raise it over my shoulder like a drawn sword. Every sense is switched to high alert, adrenaline screeching in my ears. Five not particularly stealthy steps later, I reach the door to the living room and nudge it open with my knee.

The room is empty, but the TV is on in the corner, flooding the room with dancing blue and white lights. I swallow hard, battling weariness. If an intruder is in my home, the only place they can be is my bedroom with its tiny en suite bathroom.

I'm about to head there when something catches my eye.

No.

Not something.

Some*one* . . .

'What are you doing here?'

The diminutive figure on my sofa stirs and my daft mother jumps to her feet.

'You're back! Oh, come here, my superstar news reporter!'

I'm engulfed in a delighted hug that reaches as far as my chest, hanging on to her for fear of being knocked off my feet. 'Mum, what's . . . ?'

'We saw you. On the telly. And then your dad switched to another channel and there you were again! And the radio! And on the interweb! I am so proud of you!'

'Mum, you don't drive. How did you get here?'

'I might have had a wee bit of help,' she says against me.

'How bloody late are you?' My sister walks out of my bedroom, calm as you like, as if she's always here in the early hours of the morning.

'You dragged Dacey over here, too?'

'Well, she has a car and your dad's due baking in two hours, so he wouldn't bring me.'

'Mum, you're impossible.'

'Love you too.' Dacey heads over and plants a kiss on my cheek. 'You're lucky you didn't have Granda Brady in the welcoming party, an' all. I had to bribe him with one of my traybakes to make him stay at home.'

Mum finally lets me go and we stand there, a bunch of loon-grinning, sleep-deprived Quinns in the middle of my lounge.

'You were only on the bloody telly!'

I'm so tired I can hardly stand but I'm caught up in the rush of joy when I see their faces. 'I know!'

'Conn saw it too; he's left you about a gazillion voicemails so don't be surprised if your phone melts when you open them.'

My mum beams in the way only she can. Even with sleep tugging at her words, she illuminates the space around her. 'We phoned *everyone*. You were amazing! I was in tears, of course. Your dad was in tears. Our phones ringing off the hook as soon as we ended each call . . . ' Her eyes glisten and Dacey and I gather her into another hug.

'Thank you,' I say, my words constricted by thick emotion. It's been the longest of days and I feel like I've lived several lives during the past few hours. The rumour, the meeting at Rossi's, the scoop, the letter. And Esther . . .

Esther.

I close my eyes.

'We should get going, Mum,' Dacey says, at last, forever the sensible one. 'This one needs his sleep.'

I catch Mum trying not to yawn, feeling her sagging a little against me. I love that she's even here, but we all need to sleep soon. Dacey looks done in, too.

'Why don't you stay here?' I suggest.

'We couldn't . . .'

'Look at the two of you: you're dead on your feet. If I let you drive home I wouldn't sleep for worrying anyway. I'll make up the sofa bed for you, Mum. And Dace, I've a futon chair in my room I can bring in here for you.'

If they want to protest, they don't have the energy. Mum's relief is immediate. She looks fit to drop and my sister won't be far behind her.

Pushing the final reserves of energy into my limbs I set up the lounge as a makeshift hotel room, bringing spare bedding and pillows from the airing cupboard where the boiler lives. Dacey helps, Mum leaning gratefully against the back of the sofa bed, trying her best to keep her eyes open as she watches us. When she's sent Dad a text to say where she is, we tuck her in like a baby. Within minutes, she's gone.

Grinning at my sister, we tiptoe into the kitchen.

'We figured you wouldn't have eaten, so Mum packed this.' Dacey pats a large plastic carry box stuffed with grease-spotted white paper bags, their tops rolled over in the way my parents taught me as a kid. I picture five-year-old me watching Dad in the bakery flipping the bag over and over, ever the showman, wanting so much to be like him.

'Did she bring half the shop?' I whisper, peering into each bag. Golden-topped sausage rolls, sugar-sprinkled apple hand pies, gorgeously sticky twisted yumyums, a wide speckled tiger loaf and several slices of pork and egg pie, each slice featuring a perfect circle of hardboiled egg suspended in glistening pink meat, edged with golden jelly and pastry that you can taste before you even put it in your mouth. I dive in while my sister puts the kettle on. It's home contained in an army of Quinn & Co bags – the ultimate reward for everything today.

'She had to see you. We both did. Sorry for not letting you know earlier. It was kind of a last-minute thing.'

'It's great to have you here. Thanks, sis.'

She stirs the teapot, then reaches up to ruffle my hair. 'You were amazing. How do you feel?'

'I – honestly don't know.'

'A lot to take in, I'll bet.'

'Just a bit.' *You don't know the half of it*, I think. And then I remember kissing Esther. My heart plummets.

Dacey clocks the change immediately. 'Not all good?'

Can I trust her? 'It was unreal – like I was standing behind myself, you know, watching me doing it all. But something else happened . . . Esther and me – we kissed. By mistake,' I add quickly, seeing Dacey's mouth fall open. 'I mean, we're okay and everything. Just a reaction to the scoop and, you know . . . Anyway, she was fine when I left her.'

'And you?'

'I'm not sure.' It's the truth. I haven't dared let my mind stray there in the craziness of this evening. But now the news reports are over and I'm facing my big sister in the quiet of my own kitchen, I can't avoid it. 'We finished the letter, you see. For Jessie. And delivered it.'

Dacey's eyes widen. 'Before or after you kissed her?'

I swallow hard. 'After.' Said aloud it sounds so much worse.

'Bloody hell, Arch.'

'I know.'

'So what did Jessie say?'

'She hasn't seen it yet. We left it on her desk before all the interviews started.'

'*We?*'

'Esther and me.'

'And she was okay with this?'

'It was her idea.'

'Really?'

I nod.

'How long after you kissed her did she suggest it?'

It's too much, too late for my mind to wrap around any of it. Have I just been the ultimate git to Esther? 'It's too late to go into it now. I need to think about things and my brain is shot.'

Compassion floods Dacey's expression. 'Sure. Let's get you a cuppa and then we both need to crash.'

Finally in my own bed, my entire body sore, I close my eyes in the strange stillness. A shadowed image of a white envelope lying on a dark grey desk fills my mind. Tomorrow, everything could change. Perhaps the change has already begun.

Esther delivered the letter with me. She said it was the right thing to do. I did it because I believed she was right.

So why am I doubting it now?

Twenty-Nine

ESTHER

'What are you drawing?'

A little blonde curly head nudges my elbow, a small hand depositing a well-hugged bunny on the kitchen island as Ava-May scrambles up beside me. She had a disturbed night last night and was running a temperature until an hour ago, so she's off school and officially my sweet little shadow today until her sisters come home this afternoon. I don't mind. This morning especially I want to be as busy as possible.

I reach down to lift her the final few inches onto the bar stool and stroke the soft wool of the rainbow knit cardigan she's wearing over cute unicorn pyjamas.

'It's going to be a brochure,' I say. Seeing her nose wrinkle, I laugh. 'Like a little magazine? About the people I work for.'

'Will there be dragons in it?' she asks hopefully. 'Or magic cats?'

'Probably not. I might have to sneak a few in behind the words and photos, though, what do you reckon?'

Ava-May gasps. 'Like *invisible* ones! Invisible super-spy dragons and cats. And unicorns, too!'

That would sell the charms of Concilio Cleaning to me, I think.
'Great idea.'

'Your laptop is cool.'

'Thanks. It's a bit old and grumpy now.'

'Like Daddy.'

It's so good to laugh. Ava-May joins me, our laughter dancing around the walls and units of the kitchen. My heart still stings from yesterday, but I woke this morning determined to move forward. I still have so much – including Archie's friendship. I'm stronger than I've been in months, happier too. I have new opportunities to explore, renewed hope in what I'm capable of, a bright new road stretching ahead of me, beckoning me to follow.

I still have Archie.

It could have been so different if we hadn't delivered the letter – if I'd backed away because I was hurt and had never seen it through.

There was a text from him waiting for me on my phone this morning:

Hey you. Thanks for being there yesterday. For being you.
I couldn't have done any of it without you. You mean the
world to me, Esther. Call you later? A x

I was so close to making a massive mistake yesterday. I could have lost him completely. It was just a kiss. We'll bounce back from this and be friends for life. In the end, that's what matters. Anything else would be selling ourselves short.

I wish I hadn't kissed him. But that was yesterday. Time to get over it and get on with getting my life back. My list is back where it belongs in my jeans pocket and calmness is returning to my soul.

Plus, I now have an army of invisible mythical creatures to sneak into a cleaning company brochure . . .

By the time I've finished the mock-up design it's almost lunchtime. Ava-May has been surreptitiously yawning behind her pulled sleeve for the last twenty minutes and I don't want her toppling off the stool if sleep wins the battle for her eyelids.

'Come on, beauty,' I say, hopping down and lifting her into my arms. She snuggles into me, all warm and bed-scented. 'Let's make you a cushion castle bed on the sofa.'

'With a moat?' she asks, sleepily.

I suppress my smile. 'Probably.'

She's curled up in the corner of the sofa almost asleep while I make a nest of all the cushions I can find. (This being my sister's house, that means a truckload of them.) I pull a Wedgwood-blue throw from the armchair Gavin likes to sit in and fold it into a soft, narrow length just beneath the sofa along the line where the expensive cream rug ends and the stripped wood floor begins. As a moat it's pretty impressive. Gently, I lift Ava-May and settle her in the middle of her magnificent cushion castle, fetching her favourite rainbow-star fleece blanket from the decorated blanket basket Naomi keeps by the fireplace, and tucking it around her tiny frame. She murmurs in her sleep, pulling Dave the Bunny close under her chin and popping her thumb into her mouth.

I fetch my coffee cup from the kitchen and curl up in Gavin's armchair, watching my littlest niece dreaming. In the quiet house, with the still-damp green of the garden beyond the full-length windows, calm washes over me, a gentle returning tide. I close my eyes and sink into it.

Time is what I need. Time to process everything that

happened yesterday. When I've worked out what the hell happened with us, I will feel better, I think. It's like I've lived a year in a few days, the bruises from the emotional twists and turns still raw. In all the commotion yesterday I feel like I forgot to breathe. That can't happen again.

Archie will have seen Jessie by now. One way or another, he will have his answer. I've purposefully not looked at the clock this morning, but my inner timekeeping has monitored the hours anyway.

What happens if she says no? If she doesn't feel the same?

Part of me still wants to stand beside Archie, be his shield and companion, for whatever he's about to face. But that's not my responsibility – it never was. I promised to help him because I needed to move on. It was as much for my benefit as his. Wasn't it?

If Jessie says no . . .

She won't though, will she? She'd be insane to turn Archie's heart down.

The intense green of the garden stings my eyes when I open them again. I blink away the water that rises. I'm just tired, like my littlest niece, whose gentle snores mingle with the soft rumble of the tumble dryer from beyond the kitchen. I need to cocoon myself in calm like her cushion castle and let myself rest. At least in this house, with no reminders of Archie Quinn save for a bright-orange ukulele I love with all my heart, I can find distraction.

By now, he'll know.

By this evening, I'll know, too.

Until then, I'll rest. And breathe.

Thirty

ARCHIE

It's 12.30 p.m.

Still no sign of Jessie.

What's worse is that nobody seems to know where she is. She hasn't phoned in sick, but beyond that nobody's sure what's keeping her from *The Herald*'s office today. It's quiet too, which doesn't help my stressed-out head. Elvis is at a press conference hosted by Greater Manchester Police about a new neighbourhood knife crime awareness initiative. Liam has his head down, finalising the incidental columns for Friday's issue. Callaghan is in a meeting with the distributor and will be there till mid-afternoon.

It's too bloody quiet.

And there's a good chance I'll lose the plot if Jessie doesn't arrive soon.

The letter is still on her desk, where Esther and I left it yesterday. Several times I've almost swiped it off. What little sleep I managed last night wasn't enough to dispel my nerves this morning, but I thought I'd resolved myself to facing Jessie by the time I'd driven in.

I just wasn't expecting that resolve to be tested *this long* . . .

It helped that I talked to my sister a little before she and Mum left for the bakery this morning. Dacey is the most down-to-earth, steady person I know, a fact that used to infuriate me as a kid because I could never wind her up in the way I could with Conn. She was like the Dungeon Master; calmly walking through fire, tsunami waves, cacophonous explosions and everything else that could be thrown at her. When you're the youngest of three siblings, you want the upper hand all the time: with Dacey Quinn as my sister, that was never going to happen.

I love that quality in her now. Over the years it's been my salvation and my strength. In a family where high spirits and energy often flip to thunderous drama, she is the safe, sure ship plotting a course through the worst of it.

'So, you're going ahead?' she'd asked, tucking into a huge stack of toast I'd made from the delicious tiger loaf Mum brought over.

'I've promised myself this for two years,' I'd replied.

Dacey had jumped on that like a ninja. 'That's not what I asked.'

'I'm in love with Jessie Edmonds. I've been in love with her for almost three years.'

'And how long have you known Esther?'

The knowing tone of her question had irked me, mainly because I knew she had a point. I've known Esther a fraction of the time my poor, battered heart has ached for Jessie, but that short acquaintance has thrown everything else into question. When it shouldn't have. That wasn't the deal: I know it, my heart knows it and Esther knows it.

'I am torn,' I'd admitted. 'But what do I do? Esther delivered that letter with me. She was adamant. That can only mean she believes in Jessie and me.' *And nothing else*, my traitorous head had added.

'Arch, stop overthinking this. Give Jessie the letter if you're sure: take your chances like you always planned. Esther helped you do what you've talked about for years – she sounds like a great friend to me. She wants you to be happy. Do you want that for yourself?'

I stare at the envelope on Jessie's unoccupied desk. What do I want?

I sent a text to Esther when I woke this morning. She hasn't replied yet. But until there's news either way, what could she say?

If I take Esther and the past few weeks out of the equation, if I just focus on my heart, Jessie is still there. I care about Esther – and I don't regret kissing her – but the fact remains we met because I was in love with Jessie. That doesn't go away because of a few admittedly great weeks with a new friend.

This is my fear talking, I'm certain of it.

I have to calm down. Focus on the future. With Jessie told, I can finally start to plan my escape from here.

The last live piece I did on the Sergio Totti story was for ITV Sport. The news editor from MediaCity in Salford emailed me his card directly afterwards and told me to call him if I'd like an informal chat about my career. I'm going to take him up on it – because when am I likely to get an opportunity like that again?

Manchester City finally released a statement this morning confirming the signing of Sergio Totti for an undisclosed sum.

Bigger, beefier news network journalists have muscled in on the story, but I broke it. A Google News search for 'Totti to Manchester City' features a whole page of my report in its top results. My daft face, grinning outside Rossi's. Grinning with the shock and thrill of a genuine scoop – and for my beautiful friend behind the camera, filming it all. The video has been posted and reposted thousands of times on hundreds of different networks, sport sites, football gossip sites and fan sites across the world. My words, my story, my ugly mug, all over the world! I never thought I'd see that in a million years.

It may be a coincidence, but I've also had a slew of messages and emails from my boss. Well, they *say* they're from my boss. Only they don't sound like Callaghan at all.

Great work, Archie!
Doing it for The Herald, too – a masterstroke! JC

Sky News! JC

Top trending topic on BBC News website,
Twitter and Google. Keep it up! JC

Perfect delivery on the BBC Radio 5 Live piece.
Nice mention of The Herald. Thanks, JC

Archie
Most impressed by your work. I'm in distributor meetings tomorrow till 3 p.m. but when I get in we need to talk. I have a proposition that may be of interest.

Regards,
Jock Callaghan

Has a malevolently generous spirit body-snatched my editor?

Liam made a joke about Callaghan having to clean *my* car for a month now. I may have laughed it off then, but it's a turnaround I never saw coming. Given what Elvis told me about my editor's frustrated career hopes, I'd expected a torrent of envy-fuelled abuse when he next saw me.

What with that and having to face Jessie after she'd read my letter, I'd expected a lot of noise to contend with today. This stillness in the office is too oppressive. I'm best when I'm surrounded by noise: the buzz of the newsroom, the constant thrum of Manchester life and traffic, the dubious clamouring of melodies in The Old Guys' circle of musicians. I can't think straight with nothing else to focus on.

I need to get out of here.

'Want anything from town?' I blurt out, causing Liam's head to pop up like a meerkat sentry catching a sound.

'Get us a batch, would you? Don't care what's in it.'

'Ham? Cheese? Salad?'

'Whatever. Some kind of meat and if you want to fling in something green and healthy I can tell my missus I ate, all the better. Crisps, too. And might as well get cakes, seeing as we're celebrating you being the man who brought Man City to their knees.'

His grin is a reward today.

It's fresh outside, no sign yet of the promised heatwave the news networks have been squabbling over for the past week. Just a bright summer day, all blue sky and racing white clouds in the ever-present breeze. Warm enough to go out without a jacket, but cool enough to keep you from sweating through your shirt. A perfect Manchester day. I love this place. And I need the city at its best and brightest today.

There's a queue at the sandwich shop round the corner from *The Herald*'s building, but I don't mind. I'm in no hurry to get back there and for once not in any fear of encountering the wrath of my boss, both of which are reasons to enjoy being outside.

While I wait, I scroll the latest transfer window news on my phone, which, in the absence of any significant breaking stories, seem to have returned to the vain hopes of fans and pundits for summoning fantasy starry signings. I jump when the screen disappears, replaced by a caller ID:

Greg Behrenger, NewsCal Agency

Quickly, I accept the call.

'Archie, hi. Greg from NewsCal. I take it you've seen the statement?'

'Hi, Greg, yeah, saw it this morning.'

'Great work, lad. We've syndicated your report across our global news partners. That's some buzz you've created there.'

'Thank you.' I smile against the phone. This is what I need to focus on now – in all the craziness of yesterday I never allowed myself time to let it sink in. I broke an international news story, the aftershocks of which are still being felt around the football world. It's a promise of what my career could be now I've taken the step I'd vowed I'd take. Even if Jessie says no – and I think she's bound to say no – I've proved I can do the job I've been chasing all this time. I can dare to dream about where I could be.

'Okay, I have some print article requests I'm sending over. Quick turnaround of course, but your name in the byline as promised. You okay to get them done and submitted today?'

'Yes,' I rush, not caring that I sound like a breathless teenager because this is *immense*. 'Whatever you need.'

'Excellent. I also have talkSPORT wanting you to do a Zoom call around ten tonight?'

'Happy to.' My dad and Conn will be over the moon with that one. Conn is the only person I know who can't sleep at night unless talkSPORT is playing in the background. Elodie's made him sleep with earphones in now, having been driven half to distraction by football-mad radio callers yelling in the early hours. Reckon I'll be in my big brother's good books for weeks after this.

'Great. When the dust settles, we'll have a proper chat. Get you working a bit more for us. Up for that?'

I blink in the bright sunshine. 'Absolutely.'

The call ends and I realise the queue has moved forward, leaving me several steps behind. I skip ahead, forgetting my weariness, my frustration and the still-unpicked tangle of thoughts in my head. *I made this happen.* I'm going to allow myself a moment to celebrate it . . .

'Archie.'

And just like that, there she is.

Walking towards me like a sunlit vision, blonde hair loose around her face, white shirt dress hugging her figure in the very best way . . .

'Jessie . . . ' I begin. But I don't get the chance to say more.

'*Yes.*' She smiles, reaching me, the letter I wrote with Esther in her hand. 'My answer is yes.'

Before I can reply, her lips are full on mine; the wolf whistles of the sandwich shop queue fading behind the crash of my heart as Jessie Edmonds slips like a glorious, lucid dream, straight into my arms . . .

Thirty-One

ESTHER

I'm okay.

Really, I am.

How could Jessie have said no with Archie's lovely heart laid out for her like that? At least it confirms my suspicions: she's a woman worthy of his love.

I'd hoped she would be. Strange though it sounds, given the ache of my own heart right now. I wanted her to be worthy of those years of longing. Archie deserved to fall in love with someone worth falling in love with.

All the same, it hurts to hear the breathless joy in his voice.

'I thought it would be awkward, you know, talking to her after I'd laid myself bare on the page? But you were right, Es: I just had to trust my heart and let go of everything else. I was ready for her to say no . . . '

'But she didn't.'

The rush of air from his laugh stings my ear. 'No, she didn't. I think you would call it an emphatic *yes*.'

She would have kissed him, then. Of course she would.

Was it different to our kiss?

I kick the rogue thought away. *None of your business, Esther. Thinking like that achieves nothing . . .*

'I knew she would.'

There's a pause. I wonder which words Archie is hastily discarding. 'How are you?'

How *am* I?

This doesn't feel like it did when Matt bounced over to my apartment to say he'd proposed to Nina. That felt like he'd kicked my feet out from under me and carried on kicking where I'd emotionally fallen. Archie didn't do that. I knew his plans: he made me part of them. I can't be surprised. I have no reason to resent our plan succeeding.

I just wish it hadn't happened so soon after we kissed.

Which was a mistake. Of course it was.

But it was still a kiss.

'I'm good,' I rush, stuffing away everything else. 'I've picked up some extra work, actually. Design work, like I did in my old job. Marjorie's asked me to mock up a company brochure for her boss. Paid, too.'

'Oh, Es, that's awesome! I'm made up for you! So – what does that mean for your cleaning?'

I'm imagining the edge to his words, I'm certain of it. 'I still have my job. Not abandoning Fred just yet.'

'And the Post-it King?'

I breathe against the needle-scratch of his question. 'Couldn't abandon him, either.'

'Are you coming to The Old Guys on Saturday?'

'Try and stop me! I've been driving Naomi up the walls with my practising. Reckon I can play the basic chords for those songs now.'

'Wow, you're already streets ahead of the rest of us, then. Maybe we could do lunch after? See if Lil at the pub has any more pearls of wisdom for us?'

Ahead of me the crowd of arriving parents has swelled. 'I've got to go, they're opening the gates.' I check the clock on my car's dashboard, grab my bag and open the driver's door.

'Okay – Es?'

'Yes?' I answer, clicking the auto-lock button on my car key and hurrying towards the packed school gates.

'Are we good?'

'We're fine. I'm thrilled for you, Arch. Stop worrying.'

His goodbye is only half-said when I end the call.

There are days when the sudden burst of chatter and energy that ensues when the girls arrive jars my head and it's a struggle to concentrate on the drive home. Today is not one of them. Issy and Molly's happy chatter soothes me, blasting all unwanted thoughts from my mind. I love these girls and in the last few weeks we've become firm pals. They make me laugh with their view of the world and their wry take on life. I wish I'd been that sure of myself when I was their age.

'Maddie Richards isn't talking to us *again*,' Issy informs me with a sigh my mother would be proud of. I'm currently being briefed on the latest scandals in Year 4, a veritable hotbed of drama and intrigue. It's better than any long-running drama on TV. 'You'd think she'd be bored of flouncing off by now, but oh no, not Maddie.'

'Why is she mad at you?' Molly asks. Her feet drum against the back of my seat like a particularly insistent lower back massage.

'Why is she *always* mad? Because someone came to school in the same shoes.'

I glance at her in the rear-view mirror. 'Aren't all school shoes pretty much the same?'

'You know that, I know that. But Maddie's convinced everyone is copying her. I told her, "They're just black shoes, what's original about that?" And you know what she said? "Well, *yours* might be, Issy Martins, but mine have my trademark flair." . . . '

Molly and I snort with laughter. In the back seat, Issy beams at our reaction.

'I'm seven and even I know you can't *zhuzh* up boring school shoes,' Molly observes, her dryness as funny as her sister's impressions.

'I'm just going to do everything with *trademark flair* now,' Issy deadpans. 'Look at me! I'm not just opening a pencil case; I'm doing it with my trademark flair!'

'And Auntie Esther's not just driving the car, she's doing it with her trademark flair,' Molly joins in.

'I like that,' I say, relaxing into the game. 'Maybe I wear my work tabard with trademark flair, too?'

'Definitely! And don't forget Fred's trademark flair, too.' Issy grins.

'And I do this with trademark *flair*,' Molly adds, the last word a magnificent burp that reverberates around the car. Issy and I protest loudly, while Molly giggles her little head off. Maybe we won't tell their mum about that . . .

I don't care, though: this is exactly what I need. The unbridled joy of my nieces is a gorgeous, irresistible force that sweeps everything else away. I am so lucky to have this in my life – to be part of it without ever having to ask. I love how they involve me in their fun, how I never have to jump through hoops to be approved or prove my worth to be included.

Like The Old Guys have welcomed me in without reserve. And, when I can divorce the other stuff from it, my friendship with Archie, too. *That's what I'll choose to see from now on*, I think, as I drive and we laugh and talk at a hundred miles an hour, several decibels louder than any of us needs to. I'll choose to see the fun and life and friendship I have with Archie. It was a gift when he found me sleeping in Fred's cupboard: it's a gift now.

My life is good. I have so much today that I could never have anticipated in those dark final days in my apartment, when the end of my old life seemed like the death of everything I cared about. I won't be living at Naomi's forever, I might not be cleaning offices a year from now, but I'm grateful for them both.

Will I have Archie this time next year? Only time will tell. Until then, I'm going to make the most of it.

We pull into the drive, a breathless, giggling mess of happiness, and the girls pile out of the car still buzzing, while I follow them with an armful of bags, raincoats and gleefully discarded school jumpers. My sides ache from laughing, my smile lodged in place despite the vehement protest of my face muscles.

'Pop your key in the lock, Is,' I call. 'I can't reach mine carrying this stuff.'

'No need,' my niece replies over her shoulder. 'Mum's here.'

I look up over the pile of belongings in my arms. Naomi is there, her smile tight.

'Everything good?' I ask, heading up the steps towards her.

'I'll take these,' she replies, not quite making eye contact.

Relieved of my burden, I push my hands into my pockets, the last ghosts of laughter ebbing away in the bright sunlight. 'Nai, what's up?'

She blinks. I see her swallow hard before she speaks.

'Matt's here.'

'What?'

'He arrived half an hour ago. I told him he couldn't stay but he insisted. He said he has to talk to you, today.'

I hear the words she's saying, see them moving on her lips, but there's a disconnect between them and my brain. I said all I had to say to Matt that day at the supermarket, didn't I? I drew a line under everything. What part of that did he not understand?

'Where is he?' I demand, my teeth gritted against the fury flooding me where laughter and lightness lived until I arrived home.

'I don't want any trouble, Es. I tried to get him to go but he wouldn't budge.'

'I know you did.' I rest my hand on her arm, my fingers shaking from the effort of remaining calm. 'I'll get him out.'

'If he needs to talk . . . '

'I'll tell him to pick a better time.'

'Use my garden office if you need it.' Her eyes brim with concern. 'Will you be okay? Gavin will be home any minute. I can ask him to chuck Matt out.'

'I'll be fine. He has no business coming here, unannounced. But I can handle him. I'm sorry, Naomi.'

'Don't apologise.' Her hand rests protectively on mine. 'Just – give him *hell*.'

Fire burning my gut, I power into the room where Matt Hope is laughing and goofing around with Issy and Molly, Ava-May sleepily observing from her cushion castle nest, half of which has tumbled to the floor.

How dare he?

He looks up as I approach, that bloody blasé smile of his aimed at me.

'Outside,' I snap, walking past him to the open bifold doors and out into the garden. I don't wait for a reply or look back to check if he's following: I know he will be. Sure enough, as I fling open the door to Naomi's garden office, I hear his heavy steps on the wooden floor behind me. Reaching my sister's desk, I turn to face him.

He is flush-faced and bewildered, but that smile annoyingly remains.

'What the hell are you doing here?' I don't try to be civil. He has invaded my space, my home, my peace and I'm damned if I'll let him think it's okay. It's *not* okay, and he knows it.

'I want to talk.'

'You could have called me. Oh, that's right: you lost your phone on honeymoon when you stopped talking to me.'

'I said I was sorry . . .'

'So what's your excuse this time? Because I don't remember agreeing to this.'

'I wanted to see you.'

'I don't care. You don't turn up here, shouting the odds at my sister in her own home, scaring her half to death . . .'

He laughs and I resent the way tension leaves his body. 'Nothing's likely to scare your sister. Naomi's a rock. And it was lovely to see the girls—'

'Go home, Matt. I've said all I wanted to say to you.'

His face falls. 'Well, I haven't . . .' He glances over his shoulder at the house where my family are no doubt party to all this, swears under his breath and pulls the door closed, sealing us in. 'There's something you don't know. Something you *need* to know.'

What more could he think I want to know about him? He's been happily absent from my life for over a year and only talked to me after that because he bumped into me and was shamed into it.

'I don't want to hear it.'

He folds his arms, his back firmly against my only means of escape. 'Well, I'm not leaving until you do.'

Panic grips me. I have no answer for this, no clever plan in case this ever happened. I was happy about walking away from him last time. But how do I manage this?

'Sit down,' he says, softening his voice like he always did when he was losing an argument. 'Please?'

'I'd rather stand.'

He blows out his frustration, running a hand through his hair, which has grown as messy and complicated as he has become. 'Okay, fine. I'm just going to say this because if I don't, I'll . . . ' His eyes plead with me where words have failed him. 'Just hear me out. Then if you want me to go, I will.'

I don't reply. I have no choice in listening to him but I can choose not to make it easy for him. It's the only power I have.

'I've left Nina.' He waits for me to speak but I can't. 'Six months ago. We've already started divorce proceedings. It's a mutual thing in case you're wondering.'

I keep my eyes on him and refuse to let myself sit, despite my legs becoming unsteady. I grip the edge of Naomi's desk for grim life.

'I should never have married her. It was a huge mistake: we knew the moment we came back from Antigua. Looking back, I was never certain of us working. Turns out, neither was she.'

It explains the tiredness I noticed before, the aimlessness with which he was walking up that supermarket aisle. Why didn't he tell me this then? And what does he expect me to do with it now?

'I'm sorry your marriage failed,' I begin, picking my words with care. 'But I don't know why you're telling me . . . '

'Because it's your fault!'

What?

He's breathing heavily, as if the accusation stole the air from him when it left his body.

I'm reeling, but furious. 'No way. *No way* are you dropping that at my door. Your marriage has nothing to do with me. It never did . . . '

'It's because of you.'

How can he say that? After everything I did for him?

'You didn't marry Nina because of me, Matt. You married her because you decided that was what you wanted. Don't you bloody dare accuse me! I supported you. I stood by you as you married her. I said *nothing* . . . '

'Exactly!' He claps his hands as if I've unwittingly proved a point. 'You *said nothing*. When I'd been waiting for you to say something. For *years*.'

Now I sit.

When I don't reply, he sinks into a chair, too, eyes wild. 'It's always been you, Esther. Right from the start. I thought you knew, that you felt the same. And yeah, we mucked around with other people but we always came back together. That was what mattered. You seemed so agitated when I was with someone; when you were dating I couldn't think straight either. I thought we'd work it out, eventually. Give in to the inevitable, but – you didn't say anything. Even when we'd both been single for a year . . . '

I am not hearing this. It isn't real. It's not possible Matt loved me all that time: I would have known. I would have felt it, instead of understanding in the deepest part of my heart that I was the only one holding out for him.

'I don't believe you,' I say, the power gone from my voice.

'It's true. You know it is.'

'Then why was it my place to call it? Don't you think I waited, too?'

I've said too much. I jam my lips tight shut but it's too late: I see it register in his expression. My tears begin to well and I look away.

'I thought you'd say something when Nina showed up. I kept asking you, over and over. *Should I marry her, Es? Is there any reason why I shouldn't?*'

That question.

It's haunted me since the day Matt chose Nina, but until now I believed it was my missed chance to speak, the consequences of which I carried alone. I never thought he'd asked it to prompt me into fighting for him. The revelation frees me then instantly imprisons me again. It was never my fault for not speaking. I should have believed in myself, refused the guilt I was never meant to carry.

But he's not strapping it to my back now.

'That's not fair!' I raise my head, let him see the tears fall. 'You should have said something, Matt. You had years, too. If you loved me like you say you did, how could you ever have contemplated marrying Nina?'

'Because I didn't know what else to do!'

I can't believe I'm hearing this. The fire is back – I grasp it and let it propel me. 'You could have told me. You could have marched round to my apartment, like you've marched here today, demanding to talk to me. That's what someone chasing love does, Matt. They don't use someone else to try to trick words out of the person they really want.'

'It wasn't a trick . . . '

'Wasn't it? Forget the small detail of not loving Nina like you said you did; are you telling me that pursuing her, being with her, proposing in the most overblown, public way possible, planning a wedding you knew your heart wasn't in and then making promises to her on your wedding day that you had no intention of keeping, was all an act of love for me?'

'It wasn't . . . I didn't mean . . . ' I can see him floundering now. Indignation forces me to my feet.

'You are not blaming me for your inability to know your own heart. I took a lot of responsibility for you, Matt, but I won't take that. You lied to Nina. You lied to me. You lied in front of everyone that loved you.'

'You said you loved me . . . '

'Get out.'

'You said you loved me, Es. Just then. Admit it: you wanted me to say something.'

'Then why didn't you?' I don't want to be here. I never wanted to say this aloud to him but it's too late: he knows. And that spark of hope is back in his expression. I'm losing ground and I can't claw it back. 'Just go . . . *please.*'

'I can't. I won't. I love you.' He stands, risks a step towards me.

'Don't say that.'

'I've always loved you. Nina knew that. She said there was no point hoping for my heart because it was already taken.'

Another step. I want Naomi's desk to rise like a ten-foot wall of solid stone between us to keep me safe, but I'm trapped here.

'Matt, stop this.'

'Do you have anyone else? Has there been anyone else since I . . . ?'

Yes, I want to shoot back. *Someone a million times better than you'll ever be.* But there isn't any more, is there?

'I don't want you.'

'Liar.'

'Get out.'

He retreats a little, rubbing the back of his neck as if my words are tiny arrows fired into the skin there.

'This isn't what I wanted it to be like. The words aren't coming out right . . .'

'Go home.'

'Listen to me, Es. Let me say this: I know I let you down. I know you're hurt and I hate that I made that happen. But I don't think it's a coincidence we met the other week. As soon as I saw you, I knew I still loved you. I still *love* you. I made a stupid, brainless mistake and I should have had the balls to tell you, long before Nina ever arrived.'

'Matt, please . . .'

'I'm trying to make it right.'

It's too much. 'You can't. It's done.'

'Let me try, Es. We were great together once.'

'No.'

'Imagine none of the rest ever happened and this is just me, right now, blown away by you, wanting so much to be yours.' He risks a move closer.

I'm out of ammunition, my head throbbing and my body no

longer listening to my will to fight. I don't flinch when he moves in front of me, his breath so close it prickles my skin.

'You broke my heart. And then you vanished.' My voice is barely a whisper, choked by emotion and sapped by fear. But I still say the words, hoping they have power where their speaker doesn't. 'You made me feel it was my fault. Made me beat myself up for not saying anything. And then you come here now, accusing me of the same thing. That's not something you can *imagine* out of existence. You don't get to have me now your Plan A failed – and, worse than that, trying to pin the blame for your mistakes on me. That's not love, Matt.'

'Then let me show you what love is. Let me get it right.'

'I don't think I can.'

'Think about it, please? I don't know how to make things better between us, Es. But I'll do anything. We've wasted so much time. Made so many mistakes. I'm not doing it again. This is the right thing for me – I want to love you, the way I always should have.'

I could reach out now, only a little way, and touch his face. I'm horrified by the urge to do it, digging my nails deep into my palms to stop it happening. Matt stares at me for a long time as the garden office surrenders to stillness. I'm aware of our breathing, of the barely imperceptible pull between us. Fear rises, but with it something else: something deeper, something hidden for too long. I don't want to acknowledge it, but what if it's real?

Just as I think he's about to close the gap between us, Matt pulls back. 'I mean it, Es; I'm not giving up on this. But I won't push you. I think you know what's happening here. It's your call now.' He looks back to the house. 'I'll apologise to Naomi. And I'm sorry I chucked all this at you. Just think about it, okay?'

'I won't change my mind.' My voice isn't convinced.

'Maybe.' He turns, opens the door and walks out.

I just stand there, watching him stride back to the house. He's taller again, the dancing shadows of clouds passing across the sun seeming to follow in his wake.

I bury my head in my hands and block him from view.

Thirty-Two

ARCHIE

'I've been in talks with the board this morning. And I am happy to confirm we would like to formally offer you a writing position at *The Herald*.'

Jock Callaghan is not a man for whom smiling comes naturally. I *think* that's a smile he's wearing now, although, as Mum often says, *it could just be wind* . . .

'A junior reporter?'

'A full reporter. With the commensurate salary and benefits, of course. With Brian retiring soon we need new blood to keep this team strong. You've more than proved your chops for a great story.'

I eye my boss. This all seems too good to be true. And I've always proved I have writer 'chops', whatever they are. If he'd bothered to look at the work I've done all the time I've been running around like a blue-arsed fly doing crap jobs for him, he would have seen it.

But I'm flattered. I'd be daft not to be. It's what I wanted: recognition, the chance to write without begging for column inches. The extra money would come in useful, too, although there's a good chance of a steady supply of freelance work from Greg at NewsCal, judging by the glowing emails he's still sending me.

It means I'd be working with Jessie, too. Right now, that's the most attractive benefit of Callaghan's offer. He, like everyone else in the newsroom, is well aware that we're together, largely because Jessie is a firm fan of *very* public displays of affection, especially when our boss is in the room. Her hand rests on my shoulder when we're talking to Liam and Elvis; her fingers find mine as we stand in the coffee queue; stolen kisses when we're in the lift; countless tiny touches when she's laughing with me.

I'm not complaining. Honestly, I'm not. It's just a lot to take in.

Jock Callaghan leans back in his chair, a smug look of satisfaction on his face. I should press my advantage, make him sweat a little, but isn't this what I wanted from the start?

I remember reading an interview with a novelist years ago whose eighth novel became an instant, overnight success. Number one bestsellers on both sides of the Atlantic, film deals, mega-sales, the whole nine yards. They had been at the point of giving up, mid-listed and then dropped by their publisher, the book that made it written in a last-ditch attempt to prove what they could do. But I remember being struck by how weary they sounded, as if all of the success they'd longed for wasn't quite what they'd imagined it to be.

That's what this feels like.

And it *shouldn't*. I should be the happiest sod in the city because I got exactly what I wanted: Jessie; a reporter's job; recognition for my words – everything. I need to have a long, frank chat with myself.

Esther would tell me to get on with it. She'd be right, too.

I need her to tell me I'm being an idiot.

I need to talk to her.

But she isn't answering her phone.

I knew things would change for us if Jessie said yes. I wasn't so self-obsessed to think we could carry on exactly the same as before. But I miss that. With our objective achieved, the momentum is gone: that thrill of working together to make something happen, every conversation a step closer to the goal. I knew we'd need to find new things to talk about, but I just miss talking with her. Hanging out. Twitting each other on and talking utter bollocks because it didn't matter whether we were serious or not, it was the communication that meant the most.

I hope she's okay.

I've been monumentally selfish the past few days, too caught up in the surprise of Jessie Edmonds wanting to be with me and the bright flash of career possibilities to text Esther as much as I have before. Tomorrow we're due at the community hall for The Old Guys' practice and I can't wait to see her. But something about her radio silence feels off. I want to talk to her before we go to the rehearsal.

I just need her to answer her phone.

My boss clears his throat, the edges of his alien smile straining a little now. 'So? What do you say, Archie? Want to be part of the next great age of this paper?'

'Can I think about it?' I surprise myself with my answer.

Callaghan's piggy eyes widen as far as they're able. 'Well, of course, it's a big step, I understand.' He gives a nervous laugh. 'Just – uh – don't take too long, eh?' I almost expect him to add, *you little scamp* and wag his finger at me.

254

We've reached unimaginable levels of weirdness now.

'Thanks. I'll get back to you as soon as I can.'

Walking out of his office feels like a victory lap.

'Well?' Jessie is at my side the moment Callaghan's door swings shut, Liam and Elvis heading over, too.

'He's offered me a reporter's job.'

'Oh, Arch, that's amazing!' Jessie kisses me and I lean into it, feeling the back slaps of my colleagues as they groan about having to witness another kiss.

'Put the lad down, Jess. You don't know where he's been.'

'We'll have to separate your desks, or else you'll never write a word.'

'Okay, okay.' I grin when Jessie releases me.

'So you've accepted?'

'I've said I'll think about it.'

Jessie's mouth drops open. 'But it's the job you've wanted for ages.'

'It is but there are other options I want to pursue first.'

Elvis chuckles. 'I'll bet the boss were chuffed with that.'

I grin back. 'His eye started twitching when I said it.'

Liam and Elvis roar with laughter. But when I turn to Jessie, she isn't smiling. 'You should say yes straight away. You know what Callaghan's like. He might change his mind. He does when you least expect it.'

It jars my good humour a little. I know she's right, but this is my decision. 'If he does then he was never serious about having me in the first place.'

'Give him a break, Jessie.'

'I am, I just think he shouldn't miss an opportunity.'

I take her hand. 'I'll be fine. I have a couple of phone chats lined up for later today and then I'll be able to give Callaghan my answer.'

'Don't keep him waiting. You deserve this chance, Arch.' Her hand slips from mine as she walks back to her desk.

Liam slinks away, too, leaving Elvis and me by the coffee station.

'Trouble in paradise?' he asks, handing me a mug of coffee.

'Creative differences,' I say, my heart dropping a little.

'Perils of dating on the job.' He sips his coffee and lowers his voice. 'What happened to the other one?'

'What other one?'

'Your co-conspirator on *Project Love Letter*.'

'She's very happy for us.'

'Oh, aye?' Elvis nods over his mug. 'Not returning your calls, then?'

How does he know that? 'I'm seeing her tomorrow.'

'That's not the point though, is it? By the way, if you ask me, which you haven't, well played on the job front. Make him sweat, even if you know you're going to take it. Callaghan won't like it one bit, but he'll respect you more for it, in the end.'

'Thank you.'

'And – about the other issue – give the lass time. She's a sweetheart. Could tell the moment I met her when we broke the story. Esther seemed like a keeper to me.'

I watch him as he walks slowly back to his desk, completely aware of the bomb he just dropped.

After work – and giving Jessie my apologies that I won't see her till Sunday – I head to the one place I know I'll find some common sense.

Mum is grinning in the doorway to Quinn & Co before I reach it, ushering me in with flour-dusted hands. Within five minutes I'm plonked in an armchair upstairs with a mug of tea and a plate of warm sausage rolls as Mum rearranges the sofa cushions and fusses around me.

Dad winks at me from his armchair. 'Thank goodness you turned up. Your mother's been worrying herself sick about your shiny new media career.'

'I have not, Doug Quinn, you take that back!' She scowls at my dad and ruffles my hair like I'm four years old. 'I just wanted to make sure you're still enjoying it, that's all. And that you're resting enough. And eating . . .'

'Don't ever change, Mum,' I say, as Dad snorts into his tea.

I need this today. Still no word from Esther and I've reached the point where I can't leave any more messages unless I want her thinking I'm a manic stalker.

Mum and Dad's reaction to the news about Jessie was as warm and supportive as I'd hoped, but when I tell them about Callaghan's job offer, it's a different story.

'I hope you told him you'd think about it.'

'I did, Dad.'

'That's my boy! See, Kathy? I told you our Arch has his head screwed on proper. Give yourself time, work out if it's what you still want.'

'Jock Callaghan doesn't deserve any consideration,' Mum huffs amid the cushion garrison on the sofa. 'That man's done nothing but put you down and squash your career for three years. And now the world knows what you can do, he suddenly sees your worth? *Pfft*. Find a proper news company to bless and kick him to the kerb, I say.'

'How do know that phrase?'

'She's been watching *Below Deck* again,' Dad tells me, with a cheeky grin. 'Reality TV is catnip to your ma.'

Mum shakes her head but her smile gives her away. 'I love the drama, what can I tell you?'

'They should make a show about this place,' I say, smiling. '*The Quinn Family Bakery*.'

'Nobody'd believe it,' Mum says. 'You know Mrs Hawkins from the estate's only gone and got herself a toy boy? Total scandal about it in the shop today. She retired last February; he's the lad who delivered her supermarket shopping every week. They eloped to Gretna Green last weekend, never told a soul.'

'Bloody impressive customer service, that.' Dad chuckles, rising from his chair. 'I need to check on the oven. That's an ongoing drama only I'm interested in. Back in a mo.'

Mum waits until he's gone before shuffling across the sofa so she's closer to me. 'So, what brought you here today? Besides the job thing. And the Jessie thing?'

There's no point in hiding anything from her. I'm clear glass where Mum's concerned.

'Esther's gone quiet.'

Her eyes soften. 'Ah, I wondered if she might.'

'It's more than just awkwardness. I feel like something's wrong, you know? Beyond stuff with us. Do you think you can sense when things are happening for someone you care about?'

'Well, I knew we'd be getting a visit from you today.' She reaches across and squeezes my shoulder. 'You've a heart that notices, Archie. Quinn family trait, I'm afraid.'

'I'm worried about her.'

She acknowledges this with a nod. 'And you miss her.'

I can't answer that. She smiles like I did anyway.

'Call her. Tonight, after her shift. In my experience the tough stuff feels harder the closer to midnight you get.'

Another one to add to the million reasons why my mum is *magic* . . .

I wait until 11.15 p.m. before I call, my heart in my mouth as I hear each unanswered ring. At least it's ringing this time. Every other attempt has gone straight to voicemail. That has to be a good thing, right?

'Hi, you.'

The sudden arrival of her voice makes me sit bolt upright on my sofa. 'Hello. I've been worried about you.'

'I know, I'm sorry. You send a *lot* of texts when you're worried.'

Too many, obviously. I could kick myself for not considering that. 'I wasn't stalking you.'

'I know you weren't.' Her laugh is a weary one but magnificent to hear. I thought she might be mad at me. I couldn't bear that. 'I've had to deal with some – *stuff*.'

'Bad stuff?' Was my gut right, like Mum said earlier?

There's a definite pause before she replies. 'I don't know. I really need to talk about it and I know you have loads going on, but—'

'Yes,' I rush, aware I'm gripping my phone. 'Tell me.'

'Not on the phone. Can we meet tomorrow, before The Old Guys' practice?'

'Of course. How about a walk in Heaton Park?'

'Perfect.' Her breath is shaky on the other end of the call, as if she's finally releasing it after hours of keeping it held. 'I miss you, Arch. Our chats. It hasn't been the same since . . . '

'I know, I'm sorry. I miss our chats, too. Hang tight, Es. Whatever it is, we'll sort it.'

When the call ends, I stand and walk to the window. Manchester is still this evening, the road beyond my apartment quiet and the large horse chestnut tree outside unmoved by any breeze. I don't know what I'll find when I see Esther tomorrow, but I'm going to be there for her.

Everything else can wait.

Thirty-Three

ESTHER

I love this park. I haven't visited Heaton for a while, but now I'm here I feel like I'm in the company of a long-lost friend.

And waiting to meet another one.

Archie jogs over to meet me as soon as he's parked, his smile masking concern. We meet at the edge of the car park, just as the summer sun breaks through stubborn slate clouds that have loomed over the city since I woke this morning. It's just gone half past eight, giving us plenty of time to talk, although I'm still not sure how to put into words the cacophony of competing thoughts Matt left me with. I just know if anyone can help me unpick them, it's this man.

I've missed him so much. It's only been a matter of days since we delivered Jessie's letter but this strangeness between us is alien, unwelcome. It feels like it's been forever since we were last *us*.

I don't even wait for the inevitable awkward dance when he reaches me, going straight in for a hug. The rush of breath from his surprised laugh grazes the top of my head as he hugs me back.

'I'm so glad you hugged me,' he says.

'Me too.'

In this, at least, we are equal.

'What's going on, Es?'

I pull back and look up at him. 'Not here. Let's walk a bit.'

We follow the path through stunning parkland, the sun burnishing the tops of ancient trees and gilding the swathes of summer green grass. I can breathe here for what feels like the first time in days. A large part of that is the man walking beside me. I love that he's here, that he didn't hesitate to make time for me when I asked.

I've missed that, too. Being there for each other, never more than a call away. I watched his texts arrive yesterday, not knowing how to answer any of them. How could I when I couldn't find words for myself? This is a million times better. I don't have to try and read between the lines or work out what Archie's thinking. For the next couple of hours, it's just Esther and Archie, the same as we ever were.

'Are you going where I think?' Archie grins. It's the first time we've spoken, the easy silence we've walked in enough until now.

'Depends. Where would you be heading?'

'The Temple?'

'Then you're right.'

The path begins to climb and we puff our way up until the trees clear and the Heaton Park Temple magnificently appears ahead. In the early morning sun its curved white stucco walls glow, the elegant rotunda framed by stone columns, its domed roof rising into the breaking clouds. The first time I saw this building as a kid I fell in love with it. It was an observatory once and people still come to stargaze from its high vantage point over the city. Walking up to it feels like an adventure. Today, it feels like a pilgrimage.

There are three benches in front of a grand stone balustrade that surrounds the Temple, all of them thankfully empty at this hour. We head for the middle one and sit down.

'Looking good, Manchester,' Archie breathes, gazing out across the endless green of the park to the glittering buildings of the city just visible on the horizon.

'She'll do,' I say, my dad's favourite phrase strangely comforting when I speak it.

'My dad says that.'

I turn to him. 'Mine too.'

His eyes drift back to the view. 'Hard not to love her, really.'

My stomach flips. I follow the lines of sun where they break between the trees. 'I love this place. It's been too long since I . . .'

'Tell me what's happened.'

He doesn't look at me when he says it, but his gentle smile at the city eases the tension.

'Matt's left Nina.'

'*Shit* . . .'

'He came to my sister's house yesterday, demanding to see me and that's when he dropped the bombshell.'

'Was your sister in?'

'And the kids. Lucky for Matt my brother-in-law wasn't at home – Gavin was vicious about it when we told him.'

'I bet your sister wasn't best pleased, either.'

I nod, remembering Naomi's disgust when I told her everything Matt had said. She'd just about calmed down when Gavin came home and his fury over it set her off again.

'Barging his way into the house – *our* house – like he bloody owned the place? The nerve! I've half a mind to barge over to his, knock some sense into the bastard.'

'I'll come with you,' my sister had snapped, reaching for her handbag.

'You're not going over there,' I'd said, using what little power I still possessed. 'Please. Let him be.'

My brother-in-law had relented, eyes wide with indignation. 'This is your safe place, Es. You should feel safe here. I'll not have anyone think they can threaten that.'

I hate that it happened in their house and I know they don't blame me for it. But their anger on my behalf was touching, in a shouty way.

'So how long did they last? Matt and his ex?' Archie asks now.

'Not even six months.' It hits me again: that waste – of time, of money, of worrying about stuff that never even existed . . .

'Love of his life then.' When I don't reply he glances at me, his face falling. 'I didn't mean . . . '

'You're right: she wasn't.' I stare across the park. 'I am, apparently.'

'What?'

'He said it was my fault his marriage failed. That he only married Nina to try to get me to admit that I was in love with him.'

His mouth drops open.

'Yeah, I know.'

'What kind of screwed-up logic is that? And what were you supposed to do, feel guilty because he couldn't stay married?'

At that moment, I love Archie more than I ever have. Indignation flushes his face, the words I so needed to hear flooding out of him as he processes it all. Indignation on my behalf, saying everything I've felt since Matt's visit but have been unable to express.

'What an utter, utter bastard thing to do! Who drops that on someone they say they love? Who thinks that's a declaration you'd ever consider? I've never met the man but I'd like to kick him right down that hill . . . '

'I'm so glad you said that.' I smile. But, as he turns to me, the enormity of the mess crashes down on my shoulders. It's too much: tears arrive before I can stop them.

'Oh, Es,' he says, reaching for me.

I fold into the warm, soothing strength of his embrace.

'I don't know what to do,' I sob against him.

'You should have called me.'

'I couldn't . . . '

He doesn't reply.

We stay there for a long time, my breathing slowing to fall in time with his. When my tears have gone, I lift my head and rest it against his shoulder. Archie's arm remains around me as we gaze out at the dew-soaked park and the waking city beyond.

There are things we need to say, hovering like uncertain spirits around our bench. But they can wait.

I don't know how long we stay there, watching the park slowly coming to life, the clouds dancing across the wide expanse of sky, the comforting shadow of the Temple at our backs. I listen to the birds and distant rumble of planes arcing across the city, hear the whirr of bicycle wheels down on the main path and the staccato stabs of voices. I hear the soft rhythm of Archie's breathing, the steady beat of my heart; feel the gentle kiss of sunlight on my skin and the strong, certain warmth of his arm around my shoulder.

There are moments in life I wish I could capture forever – scoop everything inside a bottle and keep it close to my heart. I don't know what lies ahead for us, but this moment is one I know I'll want to return to when the clamour and confusion of life get too much. I know it can't last. But I'm so glad I'm here, now, in this place. With Archie.

He shifts a little beside me. I lift my head and sit back, aware of his arm still protecting me along the back of the bench. 'So he wants you now?'

It's heavy, weighted with so much meaning I don't want to decipher. 'He says he's always loved me.'

'Is that enough?'

'I don't know.'

'What do you want, Es? Because I think that's all that's important here.'

'I loved him for a long time.'

Archie's head drops a little. I see him rub a finger along the line of his jaw. 'Do you love him now?'

'He lied to me. To everyone. If he really was waiting for me to say something, why use Nina as a threat to get me to say it? I mean, who does that, Arch?'

He meets my gaze. My heart crashes to the gravel path at my feet. I look away.

'Could you forgive him? For all of that? If you love him, Es, is that enough to forget the rest?'

That's the problem: my head knows it's not enough – will never be enough to make the last year and the revelation of his real motives disappear. But my heart?

'I keep thinking what might have happened if he'd just been honest with me from the beginning. We might be together now.'

'You can't know that, though. He had every chance to tell you he loved you but he didn't. You have to ask yourself why that was.'

'He was scared.'

'He was a bastard. And he doesn't deserve you.'

I sit up and stare at him, surprised by the venom in his words and the tension in his jaw. 'Probably not. But what if we started again?'

'He made you believe you weren't enough for him. And then, when the pack of lies he'd told came tumbling down around his ears, he said it was your fault. That's not love, Es. That's kicking someone twice to boost his ego.'

I know he's right, but something about his tone irks me. 'So what *is* love, Archie?'

'What?'

'We've spent weeks researching it, all those stories we collected, all those people happy now because they trusted love and found it. So what's the secret? What makes it real and not a sham? What makes it work and not break you? Because, to me, love just seems to be a load of pain you either inflict on yourself or someone else . . . '

I stop myself, far too late. I clamp my hands to my eyes and give a groan of frustration. 'I'm a mess. Scratch what I said, okay? It's my crap, not yours.'

'You can say that stuff to me. I'm here because I want to hear it.' His reassurance is tentative, as if he's not sure the words will help.

'I'm sorry.'

'Don't be.'

'So, how's stuff with Jessie?' I ask – and the ridiculousness of that segue after my rant about love tips the tension. We burst

267

out laughing, startling a scavenging wood pigeon that abandons a large piece of bread crust by our bench and flaps out across the green hill.

'She wasn't impressed at me not seeing her today,' Archie says, adding quickly, 'and no, before you ask, that isn't because I said I'd meet you. Saturdays are sacrosanct. I have a prior date with The Old Guys – *and* you.'

I flop back against the bench. 'Can we go back to the fun stuff, please? I liked it better when we were old Mrs Stanhope and the Post-it King.'

'Me too.' His eyes twinkle. 'Actually, there's a great place we can start.'

'Where?'

'Stand up.'

'Why?'

'Don't look so suspicious! I'm not going to roll you down the hill or anything. Stand up.'

I do as he says. 'Now what?'

He grins. 'Turn around.'

'Which way?'

He grabs hold of my shoulders and pivots me to face the Temple. 'That way.'

I blink at the gorgeous building. 'Am I meant to be doing something here?'

'Look down.' When I frown, he pats the bench. 'We haven't said hello to the bench name. Auntie Sue would be disappointed in us.'

'I see.' Giggling, I look at the dull brass plaque screwed to the backrest of the bench. '*In loving memory of Ethel and Jeff Bincham, who loved it here.* Aw, hi, Ethel and Jeff.'

'They sound awesome.' Archie leans in and traces his finger over the line beneath the dedication. *'Always and forever, no matter what.'* He glances at me. 'That's us, that is.'

'Eth and Jeff?'

'No, this bit – *always and forever, no matter what*. That's us. Doesn't matter what else happens, or who else comes into our lives, this is what I want us to be. No matter what.'

I love it. I love it so much. But he can't promise me that. Life threw us together and it could just as quickly break us apart. 'Archie, I don't think you can say that . . . '

'I can if we make a pact now: no matter what, Es, I am here for you. It might have been a coincidence we met, but this kind of friendship doesn't come along often. We found the words for the letter together: this is a lifelong thing.' He holds out his hand. 'What do you say? Shall we agree on it?'

I stare down at his outstretched hand. This isn't just a gesture: there's a world of meaning if our hands join now. But the last days without him have been lonelier than the year I pined for Matt. If he's serious, this means Archie Quinn will be in my life for as long as I want him.

Heart thumping wildly, I place my hand in his.

'Always and forever?'

He smiles, his thumb stroking my palm. 'No matter what.'

Thirty-Four

ARCHIE

Esther Hughes is a force of nature. But she has no idea – like a hurricane that's completely unaware of its power.

I watch her laughing with Kavi and Isaac as they try to show her chords on the bright-orange ukulele. Kavi is strumming the shape on his guitar while Isaac crouches in front, moving Esther's fingers to the correct places on the fretboard.

If anyone deserves to be happy, she does.

But what if that happiness is Matt Hope?

I think he's a lowlife for what he did to her, but ever since we talked by the Heaton Park Temple this morning, my conscience has had an itch. I wanted to defend her because she's wonderful, but is it fair to tell her to walk away from the man she loved for so long, when it turns out he loves her, too? I have Jessie – largely down to Esther believing in my right to happiness. Can I deny her the same?

And am I mad at Matt because he has Esther's heart when he doesn't deserve it?

'Must be crowded in there.'

Granda Brady nudges his shoulder against mine, handing me a mug of tea.

'In where?'

'That head of yours. Like Manchester Piccadilly at rush hour.'

'I was just thinking.'

He sucks air in between his teeth. '*Ach*, you don't want to be doing that, son. Dangerous pastime. Drink your tay and wait for the impulse to leave.'

I laugh and do as I'm told. 'It's not working.'

'Drink more. Add a dram or two. After a few of those, you'll forget how to think at all.'

'I'll bear that in mind.' I steal a look at him and decide it's worth asking. 'Granda, have you ever had to let someone make a choice you didn't agree with?'

His surprise makes the brim of his hat rise. '*Let* someone make a choice? Who died and made you the Almighty?'

'I don't mean like that. I meant . . .'

Granda blows on his tea. 'You mean watch them make a choice you disagree with? Plenty of times. But if you care about them, you care about their right to make those choices *despite* you.' He takes a thoughtful sip and I feel the same stillness around him as when he folds napkins. I wait for the ritual to be complete because I know a pearl lies at the end. 'This will be Esther, I suppose?'

'*Shh*!'

'I'll take that *shush* as a yes. And the decision is, what?'

'Whether she should be with someone who isn't worthy of her.' I catch his stare and grudgingly add, 'In my opinion.'

'But you've got your Jessie.'

'I have.'

'So what business is it of yours who Esther has?'

My head bows. 'None.'

'Exactly.'

'But she asked my opinion . . .'

'And I suppose you gave it?' He shakes his head. 'You can't keep her for yourself when you didn't choose her. You know what being lonely is, Archie, and it's a great steaming bag of shite. So why would you make someone that special carry it instead?'

Sometimes I think my granda has a sharpening tool he keeps just for words.

'Right, you load of layabouts, to your chairs please,' Big Jim bellows, holding up an apologetic hand to Esther, 'and Miss Esther, if you'd like to sit down, too.'

'You smooth-talker, Jim,' Li'l Bill chuckles.

We're settling into our seats, Esther marking out the chords Kavi and Isaac just showed her and Granda Brady watching us like an Irish golden eagle eyeing up its dinner, when Marta appears.

'Before you begin, I have an announcement.'

'Someone's making an honest woman of you at last!' Eric calls out, causing laughter to ring around the hall.

Marta raises an eyebrow. 'They tried and failed, Eric. Are you offering?' Wolf whistles meet her sly grin. She holds up a hand for quiet. 'I've just arranged your first gig!'

That silences the room.

Undeterred, she presses on. 'It's a fundraiser, to help us keep this place afloat.'

'Would we make more money asking folks to pay us *not* to play?' Granda asks, the others agreeing.

'You've been rehearsing for years. You can do this and do it well. Besides, we have a sponsor.'

'Who?'

Marta beams. 'Pennine Landscapes. Josh there says he'll match whatever we raise pound-for-pound. It could make a real difference.'

That's a huge step forward for us. This building is great but it needs so much doing to it. We've saved it from being sold to developers three times, the council eventually leasing it to us with a peppercorn rent on the understanding we fundraise to cover repairs. With a business on board, we could get some real work done. There's a hum of approval around the circle and then Big Jim, ever the realist, raises his hand.

'When is the gig?'

Marta's smile flickers just for a moment. I sense the atmosphere around me do the same, as if the power supply to our enthusiasm has a dodgy connection. 'In three weeks.'

'*Three weeks*? And you only thought to tell us now?'

'Jim, it will be fine. I hear you rehearsing every week and you've come on great guns lately.'

'In this room, maybe, with only us listening,' Old Bob retorts. Isaac and Li'l Bill nod vehemently either side of him.

'An audience is a very different proposition,' Kavi agrees, glancing at Eric for support. 'Right now, if we hit a bum note, or fall over a section, we can stop and laugh about it. You can't do that with people watching.'

'Especially if they've paid,' Eric adds, ducking a little behind his guitar. 'You don't want to go upsetting folk, especially not people round here. There'd be a stampede for refunds.'

'I think you're all panicking for nothing.' Marta has to raise her voice over the dissent, her own expression far from confident now. 'Brady, back me up here?'

As one we turn to my granda, who has fallen uncharacteristically quiet during this discussion. He nods to his audience, clearly milking the stage he's been given. Saint-like, he raises a sun-weathered hand and the room hushes in reply.

'There's an old saying where I come from,' he begins. I glance at Esther and see she's already biting her lip to stall laughter. '"Music without an audience is like a body without a soul." You can't truly appreciate the magic of melody unless it's shared.'

He nods again and I watch my fellow players letting it sink in. His 'old saying' is about as authentically Irish as Tommy Steele's accent in *Finian's Rainbow*, but Granda is unlikely to worry about minor details like that.

'Well said,' Marta breathes, surprised by the effect Granda Brady's words have had on the room. 'So how about we—'

'Failing that,' Granda interrupts, 'hire in a bar. If you get the punters blathered they won't give a stuff about the quality of the music.'

Laughter breaks out around us and Marta raises her eyes to heaven as any control she had over The Old Guys spirals gloriously out of her reach. Esther laughs too, but then I see her look over at Marta, her smile fading. Slowly, she lifts her hand.

'The lovely Miss Hughes desires the floor,' Granda announces and order is temporarily restored.

'I think it's a great idea. And three weeks is plenty of time to get ready, if we all practice at home, too.' All eyes are on her now, mine included. She has that unmistakable fire about the way she speaks that makes every word seem not only reasonable but also exciting.

'You're being very kind to us . . .'

'No, I'm not, Kavi. I think this place is wonderful. I'm so chuffed to be part of this group. Imagine how much better it would be if we had a proper water heater, or a fridge that didn't freeze the milk the minute you put the bottle in it. Imagine if we didn't have to spend half an hour on rainy days placing buckets under the roof leaks before any of us could play anything. One gig is worth all that. And so what if we hit bum notes? Let's get the audience in on the joke. Make them feel part of things, part of the magic, like you've made me feel.'

I know I'm staring, just like everyone else, but I can't help it: Esther Hughes is bloody marvellous. She's inspiring and positive and – beautiful.

Beautiful? That wasn't the word I expected to arrive.

Watching her, I suddenly realise Granda's right: I can't hold onto her, keep her from finding happiness where her heart lies. She deserves to be seen and loved and appreciated for the wonder she is.

And that starts with me.

After the meeting, with every member of The Old Guys now signed up to the fundraising gig, I wait until she's said goodbye to everyone before catching her elbow and leading her to the side of the community hall.

'You were awesome.'

'Thanks. It means you're stuck with me, though, for the next three weeks at least.' Her smile is so lovely . . . 'Big Jim and your grandad said I have to play, no matter what. Let's hope the audience are as forgiving as I told everyone they would be, eh?'

'Here's hoping.' I steel myself for what has to be said next. 'Es, what I said this morning – about Matt – no, hear me out – you shouldn't listen to me. I'm always going to be a . . . whatever the male friend equivalent of a mama bear is.'

She observes me wryly. 'Maybe I like you being protective.'

'I always will be, no fear of that. But if you love him . . . '

She stares at the floor where her orange sneakers shuffle across the scuffed lino. 'It doesn't matter what I—'

'If you *love him*, Es, go for it.'

She blinks up at me.

'You're amazing and you deserve to be happy. If Matt can do that, let him. Make him work bloody hard to prove himself, though: don't make it easy. But don't be afraid of letting him in.'

As I'm driving home, the weight of it all finally hits. Will Esther follow my advice? It's none of my business now. What I do know is that I did the right thing. Now I have to let Es do hers. Whatever that is.

I have to look to my own life and there's somebody I've been neglecting.

Jessie is a vision when she opens her door, her blonde hair damp and tousled from the shower. 'Well, aren't you a sight for sore eyes, Archie Quinn.'

'I missed you,' I say, smiling as I gather her in my arms.

'And you're not going to go running off again?'

'No way.' I push all thoughts of Esther from my mind as Jessie's arms curl around my neck. 'I'm all yours.'

Thirty-Five

ESTHER

I left the house early this morning, before Naomi, Gavin or any of the girls were awake. I needed to walk, to think.

The whole city is cloaked in a shroud of pale mist, transforming all it touches into shadowy ethereal phantoms. It isn't raining but heavy dew covers the ground. The air is still and cool, the promise of future heat present behind the veil of white.

I didn't sleep well last night. My eyes carry the heaviness of too much thinking and too little sleep, my body weary and restless at the same time. The strong coffee I bought from the tiny takeaway hut at the entrance of the park is helping a little. It warms my fingers where I hold the cup, the rising curls of steam kissing my skin where I hold it close to my lips.

Am I doing the right thing?

I still don't know.

Twenty-four hours ago, I thought I had everything sorted. Thought I knew what I wanted and what was going to make me happy. Yesterday at the Heaton Park Temple with Archie, I thought I'd made up my mind. Today, everything could change.

Archie's parting shot after The Old Guys' rehearsal surprised me. I pretty much assumed he'd nailed his colours to the mast yesterday morning. It took some time to get my head around it, but now I think I understand. This isn't about the past. It's about making something new.

I've been so hurt and confused by everything that happened during the past year – and then, when I met Archie, the waters muddied again. I care about him and I think, for a while, I wondered if we might become more. But did I fall for him or the man I saw willing to go to any lengths to win the woman he loved?

The more I've considered it, the more I'm persuaded: I wanted someone to be that committed to loving me. And yes, Archie Quinn is gorgeous and the moment we kissed still refuses to be explained as easily as the rest, but it was his heart and his passion I fell for. The letter I found that started it all was one I longed to receive.

I wanted someone to say he loved me.

On Friday, someone did. But I was too tangled in hurt and anger to realise.

I'm the only soul I can see as I make my way slowly around the small lake, watching the sweep of weeping willow branches emerging from the mist. The air around me is a breath held, the sounds of the park eerily deadened. I can't hear birds singing, or the gentle lapping of the lake against its muddy banks, but I'm unusually aware of my own breathing. I can't yet see where I'm headed. Instead, I follow my instincts and walk on.

I know this small park so well I could walk around it in complete darkness. So much of my life has played out here. It made sense to come here now, on the cusp of another chapter beginning.

Bransholme Rec isn't as grand as Heaton Park. The single

building it boasts is no temple: instead, a simple, green-painted corrugated steel park-keepers' hut peppered with bits of graffiti, including the legendary Ralph's Surf Shack, daubed in white paint on its side decades ago in honour of the late council groundsman and now a local landmark in its own right.

I reach my destination – a black iron bench encircling an old copper beech tree, facing the lake. Its iron is rusted, bent and a little rickety in places, but to everyone who grew up around here, it's sacred ground. The Beech Bench must feature in so many personal histories. I reckon it could spin a yarn or two about us all.

I sit down and imagine the curve of the lake where this morning it's hidden. My memories fill in the blanks. When the mist clears later, this place will buzz with life. The certainty of that gives me hope. Anything is possible in the hours that lie ahead.

I drink coffee and watch puffs of steam and breath meld with the mist. I'm calmer than I expected. Bransholme's stillness is helping.

Behind me the crunch of gravel sounds. I turn to see a figure moving through the mist towards me, a smudge of shadow to begin with – broad-shouldered and tall – the shape of a man becoming more defined the closer he gets. As he pushes through the mist, my heart jumps a little.

'Morning,' Matt says.

'Hey.'

'Mind if I sit?'

There's a scrabble of paws and I look down to see a bundle of shaggy grey fur skirt the edge of Matt's long coat, tail wagging wildly.

'Who's this?' I ask, my hand receiving a brisk lick when I greet the dog.

'Picard,' Matt replies, wincing a little. 'I know, lame name.'

'*Great* name,' I return, for a moment forgetting why I'm here and who is now sitting beside me, inches away. 'Who wouldn't want a Starfleet commander for a companion?'

We trade unsteady smiles.

'I didn't know whether to bring coffee,' he says, nodding at my cup. 'I didn't reckon I'd have much left in the cups by the time I arrived, the way this one pulls on his lead.'

'How long have you had him?'

'Six months. I bought him as gift for Nina when it was already too late.' The mention of his ex causes his eyes to drift to the wall of white where the lake should be. 'So Nina moved out and Picard moved in.'

'I was surprised – that time I saw you. I didn't figure you for a dog person.'

'I wasn't.' He laughs, firing a cloud of breath into the mist. 'Not sure I am now. But he's a good lad.'

Picard flops to Matt's feet and harrumphs into the dew-soaked grass. The smile Matt gives him betrays his true feelings.

No change there, I think, kicking myself for letting that one sneak in. I shift a little on the bench and drain the last of my coffee. Matt catches my movement and I feel his eyes on me.

'Thanks for seeing me, Es.'

'Thanks for coming.'

'I wasn't sure I'd hear from you. After last time, I mean. I'm sorry for the way that happened. Barging in, calling the shots. That wasn't how I'd planned it.'

I'm not about to let him off the hook for that but I have to let it go for now. 'What you said, about me, did you mean it?'

I dare to look at him. His expression says it all.

'I have loved you for a long time. But I should have told you.'

'Yes, you should. And you can't hold me responsible for your marriage . . .'

'I know. I'm sorry.' He pinches the bridge of his nose, eyes closed. 'I just – seeing you again, it all made sense. I think I held back all those years because I believed you should want to tell me how you felt. When you didn't it turned into a battle of wills.'

Picard stirs at Matt's feet, soothed when he ruffles the fur at the back of the dog's neck. I follow the movement, remembering so many stolen glances at those hands.

'It's such a mess,' I say, catching him watching me and forcing my eyes back to the mist-shrouded lake. 'You really hurt me.'

'I didn't know what to say.'

'That wasn't a reason to stop talking.'

'I know. I know, Es. I didn't trust myself when things got bad with Nina.' He shakes his head. 'I thought I'd end up saying something I'd regret or making a play for you. It was easier to stay silent.'

My heart contracts. 'It wasn't easier for me.'

He doesn't answer that. Instead he faces me, his hand assuming the slim gap between us where we sit. 'I can't stop thinking about you. You're in my head, all the time.'

'Matt, I—'

'I wonder what it would be like to hold you. To kiss you . . .'

'Wait . . .'

He's too close, too soon. I came here because I needed to hear him say this, but suddenly I'm scared. I edge back, but my heart aches with every word he speaks.

'Haven't you ever wondered that, too? What would it feel like? Because I think it would be the greatest thing, Esther. Being yours would be the greatest.'

I look at him and see the truth. For years I imagined how it might look to see Matt's lips forming those words, but now he's saying them it doesn't seem real.

'Why didn't you tell me?'

He retreats a little. 'I was scared. We'd been friends for so long – I couldn't bear to lose that.'

'I stood by you through everything. Even on your wedding day. How were you ever going to lose me?'

He bows his head.

The white stillness of the Rec billows in.

And Archie's words return to me:

If you love him . . .

I'm at the end of a painfully long road, a crossroads ahead. One decision left to make.

If you love him . . .

If I look past all the hurt and recriminations, what remains?

If you love him, Es . . .

'I want to know,' I say.

Matt lifts his head.

. . . don't be afraid to let him in . . .

'I want to know what it feels like.'

And then Matt pulls me to him, kisses I never thought possible falling on my skin like Manchester rain. I give in to them, sinking into his arms, letting go. Around us, everything fades.

You deserve to be happy. If Matt can do that, let him . . .

The memory of Archie's sad smile is the last thing to disappear into the brightening mist . . .

Thirty-Six

ARCHIE

I'm waiting in a bright, sparsely furnished reception in Media-City in Salford, wondering how in the heck I got here. I had no sleep last night; I've drunk too much coffee already and I can't feel my feet.

Esther would tell me to get a grip. I blow out against the stab of pain her name brings. I love that she took my advice – I just wish she hadn't this time. She called me after she got together with Matt. She sounded happy. I didn't hear the hesitation in her voice, I tell myself again. And even if it was there, I shouldn't have heard it. She's following her heart like I told her to. I have to be content with that.

It's only been a few days since she told me but it feels like forever. We're still texting but I'm trying to give her some space as she navigates the new stuff with Matt.

I just wish she could be waiting with me today, telling me not to be daft.

As far as my editor and colleagues at *The Herald* are concerned, this is a mid-morning dentist appointment. Further investigation following the 'X-rays' I had taken last Friday, aka a lengthy chat with Greg from NewsCal, talking about upcoming freelance work for them.

I probably should feel bad about lying to them all, but after years of Callaghan pretending every arse-end task he chucked at me was going to lead to a writing job, I reckon this makes us quits. Elvis has worked it out, though. He sent me a 'good luck at the dentist' text this morning, which is most unlike him. I like that he set the ball rolling on all of this, swiftly bypassing our boss to do it.

This meeting is happening because the casual phone chat I had with the news editor from the ITV newsroom turned into an invitation for coffee and the chance to share my portfolio. Initially I worried my portfolio would consist of a few scratty sheets of A4 paper, but I spent yesterday evening printing out all the pieces I've written in my own time for MyManc and other online publications and I was staggered by how much work I've done under Callaghan's radar. Consequently the folder in my sweaty hands is reassuringly thick.

So what is there to worry about? the Esther in my head says. *Stop being a dingbat and enjoy this, Archie.*

I miss her. I'll see her at rehearsal on Saturday, of course, but that feels like an age away.

My phone buzzes in my jacket pocket. I risk putting my precious portfolio down for a moment to check the message, trying not to notice the damp outline from my hand that beads its plastic surface when I rest it on the coffee table in front of me.

How's it going? Hope they give you a sticker for being a brave boy ☺ I'll give you something later, too . . . J xxx

I should have told Jessie where I was coming this morning.

The three kisses at the end of her text are like face-slaps to my conscience.

I would have told her, probably, if she hadn't given me a lecture in bed yesterday evening about protecting my career at *The Herald*. I hadn't mentioned it – we'd been more than sufficiently occupied by other things instead – but as soon as I went to get us coffee, she launched into her piece.

'I'm not saying *The Herald* is the only place you could work, Arch, it's just that us being there together, chasing stories together, would be so good. I've a ton more experience than you; you're fresh and new and not bound by any of the conventions of the rest of us. Together we could be a power couple in local news media.'

She could have a point. Only when she said it like that, it sounded more like one of Callaghan's emptily vague promises than a thrilling opportunity. It's a vision for my future that doesn't feel like mine.

I'm probably just overthinking things. In all likelihood this meeting will turn out to be nothing more than a kindness and then I can take Callaghan up on his job offer. I can be in and out today and Jessie will be none the wiser. I just need to try the door for myself.

Give it a go, Arch. Who knows what could happen?

I smile at the spirit-Esther hovering beside me. Stuff it, when I finish here I'm calling her. Or sending a text. Will she be at Matt's now? A ball of tension rolls to the bottom of my stomach. Yeah, a text is probably safest.

'Archie Quinn?'

A tall man in a blue-checked shirt and dark jeans stands by the reception desk, looking out across the space where several people are dotted about. I raise my hand and he smiles, striding across the highly polished cream floor towards me. I shove my phone in my pocket, grab my portfolio file from the table and stand to greet him. I hope I don't look as wild-eyed and sweat-damp as I feel.

Cool and calm, Quinn . . .

'Ranbir Sen, associate news editor.' He shakes my hand and I pray it isn't as clammy as I fear. To his credit, if it is he doesn't react. I wonder how many terrified baby journalists he meets in this place. Now I'm here I'm a fish so far out of water I might as well be flapping about like a dying flounder on MediaCity's high-shine floor.

'Thanks so much for meeting me,' I say.

He dismisses this with a wave of the folded paper in his hand. 'Pleasure's all mine. Awesome work on the Totti story – though it pains me to say it, being a lifelong United fan. I appreciate the pieces you did for us when the story broke – and when Greg mentioned you were looking for opportunities, it seemed too good to miss.' He nods towards the news building. 'Shall we?'

The next half hour passes like a high-speed fever dream. We tour the newsroom, passing desk after desk of journalists in surroundings so state-of-the-art it makes *The Herald* look like a dusty relic in a museum. There are TV studios, radio broadcast studios, production facilities, the possibilities for work here dizzying.

'Have you thought which area you'd like to specialise in?' Ranbir asks as I struggle to take it all in.

'There's so many possibilities,' I reply, sounding like a breathless kid. Dragging some of my dignity back, I manage: 'I wouldn't want to be too prescriptive this early on in my career.'

'Wise. Well, obviously we're not the only news-based providers here, you also have a range of local, national and international concerns across multimedia, multidiscipline areas.' He smiles and I'm instantly at ease. 'Between you and me, I still feel like a ten-year-old in a sweet shop in this place.'

'I can imagine.'

'Great. So, let's head to my office, grab some coffee and have a look at that portfolio of yours, shall we?'

Over an hour later, I emerge from the building. My legs feel shaky but my feet are walking on air.

It's so much better than I'd hoped.

A job offer.

'We're looking for a production journalist to work across our news and current affairs teams where needed,' Ranbir had told me. 'I think you'd be great. You have an eye for a story, your citizen journalism pieces show me you can turn your hand to write about anything, and you've more than proved yourself capable of handling stories at a national level when they happen. It's a good, solid place to broaden your skills and there will be lots of opportunities for career progression.'

It's a little more money than I'm getting at *The Herald*, but the chance to work in that kind of environment is what makes my toes tingle. It starts in three months, so I've time to think it over. But really, do I need to think at all? This is the biggest opportunity I've had in years and might just open more doors for me.

Jessie isn't going to be happy. Maybe I won't mention it, just yet. Ranbir said he needs to know in two weeks' time. That should be enough to find the nerve to tell Jessie and the words to do it, shouldn't it?

I fire off a text to the one person I want to tell.

Hey, Es, guess what? I just got offered a job – ITV! A x

I've barely made it back to my car when my phone rings. I answer the call to a shrill squeal, laughing as I settle back in the driver's seat.

'*Amazing!*'

'Ha ha, thanks.'

'Oh my life, Arch, how did this happen?'

'It was one of the news editors I did bits for with the footballer story. He asked me in for coffee, next thing I know he's offering me a job.'

'I'm so chuffed for you! I hope you said yes.'

I catch sight of my reflection in the rear-view mirror. The Archie Quinn in there looks incredibly sheepish for someone who's just had a career break. 'I'm thinking about it.'

'What's there to think about? Say yes.'

'It's complicated. I need to give notice, make sure *The Herald* has cover before I go, work out if the commute's doable . . . '

' . . . tell your girlfriend,' she adds, making my heart sink.

'That too.' The mirror-Archie glares at me.

'I'm sure she'll be over the moon for you.'

'Yeah, Jessie might not see it that way.'

'Why?'

I know exactly what Esther will say if I go into it, so I sidestep as best I can. 'I'm sure it'll all work out well. Thanks for calling me back.'

'When you send me a text like that? How could I not?'

'I thought you might be – busy.'

'No. Not unless you count tackling the Martins family washing mountain as busy and, believe me, I'll happily drop it for any reason.'

'I meant Matt?'

'Oh.' There's a pause. 'No, he's at work. I'm not seeing him till tomorrow.'

'Right.' I grimace at the mirror. 'So, I'll see you Saturday, then?'

'Just you try and stop me. That's if my fingers don't fall off from practising before then.' I'm about to reply when she continues, 'It's lovely to speak to you.'

'You too.'

'Anyway, I'd better go and fight my way through this washing pile. Congratulations, Arch. Don't you dare throw this chance away.'

After the call ends, I sit in the car for a long time.

She's right, of course, like so many other things. Now I need to figure out how on earth I make this happen . . .

Thirty-Seven

ESTHER

Fred's wheels are really showing off tonight. A double-squeak, almost a perfect half beat apart. As I push him round the office, I can almost make Stevie sing in time with it.

It makes me smile, and I need that.

I had my first row with Matt last night. I wasn't supposed to be seeing him, but he'd called me as soon as I'd finished my cleaning shift, asking if I could go over to his. To be honest, it was late and I was tired, the mammoth laundry pile I'd washed, dried and sorted coupled with a fractious school run drive home where Molly and Ava-May scrapped in the back seat for the whole journey had all but wiped me out. I'd worked on the brochure for Mr Grove, too, using every spare moment I had, plus trying to squeeze in quick bursts of ukulele practice for the gig.

'I'm exhausted,' I'd protested, but Matt had insisted. So I'd gone.

I wish I hadn't now.

I scrub extra-hard at a stubborn run of stains across *The Herald*'s coffee station. Do they heat-weld the beverage to the steel of this thing?

He's called me four times since I got here tonight but I've let voicemail deal with him for now. It'll be apologies, his little-boy-lost voice whimpering down the line. I don't want to hear it tonight, and especially not if he's asking me to go over again.

The row began because I'd told him I couldn't see him on Saturday. We haven't many rehearsals left before The Old Guys' first gig and we're going to need every minute we can grab to make us sound even halfway decent. Marta said tickets are going fast, which is both thrilling and terrifying. We have to up our game and fast.

'We've just got together,' he'd said, nuzzling into my neck as we'd lain in the darkness. 'Shouldn't we be making the most of things?'

'We are and we will. But I'd arranged to do this before we got together. I can't let the guys down.'

'You mean Archie.'

And that's where I should have made a joke or laughed it off. Only there was something in the way he said Archie's name that sharpened the syllables into a drawn dagger.

'And the rest of The Old Guys.'

'But mostly Archie. You promised *him*.'

'He's my friend.'

'Friends understand when you need to spend time with your boyfriend.'

'Archie does understand. But this gig is important to everyone. It's important to me.'

I'd felt him bristle beside me. 'Archie is important to you.'

'He's my *friend* . . . Why are you being like this?'

'Because it's like the bloke can't leave you alone. And you don't want him to, either. You're obsessed with each other.'

'How do you work that out?'

'You answer every text from him the minute it arrives. I'm pretty sure you answer his calls, too, when I'm not there. And you go rushing over to meet up with him whenever you can.'

'I don't go to meet him.'

'Naomi says you do.'

That was a kick I hadn't anticipated. I'd stared at him, the single ray of streetlight glow from the gap in the curtains marking the contours of his face. 'Since when do you talk to my sister?'

'She said it when I went over to see you.'

'As I recall she was trying to get you to leave when you'd barged your way into her home, which still isn't on, by the way.'

'I said I was sorry . . . ' he'd begun, but the fire had already risen in me. How dare he accuse me of sneaking around with Archie behind his back! Like I needed Matt Hope's permission to stay friends with the person responsible for getting us back together!

'And anyway, I wasn't seeing Archie then,' I'd shot back, already wanting to leave. 'I was bringing the girls back from school.'

'And that's another thing. Now you have me, you shouldn't have to.'

'Shouldn't have to what?'

'Live there. Do all their skivvying like you're Cinderella or something. You should move in here with me.'

Fred's double-squeak quickens as we leave the cleaned coffee station. I'm still shaken by that now. *Move in*? We've spent years not being together, have barely been seeing each other for a week and now he thinks we're ready to move in?

I love Matt. I'm enjoying getting to know him as my boyfriend instead of my unrequited crush. But I'm still working everything out. And he isn't fully divorced yet – I know that's just a formality between him and Nina and they both want it sorted quickly, but I wouldn't feel right moving in until he's mine in every sense: emotional, physical and *legal*.

Of course, I never got the chance to explain any of that because he'd taken my less than enthusiastic response as proof I was obsessed with Archie, putting myself at his beck and call when he never did anything for me in return. The row had begun with the angry snapping on of the bedside light and had ended with me getting up, chucking on my clothes and making for the door.

It didn't help that Mum and Dad had got wind of it this morning when Naomi let it slip by mistake when she'd called them and then she had to pass the phone to me so I could face the third degree.

'Are you out of your mind?' Mum had demanded, her tone leaving me in no doubt what she thought of my new boyfriend. 'That boy smashed your heart and made you feel it was your fault.'

'He said he's sorry,' I'd returned, sounding as pathetic as I felt. 'And he loves me.'

'*That* is not *love*, Esther Hughes,' my mother had snapped before Dad's soothing voice had cut across her ire.

'We're just concerned, love. If you're happy, that's all we want.'

'But it's *Matthew Hope*,' I'd heard Mum growl behind him. It's going to take a while to convince her – another bump I didn't see ahead.

We'll sort it all out, eventually. The thing is, I can't shake the feeling that it shouldn't be *this* hard . . .

'Esther.'

I look up from Elvis's mug-strewn desk to see Marjorie striding across the darkened office towards me. 'Hey.'

'I've just looked at this.' She's waving my mocked-up brochure aloft. 'It's bloody good, kid. I mean it. The words, the way you've laid it all out – I'm the world's biggest cynic but I'd hire us based on this.'

Marjorie Ollerenshaw being enthusiastic and complimentary is quite a sight to behold. I smile back, not really sure how else to respond.

'Thanks.'

'I'm taking this to Peter – *Mr Groves* – tomorrow morning. If he wanted to see you, could you get over to the office during the day?'

'Shouldn't be a problem,' I reply, mentally lining up contingencies in my mind. Naomi will be at home tomorrow so at a push she could cover the afternoon school run if I wasn't back in time. Ordinarily this wouldn't go down well, but she saw the brochure as I was working on it and seemed genuinely impressed.

'Could you do something like this for my website?' she'd asked.

'Yes, if you tell me what you need.'

'I could pay you, too, tax-deductible service and all.'

I'm still not sure I fully trust this brave new world, with my sister and my manager being so encouraging, but I'll take it.

'Right, kid, you're on.' Marjorie's expression softens. 'Proper proud of you, I am. Gotta be honest, when you took the cleaning job here I had you pegged as some middle-class, soft-fingered fly-by-night. No offence.'

'None taken.'

'I see them all the time in this gig. Thinking cleaning is the easy option then dropping us like a hot rock the minute something better comes up. Not that I blame them. I mean, if a rich businessman wafted in here offering me a top job I'd be off like a rocket.'

Strange though it is to be sharing a joke with my manager, this is exactly what I needed tonight. 'I love this job,' I say. 'Really. It's hard work – harder than I've worked before – but I think I've been happier working here than I ever was in my last job.'

A wrinkle appears between Marjorie's thinly plucked eyebrows. 'Get away with you! Even with that swanky pad of yours over in Salford Quays?'

'Well, I loved that,' I admit. 'But before I started here I don't think I'd ever really asked myself what I wanted to do. I know this isn't going to be for ever, but it arrived at the moment I needed it most. Thanks for taking a chance on me.'

Something bordering on emotional passes across my manager's face. 'You're a good kid. I reckon when Mr Groves sees this you'll be onto a winner. Hang in there, okay?'

And with that, she's off.

I glance at Fred, who is his usual sunny, mildly dented self. 'Well, I never saw that coming,' I mutter to him.

Fred says nothing, but I reckon he's surprised, too.

The call comes at ten o'clock next morning. I've cleaned the kitchen and just hung the latest batch of the Martins's laundry mountain on the line in the billowy sunshine when my mobile buzzes.

'Esther! Peter Groves here. Marjorie gave me your brochure

mock-up and I am very impressed. Could you pop into the office today, say twelve-ish?'

'Of course. See you then.'

My sister's head pops out of her garden office. 'Was that them?'

'It was.' I carry the empty beribboned laundry basket over, trying in vain to smooth wayward strands of my hair whipped up by the summer breeze. 'Mr Groves has asked me to go in for twelve. I don't know how long I'll be . . .'

'Go,' Naomi says, taking the basket from me and straightening two of the ribbons as she continues. 'I can get the girls. Go and knock his socks off, Es.'

'Thank you.'

My sister smiles. 'I do appreciate everything you do for us, you know. I hope you don't feel put upon.'

'I don't,' I lie, a little. It's been better lately and us getting on is reason enough to ignore the rest for now.

'Whatever happens, until you can find a place of your own or – you know – you and Matt . . .' her voice falters; I love her for trying to understand me being with him, even if I'm in no doubt of her true feelings ' . . . we'll work together on stuff. I've been a bit obsessed with the business lately, but I'll keep an eye on that.'

'Thanks.'

'Now stop nattering with me and get going, okay?'

The offices of Concilio Cleaning are smaller than I remember them. Brighter too, the summer's day beyond the vertical blind-draped windows making Manchester sparkle. Peter Grove stands behind his desk as Barbara, his bustling secretary, ushers me in.

'Miss Hughes, thank you for coming to see me. Apologies for the short notice, but best to strike while the iron's hot, don't you think? Have a seat. Can Barbara get you a tea? Coffee?'

I glance at bristling Barbara, whose tight smile threatens something dire if I agree. 'I'm fine,' I reply brightly, seeing the secretary's Mafia-sure nod before she leaves.

'Straight down to business, then.' He pats my brochure mock-up on his desk. 'Very impressive, Miss Hughes. I've been in charge at Concilio Cleaning for the best part of fifteen years and this, I have to tell you, is revelatory.'

'Um, thanks?'

'*Revelatory*, I tell you. The marketing company we've always used has never once offered such a concise, perfectly constructed view of what we do. This—' he stabs the brochure with a well-padded finger '—is going to win us business. So, I have a proposition. I would like to introduce you to a great friend of mine who has handled all our printing for years. Thing is, he's never had a design team working for him – we always outsourced that ourselves. But his daughter has not long graduated with a degree in graphic design and I reckon the two of you could make something special. Would you be up for me arranging a meeting with a view to us appointing you part-time marketer for the company?'

I blink away my surprise. I'd thought at best I might pick up a little freelance work, but nothing like this. 'Definitely.'

'It might only be a couple of days a week to begin with. Our marketing needs are not the most comprehensive, as you can imagine. But you could maybe start on two days a week and hang onto your cleaning shifts for the other three?'

'Yes – is Marjorie okay with that?'

Mr Groves beams. 'It was her suggestion. Marjorie – *Miss Ollerenshaw* – is a great fan of yours. Hard to say no to her when she has her mind set. On anything.'

I've long suspected that my manager and my boss may share more than a working relationship, so this admission thrills me. They are the perfect odd couple: Marjorie with her bottle-red bob and Sahara-dry wit and Mr Groves, who looks like a miniature Oliver Hardy, all smiles and bluster. Takes all sorts, my dad says.

What do people think when they see Matt and me? Are we a couple people instantly see as made for each other?

I stuff the thought away. I need to focus on what I've just been offered – which, if I can make it work, could make a massive difference. It's not a comprehensive solution, but it's a way forward I couldn't have imagined the first time I sat in this office, my hands shaking as I handed over my CV, praying I wouldn't be laughed out of the room.

I've come such a long way. I have to celebrate that. Whatever happens next is one step closer to where I want to be.

All the other stuff – Matt's petty jealousy, my parents' opinions and whatever Archie is or isn't to me now – can wait.

Thirty-Eight

ARCHIE

I sense the impending storm the moment I arrive.

The strip lights in the community hall are as garish and bright as ever but something shadowy and foreboding hangs over the space. I'm not the only one to notice, either. Marta has been hiding out in the kitchen since she got here, according to Eric. He's huddled over his guitar in the circle of chairs, fixing a string that doesn't really need fixing.

'Keepin' my head down,' he'd muttered to me earlier. 'If you know what's good for you, you'll do the same.'

As more of The Old Guys arrive, the atmosphere becomes heavier. I see accusing glances, instruments shouldered and picked up a little too roughly and hear the badly concealed mutters whenever Big Jim says anything.

Even Granda Brady seems to have left his brightness at home today.

What's going on?

It's a relief to see Esther hurrying in, five minutes before rehearsal is due to start. She shoots me a sheepish grin as she dashes to her seat, shedding her coat and rucksack and ukulele bag around her like bits of discarded snakeskin.

'Take up the whole floor, why don't you,' Isaac mutters.

'Sorry.' Only one word, but it shudders with Esther's annoyance.

Am I the only one looking forward to this?

Big Jim hustles up to his place, opening his tatty folder of music and loudly arranging it on the music stand. Eric glances at me, while Kavi, Old Bob, Li'l Bill and Granda Brady stare resolutely at the floor.

'Right, ye bastards, let's kill some music,' Jim growls. If it's meant to ease the strange tension in the room, it fails spectacularly. He isn't smiling either.

It's nerves getting the better of everybody. It has to be. We're nowhere near as good as we should be this close to the gig. And Big Jim's lengthy email we all received yesterday evening listing everything we're still crap on hasn't helped either.

Someone has to do something. And today, quite out of character, that someone is going to be me.

'Before we start,' I say, jumping a little when all eyes turn thunderously to me. 'Can I just say how much I've been looking forward to seeing you all this week? I think we're all doing a fantastic job and even though this rehearsal might be painful, playing with you guys means the world to me.'

If Manchester had tumbleweed, all of it would be blowing across the community hall right now.

'Right,' I falter. This is worse than I thought. 'Anyway, that's what I wanted to say.'

'Suck-up,' Old Bob chunters.

'*If* we're done with the platitudes, let's play some music,'

Jim barks. 'Set One, please. "Bold Jamie" into "Julia Delaney". D-minor start.'

Instruments are readied, music sheets sorted, all eyes turning to music.

Big Jim raises his hands, tapping out the rhythm in the air.

'Takes one to know one,' Li'l Bill mutters, glaring at his husband.

Groans fill the space. Instruments are downed.

'What is that supposed to mean?'

Li'l Bill shrugs, his expression thunderous. 'Oh, I don't know. Maybe you replying to Jim's email like a needy Boy Scout.'

'How? How did I do that?'

Granda Brady raises his hands. 'Gentlemen, come on now . . .'

But Li'l Bill isn't listening. '"Oh yes, Jim, we're shit, Jim, but I promise I'll be better, Jim" . . . As if you weren't seething like the rest of us for the mean-spirited attack that email really was . . .'

Big Jim reddens. 'I wasnae saying—'

Old Bob jabs a thumb at our musical director. 'He had a point. Our last rehearsal was horrendous.'

'I'm not asking anyone to take blame, Bill. I'm just trying to play some bloody music . . .'

'It's all about *him*, isn't it, Jim?' Bob bristles, glancing at his husband. 'It always is. The world isn't against you, *William*, however much you want it to be. Jim said we need to do better. I agreed with him. Is that a crime?'

There's a crash as Jim's baton slams down on his music stand. 'I can't do right for doing wrong! I give up with the lot of yous.'

'Bill – Bob – Jim, calm down.' Esther is on the edge of her seat, orange Converse stamping against the lino floor. 'What the hell is up with you all? We all need to work on our programme – that's why we're here. So how about we get on with that instead of ripping strips off each other?'

At least that shuts them up. Rattled, but satisfied the row has ceased, Esther nods at Big Jim. 'Okay, Jim, I think we're finally ready to start now.'

It's *awful*. More awful than usual – because, in addition to our regular trips and fumbles through the music set, every piece is accompanied by fierce glares and angry words hissed under breath. I get the feeling that the tension has nothing to do with Jim's email now. Everyone is feeding their own nerves and issues into the atmosphere looming heavily over the room. By the time we break for refreshments hardly anyone is speaking. Even the surprise appearance of Marta's near-mythical Battenberg cake doesn't lessen the mood.

'Fancy a coffee after this?' I ask Esther as we're walking back to our seats.

'If it carries on you might need to make it a pint,' she says, grimacing back.

The second half of the practice is no better. The Old Guys have progressed from sending evils across the community hall to stone cold, impenetrable silence. It's as if every note we produce is under duress and it's a relief when we play the final song, 'The Wishing Tree'.

Not sure even a wishing tree could rescue us now.

But it's about to get much worse . . .

People are already packing away when Big Jim clatters his empty mug against the metal music stand, the resounding clang enough to jolt everyone to attention.

'Right, listen up. I have had it with you lot and your petty squabbles. I'm here to play music. I have no idea why the rest of you are here.' He turns to Old Bob and Li'l Bill, who have moved their chairs a foot apart and are resolutely ignoring each other. 'And for the record, Bob, Bill, if you want to yell at each other, I'd appreciate it if you'd leave me out of it. Don't lay your issues at my door. You ought to be grateful for what you've got. At least you *have* someone. Maybe yous should quit the stupid spats and thank your lucky stars you're not alone.'

Stunned, we all stare at him.

Jim wipes his mouth with the back of his hand, his chest heaving as he surveys the room. 'Not everyone in this room has something else to go back to, okay? The music we make might be a pile of shite to you but it's all some of us have . . . ' He gives a loud cough, his face flushed and angry. 'Bollocks, that's what this is. Hopeless, utter bollocks. I didn't sign up for this.'

Before anyone can reply, he snatches up his music stand and strides out of the hall, the fire exit door to the car park opening with a crash as he slams through it.

Nobody speaks. Nobody moves. From the kitchen I hear a muffled sob.

And then Old Bob turns to Li'l Bill. 'You see what you made him do?'

'What *I* made him do?' Li'l Bill returns, giving a hollow laugh when he sees his husband angrily gathering his things.

'Let's all be calm, okay?' Granda Brady steps across the circle, hands outstretched. 'We need to stay together.'

'I'll be *fine*,' Li'l Bill says. 'I just need some air.'

'Me too.'

Bob glowers at Li'l Bill but at least they leave together.

Eric heads off to the kitchen to comfort Marta. Isaac and Kavi are huddled together in a corner, talking in voices too low for us to hear. The storm might have passed, but I still sense its threat.

I offer Esther a smile, glad at least that there's one friendly face remaining in the room. 'Reckon we should leave them all to it.'

To my surprise, she doesn't smile back. 'Someone needs to check on Jim.'

'Be my guest.' I laugh. It's completely the wrong reaction and I know it as soon as I breathe back in.

'Go after him.'

'He'll be fine.'

'No, Arch, he won't. I've never seen him upset like that. You need to check he's okay.'

After our drama-laden rehearsal, it's no wonder she's worried. But it's just stuff and bluster. We'll be over it by the next time The Old Guys meet. 'It looks worse than it is, trust me.'

'But that wasn't nerves. Or wounded pride because of that email he sent us. He was properly upset. I think you need to—'

'It's *fine*.' I don't know why I'm irritated now, but I am. Esther should just trust me on this one. 'I've been with this lot forever. They bounce back eventually. You've not been here long enough to see that yet.'

'Excuse me?' Suddenly I'm facing a thundercloud about to break. This isn't about her and me: why can't she drop it so we can get out of here and be *normal*? 'I'm asking you to go and see Jim. Your friend. Who doesn't look like he's about to *bounce back* from anything anytime soon.'

I can't stop my groan. 'Just leave him be. There's no problem, Es. Stop worrying. Come on, let's get that drink.' I reach for her arm but she snatches it away. 'What?'

Esther's arms fold across her body, a defensive move for her next volley. I should see what's coming but I don't until it's too late. 'That's you all over, isn't it? Happy to yell when you want something but when I ask for your help you just dismiss it.'

'What? When have I ever . . . ?'

She stabs a finger at me. 'I had to defend you to Matt this week. He said you only ever see your problems and I told him he was being ridiculous. But he's right, isn't he? If it isn't happening to you, you don't give a damn.'

I can't believe what I'm hearing. 'Glad to know your boyfriend likes talking about me.'

'That isn't the point!'

I'm rattled now and without thinking I hit back with the only ammunition I have. 'Do you think Jessie is chuffed I'm still seeing you?'

It registers immediately and I feel like a total git. But I'm not having Esther adopting her lame excuse for a boyfriend's opinion of me. So where I should shut up I just power on.

'Being your friend isn't the easiest choice either, Esther. But I told Jessie she has nothing to worry about.'

'That's big of you.'

'Now hang on . . . '

'Kids, that's *enough*,' Granda Brady calls, but neither of us is listening.

'I don't care what you think. Archie. I care about Jim. Get your head out of your backside for once and go after him.'

I should tell her to take a running jump. But if I stay, I prove Matt's point – and I am not about to do that.

'Fine,' I shoot back, my teeth aching where I grit them together.

It's a relief to leave the hall, stamping my way out to the

car park and slamming my car door so hard the wing mirror shudders. I'm going to find Jim, calm him down and then spend the rest of the weekend in the bed of the woman who loves me.

Let Esther think what she likes.

Thirty-Nine

ESTHER

'Let him go.'

I bristle as Diarmuid Brady's gentle hand rests on my shoulder. 'I've no intention of stopping him.'

The light from the open fire escape door burns its shape into my retina as I glare at it. How dare Archie speak to me like that? All I wanted was to make sure Big Jim was okay. Archie's known him since he was fourteen; why wouldn't he be the one to go after him?

Archie's grandad sighs. 'We need to check on the auld couple, too. Isaac, Kavi, would you mind?'

'No problem.' Kavi nods. 'Will you lot be all right?'

'We'll be fine. Call me when you've tracked them down, okay?'

'Sure.' Isaac swings his music bag onto his shoulder. 'Esther, what I said before . . . '

I raise my hand. 'Forget it. Bit of a humdinger all round.'

He risks a swift smile and follows Kavi outside.

Eric appears in the doorway to the kitchen. 'Kettle is on. Tea all round?'

'I reckon so,' Diarmuid replies, reaching into the inside pocket of his jacket to produce a small shiny silver hipflask. 'And I've a tot of magic to sprinkle in, should anyone need it.' As Eric returns to comfort Marta, Diarmuid pushes a chair over to me, swinging another next to it for him. 'Now sit, Miss Hughes.'

I don't really have a choice. My body is shaking after the exchange with Archie and the experience of the worst rehearsal ever. I sink onto the unforgiving plastic and bite my lip to stop myself crying.

'I love my grandson,' Diarmuid begins, stretching out his legs in front of him as if settling in for a long story. 'But here's the thing: when it comes to seeing what's under his nose, Archie is not the fastest sprinter in the race.'

His mix of metaphors brings a smile I didn't expect. I pack it away, but not quickly enough to escape Diarmuid's notice.

'I swear that boy could be strolling through the Apocalypse itself and only realise something was up when a fireball hit him.' He leans his head to one side, so that his hat appears almost straight. 'Only this time, maybe the fireball already has.'

I stare at my shoes. 'I don't want to cause problems with Jessie.'

'And neither does Archie want to annoy your man. Well, he might want to annoy him but he doesn't want to get in your way.'

'I didn't want to yell at him. I'm just concerned about Jim and Archie didn't think I should be.'

Diarmuid nods. 'Archie didn't want to see it. But I'm concerned, too, Esther. That wasn't like Jim at all. I'll call the big fella when I get home, check he's all right.'

I might be new to the dynamics of the group, but what Jim said seemed so out of kilter with the meaningless bickering he was addressing. I felt his heart breaking. There's so much more to his uncharacteristic outburst and exit than anyone else seems to see. Tension grips my spine. 'Will Jim be okay?'

If Diarmuid knows more, he isn't about to share it. 'We have to hope, Esther.'

Eric brings tea and I sit with Archie's grandad in bruised silence. The tension has lifted from the hall but I feel its uneasy ghosts crammed into every corner.

'Archie will do the right thing, you know. In the end.'

I blow on my mug. 'I hope so. We can't afford to lose Jim.'

Diarmuid takes a long sip of tea. 'And also with Jim.'

I glance at him, but his eyes are trained on the mug in his hands and his crossed feet far out before him.

'We can't lose this group. It's wonderful.'

'It is. We are. You all are. Archie'll put things right, you'll see. He's an eejit sometimes but his heart is worth waiting for.'

I'm still trying to work out what that means an hour later, as I'm pulling into Matt's drive. I don't like the way we left things after our row and I'm determined to prove to him that he's the most important person in my life now.

Because he has to be. My life is so much bigger than Archie Quinn.

The front door opens before I'm out of my car. Matt says nothing, just hurries across the gravel and takes me in his arms. I'm relieved and exhausted and all I want to do is forget the row and the trouble today ever happened.

We head inside and curl up together on Matt's sofa, Picard jumping up between us, making us laugh as he burrows between our bodies. There's so much we need to talk about, but for now I'll take this: company and cuddles and some random film playing on Matt's TV, which neither of us is really watching. The ordinariness of it is soothing after so many heated conversations that seemed to rest on a knife-edge. Years ago, I might have called this boring. Today, it's bliss.

By six, Matt's asleep, his head resting against the back of the sofa with a snoring Picard flopped across his lap. I've tried closing my eyes too, but sleep isn't coming. The film's over so I've switched to a different channel, catching the tail end of a cycling race. I'm not invested in the action at all, but the colours and sounds are soothing. Soon I should move and start thinking about dinner.

Not yet though.

My shoulder is numb from where it's been up against Matt's chest, his arm a dead weight around my shoulders. Needing to stretch, I carefully wriggle free and place a cushion under Matt's arm. Picard is so fast asleep he doesn't even stir. I glance at them before tiptoeing into the kitchen.

I'm just filling the kettle when my phone vibrates in my pocket. Snapping the kettle on to boil, I pull out my mobile, my heart sinking when I see the incoming call.

ARCHIE calling

He's got a nerve, calling me now when he knows I'll be at Matt's. My thumb moves over the red button on the screen, but a sudden memory of Big Jim storming out of the community hall makes me opt for green instead.

'Well?' I whisper, hoping the rumble of the kettle shields my voice from Matt's ear. 'How's Jim?'

'Not good. Granda's with him now but he says he needs us both.'

'I can't. I'm at Matt's . . .'

'I guessed you would be. I wouldn't ask but this is serious, Es. Jim says he's quitting the band.'

'What? He can't do that!' I say, completely forgetting not to raise my voice.

'He is. Granda reckons he means it this time. We need you, Es. I need you.'

I kick the base of the kitchen unit with my bare foot. 'I – can't.'

'I know you think I only ask when I want something. But this time it isn't me. It's my granda and he wouldn't ask unless it was an emergency.'

'You have *got* to be kidding me.'

I look up to see Matt in the kitchen doorway, most definitely *not* asleep now and not happy, either. 'I have to do something,' I say, hand over the speaker of my mobile.

'Because Archie says so.'

'No. It's for his grandad.'

Matt snorts and shakes his head. 'Oh right, so the whole family yell for you now, do they?'

'Esther? Is everything all right?'

I cringe as Archie's voice drifts like an unwelcome breeze into Matt's kitchen. 'One moment,' I return, seeking his expression for any hint of compassion but finding none. 'Matt, I have to do this. It'll be the last time. They need me.'

He doesn't move. 'It'll never be the last time, though, will it?'

'Look, go back and rest. I'll be an hour at most and then we can order in dinner and have the rest of the weekend to ourselves.'

'Not if your *friend* has any say in it.'

'I'm on my way,' I say into the phone, watching Matt throw up his hands and storm back into the lounge. I understand his frustration, but this is an emergency. And Matt has to learn that the Esther he's with now isn't like the placid, ever-available Esther he knew before. I have to be there for my friends. 'Give me the address.'

'Give me yours,' he rushes. 'I'll come and pick you up.'

'No, I can drive.'

'Parking's shocking here. And I need to bring you up to speed.'

I don't want to meet Archie at Matt's house. But I need to help them – we can't lose Jim. Closing my eyes and wishing I could be anywhere but here; I lean into my phone.

'Fine. There's a park around the corner from here – Bransholme Rec? Pick me up from the main entrance on Holme Road.'

Ending the call I lean against the kitchen island, rubbing my eyes. From the lounge I can hear the loud music and explosions of Matt's current favourite PlayStation game. He'll be taking out his anger on some poor cyber zombies. No point in trying to reason with him any more now.

I grab my shoes, bag and jacket and leave without a word.

'You okay?'

Archie glances at me as he drives. It isn't the first time. We've been travelling for ten minutes and I've felt the weight of his stare roughly every sixty seconds.

'I'm fine,' I reply, making myself look out of the passenger door window to avoid any further eye contact.

I'm not fine and he knows it as well as I do. I'm still bristling from the exchange with Matt – and the insinuation that Archie has first call on my attention all the time. I'm annoyed that he thinks that.

And yet, where am I now? On the sofa with the guy I longed

to be with for years or in a car with the man I can't stop thinking about?

It was weird seeing Archie pull up at the entrance to the Rec, too – the territory I've always shared with Matt. Unsettling. Given I've let Archie encroach upon it, along with my workplace, my Saturdays and my thoughts, maybe Matt has a point.

'What did your grandad say about Jim?'

'He's barricaded himself into his house and he won't open the door. Granda's been talking to him through the letterbox for the best part of an hour, but no joy.'

'But I thought you went after him, after the rehearsal?'

'I did.'

'Didn't you catch him?'

'I followed him home and talked to him at the top of his path for ten minutes. He seemed fine to me, but he called Granda Brady later on and said he was quitting.'

Of all the members of The Old Guys, I never had Jim as someone who would do this. It scares me to think of him offended to the point where he'd leave. He's the steady hand, steering the rest of us through everything. If he leaves, can The Old Guys survive?

'How does Diarmuid think we can help?'

'Granda reckons he's too close to Jim to have any sway in his decision, but Jim's always felt protective over me – and now, especially, you. If that's enough to get us into the house, maybe we have a chance to convince him to change his mind.'

'That's a lot of *ifs* and *maybes*,' I say, not fancying our chances of even getting inside to talk to Jim.

'It is.'

'I just don't get why he reacted like that. Everyone was on

edge today but I thought that was just nerves getting the better of us. But that stuff Jim said about being alone – that worried me.'

'Me too. I'm sorry I didn't take your concern seriously. You were right. I completely misjudged Jim's mood earlier. I thought it would blow over, but there's so much more going on there than I realised.' Archie grimaces beside me. 'I haven't dropped you in it with Matt, have I?'

My heart sinks. I could avoid the question but he already knows Matt's not his biggest fan after our row earlier. 'He wasn't happy.'

'Doesn't he trust you?'

'I don't think it's me he doesn't trust.'

'Oh, so I'm just the sneaky git who's trying to steal you away, am I?'

Aren't you? I nearly say it, biting my tongue just in time. 'How would you feel if Jessie dashed off with another fella every time he called?'

'Point taken.'

We fall silent but the car is packed with silent questions we should be asking. Just as it's getting too much, Archie turns right onto an estate then left into a cul-de-sac.

The council houses are nestled against the hill on one side, each one linked to the road by a steeply banked path of wide ash-grey slabs. It reminds me so much of my gran's house on the other side of the city – steps leading down to identical semi-detached houses, half-pebbledash and half-brick. Some of the houses in Jim's street have been rendered smooth and painted pale peach or cream. Others look unchanged from the 1950s when they were constructed. Jim's is a little shabby but the grass of the sloping front garden is neatly trimmed and an array of pots and hanging baskets are arranged along its frontage.

And, sitting with his back against the yellow-painted front door, is Archie's grandad. He gives us a weary wave as we get out of the car and descend the path towards him, pushing himself stiffly to his feet and walking over to meet us.

'And lo, the cavalry comes!'

'How is he?' I ask.

Diarmuid's perennial smile dims. 'Not good, I'm afraid. There's no talking to him.'

'What can we say that's different?' Archie asks.

'You can't say anything.' He turns to me, apology washing his features. 'This is down to you, Esther.'

'Me? What can I say?'

'Talk like you did in that room when we decided to do the gig. I was watching Jim that day: he shone when he listened to you.'

My stomach knots. 'I don't think it'll be enough—'

Diarmuid holds up his hand. 'All I'm asking is you get him to open the door. Once we're inside we have a shot.' Seeing my nerves, he places a gentle hand on my arm. 'Just give it a go. You can't do any worse than I have.'

Their hopeful smiles reveal the family resemblance more than I've noticed before.

How can I say no to that?

Gingerly, I knock on Big Jim's door, jumping when a sigh the other side reveals just how close our friend is. That gives me hope: he isn't hiding; he's waiting for us to convince him.

Waiting for *me*.

'Haven't you said enough, Brady?'

'He might have, but I haven't,' I say, suppressing a smile that appears out of nowhere when I imagine Jim's surprise.

There's a long pause.

'Jim?'

'Ah, I'm here, lassie. I wasnae expecting you.'

'Can I come in? Have a chat?'

'I don't think so.'

'I just want to check you're all right. That rehearsal was horrendous and I hate that it's upset you.'

'You've nothing to feel bad about.'

'I'm worried about you, Jim.'

'I'll be fine. I've said everything I wanted to say to Brady.'

'But you're still by the door,' I risk. I'm flying blind but the fact that Jim is there urges me on. 'I might be wrong, but I don't think I'd be there if I'd made up my mind.'

I glance back at Archie and Diarmuid. Their smiles are barely there now. Was that too far? Should I have talked more before I challenged Jim? Diarmuid looks to the slate-grey sky. Archie lifts his shoulders in a resigned shrug.

And behind me, there's a click.

I turn to see the smallest gap where the front door has opened.

'My Amy said things like that.'

'She was very wise.'

'Aye. She'd've liked you.'

'I'd love to hear more about her,' I say, stepping back a little when the door swings open.

Jim gazes out at us three. He's pale, the shadows beneath his eyes suggesting he's gone days without sleep when in reality it's been only hours since the rehearsal. I want to hug him, but we are on such fragile ground I daren't do anything until we're inside his house. 'You'd best come in, then,' he says, directing his invitation above our heads as if watching someone else further up the steps.

Diarmuid heads straight into the kitchen, the sounds of cupboards and drawers being opened and the clink of crockery following soon after. Jim clears a newspaper and a disgruntled tabby cat from the sofa and offers it to Archie and me. It's a small leather couch, so our legs and knees touch as we sit. I catch the flush of Archie's face as we wriggle self-consciously and feel the burn of my own.

Jim sits in the high-backed armchair next to an ancient-looking two-bar fire, the kind with the moulded plastic coals and orange sunburst screen behind them. The wall above the fireplace is covered in photographs, frames of all sizes and shapes jostling for position: baby pictures, family photos, fading holiday shots and a large wedding photo in the centre of them all. A much younger Jim standing proudly next to a dark-haired young woman smiling happily for the camera. There are so many that it feels like this meeting isn't taking place in Jim's lounge but in the middle of Manchester Piccadilly station at rush hour. It's more photograph than wall, more smiles than bricks and mortar.

A talk radio station is bumbling away in the background, a slate clock on the mantelpiece ticking loudly.

Too aware of Archie's body alongside mine, I focus on Jim. 'So, how are you?'

'I'll live.'

'That's not what I asked. What's made you want to leave the group?'

Big Jim sighs into his balled fist where it rests against his beard. 'All that fighting. That's not what The Old Guys is about. Never was. If times are changing they'll not take me with them.'

'It was one rehearsal,' Archie ventures. 'We were all being idiots.'

'Things were said . . . '

'Things people didn't mean.'

Jim's gaze drops to the faded brown-and-orange-squared carpet where his cat is now spread out. 'People yell the truth when it's bad, Archie.'

'Everyone's scared of the gig,' I argue. 'And people do really daft things when they're scared.' I glance at Archie without thinking, just as he turns to me. For just a second his hand finds mine where our bodies meet. A single squeeze says more than either of us could have admitted out loud.

'Tea!' Diarmuid skips into the room, swiftly delivering mugs to us all.

Jim takes a sip, his features creasing into disgust. 'What the hell did you put in here? Gasoline?'

Archie's grandad tuts and reaches into the inside pocket of his jacket. 'Just a wee tot of the good stuff.' The silver of his hipflask glints in the early evening sunlight streaming through the window before he pockets it again. 'I figured you'd need it.'

'Irish?'

'Of course.'

Jim sniffs. 'That explains it.'

Diarmuid feigns offence, grinning in case Jim buys it. 'Apologies it's not your peaty single malt, sir. Put hairs on your chest, that will.'

'Or strip 'em right off,' Jim mutters, drinking more tea anyway.

'James. You're one of my dearest friends. You can't leave the band.'

Jim stares at Archie's grandad, then us. 'Maybe it's time.'

'We can't do it without you,' I rush, the thought of what might happen to us if we don't have him too awful to consider. It surprises everyone, not least me. 'I'm sorry. I just can't bear to think of The Old Guys splitting up. It's meant the world to me to find you. I love being part of it, even if we sound horrible sometimes.'

'Most of the time, eh Jim?' Diarmuid chuckles.

'What you do is really special,' I say. 'You welcome us in and somehow you make it all work. We'd be lost if you weren't there.'

'I was lost – before.' Jim doesn't look at me but his expression softens. 'That group saved me. Being part of it – belonging. When I lost my Amy I thought I was done. Nothing mattered any more. Useless, that's what I felt. I wanted to end it all.' He nods at Diarmuid. 'And then your man over there accosted me in a pub the day I'd planned to do it.'

The shock of his admission hits home. Beside me, I feel Archie tense. Tears well in my eyes. How could such a larger than life, positive person believe the world would be better off without him in it?

Diarmuid's voice cracks a little as he speaks. 'And do you know what I saw? I saw a man with so much to give but nobody to give it to.'

'Aye, so you decided to take it.'

'I did, and I'm proud I did. Because look at what you made happen, Jim. All those people who thought they were past use, worthless: you gave them somewhere to belong. You're a rescuer, a lifesaver. Because you know how close you came to not being here.'

Jim shifts in his armchair, the cat mewling in reply. 'They didn't seem to want to be there earlier. They treated the rehearsal like it didn't matter – like they had better things to be doing.

I don't. Not since my Amy . . . ' His voice chokes with emotion. 'I miss her. Life without her – it's too hard.'

'That's why you need us,' I say. 'Why it matters to keep The Old Guys together. We all need it – like we need you.'

He won't look at me. 'I don't know, lassie. Maybe I'm done.'

'If you're done, so are we,' Archie says. 'You're the heart and soul of us. If you leave, The Old Guys don't exist. Esther's right: we need you, mate.' He lowers his voice, leaning towards our lovely friend. 'And I reckon you need us, too. We aren't going anywhere without you.'

And then Jim begins to cry. Enormous racking sobs that shake his huge frame. As one, we all hurry over to him, throwing our arms around him. Words become useless as we hold on to the shuddering body of our friend, the frozen faces of his nearest, dearest and much-loved looking down on us from their frames on the wall.

We're shaken when we finally leave, driving the first half of the journey home in heavy silence.

And then Archie speaks. 'You were amazing back there.'

'So were you. I didn't know all that stuff about Jim.'

'Me either. It was a shock to hear it.'

'I just hope he knows how much we all love him.'

'Me too.'

'To lose someone you love so much – to think life has nothing else for you when they're gone – that's heartbreaking.'

Archie nods, but he doesn't reply.

We slow to let a bus pull out into the traffic and I'm aware of that strange weight around us. So many things I want to say but where would I even begin? Archie's brow is furrowed as we follow the bus – does he sense it, too? I hunker down in the passenger seat and watch the city pass by. I don't want to feel dread about going home to Matt, but my stomach twists with every familiar landmark I count leading back to his house.

And then the gates of Bransholme Rec swing into view, Archie slowing the car until we're where our journey began. It seems an age since we left here but now we're back it's as if no time passed at all. I don't want to get out of the car. Archie turns off the engine and sits with both hands gripping the steering wheel.

'Thanks for the lift.' My voice shakes when I speak. 'I'd better let you . . . '

'You rescued me, Es.'

Air stolen from my lungs I turn to him. 'What?'

'When you found that note. When you replied. You rescued me.'

His eyes are intent on me, the rise and fall of his chest quickening. I have to tell him the truth.

'You rescued me, too.'

'Thank you.'

'I'm sorry I yelled – earlier.'

'You were right. Like you always are. But let's not fight again, okay? I like it when it's just us being us – no aggro, no egos.'

'Me too.'

He moves a little and I think he's going to hug me but instead his fingers rest on my hand, gently pulling it up from my knee to curl around my palm. 'Can I ask you something?'

Right now, Archie Quinn could ask me anything in the world. 'Ask away.'

'Before Jessie – and Matt – before the letter and everything, did you ever think you and me would . . . ?'

A million bells begin to ring in alarm. 'Arch . . . '

'I know the kiss was a mistake. But did it ever cross your mind before?'

A mistake.

I can't let him continue.

'We're with the people we love,' I say. 'And we have each other – as friends.'

'Of course.'

My heart stings when his hand holds mine for a moment before releasing it. My skin is colder without his touch. I have to get out of here.

'Thanks for the lift and – everything.'

'You're welcome.' Archie smiles as he looks back to the road. 'Say hi to Matt from me. Or maybe not, eh?'

Watching him drive away, I don't know if he was joking.

Forty

ARCHIE

'What's this?'

Jock Callaghan looks like he's just been punched in the guts. Barely concealed rage shakes the single sheet letter in his fist.

'My resignation,' I say, resisting the urge to giggle because, honestly, this is so much better than I ever imagined.

'But you've a job here. I told you . . . '

'And I appreciate all the opportunities you've promised me.' I smile. Not *given me*, you notice. So much is implied by my word choice, which, of course, is completely lost on Callaghan. Subtlety is wasted on him. 'But when ITV offered . . . '

That's the kicker. *The Herald* can't compete with a national broadcaster and Callaghan knows it.

He snorts like a newly fenced-in bull. '*Television.*'

'It's the break I was looking for. Straight onto a team, no probationary period. My new editor says I've more than proved myself.'

I'm sailing close to the wind, but I don't care. After my two weeks' notice is done I won't have to see Jock Callaghan ever again.

'What've they offered?' he blurts, beetroot-faced and seething.

'I really don't think I should—'

'I'll double it. Plus extra holiday. And overtime.'

I should be flattered but he isn't doing this because he wants me. He just can't stand losing.

'I don't think so.' I extend my hand, a serene smile on my face while my heart thumps ten to the dozen inside my chest. 'All the best for the future.'

He's so shocked that he accepts my handshake without another word.

As I leave, Beyoncé's 'Single Ladies' comes on the radio in the main office and it takes all my resolve not to strut out in time with the beat.

Jessie has her back turned to me when I return to my desk, which is no mean feat considering our workspaces are side by side. She isn't talking to me and wants everybody in the office to know it. I knew she'd be like this, but it still stings.

It's my fault: not for accepting the job, which is the right decision for me, but because like a total chicken I left it until last night to tell her.

I should have said something earlier, but she'd talked so much in recent days about us working together in this great media empire she's imagined for us that I didn't want to disappoint her.

But I was not prepared for the ferocity of her response.

She'd invited me to hers for dinner and to stay over. When I'd reached her apartment she'd gone all out – swanky restaurant home delivery, a new dress that made me almost forget to speak at all, champagne, the lot.

'We're celebrating,' she'd said, leaning so close to me as she'd filled my glass that it was a battle to hold it steady.

'Celebrating what?'

'You. And us.' She'd clinked her glass against mine, the expensive crystal making a perfect chime. 'You showed Callaghan with that scoop and all the news reports you did so brilliantly and together we'll show him where *The Herald* could be.'

For the smallest moment, I could see that, too. Jessie and me, leaving Jock Callaghan in the dust . . . But it wasn't what I wanted.

'Jessie,' I'd begun, but she had already been serving our food and distracting me with *that* dress. So I'd waited – through starter, main and dessert, my stomach tying itself in knots with each successive course. Oblivious to it all, Jessie continued to spin her dream around us.

'Liam reckons the board aren't happy with Callaghan. Seems he's been living on borrowed time at the paper longer than any of us knew. Serves him right: that man would promise you the world if it got him his own way. We've put up with it for too long. You have, Arch. But we can show the board we have a vision for the paper beyond anything Jock Callaghan could imagine – and we can deliver it, too . . .'

When dinner was over and we'd moved to her sofa, I couldn't bear to listen to anymore.

'Jessie.'

'You smell so good,' she'd murmured, nuzzling my neck.

'We have to talk.'

'Can it wait? I can think of much better things to do right now . . .'

It had taken all of my willpower to pull away. 'I'm taking the job at MediaCity.'

There had been a moment then when I'd wondered if she'd

heard me. And then she'd sat back, her smile gone. 'You're not. You're staying at the paper with me. We agreed—'

'No. You said that's what I should do. I never agreed.'

'So you let me jabber on tonight, say all that stuff, when you knew it wasn't happening?'

'I didn't want to interrupt.' It was the wrong answer and I knew as soon as I'd said it.

'What the hell is that supposed to mean? You knew you were taking that job but you thought you'd string me along a bit longer, is that it?'

'No,' I'd insisted, but then I'd heard *that* tone in my voice – the mousy, timid version of me I only ever heard when talking to Callaghan before everything changed. And I'd realised – I don't want to be that person anymore. So instead of trying to appease my furious girlfriend, I'd decided to meet the battle head-on. 'I want this job, Jess. It could be the making of me. I've wasted years at *The Herald* waiting to show what I can do – there's no guarantee Callaghan will let me do that if I accept his job. ITV want me. They've seen what I can do and they want me on their team. Do you know what that means?'

'What does Esther think?'

I didn't see that coming. 'What?'

'Did you tell Esther you were taking the job? Because you seem to tell her everything else.'

'I did, but—'

She threw her hands in the air. 'So you tell her but you forget to tell me? What else have the two of you been discussing, eh? Those Saturdays when you were meant to be with the band – were you with her, too?'

It was spiralling beyond my control but I couldn't stop myself. 'Of course. She's in the band.'

'So you can't spend time with me because you'd rather spend time with *her*. And you can't tell me you're taking that bloody job but you'll tell her because *she* understands. Am I right?'

'This isn't about Esther,' I'd protested, but Jessie wasn't listening. 'It's my job, my life, my decision.'

'*Her* influence, *her* approval you seek above mine, *her* fault everything we've worked for is being chucked away . . . '

'It's not like that at all. This is what I want, Jess. It won't change us.'

I'd hoped she'd see the passion in me, recognise the opportunity I'd been given. But those hopes had crumbled the moment she'd stood.

'Get out.'

'Jess, come on. We should talk about this . . . '

'You didn't care much about talking until now. Not to me, anyhow. Perhaps you should talk to *Esther* bloody Hughes about it, seeing as she's your first port of call for everything.'

'Don't be like this.'

'Why should I listen to you? Go home, Archie. I don't want you here tonight.'

'I thought you wanted me to stay . . . '

'That was before. You have a resignation letter to write, apparently. Close the door on your way out.'

She hadn't even stayed in the room to watch me go.

I guess I deserved that. I should have been straight with her from the beginning. I put it off because I didn't know how to say it. But all that stuff about replacing Callaghan? That isn't me – and Jessie assuming it is makes me wonder how much she really knows me. I don't like us being at odds with each other today, but she's obviously decided to make her point.

Let her. She's entitled to be angry with me. I'll give her space to work it out and then look to making things better when she's ready to hear it. The Esther thing might take longer. But she'll see I'm serious about us and then maybe Esther won't seem the threat Jessie thinks she is. When we can talk about it without yelling, I'm sure we'll find a way through this.

I hope we will.

'You did it, then?' Liam grins.

'One resignation handed in. One notice given.'

There's a crash as Callaghan's door flies open. 'I'm in board meetings for the rest of the day,' he growls, shouldering his jacket as he storms towards the lift.

'But the editorial meeting?' Jessie begins, careful not to make eye contact with me as she stands.

'I *said* I'm busy. Can't you people do anything without me baby-sitting you?'

Jessie slumps back in her seat as he leaves.

Apart from the localised storm over my girlfriend's desk, the atmosphere in the office lifts immediately.

'Mr Quinn, a word?' Elvis calls from his desk. 'Make mine a black and two on your way over, please.'

I grin as I make his coffee. I don't mind doing it for Elvis. I wouldn't be where I am right now if it weren't for his help. He's beaming at me when I arrive at his desk.

'Take a pew, sir,' he says, opening the hallowed biscuit tin to reveal three brand-new packets of branded biscuits. 'I reckon we're in need of a proper celebration.'

'You bought these?' I ask, feigning shock.

'Red-letter day, son. Only the best for that.'

'Wow, I'm honoured. Thanks.'

Elvis nods his approval, two chocolate digestives already in his mouth. 'Course,' he adds between munches, 'what we really need is a meal out. I happen to know this cracking Italian restaurant where I'm now apparently guaranteed a table for life.'

'Rossi's?'

'Where else? Tonight?'

I'm about to accept when I remember: there's a dinner for my parents' anniversary tonight. 'I have a family dinner at half past eight.'

'Straight after work then.' Elvis brushes crumbs from his shirt and tie. 'Half-five. We'll just have mains if you like. Come on, Archie! It's not every day you get to sack off a git like Callaghan. Liam! You up for early scran at Rossi's?'

'Try stopping me!'

'Excellent. Jessie?'

'I'm busy.' Her reply cuts deep, but it's what I expected.

Elvis raises an eyebrow at me. 'No problem. Archie'll bring you a goody bag. So,' he says, grinning, 'do we have a date?'

Put like that, how can I refuse?

Jacopo Rossi greets us like long-lost family. He's prepared us a table in the centre of the restaurant and is already chattering about today's special menu we absolutely must have. Over his shoulder Ciro rolls his eyes at his father and grins at me as he pulls out chairs for us to sit.

If I thought we'd get away with a swift bite I was wrong. But, thankfully, my parents are cool about me being late. Turns out

Dacey and Conn won't be getting to the bakery until almost nine tonight, so Mum and Dad have said they'll make it a late supper instead. This is nothing new for the Quinn family: most family celebrations in my life have happened past 9 p.m., once all the work in the bakery was done.

'Thanks so much for having us early,' I say.

Jacopo bats this away with a flourish. 'Anything for my best customers.'

'How's business?' I ask, glancing around to see RESERVED signs on every other table.

'Booked out. For *months*. Everybody wants to eat where Totti ate.'

'But he didn't eat anything,' I whisper to Ciro.

He laughs. 'That's not what Dad's told everyone. And that's fine by me.'

An hour later, the restaurant is packed with diners, proof that the *Totti Effect* is still very much in operation. And while I'm conscious of the time, I'm secretly pleased that Jacopo insisted on us having the special set meal. It's gorgeous – stuffed courgette flowers with ricotta, toasted almonds and fennel drizzled in olive oil to start, pan-fried sea bass on a bed of caraway-spiced orzo for the fish course, Parma ham–wrapped chicken with honey, balsamic vinegar and pine nuts served with a rainbow of roasted Mediterranean vegetables for the main and my favourite rose panna cotta with a pile of tiny, pistachio cream–filled bomboloni doughnuts for dessert.

I'm stuffed but happy, enjoying the banter with Elvis and Liam. I won't miss working for Callaghan or the job I've had at *The Herald*, but I'll miss this: the three of us hanging out. We'll say we'll keep in touch when I go to MediaCity, but will it actually happen? When you don't see people at work every day the gulf between you can grow.

I can't think about that now. Tonight, I'm celebrating.

'We should have bubbly,' Elvis says, raising his single pint of Peroni and clearly wishing it was an overflowing champagne glass. 'But I know you're driving.'

'Also, I'm seeing my mum,' I remind him. 'If I turned up in a taxi drunk I'd never hear the end of it.'

'Fair point. We'll toast you anyway. To Archie, the longest-serving tea boy in the business, and his glittering new career. About bloody time!'

'About bloody time!' we chorus, drinking together.

'Shame Jessie couldn't make it,' Elvis says, carefully.

'She's a ton of work on,' I reply.

'She'll come around.'

'I know.' I hope so. The way she evicted me from her flat last night and her determined silence today don't look like she's about to change her mind any time soon.

Liam polishes off his pint. 'She'll be reet. Jessie's a good 'un. And she knows a good thing when she sees it.'

'Well, I'm flattered, thank you.'

'Pleasure.' He tries unsuccessfully to hide a burp behind his hand. 'Besides, you've me to thank for you two being together.'

I laugh as I lean back in my chair, my stomach aching in a good way. 'If that's your lame attempt to get me to buy another round you're about to be disappointed.'

'I can buy my own. But you still need to thank me.'

'What's that?' Elvis asked. 'Liam playing Cupid?'

'Not a mental image I want on a full stomach. He's having a laugh.'

My colleague's grin drops. 'I'm serious.'

What is he talking about? 'I got us together. Because of the letter I wrote with Esther.'

'Oh, Esther's part of it, for sure. But the letter's immaterial.'

'Give over.'

Liam leans his elbows on the table. 'Jessie's with you because I told her you were a far better prospect than the other git she'd been seeing.'

The muscles in my stomach stop complaining and start to tighten. 'What?'

I see the look Elvis shoots at Liam and it dawns on me that I'm the only one out of the loop.

'What? He *is* a better prospect.'

'Hush your noise, kid.'

The first time Jessie had mentioned being single she'd said something about a guy not being on the scene anymore. 'Who was she seeing before?' I ask, my mind racing.

'Trust me, it's better you don't know.'

'Clearly both of you do, Brian.' I turn to Liam who is hastily downing his pint and raising his hand to Ciro for another. 'Who was it?'

He hesitates. Elvis stares at the table.

'It's not a difficult question. *Who* was Jessie seeing before me?'

All glimpses of humour have vanished from my colleague. Liam adopts an apologetic look before he launches his reply.

'Callaghan.'

Elvis groans into his pint.

What?

I don't know what to think. I know Callaghan often met

with Jessie for editorial stuff, but he yelled at her as much as he did me. Didn't he?

'Jessie – and *Callaghan*?'

'Oh, don't worry, it were all over weeks ago,' Liam offers, as if this makes everything okay. 'He was shagging some girl from Accounts, apparently. CCTV caught them doing it in the office late one night and when Jessie found out she dumped him.'

'Are you kidding me?'

Liam shrugs. 'Don't sweat the fine print, Arch. She was hacked off with Callaghan and needed a real bloke to be with. I did you a favour.'

'How, exactly? By suggesting she use me to get back at Callaghan?'

'Don't be daft. Callaghan never saw you as a threat. Besides, he's more concerned about the warning he's on with the board after his late-night hot-desking. I knew you liked Jessie and she needed a nudge in the right direction. And when Esther came along . . .'

My head is swimming now. 'Esther? What's she got to do with it?'

'Everything. I saw the way you lit up every time she sent you a message or you legged it out of the office to call her. Everyone noticed the change. I just pointed out the obvious to Jessie, told her she'd miss her chance of bagging a decent bloke if she didn't get in there first. And if there's one thing Jessie Edmonds hates it's losing.'

I can't believe what I'm hearing. Jessie and I got together because of the letter – that was the whole point of Esther and me writing it. Wasn't it?

But then I think of the timing – the moment Jessie started

talking to me, the attention she paid me that seemed to come out of nowhere. And those strange chats I saw her having with Liam . . .

'It doesn't matter, son,' Elvis says, shooting a warning look at Liam. 'Let's drop this, eh?'

'Fine by me.' I eyeball Liam. 'It doesn't matter how it happened. Point is we're together now. And she loves me.'

'Okay, whatever.' He flicks his napkin in surrender. 'But a thank you would be nice. See, the letter might have sealed the deal, kid, but her mind was made up long before that.'

I don't remember the drive over to Mum and Dad's. My head is a mess of countless questions with answers I don't want to find. All this time I've thought Jessie was with me because of my words – the words I found with Esther. But what if she isn't? Did she want me just because she wanted to win?

I don't want to think that about her, even with her current radio silence. I don't want to consider that everything she's done with me has been driven by jealousy. But her reaction to Esther whenever I mention her makes sense when I look at it like that. Is this all about Jessie winning, not about her loving me?

The celebration is in full swing when I arrive at the bakery. I let the warmth and noise and life of my family wrap around me like a warm blanket after a rain soaking, accepting hugs and smiles like life-saving medicine. Mum and Dad are in their element, holding court at the top of the large steel table in the bakery, which has been transformed into a dining table for their meal. Granda Brady is regaling everyone with his suspect tales, his cheeks red from a tot of whisky too many, too drunk and happy to care what anyone thinks. Dacey and Conn flank me on either side and we're squeezed shoulder-to-shoulder between near and distant Quinn relatives and friends. I pick at the food, too full from Rossi's and my stomach too churned by emotion to eat more, but nobody seems to notice amid the noise and laughter.

In a break between courses, my sister nudges my arm.

'So what happened?'

I force a smile. 'Handed in my notice today. Two weeks and I'll be out of *The Herald* for good.'

'Congrats, little bro,' Conn says, the other side of me. 'But that's not what Dace was asking.'

I look from one to the other, my spirits sinking when I realise I've been sussed. 'I don't think Jessie is with me because of the letter.'

I catch their exchanged glance and wish I hadn't seen it.

'Maybe not in the beginning, mate, but now . . . '

'Now she flies off the handle whenever I mention Esther,' I say, the pieces finally fitting together. 'And Jessie only started speaking to me when I was meeting up with Esther to write the letter. I saw her talking with Liam – they were always weird afterwards. I knew they were hiding something. But Callaghan . . . '

'Your boss? What's he got to do with this?'

'Jessie was with him before she found out he was sleeping with someone else. She was on the rebound and when Liam told her I'd met Esther, she wanted to get me before anything happened.'

'Wow,' Conn says, shaking his head. 'And I thought my love life was messy when I was single.'

'What do you want, Arch?' Dacey leans a little closer against my arm. 'Because really that's all that matters.'

'I want . . . ' I begin. But my words stall.

I have a sudden, unwelcome recollection of the moment I kissed Esther – when I'd wondered if my words in the letter were about her and not Jessie. And that conversation in the car after going to see Jim, when I nearly asked her the question that's been buzzing in my head for weeks: has she ever considered we might get together?

'He wants his head examining,' Granda Brady states, sliding a chair between Conn and me. 'See if there's an ounce of common sense left in there.'

We groan as one, but our granda is not one for taking a hint, especially after whisky.

'Go easy on him, Granda,' Dacey warns. 'He's had a rough night.'

'With all that shite he's wading in, no wonder. Archie Quinn, is that auld heart of yours in trouble again?'

'No,' I begin, but as usual Granda isn't listening.

'Your woman and the job offer and the friend who isn't just a friend but sure your heart isn't to blame for any of it.'

'Jessie might not have chosen me because of the letter.'

'The letter you wrote with Esther.'

I nod. 'She'd just dumped our boss before she decided to say yes to me.'

'So the girl has some taste,' Granda says, his smile fading when he sees his grandchildren's mirrored expressions. 'You wrote her a letter with your heart inked into every word.'

'Which meant nothing in her decision to be with me . . . ' I say.

'Who said I was referring to Jessie?' The warmth of my granda's hand on my shoulder is comforting. 'I don't claim to be an expert,' he says, ignoring Dacey and Conn's laughter at this, 'but it appears to me that your letter *did* work for you, only not with the woman you thought you were in love with.'

Reeling, I close my eyes as my brother, sister and granda gently return to the happy chatter around me.

What if they're right? What if everything I've believed is wrong? Does my heart belong to Esther Hughes, not Jessie Edmonds?

And if that's true, where does that leave any of us?

Forty-One

ESTHER

It's funny how life turns around when you least expect it.

I knew Mr Grove was talking to his printer friend about a potential meeting with me, but I never expected to receive a job offer on the strength of a phone call.

I was just working my way through the latest batch of ironing after dropping the girls off at school this morning when my phone rang. It was a landline, an 0161 number that I didn't recognise.

'Miss Hughes? Hello, I'm Sid Maven. I run Maven Print in Oldham – we work closely with Pete Grove at Concilio?'

It was such a shock I almost dropped my phone as I left the ironing on the board and sank into the nearest armchair.

'Hi. Great to speak with you.'

'Pete showed me the brochure you designed for him and I've just this minute shared it with my daughter Greta. She loves it and so do I.'

'Thank you.'

'I think the two of you could be a fantastic creative team. It's been what's missing from my business for too long. Pete tells me you have project management and marketing experience?'

'I do,' I said, trying to snatch enough breath to speak.

'I could start you on two days a week, see how you and Greta get on. Pete suggested releasing you from two nights of cleaning and together we'll work out a remuneration package more suited to the role.'

'How much are you suggesting?' Thrilled though I was, I needed to make sure I could afford to make the change. Two trips to Oldham and back a week would be a significant change from what I've been doing.

When he mentioned the figure, it was all I could do not to squeal out loud. Almost three times the hourly rate of my cleaning job.

'Yes,' I rushed. 'Yes, I'd love to.'

I start the new arrangement on Monday. Everything is suddenly brighter, my plan to afford to rent a place of my own again so much closer than before.

So tonight is going to be a celebration. I've good news and a whole evening alone with Matt.

And Picard, of course, but he's had extra treats today and is merrily snoozing in front of the TV. I don't reckon he'll wake for a couple of hours.

I've made a huge pot roast – Matt's all-time favourite meal – and my mobile is turned off for the night. I felt bad about dashing off to Jim's with Archie last Saturday and while I don't regret going, I do need to spend more time with my boyfriend. I waited so long to be with him, so I should make the most of every moment we have together – especially when it looks like there will be more coming soon.

He hasn't apologised for his mood last weekend, or the couple of days of sulky silence that followed. He should, but it isn't worth holding out for. I just want to get on with my life as peacefully and happily as I can. It's what Archie's doing with Jessie, so I should do the same. Maybe that will finally put the questions to rest . . .

'What's this?' Matt appears in the kitchen, shrugging off his rain-splattered jacket.

'Special dinner.' I smile, sliding my arms up around his neck and kissing him. It works: he eagerly returns my kiss.

'Wow. Let's skip dinner and take this straight upstairs . . .'

'Later, Mr Hope. Right now we're celebrating.'

'Celebrating what?'

'Us. And the future.' I slip out of his embrace and hand him a glass of ice-cold Prosecco, silently thanking Naomi for donating it from her worryingly large stash in the garage.

'You should celebrate properly,' she'd insisted earlier, pushing the bottle into my hands. 'Even if he doesn't deserve it, you definitely do.'

She hasn't exactly welcomed Matt being back in my life – she hasn't forgiven him for everything, either – but she's trying. Gavin remains resolutely tight-lipped about it all, but I feel his support for me at least. Dad just wants me to be happy: if he has misgivings he's careful to keep them to himself. Mum will take longer to come round, I know. She might never fully welcome Matt into the family.

But the Prosecco from Naomi is a start. Time will be the only test of Matt and me. We just have to prove this is real by hanging in there.

I'm only having half a glass of Prosecco, needing to get home in the morning for the last school run of the week.

We clink glasses, then I usher Matt into the living room where

I've already set the table, candles and best china and all. I can't remember the last time I did this but it feels wonderfully hopeful.

I've thought a lot about last weekend and Archie's question I almost answered. Thank goodness he admitted our kiss was a mistake before I said anything I'd regret. I think I've projected my worries about Matt and me onto the situation with him. I can't let myself think of Archie as anything other than a friend – I need to learn from the past and just accept what a gift Archie's friendship is. I don't need it to be anything more. Knowing I have him as a friend is enough.

It *should be* enough.

Tonight is about righting the balance. Matt is my boyfriend; Archie is my friend and right now I need to be with someone who loves me. Especially with the news I'm about to share.

I wait until we've finished eating, which is its own special torture when I want Matt to know everything. It means we'll have more time together, less evenings taken up with the cleaning job – every way I look at it, this is progress. Another step to getting where I want to be, in life and in love.

Finally, it's time.

'So, what are we celebrating?' he asks, pouring the last of the Prosecco into his glass.

'I have a new job.' My face aches from smiling already.

His eyes widen. 'You're jacking in the cleaning?'

'Not entirely, but I'll be doing fewer shifts. Three nights a week, that's all. Because two days a week I'm going to be a marketing manager.'

'Where?'

'For the cleaning company. Well, working in conjunction with the printers they use for all their leaflets. I start on Monday.'

I wait for his reply. It doesn't arrive.

I wasn't expecting a twenty-one-gun salute, but I thought I might at least get a smile from him. There's no smile. Just a frown.

'How much marketing does a cleaning company need?' he asks, at last.

'More than they have right now. And I'll be working with Greta, the printer's daughter, so we'll do other work when Concilio don't need us.'

Matt sniffs. 'Part-time, then?'

'To begin with. If it takes off, who knows?' I stare at him. 'It's good news.'

'Is it?'

Irritation flicks at my good mood. 'I think it is. More money, a chance to do something I love. And it means I won't be working every weeknight, so more time for us to be together.'

'You could go for a full-time marketing manager job. They're ten to a penny in Salford.'

I sit back in my chair, my excitement deflating. 'They're not. I know; I tried to find one for over a year.'

'I'm sure you tried. But you shouldn't have to.'

'What's that supposed to mean?'

'If you moved in with me you wouldn't have to worry.'

What? Where did that come from? Is he even listening to me? 'We're not talking about moving in . . . '

'Why not? It makes perfect sense: you move in and look for a proper job without the pressure to earn. I earn more than enough to pay the bills so you could just relax. Not have to push a cleaning trolley or do crappy little flyers for a tiny printing company.'

'Who said anything about crappy? Maybe they'll be the best in Manchester.'

'Move in with me, Es. It'll solve all your problems. Then we would have something proper to celebrate.'

'This is something to celebrate! It's a huge step forward for me, don't you see that?'

'Sure, it's nice someone sees you as more than a cleaning lady. But I want you to live with me because I love you. Isn't that more important?'

'I'm not ready to move in with you.'

Matt looks at the remains of our meal on the perfectly set table. 'You look pretty at home to me. Cooking in my kitchen, meeting me at the door, making *this* for us . . .'

I stare at him. Is he really suggesting I play the little woman waiting for his return with his dinner on the table? 'That's not the same as living together! We aren't ready.'

I hate his shrug that dismisses my words. 'I am.' Seeing my expression he reaches across the table for me. 'Es, I love you. I want to be with you, all the time. Don't you think we've waited long enough?'

'We've only just got together . . .'

'And it's everything I hoped it would be. I'm happy, Es. I can make you happy. When we know how we feel, why wait?'

I go cold. That phrase, so like his excuse when he announced he was marrying Nina. Can't he see how foolish that turned out to be? He was in such a hurry last time – what if we end up like they did?

'I'm not ready,' I say.

'But you will be.' He stands and holds out his hands. 'Let's forget this, okay? I love you. I just want to spend time with you.'

*

That night I lie awake beside him, staring at the ceiling. We didn't mention the job or moving in again and I was too tired to fight it, so I brushed it aside. But in the early hours of the morning it all becomes horribly clear. He used exactly the same line to justify us moving in together as he'd used to marry Nina far too early. There was no heart in it, no originality. And instead of fighting back I gave in. Has Matt learned nothing from the mistake he made with Nina?

Have I?

I set aside my own feelings to keep him close to me tonight, just like I did back then. The only difference is that he spent the night with me this time instead of Nina. I made it easy for him to call the shots. All things considered, is Matt worth doing that for over and over just to be able to call him mine?

I longed for him to love me for so many years. Shouldn't him wanting to live with me feel more of a thrill than this? And why doesn't he seem to listen to anything I say?

Just before 3 a.m. I slip out of his house, closing the door quietly so I don't wake Picard. I drive slowly through empty streets, my skin buzzing with adrenaline while my mind craves rest. When I reach Naomi's I let myself in and head straight for my room, collapsing with relief on my bed.

I must sleep because when I open my eyes my 6 a.m. morning alarm is going off. Aching and weary I wash and dress and head downstairs.

'She's *here*!' a small voice squeaks – and suddenly I'm being hugged by an armful of little blonde beauties.

I laugh in surprise and look up to see the kitchen decked out in brightly coloured homemade bunting, each triangle decorated with the girls' exuberant drawings.

'We did it last night,' Ava-May says, grabbing my hand and dragging me over to the kitchen with her sisters. 'To *ceb-re-late* your new job!'

'Celebrate,' Molly corrects her.

Ava-May scowls. 'That's what I *said* . . .'

'Do you like it, Auntie Es?' Issy asks, leaning her head against my arm.

Tears flood my eyes. 'It's wonderful! You're all wonderful.'

'Does that include me?' Gavin grins, arriving with a plate laden with pastries.

I smile through my tears at my brother-in-law. 'Always.'

'We're just so proud of you,' Molly says, sounding at least thirty years her senior. 'You worked really hard and got the best job because of it.'

'Okay, girls, put your auntie down,' Naomi says, planting a kiss on my cheek as she walks past. 'Don't forget the *other* surprise we have.'

I look at their excited faces, my heart so full I can barely breathe. 'What other surprise?'

Issy, Molly and Ava-May huddle together, bare feet dancing excitedly on the slate tiles.

'We got tickets!' they chorus.

'Tickets for what?'

'Your concert!' Issy smiles.

I turn to my sister who is smiling over her coffee cup. 'I thought you were busy tomorrow?'

'We are. Watching you and your ukulele.'

It's too much. This is how I should have felt last night:

I expected to feel it from Matt, never from my family. But as I gather Naomi and the girls into my arms, tears running freely down my face, it all becomes clear. It should be this easy to celebrate with me. Matt couldn't be happy for me – about my job or the gig. He's coming tomorrow but under duress. I should have his support and belief in me like my family are demonstrating so readily this morning.

I've made the biggest mistake.

Matt Hope isn't right for me.

And after the gig tomorrow, I'm going to tell him . . .

Forty-Two

ARCHIE

It's here. The day of the gig we almost didn't get to play.

Thankfully, Big Jim is one of the first to arrive, which is more of a relief than I was expecting. I know we coaxed him back when we visited his house, but a lot can happen in a few days.

A lot's happened for me.

I'm still getting my head around what Liam told me, and what Dacey, Conn and Granda said. It's weird that, although neither Dacey nor Conn has met Esther yet, they completely understood who she was and why she mattered to me.

Why she *matters* to me.

I lay awake for hours last night, trying to work out what I'd say to her if I got the chance today. I don't know that anything I could say would make any kind of difference, but I'd like to try. It matters to me that she knows what I've worked out about the letter.

I thought about Jessie, too. About the mess I've made for myself because I couldn't admit I'd fallen for Esther instead. I should have refused to deliver the letter. I should have told Esther *she* was the reason I wrote it; that it was and always will be hers. I should have said *something*. Because now three people stand to be hurt by the truth: Jessie, Esther and me.

How I feel was never Jessie's fault and I feel awful for pursuing her when my heart was already spoken for. I am such a coward. Moving on, whatever happens, I'm going to make myself be honest every time. Right now, I feel like the lowest of the low. And it's only going to get worse with what happens today.

I sense it, in the dust-scented air around me: today is the day things will change.

'You okay, Archie?' Granda Brady is carefully lifting his beloved accordion from its tatty velvet-lined box.

'I'm grand. Just nerves, you know?'

'Nerves. Right.' He gives me that look of his that says how transparent my excuse really is. 'Well, I hope the poor unfortunates subjected to our din today appreciate the effort.'

'Marta says all the tickets sold out?'

'Aye. Poor unsuspecting beggars, the lot of them. Still, she's brought extra cakes and tay to soften the blow.' He grins, shouldering his accordion straps. 'Is the lovely Miss Hughes with us yet?'

I feel my shoulders prickle. 'Not yet.'

'She'll be bringing her man with her, I suppose?'

'I guess.' I try to look disinterested, fiddling with a tuning peg on Béla Fleck, but I'm fooling no one.

'And will your Jessie be here?'

The truth is, I don't know. She has a ticket and the last time we spoke she said she was coming, although she did ask very pointedly if Esther would be here, too.

'Mm-hmm,' I reply, hoping it covers every eventuality.

'Life,' Granda Brady says, shaking his head. 'It can be a twisted ball sack sometimes.'

Not sure you could put that on an inspirational meme but you can't fault my granda's knack of getting to the crux of an issue . . .

The rest of The Old Guys are here now, each doing their best to look confident as they fuss over music stands and instruments. I don't think any of us would win any prizes for our act but at least we're all in the same boat: a trembling, stomach-sick, cold-dread, fear-filled boat of terrified almost-musicians.

'And the team is complete!' Kavi, the calmest of us all by a mile, looks over towards the door and raises his hand.

I turn to see Esther walking in, her ukulele bag with its rainbow strap slung across her body. Behind her is a skyscraper of a bloke, wearing a scowl not unlike Jessie's the other night. I'm guessing that's Matt. He has one hand protectively on her shoulder and appears to be scanning the room ahead of them like a professional sniper.

He could eat me for breakfast.

I swallow hard.

I hadn't imagined what Matt Hope would look like but I don't think I expected someone quite so tall and with that much presence. Esther looks small by comparison, not helped by the nervous way she's creeping into the hall today.

I have to stop this. I have no right to judge who Esther loves. If she sees something worth loving in Matt, it's none of my business to wonder why. Esther didn't stuff this up: I did. If I hadn't mentioned Jessie just after we'd kissed . . .

'Ah, your girl is here,' Granda Brady says, far too loudly not to be heard. When I glare at him, he nods back over the shoulder of Matt the Giant towards the entrance. Jessie is there, her hair newly curled into golden spirals, dressed in a white shirt and blue jeans that hug every curve. Several of The Old Guys gaze over and I kick myself for being torn between watching her and following Esther's progress across the community hall.

Esther, whom I shouldn't have kissed. Jessie, who used me to get back at her ex. It should be easy to work out how I feel about them both. Why isn't it?

'Hey,' Esther says, reaching the edge of the makeshift stage. 'Please tell me you're as nervous as I am.'

'Probably more.' I smile back, glancing up as the ominous shadow of an unimpressed boyfriend falls on me. 'Hi, you must be Matt.'

My offered hand is ignored at first, then – following a nudge from Esther – grudgingly accepted. *Man*, he has a firm grip . . .

'Wouldn't miss it,' he grunts, squeezing my hand just a little tighter before releasing it. A warning shot.

'Should be good,' I reply, aiming my words at Esther instead of her scary companion.

'Looking good, Arch,' Jessie trills, arriving at my side. It's forced, too bright, and I wonder if this is Jessie wanting to win at all costs. I think of her trading Callaghan for me when she couldn't win with him, and it makes me go cold.

Matt the Giant's eyes light up and it feels like a point scored. He should be looking only at Esther, though, and as Jessie kisses my cheek, I glance at my friend to gauge her reaction. But Esther is far too consumed by nerves to notice any of it. That's good, I think.

Tentatively, I curl my arm around Jessie's waist. 'I wasn't sure you were coming.'

'Where else would I be?' Smooth reply, Jessie Edmonds. Does she mean it?

'You should probably get your seat,' Esther says to Matt.

I see him eyeballing me. 'Sure, babe. Just think, when you're living at mine you can play for me whenever you like.'

What?

I try to catch Esther's eye, but she's glaring at the floor.

Moving in? When did that happen?

'Personal gigs I don't have to pay for,' Matt continues, oblivious. 'Or share with anyone.' I hate the way his fingers move in possessive circles over her shoulder. I hate the glances he shoots at me. *Yeah, fella, like hell I don't know what you're doing . . .*

'That's what I was saying to Arch the other day,' Jessie says, looking between Matt and me as if she's trying to guess the winner.

Now Esther looks at me. I can't hold her gaze.

'I mean, we work together right now, but once he takes his new job at MediaCity, it makes sense for him to move in.'

Hell, no.

I wanted Jessie to accept my job, but this? The last time we spoke she didn't know if she wanted to be with me anymore. Now she's moving me in?

I hadn't anticipated this. It's like witnessing an out-of-control juggernaut thundering straight towards me.

'New job, huh?' Matt says, the glint of victory in his eyes.

'At ITV,' I say, instantly wishing I hadn't because now it looks like I'm backing up everything Jessie is saying.

'For a while,' Jessie continues, breezily unaware of the carnage she's causing. 'But our boss at the paper is getting on. Pretty soon he'll be gone and then, who knows? Maybe we're destined to run *The Herald* together. Archie would make a fantastic co-editor.'

I'm sorry, *what?*

I stare at her, my mouth dropping open. Jessie keeps her smile fully on Matt.

When she talked about us 'showing the board' what we could do, was this what she had in mind? I don't want to be an editor. I want to find the stories and write them. It's all I've ever wanted. Does Jessie even care?

'So you won't be working at Esther's place?' Matt asks.

Jessie frowns. 'Esther's place?' She turns to Esther, most definitely observing her down her nose. 'Sorry, do you work at *The Herald*? Only I've never seen you there. Where are you, in Sales?'

Esther makes to speak but the man-mountain gets there first. 'Oh, you wouldn't have seen her. She's a – what's the official term, babe? – night operative.'

'We really need to get up on the stage,' I rush, seeing exactly where this conversation is headed and knowing Esther is in the firing line from both sides.

'Yeah, we should . . .'

'Cleaner!' Jessie exclaims, snapping her fingers. 'You're a cleaner at *The Herald*?'

Shit. My heart hits the cracked vinyl floor.

Esther seems to shrink and I am powerless to stop it. At a loss for what to do, I'm about to reach for her arm when something amazing happens. She lifts her head, straightens her shoulders and squares up to my girlfriend.

'That's right. I'm part of the skilled team that keeps your office serviceable. Which is a good thing, considering most *Herald* employees don't take responsibility for the *mess* they create.' Her eyes slide to me. I can't read them. I'm scared of what waits for me there.

Beside me, Jessie fumes.

'We need to get going,' I say, watching Esther already walking up to the stage. 'Sorry, I didn't introduce you: Jessie – this is Matt, Esther's boyfriend. Matt, my girlfriend, Jessie.'

My girlfriend. My girlfriend who just announced we're moving in together – which is news to me – and then tried to belittle my loveliest friend. She is not the woman I thought she was – getting with Callaghan, chasing me because she wanted to win, hurting my friend. Who is Jessie Edmonds? And who does she think I am?

Oblivious to all of this, she turns to Matt.

'Ready for an hour of torture?' she asks, completely blanking me.

'Not sure,' Matt replies. 'We could sit together, if you need an ally?'

My girlfriend beams. 'Love to.' She turns to me, as if she's only just remembered I'm here. 'You don't mind, do you, Arch?'

'Not at all. Enjoy the pain, both.'

I watch them stride away together.

Nerves ball in my stomach.

What the hell just happened? Why didn't I challenge Jessie when she was mocking Esther? And will Esther ever forgive me?

A trill of a whistle sounds and I turn to see my entire family walking in. Granda Brady's reserved the whole of the second row for them – and the sight of the marvellous Quinns warms my heart. Conn and his girlfriend Elodie, Dacey with her husband Griff and their twin girls Carys and Tirion, and, right in the centre of the row, beaming like nutters, Mum and Dad. Dad gives me a thumbs-up sign and I send one back, my heart dropping to my red sneakers when they all start chatting together.

I need to check Esther is okay.

She's already sitting in place when I go up onto the stage. Old Bob and Li'l Bill flank her on either side – thankfully all smiles and flushed-face chatter once more after the disaster that was the Dress Rehearsal of Doom. I take my seat across the semi-circle of chairs from her, noticing her thunderous glance in my direction before she turns to chat to Big Jim, who is checking everyone's sheet music.

'You're going to be great,' he's saying, loud enough for all of us to hear and several of the arriving audience besides.

'We're going to bomb,' Eric mutters beside me, drumming his silver ring–stacked fingers against the scuffed wooden body of his guitar. 'Spectacularly.'

'I wish we'd had more time to rehearse,' I say, still reeling from the exchange with our significant others and wishing I could steal a moment with Esther alone.

Eric's loud laugh is a shock. '*More* rehearsal? You think we'd have survived that? The last one nearly finished us off!'

'Gentlemen, calm yourselves,' my granda says, leaning back in his brown plastic chair. 'In the words of the great Irish philosopher – I forget his name – "if it's good it'll be great; if it's shite it'll be over soon".' Pleased with himself, he clicks the keys of the accordion fingerboard and starts to play a few experimental notes.

'That'll be the great philosopher Diarmuid Brady of Wythenshawe, I take it.' Eric grins at me.

'The one and only.' I smile back. If I could just talk to Esther . . .

'Right, lads – and lassie – are you ready?' Big Jim is rubbing his hands together, looking expectantly around the group. 'It's time.'

As one The Old Guys shrink in their seats.

Jim turns to face the audience and the room begins to hush.

A few latecomers hurry to their seats. I catch Esther's eye and mouth *good luck*. She blinks and looks back at her music.

'Welcome to our charity performance,' Jim booms. 'Before we begin, let me just say this is the first time The Old Guys have performed in front of a live audience, so please bear with us and be kind. We hope the pleasure of the music will outweigh the pain of listening.'

A ripple of amusement passes across the hall.

Then Jim raises his hands and we start to play . . .

Forty-Three

ESTHER

It's awful.

Every laboured, out-of-tune note, every slip of the rhythm. We trip and stumble our way through the first medley of three reels, deliberately run together by Big Jim to beat the audience into submission. My hands are cold, my fingers so numb I can't feel the strings, as I try my best to play. But it isn't nerves, or lack of practice that's causing this.

It's Matt.

And Jessie.

And Archie.

The moment Matt spoke of us moving in, when I thought we'd already had the conversation where I said I wasn't ready – and when I'm not even certain I want to be with him anymore. That bloody awful, sneering remark Jessie made about my job, thinking she could lord it over me like some menial skivvy to her far superior job description. And the moment I discovered Archie is so much more invested in her than I thought – their whole lives planned out, apparently.

And none of it, not one single detail, includes me.

I'm a possession to my boyfriend, an object of derision to Jessie – and to Archie? What am I to him?

So the notes and the timing and the music score pass me by as all of the utter, shambling mess of my life tumbles and crashes around me.

I can see Naomi and Gavin at the end of one row, Issy, Molly and Ava-May sitting with my parents on the row behind. Dad is grinning and appears to have found a ukulele T-shirt to wear. Even Mum is sending me encouraging smiles – I never imagined that happening today. I wish I could smile as brightly back at them as I want to: all I manage is a weak wave when the medley ends.

Archie's grandad is up now, charming the audience as they recover from the first onslaught of our music. He's bringing them in on the joke, which of course was my idea, and to their credit they are responding, their laughter becoming surer and the strained atmosphere lessening its grip on the hall.

'Of course, I cannot claim this confession as my own idea,' Granda Brady continues. 'It was the wisdom of our only lady player that made this happen. Give us a wave, Esther Hughes.'

I'm so surprised I wave blandly back. A good-natured murmur from the hall greets me, but when I look over at Matt and Jessie in the centre of the audience, they're too busy talking to notice.

'And so, knowing the terrible truth about our musical capabilities, I invite you all to revel in the chaos that is the next part of this afternoon's programme. With deepest apologies to the great and noble Robert Burns, please accept our earnest murdering of his classic, "Ae Fond Kiss".'

As I turn to look at my music, I notice Archie across the stage. He is staring at me. I wrench my gaze away to the safety of the printed score. I can't think about him, or any of them. Instead, I take my solace between the lines of manuscript, allowing the flow of notes and bars to soothe my aching eyes.

Four more pieces pass by, each one met by building applause as the audience enters into the fun of the event. And then Big Jim announces a thirty-minute break, 'to soothe your poor heads with refreshments from our saviour, Marta'.

Archie makes a move towards me but I'm not speaking to him right now. I smile quickly as I pass my family, seeing their surprise as I hurry past. There's somebody else I have to talk to first.

Matt is sitting back in his chair laughing with Jessie when I reach the end of his row. I have to say his name three times with increasing volume to catch his attention. He mutters something to her as he stands – and the way she sniggers makes my hackles rise.

'Please tell me you're sending me home early,' he says, reaching my side.

You have no idea.

'Can we talk? Outside? I need some air.'

His smile is mean and he doesn't even realise it. 'I'm not surprised after that display,' he says, following me to the door. 'Whatever made you lot think you were ready to perform?'

I don't reply until we're out in the car park, a little way from the entrance to the community hall. Then, summoning all my breath and courage, I face him.

'I'm sorry it offends you.'

His mouth flaps a little. 'I – didn't mean . . . I didn't know . . . '

'It seems there's a lot about me you don't know. If you did, you'd know what playing with those wonderful people means to me, however awful we sound. You'd know that this is the first place I've felt welcomed for a really long time and that learning this instrument has been one of the loveliest serendipities of my life . . . '

'Oh, come on, Es . . . '

'And you'd know that when I say I don't want to move in with you yet, I mean I don't want to move in with you.'

'Yeah, but you will eventually. I mean it makes sense . . . '

'To *you*.' I stab a finger at his chest. 'It makes sense to you because that's all you ever see: your way, your plans, your wants. I don't think you even listened to me the other day.'

His expression darkens. 'Well, maybe if I didn't feel like you were holding off committing to me fully because you think your little mate with the banjo might change his mind . . . '

I can't believe he just said that. 'You're not listening now! I'm not talking about Archie . . . '

'Not out loud, maybe. But your body is screaming it.' Stunned, I just stare at him. 'And don't give me that shocked look, Esther. I've seen the way you've been gazing at each other right through the concert. It's embarrassing, frankly. Jessie said she's had the same battle with Archie. Do you take us both for mugs?'

'Jessie said . . . ?'

'Oh, I've learned a lot in there while you've been murdering music. That poor woman's thought you were over her shoulder the whole time, waiting to tempt Archie away . . . '

At my side, my fingers curl into fists. 'That's not true!'

'Not how Jessie sees it, and I have to say I found a lot resonating with me.'

'I helped Archie write a love letter to her. I'm the reason they're together.'

'Not the way she sees it.'

I can't believe he's saying this, that he actually believes any of it. 'Why would I get Archie and Jessie together if I wanted him for myself?'

He shrugs, his scowl deepening. 'Oh, I don't know; maybe because you changed your mind? Wanted him for yourself the moment Jessie had him?'

'No.'

'That's what it looks like to me.'

'Then you're not looking very far.'

'Tell me you're not in love with him.'

'I – I . . .' I falter, the rising rage in me causing me to stumble over my words. Matt throws up his hands and starts to walk back towards the hall.

This is it: another crossroads. A moment to speak. Last time I backed down and all the heartbreak of watching Matt marrying Nina followed. In this moment, I don't feel any stronger than I did back then. But I made a promise to myself to never fail to speak when it mattered.

It matters now.

'I loved you,' I shout.

Halfway across the car park, Matt freezes. He doesn't turn round. But I don't need him to.

I summon every ounce of breath and nerve I can and aim them squarely at his back. 'I loved you. For years. I didn't tell you because I thought it would end us. But what I imagined we could have together was never like *this*. I wanted it to work, but it isn't.'

Slowly, he turns back, his shoulders rounding as if under the influence of a significant weight. 'Because of Archie.'

'No. Because of you. And me. And the fact that we aren't what I thought we were.'

'You know what you're saying?'

Tears burn my eyes. 'Yes.'

'Because you can never take that back, Esther.'

'I don't want to.' I feel the weight of it now, slamming onto my head, threatening to crush me. 'You don't know me, Matt. Even after all these years. You just see the Esther you want and superimpose it on me. You don't hear me because what you think I should be saying blasts out my words. I don't even think you love me, not in the way you say. I think Nina was a mistake, I think you married her before you were ready and when it didn't work out, you looked to me as the solution.'

'That's not true . . . '

'I can't make everything all right for you, Matt, because you only see what you want to see. There's no future there. I don't want to end up hating you.'

'Because of Archie,' he says again. And that's my answer. He hasn't listened to me. He isn't listening now. It doesn't matter how loud I speak or what words I choose, Matt Hope is never going to hear me.

I think, if I'm honest with myself, I've always known this. Wishing it could be different isn't enough to change the truth.

'Go home,' I say, my voice steady and controlled and startlingly weary. 'You don't have to stay here.'

'Come with me.'

'No.'

'Just to talk?'

'You won't hear me.' The truth hangs heavy on my heart.

'You're dumping me and you won't even give me a lift

home?' If it's an attempt at humour it's too pathetic to amuse either of us.

'Two buses to get back to yours,' I say, sounding eerily like my mum. 'Or one taxi. Your choice.'

He doesn't say anything. Instead, he just strides past me like I'm not even there.

Shaken, I hurry back inside.

Big Jim is calling everyone back to their seats. Archie is at the edge of the stage with Brady. He frowns when he sees me but when he reaches out I hurry past. I can't trust myself to explain why yet. I keep my head down, fiddling with the ukulele's strings as Eric passes me the second-half music sheets. I can feel Archie's stare even though I daren't look up.

I won't cry.

I blink the beginnings of tears away.

I *won't* cry. I'll finish this concert with the people I love and then I'll deal with what I've just done. I'm so numb I don't even know how I'll feel. Right now what matters are the tunes and the group around me.

The second set passes in a haze of effort and applause. We finish with 'The Wishing Tree' – the first piece I heard The Old Guys play – and I sense things coming gently full circle. I didn't belong then: I do now. There's comfort knowing I've moved forward.

The audience's applause swells around us as we shakily stand to take our bows. Relief is at work both on the stage and in the hall, but we did it. As we retake our seats, Granda Brady walks to the front of the stage.

'Well, you're made of sterner stuff than we thought,' he begins, his smile widening as laughter fills the room. 'But bless you for it. Before we grant you your much-deserved freedom, allow me to charm some money from your pockets.' He shrugs, the smile broadening further. 'Ah, come on now, did you think you'd get away with the ticket price alone? We are here for one reason only: to raise funds to keep this marvellous project going. Let me let you in on a little secret: this whole shindig was my idea. The group, I mean. You have Marta to blame for the gig.'

Marta raises an apologetic hand over by the kitchen hatch. More laughter meets her gesture.

'I started this group not long after losing my wife. Now, I was lucky: being from the Emerald Isle we'd ensured a large, loud and loving family would always surround us. But even in the clamour of Bradys and Quinns, I felt alone. I knew Big Jim here from my local pub and so he was the first Old Guy I approached. I knew he'd had a tough time of it, too – and something he said to me back then really stuck in my mind: he said, "I feel like I'm past use. Someone should just chuck me in a skip and be done with it".'

I remember Big Jim revealing this to Archie and me: how we gathered around him in his many-pictured lounge, hugging him as he sobbed. I'm looking at Archie before I realise. When Granda Brady continues, I force my eyes away.

'Nobody should feel they are past usefulness, past redemption. So I started this group with just two rules: one, that every member should feel important, regardless of their musical ability; and two, that every instrument should be rescued. Only those considered worthless or too broken should qualify. Hence the punishment we've inflicted on your ears tonight. The music is immaterial. What matters is how being together feels. Because no matter how battered and broken we think we are, when we're together something magical happens.'

He glances at me, then over to Archie, before turning back to the crowd.

'And here's the thing: we're all on this stage because somebody arrived in our lives at the right time. Someone saw the worth in us, the value. My dear friends in this hall, you have arrived at the right time to ensure we have a future.' He holds up his bony hands. 'No pressure, obviously.' Laughter pools warmly at his feet like an incoming summer tide. 'So, dig deep, we ask. And if you donate enough, we'll promise *not* to play for you again for a good while.'

It's too much.

I know what he's trying to do and it doesn't surprise me at all that Granda Brady had us sussed all along. But Archie is looking over at Jessie in the middle of the room – and I see the truth: he sees her like I see him. It's unmistakable.

I don't want to see any more.

I have to get out of here.

Grabbing my ukulele bag and jacket, I jump down from the stage and skirt the volunteers with donation buckets before I duck my head to avoid eye contact with my family and run out of the hall.

Forty-Four

ARCHIE

She can't leave.

She just *can't*.

Matt disappeared at the interval and from the look on Esther's face it's clear he isn't coming back. I know she hasn't sent him packing for me, but I have to talk to her – about the letter, about Jessie, about everything.

I'm scared if I don't say it now, I might never get the chance.

It's chaos when I jump down from the stage, people from the audience swarming around the donation buckets, friends and family of The Old Guys keen to congratulate their loved ones and a tide of bodies in a last-minute rush to the kitchen hatch for the remaining pieces of Marta's delicious cakes. I apologise and weave and wind my way through them all, pushing as hard as I dare, aware of the seconds passing pulling the gap wider between Esther and me.

'There he is! My beautiful banjo-playing boy!' Mum is suddenly ahead of me, her cool hands resting on my cheeks. *Pastry-making hands*, Nanna Brady used to say, proudly. *Your*

Dougie's the bread man, Kathleen, but your hands will always bless the pastry. It's a heaven-made match for sure! It's been nine years since my grandma died, but in moments like this she's as present as any of my family in the hall.

'So glad you liked it,' I hurry, my eyes straying over Mum's shoulder to the open door beyond. Is Esther still there? Have I missed her?

Dad slaps a hand against my back, forgetting as always just how strong thirty-five years of breadmaking has made him. 'Bloody good, Arch. Even the dodgy bits.'

'Thanks, guys.' I gently pull Mum's hands from my face and squeeze them. 'I've just got to dash, but I'll see you later, yeah?'

'Where are you off to?' My big brother steps into the narrow gap that had opened ahead of me, Elodie smiling at his side. 'Dashing off to avoid your fans?'

I can't explain now, I've lost too much time as it is. I'm about to reply when my sister enters the Quinn family huddle, reaching in to grasp my shoulder like a security guard at a concert barrier rescuing a stricken fan.

God bless Dacey Quinn-Roberts.

'You need to get a wiggle on.' She smiles at me, edging ever so gently between Mum and Conn to create a narrow escape route to the door.

'I'm trying to,' I hiss through my teeth.

'Archie has to go now,' Dacey announces, her authoritative tone shocking everyone into submissive silence. 'He'll tell us all about it when he gets back.' She nods at me as she propels me towards the gap. 'Go. And don't stuff it up this time.'

I have always loved Dacey, but in this moment she has claimed top spot on my Favourite Human Beings on The Planet list.

Leaving her fielding a vociferous inquisition from our family, I make my break for freedom.

Please be outside, I will Esther, as if she can hear my telepathic plea.

What do I do if she isn't there?

I'm almost at the door when someone steps into the light. I stop inches from slamming into them. When I blink my focus back, I find Jessie glaring at me.

Around her the late afternoon sun is glowing like a pink-gold halo. She is every bit as gorgeous as she ever was, hair down, skin flawless, body perfect.

But . . . I don't love her.

Maybe I loved the thought of her because for years she was unattainable: it's crass to call her a goddess but that's how she seemed. Beautiful, remote, out of reach. I could imagine that being with her would be completely perfect because it was never going to happen. I couldn't even form a decent sentence in her presence until Esther arrived in my life.

Because *that's* why I don't love Jessie.

Without knowing it, Esther won my heart, not by being some out-of-reach siren but by being exactly who she is. I loved the idea of Jessie Edmonds, but my heart loved the reality of Esther Hughes. Crazy Esther Hughes, who rescued a half-written love letter and decided it needed completing. Esther Hughes who fell asleep in a cleaning cupboard and changed my world when she awoke. Esther Hughes aka Old Mrs Stanhope, giggling her way out of *The Herald*'s building in an old coat and paper-towel headscarf, hand in hand with me. Co-conspirator, fellow love letter researcher, constant cheerleader – stealer of my heart.

I've made the biggest mess of it all, dragging Jessie and Esther into the fray. I'm going to lose Jessie because she never really wanted me. But if I lose Esther trying to make things right... I don't dare consider what could happen then. But I have to brave all of that because carrying on ignoring my heart is no longer an option.

'Don't,' she says.

'Jessie . . . '

'I know where you're going.'

'I'm so sorry.'

She lifts her chin, eyes filled with fury. 'If you leave this hall, we're done.'

'It isn't you,' I say, hating every word.

'I swear, Archie, if you leave . . . '

'I'm so sorry, Jess. Thank you for taking a chance on me. But it isn't going to work. You deserve someone better. I'm sorry I can't be him. Be happy, yeah?'

I don't wait for her reply. Stepping around her, I hurry out of the hall.

The late afternoon sun rushes at me, my eyes taking precious seconds to adjust. I can't see Esther. I've taken too long getting out, just like I've wasted so much time dancing around the truth.

Shit.

And then I hear a car door slam. I follow the direction of the sound and see her. Esther is in the driving seat of her ancient blue car and the engine is starting.

I don't stop to think – I race to my own car, parked near the door, and get in just as Esther's car races past. I start the engine and speed off after her. As we pull out onto the main road, I consider which direction she might be going.

She isn't going to see her family because they're all in the hall. But she might be going home.

She could be going after Matt, though – I didn't think of that.

I can't let that possibility stop me from following her. Wherever it is she's heading, I'm going there, too.

We reach the first set of traffic lights and I just manage to nudge through behind her as green turns to amber. There's a van between us, but the blue roof of her car catches the sun up ahead, so I keep my eyes trained on that. We go over a roundabout, and there's a breathless second where I don't know which exit she's taking, then a blessed sight of her steers me onto the right road. As we skirt the city the traffic becomes heavier, people going out to enjoy what promises to be a warm summer evening or heading home to spend it in their gardens. Through my open windows I catch the scent of countless barbecues, interspersed with the fragrant rush of newly fried chips and pizza from the many takeaway places I pass.

It's a gorgeous late afternoon, the kind you're meant to enjoy at leisure, but, unlike everyone else in the city, I'm dashing through it. My hands are damp where they meet the steering wheel, the fresh air blowers in my poor old car no match for the seasonal heat. If I do catch up with Esther, will I be one great sweaty lump of desperation? A heart-pounding chase across a sunlit city might be the zenith of romantic endeavours, but being a damp, red-faced idiot at the end of it pretty much ruins the picture.

That's *if* she talks to me.

I don't think she's noticed me behind her yet. The van turned off at the last set of lights so now I maintain a healthy distance, hoping Esther doesn't recognise my car. I think of the last time we were in it together: that strange moment when we celebrated bringing Big Jim back into The Old Guys' fold, remembering mid-hug that everything had changed between us. All I want to do is hold her now and tell her what I should have said weeks ago. But will she listen to me when I—?

—Wait, *no*!

A double-decker bus edges out into the narrow gap between our cars. There's a pedestrian crossing in the centre of the road and I can't get round it before the bus pulls out.

Crap!

Scanning the road ahead, I see the final glint of sunlight on the blue car roof before the bus completely obscures my view.

There's another large roundabout ahead, leading to two major routes Esther could be taking. From behind the bus, I can't see which one she's going to choose. Finally, the great lump of metal barring her from my view slopes off to the left and I drive onto the roundabout.

No sign of her.

I scan the first exit, earning a sharp horn blast from the driver behind for taking too long to pass it. I ignore his frantic middle-finger-waving as I round the roundabout and check the next option. She isn't there. My heart in my sneakers, I make another circuit of the roundabout, this time looking at the road signs. She hasn't gone back the way we came. She probably isn't going to the middle of town. The next road isn't a main road and doesn't lead to the area I picked her up from last week when we were going to Jim's.

Okay, Archie. Keep looking.

The fourth sign makes my breath catch.

Of course.

It has to be.

Raising my hand to apologise to yet another driver my erratic driving just insulted, I choose the fourth road.

I know where she's going.

Forty-Five

ESTHER

I'm here.

I wasn't sure I'd make it, the way the traffic built up around me as I drove across Manchester. I don't have long before they close, but it'll be enough.

I just need to breathe.

I'd considered going to the Rec, but it's too close to Matt. I won't be going there again. This place will always be special for me and recently it's become significant again.

Because of Archie.

There's only one bench unoccupied when I reach the Heaton Park Temple, but that's fine by me. It affords me a slightly different view across the park to the sun-glittering city far in the distance. I think that's what I need right now: a different view.

Driving here, I kept wondering if I should feel worse about breaking up with Matt. The thing is, I don't: I'm relieved – and I think that's the biggest indicator I could have of how I'm meant to feel. I tried so hard to fit him into the mould I'd imagined but it was never going to work. Also because by the time we got together, my heart had changed the requirements. Matt was never going to fit a mould that looked like Archie.

I know it's hopeless. I know I've just exchanged one unrequited crush for another. In many ways I'm right back where I started, wondering if this daft heart of mine is ever going to learn.

The early evening sun is warming everything in its path: the swathes of majestic green sweeping away at my feet, the smooth walls of the Temple at my back. The sky is that deep, impossible blue you dream of for most of the year and only get to see for a few weeks if you're lucky. Tiny white clouds are scuttling over its expanse – the kind Ava-May and Molly draw in their ever-sunny pictures. There's a skylark somewhere, tweeting its little heart out as it rises endlessly. It's as if I'm being granted a rare view up here, far away from the noise of the city. Manchester looks like a glittering gem this evening and once again I thank my lucky stars that I get to call this place home.

Thankfulness. Not the most epic of superhero abilities, but I reckon I'm getting pretty good at it.

The air is so fresh up here. I fill my lungs as I gaze out across Heaton Park. And I start to line up my reasons to be thankful, like the rows of mature trees traversing the park: I'm here, in this place; I've a job I enjoy and the possibility of more work; I have a family I've reconnected with after the darkest, loneliest time in my life; I've an instrument I can pretty much play and a fabulous group of friends who don't mind my worst notes.

That's a lot to be going on with.

But my heart is still stone heavy.

I wish I wasn't in love with Archie Quinn. But I am.

I saw him watching me, all the way through the concert,

felt his gaze on me even when I made myself look away. I don't know what that means. Did he see Matt leave? Has he guessed what happened?

And that stuff his grandad said at the end – did it hit him like it did me? I know what Diarmuid Brady was trying to do but it was ill-advised. Archie has never wanted me. The letter was for Jessie. And our kiss was a mistake.

It *was* a mistake.

So why didn't it feel like one?

If I look at everything rationally, the only mistake I made was letting my heart run away with itself. Again. The problem I keep repeating. My dad subscribes to the theory that our problems are like unclaimed suitcases on an airport luggage carousel: they just keep coming around until you claim them. I know what my problem is. Next time, I'll watch my heart like a hawk and pounce on it the moment it's tempted to run after something. Or someone.

What's this going to mean for our friendship?

I haven't wanted to consider it, but now, in my elevated position over the city, I know I have to. It would kill me to lose him as a friend. Whatever else I've thought about Archie Quinn, his sudden arrival in my life and immediate connection has been a gift. I have loved being his friend. I *love* being his friend. I can't imagine my days without constantly finding stuff I want to share with him. Our rapid-fire texts have been brilliant, his messages arriving with uncanny timing, always at the precise moment I needed to hear from him most. Archie, my wonderful, unexpected friend.

But he has Jessie now. And Matt said Jessie thinks I'm out to steal him. How long can you survive as someone's friend when the person you love hates them? I want to protect this magical, daft *thing* that we have together, but do I want Archie to risk the love of his life to keep it? We spent all that time getting him and Jessie together: why would I want to destroy that?

It's a mess.

And I can't see a way around it that keeps Archie in my life.

I have to do what's best for him. Maybe if I don't see him again my heart can learn to behave. And he can be free to be everything to Jessie that he wants to be.

It means stepping away from The Old Guys – from the place I've found the most joy and acceptance ever. It means blocking Archie's number from my phone, so I won't check it every ten seconds for messages from him. It means smashing my own heart to let his breathe.

Am I ready to do that?

I know what I have to do, but the thought of it destroys me. I drop my head into my hands and let the full weight of what I'm considering come crashing down on me. I need to feel this. I need to understand what's at risk so I never make this mistake again.

As tears fill my palms and breach the line between my hands and my face, the sounds of the park continue around me: Manchester life in all its bright, bold, unashamed glory. Distant conversation, the rising skylark above, shouts from kids far down the hill and excited dogs out for an evening walk, the hum of an aeroplane traversing the summer sky.

And the sound of running feet . . .

Forty-Six

ARCHIE

I *knew* it.

I didn't check if her car was in the car park, or head to any of the other places Heaton Park has to offer.

I knew Esther would be here.

I don't stop to consider what kind of a frantic mess I look like, or even what the hell I'm going to say to her when I arrive. I just run.

She's sitting cross-legged on the farthest bench from where we sat before, every other seat already taken. Her head is in her hands and I think she's crying. From the bottom of the path leading up the hill to the Temple, Esther looks so small and sad.

And I'm the reason for it.

Halfway up the hill I suddenly wonder if she'll even talk to me. What right have I to demand she listens after all the times I *haven't* spoken?

It's too late to reconsider. I'm almost there.

Just as I reach the edge of the path that circles the Temple, she lifts her head.

I definitely can't backtrack now.

'Archie?'

'Surprise!' Is that the lamest thing I could have said? I think it is.

She stares at me, saying nothing. *Great start, Archie Quinn.*

'I wanted to check you were okay.'

'Well, I just left my family in the hall and legged it across Manchester, so . . . ' She doesn't smile when she says it.

'So did I.'

'You followed me.'

I nod, suddenly ashamed of my rash action.

'Why?'

'I needed to know you were okay.' I glance at the bench. 'Can I sit?'

She blinks, stabbing at her cheek with the heel of her hand. 'If you want.'

'I left Jessie.'

Her sigh is long. 'Yes, I know.'

'No, I mean I *left* Jessie. Not just in the hall. In . . . *life*.'

Unexpectedly, she snorts with laughter. 'In *life*? What are you like?'

I don't know if this is an open door I can trust. Tentatively, I return, 'Rubbish with words?'

'Oh, you're that all right.' She sniffs, looking away from me out across the sunlit park.

Where do I go from here? When I was tearing across the city after Esther I didn't think words would be a problem when I caught up with her. I thought I could confidently seize the moment and declare my love with words that would win Esther's heart. But they just aren't arriving like I assumed they would. I'm as tongue-tied now as I used to be with Jessie, my heart too full to let the words squeeze out. How am I still like this, after everything we've been through? Have I learned nothing since Esther left that note on my desk?

'There's so much I want to say . . . ' I begin, already aware that the words aren't enough.

'You'd best be quick. They're closing the park in half an hour.'

I turn to face her, reaching my hand out to gently rest on her knee. She doesn't flinch, which is good. But she doesn't look at me, either.

Keep going, Archie. This could be your only chance . . .

Imagining my granda peering over my shoulder is *not* helping. I gently coax the thought of him away. This is all me now. My words or nothing.

'I'm so glad we met. And you helped me so much, Es, with the letter and everything. I'm sorry that I stuffed it all up for everyone. I should have said . . . '

I'm shocked when she looks at me, the intensity of her gaze making my heart screech to a halt.

'You don't have to say that to make me feel better.'

'I'm not . . . '

'Because honestly, Arch, it's my fault we're in this mess.'

I can't believe what I'm hearing. 'What are you talking about? It's my fault.'

Her smile is so sad. The sight of it squeezes my heart. 'You're very kind but let me take the blame for this at least. I should have said something earlier . . . '

No. No way is Esther going to let me off the hook.

'This is all *my* doing, Es. Because I knew . . . '

'*I* knew. And I should have told you . . . '

'I should have said . . . '

'*How I felt.*' We say it together, then stare at each other like we've both lost the plot.

'What did you say?' she asks, her voice so quiet I can only just hear it over the noise of the park.

I take a breath and hope the words will appear. 'I should have said how I felt about you, long before we kissed.'

She reddens, turning away. 'Arch, don't . . .'

'No, I have to say it now. I made a mistake. I didn't know how I felt about you until I didn't have you.'

'You've always had me . . .'

This is purgatory. The words I want just won't come. In desperation, I turn to the small brass plaque screwed to our bench, praying for an Auntie Sue moment of divine inspiration. But my heart thumps to the ground when I see the words:

Deefur Dog 2004–2018
Best whippet this side o' th' Pennines

I could laugh at the utter uselessness of this well-meant dedication but right now my heart is on the line in the shadow of Heaton Park Temple. If I don't do something drastic I could lose my chance to love her.

I look over to the bench where we sat before – the one with the word-perfect dedication. A large bloke in a too-tight Happy Mondays T-shirt is occupying it, munching chips and battered sausage from a grease-stained polystyrene tray. Every few mouthfuls he pauses to swig from a can of beer. He isn't smiling. In fact, the scowl he's wearing could probably snap me like a twig if he turned it on me . . .

'Stay there,' I urge Esther, standing up.

'What are you doing?'

'Just trust me – and stay where you are – please?'

She gives an uncertain nod, her frown not exactly encouraging.

I can't lose my nerve. This is my last, best chance. And it involves a delicate negotiation I suddenly feel completely unprepared for. With one last glance at the woman I love, I push steel into my spine and stride over to Chip Man.

'Evening,' I begin, the brightness of my tone fading the moment he turns his killer frown on me.

'So it is.'

A large part of me wants to turn and leg it down the hill like the coward I've always been. But I make my feet stick to the path, jamming a smile onto my face.

'This is not going to make much sense, but it's life or death for me . . . '

Nothing. Not even a flicker.

I'm struck by the urge to grab his half-empty beer can and swill my throat, which has suddenly become drier than Death Valley. I press on. 'I need this bench.'

'You've got a bench.'

'I know. But I need *this* bench. Ordinarily I wouldn't ask. But you see, the young lady over there is the love of my life and I am making a total pig's ear of telling her. Being on this bench would help. So, could we swap? You get a much better view of the city from the other one.'

I don't think Chip Man blinks, ever. He's just staring at me like I dropped off Mars, chewing his chips in the same, slow, some would say *menacing* manner. I keep my smile steady, but my heart is sinking so far it's halfway to Australia.

'You . . . want *me* . . . to swap benches?'

I nod.

'Now?'

'If you wouldn't mind? Only they're closing the park soon and I really have to do this today.'

Now he blinks. And it is hands-down the most terrifying blink I have ever witnessed. I brace myself for the torrent of abuse – or fists – that are bound to come my way . . .

And then Chip Man rolls his bulbous eyes and stands, hugging his chips to his chest.

'Right.'

He raises his eyebrows and passes within inches of my face. As he trundles away I hear him muttering, 'Always the same. Highest park viewing point in Manchester and you can't move for bloody romantics . . . '

I'm shaking. But I did it. That *has* to be a sign.

My knees want to buckle against the bench that's now ours, but I wave over at Esther who is being unceremoniously evicted from the other bench by Chip Man's arrival. I watch her spring up in shock as he slides across to claim the seat. I wave again, scared for a moment that she might head down the path away from me. But to my relief, she walks slowly over.

It's a start.

I glance at the brass plaque: at the magic words that might just save me.

In loving memory of Ethel and Jeff Bincham,
who loved it here.
Always and forever, no matter what.

'Cheers, Eth and Jeff,' I whisper, as Esther arrives.

'*What* is going on?'

'Sit down, please?'

'That bloke just said you were a soppy git.'

Nice. 'Well, he's right.'

I look at Esther Hughes – and in the warm glow of early evening she is more beautiful than I have ever seen her.

This is my last chance. I have to just speak.

'My words are rubbish when I talk about my heart. You know that. So I'm going to borrow someone else's.'

I pat the brass plaque between us.

'Look at this, Es. The last line,' I add quickly, in case she thinks I'm talking about the couple who loved it here so much it warranted a bench dedication. 'This is all I have. It's the truth. I want to be with you, Esther. Always and forever. No matter what.'

She blinks at the plaque then turns her lovely head to me. 'Are you saying . . . ?'

'My heart is right here for you. Even if the words need work.'

She says nothing, her eyes on me.

My nerve finally failing, I sink to the wooden seat.

And then, Esther smiles. 'Don't stop. You're almost there.'

Does she mean . . . ? My heart jumps straight out of my chest and starts doing laps of Heaton Park.

'I might need help to finish it,' I risk.

The air stills between us.

'Are you asking me?'

I dare to slide a little closer to her. 'You're the only one who can help me. I can't find the words without you.'

'You daft beggar.' Her fingers are warm when they brush my cheek. 'You've already said all the words I need to hear.'

I don't know who kisses who first, only that it happens easier than breathing. Esther is in my arms and I'm in hers, our kisses sweet – the park and the Temple, the swathes of green and the far city melting away as we finally admit the truth.

And as it turns out, words weren't that important after all. Sometimes you just have to let your heart speak . . .

Forty-Seven

ESTHER

'This feels right. You know how sometimes you just *know*? That's how it feels. It's exactly what I need and I can't wait to get started.'

Fred says nothing, his wheel-squeak strangely muted tonight.

I smile and pat his scuffed yellow side. 'I'm still going to see you. For the moment, at least. You've been my best work colleague. It's just that Sid has been talking about Greta and me going full-time. The work's coming in so fast since the first brochures we designed went out. It's not going to be yet. But in the spring, maybe.'

I stop pushing him and rescue the side of my tabard that's slipped off my shoulder again. This place is surprisingly tidy tonight, apart from Callaghan's office, which was more of a pit than usual. I reach down to empty a wastepaper basket into the black sack in my hand, glancing under the familiar desk. No red sneakers there tonight. There'll be none there ever again. But I've seen where they live now they've been freed from *The Herald*'s office and they look happier than they've ever been.

I know how they feel.

The top of the desk is no longer covered in Post-it notes, the new occupant clearly not a fan. There's nothing on there to indicate who they are. No photographs. No mugs. No lists. Archie says Callaghan's on his third intern in as many months. The only difference I've noticed is the amount of rubbish in the bin beside the desk. Some weeks there's none at all.

And I wonder, what would have happened if I'd started cleaning here now, after the ghost of Archie had left? If there had been no discarded love letter in the bin, no indication of the beautiful soul who'd written it at his most desperate? We could so easily have missed each other.

Fate, my dad says, is a tricky sod. I'm inclined to agree.

He's abandoned the autobiography for now, much to Mum's relief. On the other hand, he's discovered a passion for power tools . . .

I've left the desk next to Archie's old workspace till last. The perfume is still there, hanging spectral-like above it. Last Archie heard, Jessie was dating someone else. I'm not surprised: beautiful people like her don't stay single for long. I should feel bad about what happened – and I wouldn't ever wish hurt on anyone – but in a strange way I have her to thank for Archie and me finding each other. If he hadn't needed words to express his heart we might never have met.

Fred's squeak returns when I wheel him around. Just the coffee station to tackle and then I'm done.

'We're good for the time being,' I assure him. 'I like seeing you and doing the other job as well. It works for now.' As I lean against his handle I catch sight of the three new friendship bracelets tied around my wrist. Lots of things work for now. I'm still at Naomi's, saving everything I can. It's giving me time to spend with her and the girls, not just on the school run three mornings a week. And it helps that Uncle Archie is practically a rock star in their eyes.

The list in my back pocket is gone for good: I have everything I need for now. Everything else will come in time.

A bell sounds behind me and I smile as I clean the coffee station.

'I reckon they weld those coffee dregs on there,' says a voice that makes my heart flip.

'I reckon you're right.' I giggle as strong arms slide around my waist and soft lips kiss my neck. 'How did you get in? I thought you surrendered your pass?'

'Ways and means, Miss Hughes.' Archie smiles, the curl of his lips tickling my skin.

'Oh right?' I wriggle around until I'm nose to nose with him. 'Sneaky journalist trick, was it? I should report you to my manager.'

'Be my guest.' He steals a kiss. 'Who do you think sent me up in the lift? Marjorie loves me.'

He looks tired tonight, three late shifts in a row at MediaCity taking their toll. With his demanding schedule and me working two jobs, it's a constant challenge to find time to see each other, so I love this unexpected visit. Everything's a challenge at the moment, but we have each other and our families and The Old Guys. A lot of love all round. That's more than enough to be getting on with.

Archie waits – *mostly* patiently – while I clean the coffee station, then helps me to wheel Fred to bed. When he's safely back in his cupboard, we walk hand in hand to the lift.

'Do you miss it here?' I ask, watching the lift numbers on

the screen above the steel door marking its slow journey up to meet us.

Archie looks back at the darkened office floor, with its blank computer screens and empty chairs and that low hum I've yet to find the cause of. 'No. But I'm grateful to it. Because it brought you to me.'

I smile up at the loveliest man in Manchester. 'Get you and your lovely words, Archie Quinn.'

'I'm getting pretty good with them now.' He glances up at the lift marker. 'And when this bloody lift turns up I'll show you what else they can do.'

'Is that right?'

'It is.'

'I see.' I snuggle into his arms, loving our game. Loving *him*. 'So what are we going to do while we wait?'

His kisses are all the answers I need.

THE END

Acknowledgements

BREAKING NEWS… (Miranda's Thank-Yous…)

Just like at *The Herald* (with no sign of a Jock Callaghan, of course), an unseen army of brilliant lovelies have been at work behind the scenes to bring Esther and Archie's story to these gorgeous finished pages. Here they all are, with my huge thanks and appreciation:

Ace Agent
HANNAH FERGUSON

Editor-in-Chief
MANPREET GREWAL

Features Editor
MELANIE HAYES

Copy Editor
DONNA HILLYER

Proof Reader
ELDES TRAN

Design Ace (cover)
THOMAS WRIGHT

Production Superheroes
ANGIE DOBBS
HALEMA BEGUM

Marketing Ace
BECCA JOYCE
JANET ASPEY

Sales Team
GEORGINA GREEN
HARRIET WILLIAMS
ANGELA THOMSON
SARA EUSEBI

Rights & Legal
HARDMAN SWAINSON – with particular thanks to
NICOLE ETHERINGTON

Star Columnists (Fab Friends)
AG SMITH, CLAIRE SMITH, KIM CURRAN, CRAIG
HALLAM, RACHAEL LUCAS , CALLY TAYLOR,
KATY & WILLIAM AT TEA LEAVES AND READS,
TAMSYN MURRAY, KATE HARRISON, THE
MINTS, THE DREAMERS, JEN AT MISS BOHEMIA,
RAEGON GUEST, THE WHITES & DICKINSONS

Board of Directors (The Big Bosses)
MY LOVELY BOB & FANTASTIC FLO xx

Honourable Mentions
YOU, lovely Reader, for enjoying this book!
MY AWESOME FAB NIGHT IN
CHATTY THING VIEWERS
TEAM SPARKLY – for all your cheerleading and sparkly GIFs
MY FAB FOLLOWERS ON TWITTER,
INSTAGRAM & FACEBOOK
THE CITY OF MANCHESTER – for inspiring this story
No characters were harmed in the making of this book
(although their ears might have taken a bashing from The
Old Guys' musical renditions…)
This book is a story about following your heart, making the
most of whatever life throws at you and believing that better
things are possible. Hope is a powerful weapon and love is our
greatest ally. Lovely Reader, I wish you both xx

ALL MY LOVE – Miranda's Book Soundtrack

These are the songs that inspired me as I wrote *All My Love*. Many of the traditional songs inspired The Old Guys' set-list for their concert. All of these musicians and artists are wonderful – please support them and buy their music!

- Esther & Archie's theme: 'BRAVE' – Sara Bareilles – *The Blessed Unrest*
- 'TAKE THE JOURNEY' – Molly Tuttle – *Take the Journey (single)*
- 'HOLD ON' – John Smith – *The Fray*
- 'FEELS LIKE THIS' – Maisie Peters – *Dressed Too Nice for a Jacket (EP)*
- 'ONE OF THESE DAYS' – Teddy Thompson – *A Piece of What You Need*
- 'THE WISHING TREE' – Mike McGoldrick, John McCusker & John Doyle – *The Wishing Tree*
- 'JIM WARD'S JIG' – Comhaltas – *Foinn Seisiún 3*
- 'COME AROUND' – Sarah Jarosz – *Follow Me Down*
- 'SWEET HONEY IN THE ROCK' – Kris Drever – *Mark the Hard Earth*

- 'ANOTHER DAY' – Karan Casey – *Folktopia: Music of Vertical Records, Vol.1*
- 'SOMEBODY TO LIVE' – Kacey Musgraves – *Pageant Material*
- 'PLANETS' – Kate Rusby feat. Sarah Jarosz – *20*
- 'WALTZ #2' – Elliot Smith – *XO*
- 'ALL MY DAYS' – Alexi Murdoch – *Away We Go Original Motion Picture Soundtrack*
- 'FIND MY WAY' – Keston Cobblers Club – *Find My Way (Single)*

Turn the page for an exclusive extract from Miranda Dickinson's wonderfully romantic and charming love story

Available to buy now!

Chapter One

LACHLAN

'Try to stay focused.'

'I *am* focused.'

I'm not. But I won't tell *her* that. What does she know about me, other than I'm the grumpy sod she has to wrestle into shape four times a week?

'You're forgetting I know you, Lachie. I can see you sneaking glances out of the window.'

'I'm not.'

I am, but only because the world out there is far more appealing than being pummelled by a self-righteous physiotherapist. I drag my gaze away and let her see it.

'That's it. Good. Try and lift that leg a little higher.'

She says it like it's easy. Like I haven't been trying for the last eight weeks. Easy for you, Tanya, walking in with that hip swing I thought was cute the first time I met you. Now it's just another kick to me: another thing your body can do that my body's forgotten.

I know what she's thinking: it's what I'm thinking, too. There should be more progress by now. Back when we started, the plan was ten to twelve weeks to regain at least 80 per cent mobility in my left leg. Doctors and surgeons, the hospital physios, they were all so sure of it. It was their job to be pessimistic, my doctor told me; whatever they'd told me about how long it will take was supposed to be worst-case scenario. But I'm eight weeks in and nothing's changed for a fortnight.

Tanya's smile is as annoyingly bright as ever, but recently a crease between her eyebrows has joined it. No amount of grinning is shifting it. That worries me.

I push harder and the pain forces a yelp from my lips. *Damn it*. Normally I can do this in silence, but now Tanya knows.

'Don't force it. Let's take a break. I'll get you some water.'

I can't tell which of us is more relieved as she hurries into the kitchen.

Shit.

Next time, I'll have to bite my tongue.

I let my gaze drift to the window again, to the building opposite. There's something going on in the flat directly over the hedge from mine. Its windows have been dark for a month now, ever since the old lady who lived there moved out. But last night, lights were blazing in it well past midnight. And today, all the windows facing my building have been opened. From time to time a carrier bag or a box will appear on the windowsill, only to be removed a few minutes later. Now the window is empty again, save for a pair of very worn gardening gloves resting against the glass. Looking closer, I can see a single naked light bulb burning in the ceiling. Something that looks like it could be a stepladder edges into view at one side, but it's draped in white – a dustsheet, maybe?

I look back just as Tanya returns with the glass of water. As she hands it to me, the chirpy dance tune of her mobile begins. She raises an apologetic hand, pointing towards the front door. She'll take it on the landing outside the flat as she always does. Judging by her tone as she answers the call hurrying out of the room, I reckon I have a couple of minutes at least.

Taking my chance, I push myself off the dining-table chair I've been doing my exercises on and hop to the window. My favourite spot. Funny, when I bought this place an age ago it never occurred to me to look outside. Now it's my lifeline. My safe place.

Standing by the glass, I can see the corner of the building next door and the wide sweep of communal garden that separates it from the main road. Two people are chatting on the pavement, their dogs making an enthusiastic appraisal of each other's behinds. I wonder if they might be connected with the activity in the opposite flat, but then they wave and go their separate ways. There's no decorator's van in the curving driveway, which is where I've seen tradespeople park their vehicles before. I glance at the car park at the rear of the building, but there's no van there, either, as far as I can see.

Yes, I know it's sad.

I never expected to become an expert in my nearest neighbours' lives, but here we are. I'm not proud of it – and I would be mortified if anyone spotted me. But – it helps. It helps to know the world is spinning on beyond these four walls. It's a promise that I'll see it again – that my own life waits there, just out of reach.

It's done more for my head than eight weeks of physio, that's for sure.

I look up from the road to the window of the flat opposite. My breath catches. Someone is standing there. They have their back to the window, but I can see a dark ponytail and a paint-splattered T-shirt that might once have been a souvenir from a rock gig. Two hands appear at the small of their back, the shoulders rolling in a stretch. I imagine the satisfying crack of vertebrae coaxed back into line and I'm instantly jealous.

Turn around.

I want to see their face. I'm ashamed and fascinated at once: it is none of my business who owns the ponytail and tour T-shirt, and yet I want to know. I'm guessing it's a woman, but from this angle it's impossible to tell. Whoever they are, they look tired. I see it in the heavy lock of the shoulders, the slow progress of the stretch. I know how that feels…

'I thought we said no looking out of the window.'

When I turn, Tanya is standing in the room, hands on hips, like my mother does when she's about to deliver a bollocking. Better knuckle down, then, until it's done and she goes away.

When I look back an hour later, the flat is dark and the windows closed.

Chapter Two

BETHAN

It's done.

I nearly broke my back in the process and I don't think I'll shift the smell of paint from my nostrils any time soon, but the flat is decorated and I can start to consider it ours.

Gwych. Excellent.

Now I just need to make it feel like home.

Everything is white. Boring, maybe, but better than the weird magnolia-beige the previous tenant had. Utterly disgusting it was, like the colour of tinned rice pudding – and I can't stand that, either. This way I can buy some cheap colourful curtains, bedding and cushions and get all my colour from that. Noah adores colour. He told me last week he'd like to live in a rainbow. So I'm going to give my boy the closest thing to his heart's desire and paint a rainbow around him.

The thought of that makes me smile.

I check my watch: thirty minutes until I'm due to pick him up from Michelle's. Thank heaven she stepped in and had him to stay last night. Without her help I don't know what I would have done. And thank goodness my new landlord was okay with me redecorating the place before we moved in. I think he was relieved, to be honest. That yucky beige and the last tenant's gross mid-wall floral borders I think they used superglue to stick up were a nightmare to get rid of, so I saved him the trouble. Landlord brownie points are important, in my experience.

Now the space is closer to the potential I saw the first day I viewed this flat. The light is incredible, and being on the end of the building means three corners of windows. No more having to put lights on in the daytime, trying not to think about whether we could afford it. It's dry, too. No telltale black spots or heavy smell in any of the rooms. We might even save on heating bills, if the way the sun has warmed the living area is anything to go by.

Any way you look at it, this is a step up.

And thirty minutes to myself? Now *that's* a luxury.

I refill the kettle and set it to boil, fishing out the remnants from the Hobnobs packet that's been dinner, breakfast and lunch for me while I've been working. While I wait to make tea, I wander over to the window at the side of the kitchen area. It looks directly into the identical building next door. There's a large grey cat spread across the windowsill in the flat opposite mine. One of its front paws is pushed up against the glass, little pink paw pads a spot of colour against the steel-grey fluff. Noah will be overjoyed if he can see a cat from his new home.

Cattttttttttt!

He's never lived in Wales, but he says that word in a pure Cardiff accent. A long *t* – almost an *s* by the time it ends. Mam would be proud. If she ever looked up from her own dramas long enough to notice, that is. I should call her. It's been too long. Once we're settled in, we'll attempt a FaceTime call. I'll have to get Emrys to go over and show her how it's done – again – but I know my big brother won't mind. When Noah starts chatting to them, everything else is unimportant.

Secretly, I'm proud of Noah's assumed accent. Last time I spoke to Mam she accused me of losing mine. Which proves she doesn't know me at all. Since I ended up in North Yorkshire, my accent has strengthened. Like a shield I hold in front of me. It's a confidence thing: that and the conversation starter it always provides. *Oh, you're Welsh?* Makes me laugh when people say that. I'm always tempted to feign shock and reply, 'Bloody hell, you're right!'

I keep that hidden, too, from most people. The cheeky side of me. Strange how people think they have the measure of you the first time they meet you and then never bother to revise it when they know you better. So they see a meek Welsh single mum who'd never dare crack a joke? Suits me.

Noah knows, though. That's all that counts.

When we're together, we have all the fun in the world. With him in my arms I can forget everything else. The worries, the circumstances I didn't choose, the list of demands on my time – none of them come from us. In our team of two we are strong. Defiant dreamers. Life-lovers. And in this flat, we're finally going to find our feet.

The kettle's click echoes in the empty space, an unfamiliar sound I will soon take for granted. Drowning the teabag in a mug, I smile. One more night in that awful bedsit and tomorrow Noah and me claim our new kingdom.

Outside the wind has picked up, sending wispy white clouds dancing across the sun. I watch the pools of light and shadow sail across the building next door and the tall beech hedge that separates us. The cat in the window opposite is sitting upright now, staring at me. Well, not *at* me. It probably doesn't even realise I'm here. Without thinking, I wave. It's such a daft thing to do, but this is my first encounter with anyone in our new neighbourhood and it feels right.

'Hello, cat.' My breath fogs the glass for a second as I speak.

The cat gives a long, slow blink. There's a moment of connection – and then it jumps out of sight.

Fifteen minutes left.

I move the paint-splattered dustsheet from the rickety old stepladder the landlord left for me and perch on a step to drink my last cuppa before we officially move in. I'm so tired it hurts to blink and I don't think my body will love me in the morning, but I don't care. I did it. Painting walls is another thing to add to my list of dubious new skills.

I glance at the now cat-less window and wonder who it shares its space with. Who its *slave* is, as my boss, Hattie, would say. She's got four of them at home and when she returns from a long day at work running the garden centre she owns she's totally at their furry beck and call. What does Grey Fluffy Mog's human look like? Older, like the previous tenant here, or younger, like me? There are so many questions in my new neighbourhood I've yet to find answers to. Even that will be a change – where we're living now it's best not to know anything about the others who share your space.

I saw signs of other younger people in the building when I came to view the flat, a month ago. A baby buggy by the communal entrance; folded toy boxes in the blue recycling bags inside the door, small muddy welly-boot prints along the vinyl in the corridor to the stairs. The landlord said it was a popular area

8

for new families. It's around the corner from Noah's preschool, so I hope some of the mums I see there might live nearby.

Does the cat have a little human living there, too?

I guess I'll find out eventually. Maybe not about the cat. But about the rest. I like how that makes me feel. Possibility, after a long line of slammed doors.

Crap, I need to get going.

I rinse my mug and dash around my new home, closing windows and turning off lights. Then I grab my coat, hefting my overnight bag onto my shoulder that I used as a pillow last night when I snatched two hours' sleep on the floor. At the door, I turn back.

'See you, flat,' I smile. 'Back soon.'

I don't think my feet meet the stairs once as I hurry out.

Want to read more from Miranda Dickinson?
Don't miss her heart-warming
and feel-good romcoms

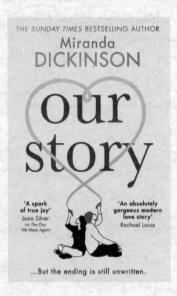

ONE PLACE. MANY STORIES

Bold, innovative and
empowering publishing.

FOLLOW US ON:

@HQStories